Julia Fitzgerald was brought up on the Yorkshire Moors, which, she says, inspired her with their wild beauty. Her passion for history first showed itself through art, when she would spend hours painting queens and princesses in historical costume. She wrote her first historical novel at seventeen, though she had been writing short stories from the age of six.

Julia Fitzgerald also writes under the names of Julia Watson and Julia Hamilton. She is the author of *Royal Slave*, *Slave Lady*, *Scarlet Woman*, *Salamander* and *Venus Rising*.

Also by Julia Fitzgerald:

ROYAL SLAVE
SLAVE LADY
SCARLET WOMAN
SALAMANDER
FALLEN WOMAN
VENUS RISING
LOVE SONG (as Julia Watson)

Julia Fitzgerald

The Princess and the Pagan

Futura

A Troubadour Book

First published in Great Britain in 1983
by Futura Publications, a Division of
Macdonald & Co (Publishers) Ltd
London & Sydney
Reprinted 1985

ISBN 0 7107 3034 9

Filmset, printed and bound in Great Britain by
Hazell Watson & Viney Limited,
Member of the BPCC Group,
Aylesbury, Bucks

Futura Publications
A Division of
Macdonald & Co (Publishers) Ltd
Maxwell House
74 Worship Street
London EC2A 2EN

A BPCC plc Company

While I was writing this book, military rule began in Poland and as this story concerns another country's fight for freedom under the oppressor, in the early nineteenth century, I thought it only right that it should be dedicated to all those who are struggling for freedom in the world today.

Julia Fitzgerald, Chester, 1982

I would like to thank my father, Joseph L Watson, for his kind help with the battle of Navarino research, which was greatly appreciated.

Author's Note: The Queen Atalanta referred to in the legend in this story has no connection with the Atalanta of foot-race and apple fame.

CONTENTS

PART ONE

The Palace of the Silver Cicadas

'A long time now I've lain in wait for you;
   my eye singled you out from all the others
   as though you lived among them like a star;
   your grace and beauty gratify my heart.'

Angelos Sikelianos (1884–1951)

'Wearing her silk bridal gown
   and her lily-white veils
she roamed through known crossroads, and in her
   dream
   she imagined the roads new.'

Sikelianos

CHAPTER ONE

The musk-scented satinwood casket contained the most glorious emeralds Lady Flavia Audlington had ever seen. Dazzling green suns, they lay across the palm of her slender hand and stared at her like living eyes. In the base of the casket was a note written in green ink on buff-coloured parchment, a note from Prince Zebukar Alhan Ahman, the governor of the Morea, in Turkish-occupied Greece, and the man Flavia had been betrothed to since she was an infant.

It was written in Turkish, of which she had a little knowledge, for she had been studying the language in readiness for her marriage.

'Sevgilim, batinin güzel gülü, Süt derili, mavi çicek gözlü, sensiz öyle yalnizdim ki. Sen oğlumun anasi, benim kadinim olacaksin.'

'Beloved, beautiful Rose of the West, one with skin like milk and eyes like blue flowers, I have been so alone without you. You will bear my son and be my First Kadine.'

Flavia's cheeks were rosy by the time she had finished the painstaking translation. It did not matter that he had got the colour of her eyes wrong. There was every excuse for this, as they had never met. All she had dreamed of for as long as she could remember was her future husband, Prince Zebukar. Marriage to him would make her a princess, but that was only a minor concern. What really mattered was that she loved him fiercely, dreamed of him every night, and thought of little save him for most of her waking hours. He was twenty-seven and she was eighteen. He had sent her a recent portrait of himself so that she could see what he looked like now. She had hung it beside the other portraits which he had sent her over the years. There was one of a slender, black-eyed young boy aged sixteen, wearing a turquoise silk coat and with a bright blue silk turban studded with sapphire and ruby brooches. Three years later, much taller, he had also broadened out, and was dressed in ceremonial robes, amethyst shot-silk, a cloak of rich purple brocade gemmed with black pearls, and the most enormous black pearl displayed in his matching turban. He was being prepared to rule in place of his father, Prince Bastan. When he sent her that painting, he wrote, 'I think of nothing but the day that my beautiful wife joins me here in Greece.'

Flavia had been very young then, and of course there was no question of her travelling to her future husband's country until she was an adult. In any case, she would never have left her father then, for she adored him. They had been everything to one another since her birth, when her mother had tragically died.

Now the final portrait of Prince Zebukar hung facing Flavia's four-poster bed. How dashing he looked – so tall and straight, his shoulders broad, his waist narrow, his stomach flat. He had the boldest, blackest eyes she had ever seen, and a sensual, full and curving mouth with a deep dimple in a strong chin. His brows were arched, and black as the pearls he wore in his ears, which, in fact, now that she looked more closely, also resembled his brilliant dark eyes. In his silk sash was a curved dagger, its hilt studded with huge diamonds, emeralds, pearls and rubies. Rings containing these stones were on each of his strong brown fingers.

In the background crouched a mountain lion about to leap on its victim. She knew what this meant. The reason for her betrothal to the Prince was that his father, Prince Bastan, and her own father, Acteon, Duke of Audlington, had gone to college together, travelled the world together, and shared many adventures. The Duke, an anthropologist and explorer, had accompanied Prince Bastan on some of his most daring and venturesome expeditions.

During one of these, a ravenous lion had leaped from its mountain lair, a few yards above the valley where the Duke and his bearers were walking. The lion had landed with its full weight on the Duke, crushing him into the stony dust. With tremendous courage, Prince Bastan had tackled the lion single-handed while their native bearers had fled, terrified.

The fierce battle which ensued was between Bastan and the beast, for the Duke had been knocked unconscious and there was no one to aid the young Turk. Finally, the lion was weakened by loss of blood after being repeatedly stabbed by Bastan with the jewel-studded dagger which was now in Zebukar's possession. Bastan, gasping for breath and breathing raspingly, watched the lion stagger away, to fall, dazed and blind with exhaustion, over the edge of the crevasse a little way ahead of them.

The Duke recovered consciousness, the bearers tiptoed back, shame-faced, and Bastan was doubly revered from that moment onwards. A pact had been made that night – a pact which one would have thought not only improbable but impossible. Bastan's heir was to be betrothed to the Duke's first daughter, should there be one.

'Imagine it, my good friend,' Bastan said. 'Your daughter, who will be as beautiful and brave as you are handsome and famous, will be united with my son. Together, they will share Greece. Together they will found a glorious dynasty of sons who will reign supreme in Greece for centuries, millennia, to come . . .' Bastan's earth-brown eyes glittered with his vision. At the time, he was nineteen, and Acteon twenty-two. Neither were married, nor had they so much as considered the selection of a bride, although Bastan's aged father had completed a list of possible princesses, including one of the daughters of King George of England – a lady who had possessed the foresight to faint at the suggestion that she marry a Prince of Islam.

Back in England, Acteon fell crazily in love with two young heiresses. One, the Lady Jemina Spartles, was golden-haired, brown-eyed, petite, shapely as a miniature Venus, and possessed of a steely spirit. In fact, she had so much of the latter that she turned down the Duke's

13

proposal no less than four times, and, on the fourth occasion, pushed him into a flower-bed, to boot.

Undeterred, the Duke arrived at Spartles Manor on a fifth occasion, laden with gifts. There were exotic ornaments and bolts of material hand-woven by Mexican Indians, necklets of lapis lazuli, turquoises and seed pearls, fans of enormous ostrich feathers, and strange, almost frightening gargoyle masks created by the self-same Indians. Having presented all these to the Lady Jemina, in a somewhat disorderly heap at her feet, the Duke knelt and begged her to marry him, or he would die. His answer was peal after peal of uninhibited laughter. Looking down, he saw why. Lady Jemina's pet spaniel had chosen the Duke's right knee on which to deliver a plethora of waste products.

'*That* is the end!' the Duke raged, leaping to his feet. Stalking out of the gardens, he vowed never to approach the lady again. Such insufferable heartlessness! She was making fun of him all the time and she did not deserve his devotion. He would not make the same stupid mistake again. The lady with whom he fell in love next time would be the exact opposite of the arrogant, cold-hearted and cruel Lady Jemina.

Six weeks later, the Duke and Jemina were married. It was the wedding of the year, this love-match between quite the most eccentric duke England had ever produced, of whom it had been said that he would die a bachelor, and the lady of whom it had been said that no man, civilized, savage or barbarian, could tame her.

Flavia knew the story well, and it brought tears to her eyes whenever she recalled it. She wished that she had known her mother, but the Duchess had survived only eight months of married life. It had not been marriage itself which had killed her, but the arrival of her first child, a large, healthy and squalling baby daughter.

The Duke went into deepest mourning for a year. He would never marry again. Knowing that Jemina would have wanted it, he saw that their daughter was christened,

14

but other than that he did nothing for the child. He surrounded himself with paintings of Jemina and wept whenever he looked at them. He spent hours at the family vault, kneeling by her tomb, kissing the carved stone effigy with the little stone spaniel at its feet – for Jemina's dog had died of a broken heart a few weeks afterwards. Guilt, grief and desperate loneliness had twisted inside the Duke's heart. A man of fiery passions, he now had no outlet for them. It was rare for a man with such fierce desires to be by nature monogamous, but he was. A lifetime of sleeping alone in bed lay before him, a never-ending torture devised by the most callous executioner. Not death, but living death.

And as for the child who had caused his beloved's death? After the christening, during which he did not smile or speak, he would not so much as look at her. She was cared for by her nurse and servants in the farthest corner of the house from her father, and he refused to have her name mentioned in front of him. That she had a name was entirely due to Jemina, who had left a letter stating that, in the event of her death in childbed, she wanted her daughter to be christened Flavia.

In vain did Flavia's nurse beg the Duke to look upon the little girl just once, once only. He would not do it. Raging at the woman, he would storm off on his horse into the wildest part of his vast estates and disappear for hours on end. He knew that he must go back to his former life. The world lay out there, so much of it begging to be explored by him, and it would free him from nauseating domestic tentacles.

Mexico beckoned again, but it was not the same without Bastan, who was busy founding his own dynasty now. After three months in the steamy tropical wilderness of the Mexican Indians, Acteon headed for Greece and the palace of Bastan. There Acteon saw the nine-year-old Zebukar, along with his mother, the Princess Fira, first wife and chief Kadine of Prince Bastan. Fira was radiantly beautiful. The daughter of a Caucasian chieftain, she had been abducted by corsairs when she was twelve-years-old. Bastan had taken one look at her, and ordered that she be prepared for marriage to him when she was sixteen. (He was not, nor ever had been, a man who would corrupt or debauch children.) Fira had been fruitful, and Zebukar was conceived on her wedding night. He was a lively, bright-eyed boy, healthy, vociferous and beautiful.

If Fira was seen to look at him with fear in her eyes when she thought no one was observing her, no one spoke of it. It was put down to natural fears of a young mother for her infant son. Fira kept her secrets to herself. She was ivory-skinned, with flaxen hair so long and thick that it covered both herself and her husband when they lay naked in bed together. Her eyes were a very dark brown, which gave her a striking beauty, and she had a tiny mole on her chin, which Bastan loved to kiss. He was, for a Muslim and a Turk, a most devoted and faithful husband.

Acteon was not soothed by such scenes of intimate domesticity, although, on seeing the Prince, he did remember – but dimly – that he had a daughter in England – a daughter at whom he had never looked, whom he had never held. Bastan was swift to remind Acteon of their pledge: that Bastan's heir would marry Acteon's eldest daughter and found a dynasty.

'What is the Lady Flavia like? Is she beautiful? Does she have her mother's colouring?' Bastan asked, imagining that Zebukar's wife would be as fair as his mother. Being so much in love with Fira, Bastan considered blonde women to be the epitome of female beauty.

Acteon flushed and tried to change the subject, but Bastan persisted. 'The Lady Flavia *is* healthy? She is not, Allah forbid, damaged in any way?'

Acteon frowned, for the truth was that he did not know what his daughter looked like, or how fair she was. He did not even know whether or not she was a normal infant. But he thought that his servants would have told him had she been deformed in any way, and although the nurse had tried to tell him many things, that had not been amongst them.

'She is a healthy child, Bastan,' he said finally.

'Then we shall go ahead with our plan? They shall marry one another? You know it is the custom for Muslim monarchs to marry women who are not of their race? Flavia will be welcomed here – my wife will teach her all that she must know. She will find it strange at first, but that will soon pass. Will she be raised as a Muslim?'

It was not such a strange question. Bastan knew that Acteon had been a discreetly-practising Muslim ever since the Prince had saved him from the mountain lion.

'Is there so much difference between God and Allah?' Acteon had asked then. 'They are so very similar that one is tempted to consider them one and the same. Their teachings are alike – that it is folly to amass great fortunes, that the true believer will humble himself in prayer, keep aloof from vain words, give alms, restrain his appetites.'

'I believe it is your Bible which says good men are blessed. So does our Koran, our holy book. We believe that those who tend well their trusts and their covenants, and who pray as they have been taught, shall be the inheritors of paradise.'

'And the Muslim who preserves the life of a Christian when he is attacked by a wild beast shall have the joy of knowing that his once Christian friend is now a Muslim,' Acteon replied and the two men grinned at one another, earth-black Turkish eyes staring into peridot-green ones.

Now, in answer to Bastan's question, Acteon said that his daughter would be taught the tenets of Bastan's religion, but that he would not have her forced into practising a creed which she did not relish, and as he spoke, Acteon realized that he meant what he said. He would not have Flavia bludgeoned into doing anything that did not meet with her approval.

'That is as it should be,' Bastan agreed. 'As you know, I am not a man of force. What Allah decrees shall be so. I will leave it in His hands, and He shall convert the Lady

17

Flavia if it be His will. If not, then so be it. The harem here is filled with non-believers – it means little.'

'You have younger sons?'

A shadow darkened Bastan's face. 'Twin boys died at birth. They were the sons of Kadine Electra, a woman of Greek birth, from one of the islands.'

'No doubt Allah will send you many more – you are young – you have years ahead of you to sire more heirs.'

'Allah has been good sending me one healthy son. I shall be happy to leave my lands in Zebukar's hands. He is a noble child, he has a bright spirit and a keen mind. What more could a man ask in a son?'

The two men had not noticed Kadine Fira sitting on the edge of one of the lilting fountains in the outer courtyard of the palace. Dabbling her fingers in the water, longing to throw off her heavy, constricting veils and run on fleet feet as she had done in her father's land, Fira listened and prayed to her own gods.

'Make Zebukar as noble as the Prince my husband believes him to be. Let him grow straight in body and in mind. Let – let there be no streak in him of – of – the bad blood in my own family. Let it be dead now. Dead *forever!*'

Racing through Fira's mind were images of her early life. On her mother's side, one generation of normal sons and daughters, then one generation in which there would be one, sometimes two men with homicidal tendencies, debauchers of children, men with decaying minds who left a trail of devastation wherever they went. And, on her father's side, the side descended from Genghis Khan, the men with inhuman strength, inhuman desires. Her father, Lord Gudulf, had kept a harem of his own – thirty wives, seventy children before he was forty-years-old, bedding with sometimes as many as five wives in one night, and sometimes fertilizing them all in one night . . . That was Lord Gudulf, descendant of the dreaded Ghengis Khan.

Looking at Zebukar, she was sometimes content, sometimes uneasy. He was, so far, so easy-going, so charming – too charming. Yet she felt that she should have more trust in her gods, for if she left her fears in their hands, would they not care for her son and ensure that he was a good ruler? She had seen the misery and chaos brought about by evil rulers, the persecution of a people, the rape, pillage and looting, the burning, savagery and destruction of the barbarian hordes. She did not want that for Zebukar, for Turkish-occupied Greece.

Bastan was a just and caring governor. He had been one of the few Turkish rulers of Greece who had created peace and industry out of desecration and havoc. Secretly, Fira thought it was shameful to occupy another's country, to conquer and take for one's self what belonged to someone else. She would never say this, of course. She loved Bastan too much. But she could not forget that she had been carried off by corsairs when out riding with her women and sold into the harem of Prince Bastan, via his Kislar Agha in Constantinople, a city which thronged with thousands of Christian slaves. She was not a Christian, and she had quickly learned to love her new husband, but she could not forget that to take what belonged to another was a crime.

She had never mentioned her family to Bastan, except to say that she was daughter of a chieftain in her homeland. Loving Bastan as she did, what good would it do to tell him of her dread?

How could she say, 'My ancestors have been monsters, vile and terrible savages who slaughtered, tortured and raped their way through our country for centuries,' when she knew that the Turks had behaved likewise for centuries too? Bastan would only shrug and say, 'Allah watches over his faithful', and that would be that. But she could not banish the dread, all the same. It lingered within her, like a meal that was too large and weighted her down, and nothing that she had ever done over the years – not even hours spent in prayer – had freed her of this ominous foreboding.

Now she knew that her son was to marry a girl from a country far from the one her son would one day rule. From her own experience, she knew how well such a marriage could work out. For centuries, the Grand Turk had taken foreign women into his harem, women from all over the world, of different colours, creeds and beliefs. Usually, save for one or two notable exceptions, it had worked well. Fira knew very little about the girl who would one day be First Kadine in Zebukar's court, but she liked the look of Acteon – he was noble both by birth and inclination, handsomely built and fair of face.

Bastan was not the kind of Muslim husband who shut his wives away in their harem, to be slaves of indolence and voluptuousness. Fira was allowed out to meet notaries who visited the court, although of course she must remain veiled at all times save when alone with her lord. To a woman who had spent her developing years riding bareback, wearing loose, belted shirts and baggy trousers, with high boots to the knee, this had been not the least of her ordeals after marriage. The daughters of Lord Gudulf had been raised like his sons, for their country was a wild and savage land with its plains and steppes, the wolves and bears which lived in the mountain regions, the barbaric climactic changes, the villainy of the people Gudulf had ruled with an equal villainy, not to mention those from bordering lands who had made regular assaults upon his domain.

From the age of ten, Fira could fight with a dagger, ride bareback for days on end, go for hours without food and water, survive with four hours' sleep at night, wrestle with boys of her own age, and handle the most spirited horse. It was necessary for survival, and, being intensely practical, she had colluded with necessity. Now all that must be put aside. The First Kadine of a Muslim Prince did not ride horses, show her face in public, appear without the adornment of a fortune in gold and jewels, or so much as speak to those of the opposite sex without her husband being present, and only then with his total approval. Then, she had been like a boy. Now she must be a woman at all times.

In England, girls wore long skirts, stockings and shoes, and they behaved with what Bastan called 'dec-or-um'. English girls did not need to be taught how to be women, he said, with a twinkle in his dark eyes, for they were born ladies. It seemed that Zebukar would be ideal for such an English lady, for he was amiable, well-mannered, charming and polite. She must pray that the English lady would be the saving of Zebukar. She must also pray that the union would be a love match, for, as far as Fira was concerned, nothing else mattered in life.

When all the relevant matters had been fully discussed between Bastan and Acteon, the Duke returned to London where his daughter waited for him. She was now eighteen months old and could toddle remarkably well, considering the plethora of skirts, bodices and bonnets with which infants of her day were burdened.

Walking into the nursery, shoulders hunched, mouth grim, Acteon saw the little doll toddling towards him, on tiny plump feet in little satin shoes, her eyes alight. They were such a bright green, yet so pale. They were Jemina's eyes. Tears began to pour down his face, and he slumped in a chair, but it was a nursery chair and too tiny for his massive frame. Overflowing in more ways than one, he sat and stared at the little girl with her topknot of bright russet curls, the very same colour as his own. Another red-haired Audlington, he thought. The line goes on, it does not end with me. And then a slow smile started, followed by gentle laughter which grew to hearty roars of delight. Scooping up the little laughing doll with the peridot eyes, he planted her on his knee and, from that moment on, father and daughter were inseparable.

Since that day, seventeen years had passed. Acteon was no longer in good health; he had strange pains which sent him to the comfort of his bed, and there he would lie, very pale, very anxious, being tended by Flavia who had learned a great deal about the treatment of invalids – especially ones who were sometimes querulous. As a child she had prayed that her father would find a woman to love, but he had never seemed to notice that women thronged around him, exerting all their charms to try to engage his interest. He was still one of the most eligible bachelors in the land, but he would rage if anyone said as much to him.

In his heart he was married to Jemina and always would be. There was no one else he could desire in that way. As for Flavia, she was his comfort, his consolation, but, much as it would pain him to part with her, he knew that she must go out into the world – as he had done years before – and find her own fortunes. It had always been thus with the Audlingtons, male or female. He knew that he would not find anyone to take her place, and the thought of placing himself in the inept hands of servants filled him with misgivings, but it must be done. When his daughter set off to marry Zebukar, he would be smiling as she went. The tears would come after.

Flavia was torn between excitement and unhappiness. All her life had been a preparation for this moment, for the magnificent union between a British Duke's daughter, and the heir of a Turkish Prince, first cousin to the Grand Turk. It was not the wealth, the splendour or the position that she wanted, but the arms of her handsome young husband around her. In flesh and blood and passions she was a true Audlington, fiery, indomitable, proud and sharp as a scimitar blade. She could cut right through to the heart of a situation in seconds, perceive truths, which others would never see in a whole lifetime, in a moment. Out there, the Universe, starry, wide, and spectacular was awaiting her. To rule with her husband, and share his life and help his people – what could be more blissful than that? Then there would be children to raise. She would take this on as her own cherished task.

She was fully aware that Muslim wives were subject to their husbands' wills and must be more obedient than

English spouses, but she was sure that Zebukar would love her so devotedly that she would be allowed a special place beside him. In time, she had no doubt, she would be able to dispense with all the nonsense of wearing the concealing *yashmak* and *chador*. After all, who would want to be parcelled up like that in public? As Princess Flavia, she would wear sedate and respectable gowns, but they would also be beautiful and elegant, of course. She adored clothes and chose them carefully to match her moods. She had a strong feeling for colour. Some she loathed, like bright, harsh green and dull, sombre grey. She imagined that it would be distressing to be swathed in the black *chador* in public – and also very hot and uncomfortable.

Perhaps she could devise a light veil which she could wear over the lower half of her face when in European dress. She smiled at herself in the mirror. She was sure that she could twist Zebukar round her little finger as easily as she did her father.

Princess Flavia – how strange it sounded. Prince Zebukar and Princess Flavia, Their Most Illustrious Highnesses, Allah be praised, Allah the all-merciful, the all-powerful . . . She knew so much about her new religion. She also knew that her father had been a secret Muslim for as long as she could recall, so it was in no way alien or unthinkable to her. Indeed, she believed that there was only one God, whatever He was named by different creeds and races, and as Muslims spoke of Allah being the one true God, she did not find their beliefs unacceptable. Far from it. Having been raised as a Georgian daughter was an excellent grounding for becoming a Muslim wife. The two held much in common. A wife should obey her husband. A wife should put her husband first. A wife should bow to her husband's wishes. Was there all that much difference between England and Turkey? No, she thought not.

She had studied the Koran carefully. It was very similar to the Christian Bible, she thought. So many words and phrases were familiar to her, as if they too, spoke of Christianity.

'Judgement belongeth to God alone. He hath bidden you worship none but Him. This is the right faith, but most men know it not.' And, 'Thy Lord hath not forsaken thee, neither hath he been displeased. And surely the Future shall be better for thee than the Past. Did He not find thee an orphan and gave thee a home? And found thee erring and guided thee? And found thee needy and enriched thee? As to the orphan, therefore wrong him not; and as to him that asketh of thee, chide him not away, and as for the favours of thy Lord tell them abroad.'

Could those words not have come from the Christian Bible? Having finished brushing her waist-length auburn hair, Flavia tossed it back over her shoulder. She would see that her father was settled for the night and then she would go to bed. She had sent Alice early to her bed, and it seemed an excellent idea for them all. The nights were still cool and to be tucked up cosily with a fire crackling in the hearth was a pleasant prospect. She smiled to herself. Because she had been caring for her father for nearly a year, she had allowed the pace of her life to slacken, and perhaps lost touch with the outside world. Parties and gossipy gatherings had become pleasures of the past. She would dearly love to get herself up to date on what was happening in the world, but she knew that was now impossible.

As she slipped out of her room, she threw a kiss at Prince Zebukar's portrait, as she always did. Those fierce, dark, burning eyes were glowing with passionate love just for her, she knew. How dazzling he was; how virile and beautiful, and how she adored him. As to the odd snippet of news from Greece which had reached them lately, well, she knew it to be lies. How could her darling Zebukar be anything other than perfect? As his bride, it was her place to support him with the utmost loyalty. If she were ready to listen to tales against him at this early stage in their relationship, what hope was there for trust later on? She had heard that a Society had been formed in London, its aim to release the Greek people from their Turkish overlords, whose rule was increasingly savage, or so the Society claimed. Flavia thought them romantic dreamers. Everyone knew that if the Turks withdrew from Greece, the Russians would step in and add Greece to their empire. The Russians already had a Greek emigré for their foreign minister, by the name of Capodistria.

Leaning over her father, she smiled. 'Do you want anything else before I retire, Papa?' Her fingers touched his forehead lightly.

'Sweetheart,' the Duke's gnarled fingers gripped her wrist and lifted her palm to his lips for a kiss. 'I have missed you so much, so much. You cannot *ever* know how much!'

An eerie sensation trickled along Flavia's spine. Was her father fevered? He seemed to think she was, well, could he have been dreaming and imagined that she was her mother? That had happened once before, when he had been suffering from a quartan fever. Luckily it had passed, but she had been frightened at the time – frightened that his mind had gone completely. The thought of the bold and fearless Acteon with his mind destroyed had nearly broken her heart.

'Sweetheart, I would love some hot milk with a little Madeira in it – and a madeleine, or one of cook's sponge fingers. Remember how we used to joke when you were little – how we used to say that we did not know how cook managed all her work with those soft, spongy fingers of hers?'

'I remember, Papa. I will get them for you now. I won't be long.'

Flavia did not wake Alice, who had been pale with a cold. She went to the kitchens herself. It was the least she could do for the father she would soon be leaving. Thousands of miles would separate them. How would she survive it? Worse, how would he? A glass of milk and a sponge finger . . . How simple were his needs. If only her husband could have lived on a neighbouring estate, and she could ride here to Audlington House every day to see that the Duke was being well tended, that he had all he needed.

Heating the milk on the sturdy iron range, she thought of the long months to come. Never again would she have to endure the caprices of the Great British Weather, frozen one day, steaming the next, drenched another, blown in circles after that. In Greece, so clement and temperate, she would bask in glorious sunshine, stare out across the sumptuous Aegean, blindingly blue, richly beautiful. She had been told that Prince Zebukar's palace overlooked the sea. It had singing fountains in the Turkish style, with prettily carved stonework and trellises strewn and coiled with rioting blooms. The marble-tiled floors were picked out in cool colours of powder-blue, rose, ivory and almond-green. She could not wait to see it all – if only her father were well enough to come with her, to make his life with them in the Morea in Greece. He had said that he would come, as soon as his old relics had recovered, and by that he had meant his old bones. But he had been failing for over a year now, with little sign of improvement, and the doses of the physician's painkilling medicine were larger all the time. Once, a dash of Madeira in hot milk would have settled him for the night, but now that was just a formality, coming as it did after the deep draught of laudanum.

The kitchens were chilly and silent. Genghis, the mouser, snored in his corner by the range, his pallid coat tufty and ungroomed. He was an odd cat, for he hated to be touched, and Flavia had never seen him licking himself. He must be all of twelve years old now. Reaching out, she touched his bristly fur, but he did not even flick an ear, although his snores became a little fainter before deepening again. Much good he was at mousing these days, she thought fondly.

Dark shadows hovered in the corners of the room, threatening, dangerous with secrecy, but she had never been scared of the dark. That was for weaker mortals, not a daughter of the House of Audlington. She was not aware that anything frightened her now, except the thought of her father dying alone, without her by his side. But she had been raised to put duty first, and she lived in an age which expected a wife's loyalty and devotion to her husband to be paramount. She knew that she would be such a wife, that Zebukar would fall wildly in love with her, and that they would live happily ever after. Just as her Papa and Mama would have done had not Mama died so tragically. Or was she building a fantastic dream? *Turkish oppression in Greece.* She remembered the shock of reading that headline in one of her father's papers, and then throwing off her shock along with the disloyalty to Zebukar which it represented. *The vicious yoke of the Islamic conqueror.* That had been another headline. All lies, of course. How could they be true? Bastan had been revered, a good, kind and cultured man. Had not her own father said as much, and often? Her father would never have spent so much of his youth with a cruel tyrant. She knew that her marriage to Bastan's son was Acteon's greatest dream. The culmination of his lifetime's ambition, the apogee of all he desired. She could never disappoint her darling, dying Papa.

The milk was sizzling, announcing its readiness. Filling a tumbler with the steaming liquid, she added honey, made by their own bees from the pollen of wild blossoms. Walking back alone through the dim corridors to her father's chamber, she savoured the experience. This would be one of the very last times she made this journey. That thought brought a flood of mixed emotions. Joy, that she could care for her father, sadness that soon she must leave him.

A new life, that was what he called her future. A new life full of promise and excitement. Beside her husband, ruling a great country, helping its peoples, nurturing thousands instead of one old father, he had said, bringing tears to her eyes. The Prince needed a wife's warmth and comfort in the troublous times he was having. A renegade rebel was causing chaos with his attacks on the Grand Turk's government. The man was a Greek, a so-called 'freedom-fighter' who had led his followers to make war against the Turkish occupation forces and their leaders.

'He is insane, of course, my love,' Acteon had told his daughter. 'The Turks have ruled Greece for three hundred years now – what need is there of insurrection and such revolting cruelties as this rebel leader has inflicted on the occupation forces? Terrible, indescribable atrocities which have ensured that the man – they call him the Pagan – will pay the ultimate penalty when he is caught. And that will not be far off . . .'

'Greece is at war?' Flavia had asked, fearing for her Prince's life, longing to be with him despite the dangers.

'No – no, nothing like that. Do you think that I would let you go to a war-torn country? No, this man, this fiend, the Pagan, is leading minor revolts here and there throughout the country, and perpetrating the most appalling crimes.' The Duke shuddered, recalling what he had read in the letter from Prince Zebukar, which had been for his eyes only, and which had accompanied the flowery love letter for Flavia.

Turkish soldiers – poor, suffering men only carrying out their orders – had been hacked to death, tortured, their hands, tongues and ears cut off – and worse. Some had been buried in sand, the tide coming in as they watched, its waves putting an end to their lives. It was said that the Pagan and his followers had stood by, laughing, while their wretched victims drowned. What manner of man was he? Everyone knew that Prince Zebukar was a generous, just man who cared deeply for the Greeks whom he ruled in the name of the Grand Turk. How could the son of Prince Bastan and Princess Fira be anything else?

Acteon remembered the Greeks as loving Bastan whole-heartedly. Worshipping him almost, for he had improved their lives so much. He had never been a lofty, distant prince who kept a barrier between himself and his subjects. He had gone out amongst them, spoken with them, asked to hear their problems. And he had raised his son to carry on his work. The country had flourished, and prosperity was now the order of the day, all thanks to him and now to Zebukar. Yes, Acteon had read the conflicting news items in the papers, but he could not believe that matters were deteriorating in Greece, in spite of the temporary anarchy brewed by the rebel called the Pagan. Had the Turks been villains, would they not have persecuted the Greek Orthodox Church? Yet they never had, as far as he knew.

All the same, to allay his misgivings, he contacted his friends in the government and a deputation had been sent to the Morea by King George, to ascertain the truth. While there, the deputation had been fêted and lavished with attention, balls and soirées were held in their honour. There had been an opportunity to meet the ordinary Greek people, too, and to hear what they had to say about their Turkish overlords. They had heard nothing but good of them.

Acteon had been thoroughly reassured by the deputation's report. Greece had never been more peaceful, more contented. There was no poverty, no starvation, no privation. Greeks and Turks worked and lived happily together, and all were eager to meet and honour their new princess when she arrived. All through the length and breadth of the country, its hospitable people were busily preparing and making wedding gifts for her. Acteon was heartened beyond belief by the report, which had been prepared by staunch men of the King's government, all old friends of his, whose word was unimpeachable. Flavia's arrival could do nothing but bring even more happiness to Zebukar's domains, the Pagan would see the error of his ways and the insurrections would be brought under control swiftly.

As he sipped his nightcap, his eyes adoring his one and only child, the Duke thought back to her infancy, regretting bitterly how he had neglected her in the first months of her life. What an idiot he had been, arrogant, blind and unreachable, only his sojourn with Prince Bastan and his wife had showed him the stupidity of his ways. Children came from Allah, and as such should be cherished. Well, he had more than made up for those early months of neglect, and now he was giving his beautiful daughter into the hands of the man who called himself Allah's Servant, the man whom he had last seen as a handsome, amiable little boy at Bastan's court.

The son of such a happy marriage as that between Bastan and Fira would know all that needed to be known about making his new bride happy. Acteon had no fears on that score. And if he fretted over having to part with her, he must console himself with the knowledge that she was safely betrothed, protected from the vulpine world of avaricious suitors, after his death. They would have torn her to shreds for her fortune, not caring for her heart . . . He could die content now.

'Flavia, my sweet.'

'Yes, Papa.' She leaned even closer, eyes tenderly luminous.

'You will be happy for my sake, when I am gone?'

'Do not speak like that, dearest Papa!' She held his hands tightly in her own.

'You know that this marriage is my dearest wish? My dying wish. The vow I made to Bastan who saved my life so heroically, and but for whom I might never have learned how to love you. He was willing to die to save me.'

'I know, Papa. Yes, I shall be happy, always, for *you*.'

'Never take love for granted, my sweet. Cherish what you have, for it can so easily be taken away. Think of me often, for I shall be thinking of you.'

'You will always be in my thoughts, dearest Papa. Now sleep, and in the morning I shall bring in your breakfast.'

The Duke's lids were drooping as the sleeping draught took effect. Smiling indulgently, Flavia took the tumbler from his hand and gently pulled the coverlets up round his shoulders. Even if Muslim traditions would not allow her to call her first son Acteon, she would always secretly think of the boy by that name. Or perhaps the Prince would allow Acteon to be their son's second or third name? Nothing would make her happier.

Taking one last fond look at her now sleeping father, Flavia tiptoed from the room, carefully closing the door behind her.

CHAPTER TWO

He was beautiful. She had never seen anyone so beautiful. Shivers of excitement and anticipation thrilled through Flavia. This was her betrothed, her prince. Soon, he would be her husband, his arms would be around her, his lips on hers. She could not wait. Watching him from a distance was sweet agony. Zebukar . . . His name was on her lips, in her heart, aflame in her soul.

Between them stood the Prince's Prime Minister – or that would have been his title had they been in England. Here, at this Turkish court, he was called the Kislar Agha and he was grotesquely fat, his stomach like a swollen moon which looked as if it would drop to the ground at any moment. The thought of this made Flavia want to laugh, so she compressed her lips tightly. The Kislar's face was strangely thin, sharp bones sticking out like blades, and his nose was crooked, having been broken at some time and set badly. Nonetheless, his humourless mouth smiled a broad welcome and he looked immensely pleased that his master's bride had arrived at last. In a carefully rehearsed speech, he told Flavia that the whole of Greece, and indeed of Islam, was enraptured at this union between herself and Prince Zebukar.

'There are gifts awaiting you, My Lady Duchess – jewels and silks from Allah's Most High, Most Glorious and Most Revered monarch, the Grand Turk himself if My Lady Duchess would care to be shown to her suite, she will find all in readiness for her . . .'

Flavia replied politely, conscious of the splendidly handsome Prince watching her from across the prettily-tiled court. Was she not to be allowed to speak to him? Surely he would approach her and welcome her himself? But no, like a sphinx he looked on from afar, studying her so intently that she felt scoured by his eyes. Was this the custom, then? She had always thought it to be the exact opposite here – that she would converse only with her husband, not with his ministers, certainly at first.

Bevies of richly-robed men and women were standing to one side, also observing her. Husbands and wives, she imagined. The women were of course swathed in heavy, dark robes, their faces masked with rigid black *yashmaks* which she thought looked quite horrifying, and somehow brutal. She tried to concentrate her thoughts on these people for it became obvious as the minutes passed, that the last thing she would be allowed at this point was conversation with the Prince.

Anguished, she felt desperately homesick in a way piercingly new to her. Not even during the long, bleak months at sea had she felt like this. If only her Papa were here . . . She could not bear this terrible loneliness a moment longer . . .

Then suddenly, the people were ebbing away, on silent, slippered feet, and the beautiful, lushly-coloured court was empty – save for Flavia and the Prince. Colour dashed to her cheeks, her heart thumped, her knees shook. He was coming towards her, her beautiful handsome fiancé . . . Yards, then feet, then mere inches separated them, while her heart thundered ever more loudly and she had an image of herself fainting away at his feet. What an impression that would make on her new husband! Clenching her hands, she waited to hear him speak, wanting with all the longing in her to know what his voice sounded like.

'Beloved wife, Chosen One of Allah, welcome to my palace. This is your home from this moment. Here, you will know nothing but happiness and comfort. All you ask shall be yours, silks, rubies, pearls, gold, honour, love. All that I have is yours, beloved wife-to-be.'

The words flowed over her, through her, like multi-coloured liquid silks undulating their way through her senses. Heaven bloomed in her mind. She saw it, felt it, welcomed it. He loved her; she loved him. What more was

33

there to life than this? If he would but take her into his arms now, and kiss her, she would want nothing else on earth.

'Your Highness, I want nothing but your happiness, and I hope to spend the rest of my life ensuring that you enjoy that state,' she whispered.

Zebukar grinned, his pearly black eyes flashing, his strong teeth white as pebbles bleached by the sun. There was vigour in his face, a lively, powerful energy which instinctively she knew would make him a good lover. She was no faint-heart, no pale, passionless creature – she was her father's daughter, her mother's too. What no one would tell her about life and its intimate secrets she had learned in the Duke's library, devouring his books. She had wanted to know everything there was to know – especially about the relationship between men and women. And she had learned a great deal, but never enough. Soon, with this masterful, dashing man, she would find out the last, vital secrets . . .

A gust of wind swept through the court, making the Prince's scarlet silk cloak billow out so that he looked as if he were about to take wing, and then, to her overwhelming delight, he swept her into his embrace, and for the first time she felt his lips on hers. Not even years of sensual imaginings could have prepared her for such tumultuous bliss; her skin teemed with sensation wherever his body touched hers, and her mouth was seared.

What would happen now? Her knees felt powerless at the thought, her senses craving unity with this adored man. Her Prince, her very own beloved Prince . . .

Above them as they kissed, a bird wheeled, dipping and fluting through the air, as if taking stock of them. Beautiful, streamlined, autonomous bird, the Prince's own, which he had trained to kill, to peck out the eyes of its prey, then leave it to bleed to death on the ground.

Prince Zebukar was murmuring love words in her ear, a passionate mixture of Turkish and English, so ardent that the colour thronged in Flavia's cheeks. She was as

34

malleable as silk in his arms, his offering, his eager bride: she wanted him as much as he wanted her. Crushed against him, she could feel the power and hardness of his masculinity stabbing into her, and, despite her ignorance she knew that this was what she had been waiting for. Instinct, race memory, urged her to respond, to give so that she might receive.

'Allah has blessed me, sending me the most fair and virtuous of women to be my bride. No one shall ever stand between us, my Western Rose, my Lady of Mysterious Delights. You will bear me sons whose names shall be famed for centuries to come – black-eyed, red-haired boys. Allah has willed it, and so shall it be. All praise to Allah the Most High.'

'All praise to Allah the Most High,' echoed Flavia, feeling that she had stepped into another world, the Garden of Allah, where pain, bad memories and suffering could never intrude. With Zebukar's mesmeric eyes searing into hers, how could she think otherwise, or want to? Heaven was here, and she wanted to relish it with her husband-to-be.

A servant appeared from nowhere on silent, slippered feet, and Zebukar himself poured a drink for Flavia. It was orange fruit sherbet, sweet and scented, but she did not notice the overpowering taste, only the hypnotic gaze of the man who handed it to her, and the smile playing on his lips. A jewel blazed in his cloth-of-silver headdress; it was a ruby as big and red as a peony and it, too, seemed to be staring at her immobilizing her senses, entreating her to be its willing, eager slave. She did not want to disobey! Nor would she have known how even if she had wished to.

When she had emptied the jewelled goblet, the servant took it away, vanishing in a swirl of robes. Zebukar grinned, his black eyes glittering.

'You will become accustomed to being served as befits a princess and chief Kadine of the first cousin of the Grand Turk. Whatever you wish shall be yours, you need only ask. Now I must leave you, but you will be in excellent hands. The Lady Orlinda will attend you, and she speaks English.'

And with that Zebukar was gone, as swiftly and silently as the royal falcon which had now vanished from the sky. Seconds later a tall and heavily veiled woman approached Flavia, saying in a low voice that she was the Lady Orlinda, and her dutiful servant.

'If Your Ladyship would follow me . . .' Orlinda whispered, beckoning Flavia into the palace. They bypassed the main entrance, walking through rose gardens and trellised walks, arbours bursting with vivid colour and pungent scents. Here, the blazing sun was so bright that Flavia had to narrow her eyes to block out some of the glare. She knew that her fair, delicate skin would not survive the onslaught of such a dry, piercing heat, so she would have to protect it carefully. Her father had warned her to spend only a short time in the Greek sun on the first days there, lengthening the time gradually. She thought it excellent advice.

She could not tell what the Lady Orlinda looked like, for even after they had stepped inside the palace and reached the entrance to what were obviously private apartments, she did not remove her veiling. It was a new experience to Flavia, trying to engage someone in conversation when she could not see their face, or know whether their mouth were grim or smiling. She supposed that she would have to get used to it – in public, anyway, but she had been led to believe that women removed their veils when alone and in private. Normally, she would have put her thoughts into words, but this country and its ways were still very new to her, and the last thing she wanted to do was alienate her future husband's people. Smiling, she allowed Orlinda to show her round the sumptuous suite where refreshments, robes, and chests filled with gems awaited her. There was a sunken bath of delicate almond-green marble which was being filled with steaming, scented water by two obsequious tiring women who kept their heads bowed and shoulders hunched as they worked.

When they had gone, the Lady Orlinda flung open the lid of a scented coffer and drew out a handful of rose petals which had been steeped in delicious attar of roses. She walked over to the steaming bath and flung the petals into it, bowing her head as she did so – almost as if she were making a libation to the gods. There was a reverence in her gesture which was not wasted on Flavia. Was Orlinda praying? She kept her head down and her lids closed for some moments before turning to Flavia.

'My Lady Duchess,' she erroneously addressed her new mistress. 'We all wish you well here. We look to your arrival as the start of new blessings for us – which we-we—' Orlinda's voice quavered and Flavia was startled to see what she thought were tears in the woman's dark eyes.

'Are you ill, Lady Orlinda? May I get something for you?'

'No – no, I am not ill, My Lady Duchess, not ill.' Orlinda seemed to be visibly bracing herself, straightening her back and shoulders, lifting her head high. 'All my people, that is, the people of Greece who are – who are, needful of a new mistress, are eager to welcome you.'

'I am delighted to be here and to receive their kind greetings. As soon as I can, I will hope to meet my future husband's subjects.'

A strange look came into Orlinda's eyes at that last word. The veiling of her *yashmak* shivered as if she were grimacing behind it. Flavia thought that she knew what was the matter: here was a woman with a very powerful feeling of national identity – a Greek woman who could not help but look on Zebukar as a despotic ruler. To raise this point would require a delicacy which Flavia did not think she possessed at this moment, tired and strained as she was from her long sea journey. Also, it would be disloyal to her future husband. She would tackle that later, when she was revived.

The bath elevated her to the realms of divinity, stealing the aches from her body, breathing vigour into her blood. She was not prepared for the tiring women to stand over

37

her as she bathed, which they did, their unmasked faces blank, their eyes darkly empty. Now and again, they cast more scented petals into the water, and emptied unguents of musk oil, jasmine and ambergris after them, so that even the steam was heady and rich. Her hair could not be washed in such oily water, so it had been pinned up by Orlinda, who now waited with fluffy towels into which her mistress stepped.

Even the towels were scented with attar of roses, and because of the priceless oils, Flavia did not come out of her long soak looking like a shrivelled almond. Her skin was soft and velvet, smooth and silky.

Once she had dried, Orlinda washed her hair. She sat in a carved chair, leaning her head backwards on a velvet hassock. The woman was dextrous, gentle and swift and soon Flavia's ample auburn tresses were swathed in a turban to dry. She felt so much more relaxed now, and ready to choose her gown for the evening's entertainment which would consist of a dinner in her honour to be attended by all the major dignitaries of Zebukar's domain. Each was to pay homage to her in front of Zebukar, and they would be bringing wedding gifts. It was exhilarating – but her thoughts did not dwell on the gifts. She was eager to see her future husband again, to sit beside him in the place which was now allotted to her as his future Princess, to let their people know that she cared for them, cared deeply.

When she was dry, Orlinda led her to a plump velvet couch buttoned in almond-green silk, and she lay on this while Orlinda massaged unguents into her limbs. After a time, it became less embarrassing, but how unlike bath-times in England, Flavia thought, recalling the hefty iron tub with its huge clawed feet lurking in wait to stub bare toes; the enormous vaulted bathroom which was like a wind chamber with its draughts and breezes, and the water itself which was always tepid after being carted from the distant kitchens; the bony fundament of the bath which nearly paralysed her muscles. England, dear England, with its unschooled climate, and all its inconveniences, discomforts and blemishes – how she loved it. And Papa . . . Her eyes misted over. She had written to him every day while at sea, and would continue to do so. Indeed, she had hoped that there would be letters waiting for her here, brought by swifter ships than hers.

'Lady Orlinda, is there mail for me – letters?'

'I do not know, My Lady Duchess – please to ask His Most Great Highness the Prince, your betrothed. Please to ask him always such things. Always.'

'Of course. Thank you.'

The tiring women had begun to show new robes to her. One by one, they stepped in front of her, a gown over their outstretched arms, their faces as mute of expression as ever. Gorgeous, blazing gowns they were, scarlet-gemmed with silver beads, fringes and embroidered ferns fragile as gossamer; almond-green silvered brocade studded with tiny glittering diamonds; butter-yellow velvet trimmed with citrines and topaz; china-blue cloth of gold petalled with sapphires – and each gown in the loose, voluminous Eastern style, each with its own matching *yashmak* . . .

Flavia had hoped to be able to wear one of her own gowns. There was a silk dress in the very latest English mode which she had planned to wear on her first night. Gleaming white, with serene, stylish lines, caught beneath the bust with diamanté, the neckline scooped but not too daring, the sleeves beribboned and tucked in the style of Renaissance Florence. Her father had always loved her in white, and she had worn the dress for him to see before she left. It had cost many guineas, more than she had ever spent on a gown before, more than she would have spent on three gowns, but they were not impoverished and she was after all to be a princess, as her Papa reminded her, a fond smile lighting his tired face.

She felt that she was cheating him somehow by not wearing it, but it would look very rude if she waved away these splendid outfits and wore one of her own.

Finally she decided on the almond-green. It was ablaze

with diamonds and in the light from the tapers would dazzle all those present. 'Make an entrance, my love – stun them all, show 'em the English can be peacocks too,' the Duke had grinned.

The underdress was sumptuous, liquid silk against her body, and she was silent with admiration as it was slipped over her head, susurring about her ears like the soft waves of the sea. Virtually every inch of the overdress was emblazoned with diamonds, so that when she looked down she was blinded. The boat-shaped neckline was encrusted with diamonds and tiny emeralds which were as pale green as her peridot eyes. But how heavy it was.

At home, she would now be coiling up her hair – which she preferred to do herself – but she could see Orlinda approaching with a vast expanse of pale-green silk which floated behind her as she moved. The edges of this too were weighted with gems.

At first, Flavia put the silk round her shoulders like a wrap but Orlinda shook her head. Taking the silk back, she gestured to Flavia to put it over her head, veiling her face. Flavia clamped her mouth shut. So she must be hidden behind a veil like a Turkish woman. The silk eddied round her face like a mist, and was sucked into her mouth when she spoke. She thought it a most impractical mode of dressing, and very much wanted to tell the Lady Orlinda so, but she did not. Silence fuels the sunshine, her father had always said.

'Shall I meet the Prince's mother tonight?' Flavia asked, and was shocked by the effect her words had upon Orlinda. The woman shrank back, her eyes staring. Then, after an obvious struggle, she managed to mumble something inarticulate.

'Is the Prince's mother ill?' Flavia asked, concerned.

'Oh no, she is not – that is . . . *Aiee!*' Orlinda made a strange keening noise, her fingers to her lips. The tiring women were watching, waiting to be given their next commands, unable to understand what the two women were talking about.

'My Lady, what is wrong?' Flavia insisted.

'Ask – ask His Most Serene Highness. He will tell you, My Lady Duchess.'

Then Orlinda was hurrying the tiring women out of the room and rushing about in search of a handmirror in which she insisted Flavia view herself. Flavia agreed, but as she could see nothing except for an almond-green veil she thought it a totally wasted exercise.

'My Lady Duchess has the emeralds of Bastan?' Orlinda then asked, at which Flavia nodded. 'His Most Serene Highness will be expecting Your Ladyship to wear them.'

'Of course.' Flavia went over to her suede dressing case, lifted its lid and drew out the jewels. Instantly she was back in England, in her father's house, gazing at the vibrant emeralds for the very first time. They were ridiculously large, and she often experienced a feeling of disbelief when she looked at them. She knew without doubt that they were real – a wedding gift originally given to Bastan's first wife by the Grand Turk himself. Now she was to wear them, for soon she would be First Kadine here. She dearly wanted to meet the Prince's mother, for Acteon had told her much about the beautiful and spirited Fira.

A butter-haired princess descended from Ghengis Khan, that was how Acteon had described Zebukar's mother. The Princess Fira had lived a life of seclusion since the death of Prince Bastan, so Flavia had been told. Perhaps she was ill? Perhaps she was dismayed at seeing a newcomer and a foreigner taking over her position as First Lady? Who knew?

Iron-muscled guards were waiting at the doorway to the suite, huge fat turbans on their heads, their arms and chests naked and bronzed, their legs encased in loose, silk trousers which ballooned to the ankles. Flavia must have looked startled at their sudden appearance, for Orlinda put a hand on her arm.

'Do not be afraid, My Lady Duchess, they are *castrato*, quite safe.'

And then Flavia was thankful for the veil, for she was blushing hotly. Yes, she knew what that word meant, for she had studied every book and tract she could find on the Turkish and their way of life. *Castrato*, castrated, their manhood cut away when they were young boys so that they could be safely allowed near the concubines and Kadines.

Flavia stared hard at the men. They could not see her eyes upon them. Did castrated men look any different from ordinary ones? They were broader, fatter, but still muscular, and as sturdy as barrels. Their chins did not look bristly and she wondered if the operation affected their body hair. She would also like to have known more about their private feelings. She could not imagine that they welcomed being castrated, but she knew that many eunuchs had risen to posts of immense power and wealth in Turkey's history.

The eunuchs, with gleaming scimitars tucked in their folded arms and jewelled daggers in their sashes, led Flavia along a series of corridors, while Orlinda fluttered behind her like a moth. The Palace of the Silver Cicadas was vast and echoing, and they walked for a very long time without seeing anyone, or hearing the slightest sound but their own footfalls. Then the noise of drum and tabor floated out of the distance towards them. It was like hearing ghostly pipes in a haunted Scottish castle, and made the hair at the back of Flavia's neck stand on end.

'We are nearly there,' Orlinda whispered. Suddenly the noise of the music became piercingly loud; the instruments made a harsh wailing sound like a banshee's complaint. The notes wavered and dipped, rose, then dipped again, and a drum was being beaten steadily, without emotion. There was something else too – the chink of what could be bracelets.

A girl was dancing in the centre of a richly-coloured, vaulted hall whose floor was tiled in ivory, geranium-red and primrose-yellow. Rich mosaics in blending hues lined the walls and scarlet silk curtains hung down one side of the chamber. The air was musky with the scent of incense, oranges and spice.

The girl was little more than a child, her body slender but shapely. She was half-veiled, and her eyebrows were thickly made up with kohl, a black line joining them together over the nose, a tiny ruby gleaming in the centre of her forehead. She had long hair reaching to her ankles, but it had been ineptly bleached and was streaky and crisp looking. The dusky down on her body and the darkness of her skin and eyes proclaimed that she was the possessor of a mixed heritage. On her wrists and ankles jangled dozens of silver bangles and a swirling scarlet silk skirt flew round her legs as she gyrated to the wailing music. Her slightly swelling breasts were covered by a stiff bodice of lemon brocade, heavily embroidered with green and scarlet silks and polka-dotted with spangles which reflected the light like mirrors.

The girl's body was gleaming with sweat, and she looked tired, but she continued to execute the vigorous contortions, watched covetously by all the men present. There were many men, Flavia noticed, and one heavily-veiled woman sitting beside Prince Zebukar. The woman's shoulders were hunched – she looked weary and dispirited. The Prince's mother? Then perhaps it was true that she was in bad health?

On seeing his bride, the Prince clapped his jewelled hands together impatiently and the dancer fled, not looking to left or right, her veils and hair streaming behind her as if windborne.

Seconds later, the Prince was taking Flavia's hand and leading her to the main table where he showed her to the carved throne on his left hand. He did not attempt to introduce her to his mother – if indeed that is who the veiled lady was.

All eyes were now upon Flavia – or rather upon the little that could be seen of her behind her veil. She was finding it increasingly steamy inside the silk tent and was longing to breathe air in the good old-fashioned way, but of course

43

the last thing she could do before all these Muslims was fling off her purdah. Only Muslim women of loose morals showed more than their eyes to men other than their husbands. She must give them time to adjust to her, to realize that she was not going to be subjugated. Her dream of sharing Zebukar's throne, of working with him, beside him, to bring contentment and happiness to their peoples could not be accomplished if she remained a veiled, mysterious and voiceless wife.

As Flavia took her seat on the carved throne, Prince Zebukar made what seemed to be a welcoming speech in Turkish, gesturing first to his betrothed and then to the assembled guests. She was able to pick out one or two words, although the Prince spoke rapidly. 'Pearl', 'success', 'overcome', and 'Pagan', being the words that she managed to translate before the Prince sat down, beaming broadly.

Flavia leaned towards him, her voice low.

'My Lord Prince, might I be introduced to Her Highness your mother,' she whispered.

Zebukar's smile faded instantly, a warning look darkening his eyes.

'Her Highness the Princess does not converse in public places,' he said, his voice reproachful. 'In her own good time, Her Highness the Princess will speak with you.'

'Of course.' Suitably chastened, Flavia felt her cheeks burning. Then enormous solid-gold platters were being carried in, their edges gleaming with sapphires and rubies, their centres piled high with a magnificent array of Turkish food. Heavily oiled, with oils from Corone and Modone in Messenia in the Peloponnesus, the main dishes consisted of mutton, lamb and kid, geese, poultry, guinea fowl and pigeons, with fruits in season to follow, fresh figs – which Flavia had never tasted before and which she found were heavenly – and fruit sherbets in orange, lemon and other assorted flavours, heavily sweetened with honey. Almonds, plump, black raisins, pistachios, honeyed-ginger and hazelnuts, with dishes of *Rahat Lokum* ended the meal.

'What is this called?' Flavia asked the Prince, as rose-pink, ivory and lemon-yellow sugar-dusted squares were offered to her.

'*Rahat Lokum*, Fair One. It means "giving rest to the throat." It is also known as Turkish Delight, and is made from grapes or mulberries, with semolina flour, rose-water, apricot kernels and honey. I am extremely fond of it and eat it all day. It helps me to think.'

Flavia smiled, thinking of her nurse's abjuration to avoid all sugary confections because they blackened teeth and made the bones ache as age advanced. The Prince's teeth were splendidly shiny and healthy.

Eating while veiled was a virtually insurmountable problem. No napkins were provided, but silver bowls of scented rosewater were brought round between every course, to clean the fingers of the diners. This Flavia took generous advantage of. The veil was apt to billow into food as she carefully lifted it to her lips, and eventually she had to sit forward, slightly stooped, in order to eat more easily. Even so, she could not manage as much as she would have liked of the strange and exciting-looking food. Fighting back a violent desire to fling her veil off and throw it across the room, she savoured a piece of pink *Rahat Lokum*, then a white one, then a yellow one. The confection felt like velvet in the mouth and melted away like magic, disappearing down her throat like liquidized silk. Yet it looked so solid and square in its dish.

The Prince's mother did not eat, but now and again sipped at a jewelled goblet of wine. Flavia felt a great wave of empathy for her. Poor woman, shackled for her entire life by the rigid controls of the Muslim religion, veiled and shrouded, her spirit hidden away in purdah. I shall *never* be like that, Flavia vowed. No one is going to close my mouth, or imprison my spirit or my body!

She longed to call the Princess's name, to speak to her across the Prince, but there was something powerful and forbidding about his strong yet slender form in its bright silk clothes encrusted with emeralds and diamonds. He was an autocrat – and something else with which she was not familiar. Despotism came into her mind, but she silently laughed it away. Zebukar was dearly loved by his peoples, even if the majority of them were Greek and his forefathers had invaded this country to take it by force. All that was forgotten long ago; all was happiness and success now, as King George's commission to Greece had reported only recently. Authority must be the word that she had meant. Yes, of course it was. Authority. Would not any monarch need that?

The musicians had been playing continually during the feast, their music varying between the plaintive, the eerie and the impassioned. They leaped to their feet as Prince Zebukar clapped twice loudly; it was obviously their signal to leave. Now Flavia saw that they were blind, and had to be led from the room on the arms of eunuchs. Poor creatures, blind. Her heart went out to them, for they were even more constrained and confined than women in purdah, for they could see nothing at all, not even through the space allowed women between veil and *yashmak*. But how generous and thoughtful of her future husband to give these poor men work here at his court, for they would surely have led a life of poverty and subsistence anywhere else. Dear, good, kind Zebukar, how she loved him.

The meal was over, the guests departing. She had not been introduced to any of them personally, which was a great shame, but possibly that would come later. After all, she was here for the rest of her life. Not too sure what to do now, she looked to Zebukar for his help, but he was talking to a grim-faced man wearing a huge, orange silk turban. She looked towards Princess Fira but saw that her seat was empty. She was disappearing out of a far doorway on the arm of a tall woman. Standing, the Princess was frail-looking and bent over the arm of her attendant as if she were very weak. How old would the Prince's mother be now? Surely not much more than forty and five years, if that? And she had borne only one child, so she could not have been affected by excessive childbearing, which was a woman's greatest enemy. She dearly hoped that she would be able to prove of some comfort to the Prince's mother, and build up a good relationship with her. So much depended on amicable relationships.

She thought of her father, a lonely widower since the death of her mother, and of the Princess Validé, also alone since the death of Prince Bastan, with whom she had shared an idyllic love. Why did some have so much and others so little? If she could, she would like to help right the balance a little, by being a loving and devoted daughter-in-law.

Zebukar was at her elbow, his face alight with admiration and possessiveness.

'My beautiful Western Rose, lover of *Rahat Lokum*,' he teased, 'your women will take you back to your apartments now. We must not meet alone until after the wedding. Just a few weeks, and then you will be in my bed, my beauty, my English virgin, and I shall make you mine as no one else has ever done before. Keep my heart with you until we meet again . . .' Slowly, he lifted her veil, which fluttered as tremulously as her heart, and then his mouth was on hers, and life was flowing between them, wild, warm, and passionate.

Seconds later he was gone, and she was being led away by the Lady Orlinda and half a dozen deferential veiled women.

Had that kiss really happened? In her bed that night, Flavia touched her lips with her fingers, feeling, in her imagination, a flame of heat as if it sprang from the Prince himself. He had marked her as his with two kisses. She had known that she was his alone, wanting no other man, for years. Now it was fact. Beautiful, unchangeable, ineradicable fact.

CHAPTER THREE

As a rule, concubines did not enter into marriage with their Turkish lords. It was enough that they entered his harem, and became one of his goods and chattels, as much his property as his couch, his footstool, his scimitar.

There was no danger that Zebukar would treat Flavia, a British girl, as a concubine and not make her his princess and chief Kadine. Not only that, but she would be his only Kadine. That had been agreed years before by the two fathers, Bastan and Acteon. In return for the immense privilege of having a Western bride, Zebukar had promised to treat her as she would have been treated had she married a man of her own country. That was all understood. So Flavia had no fears on that score, even though she knew that Turks were lustful and passionate by nature, and that various Grand Turks in Constantinople had thought nothing of having five hundred concubines for their delectation.

It was Bastan who had introduced the Western concept of true love and monogamy, a concept his son respected and would put into practice.

Once or twice, when she looked from the windows of her sumptuous apartment, Flavia saw a stream of lovely young girls passing by. Their heads were high, their shoulders straight. They were young – too young to be veiled – and they were richly-dressed. All were black-haired, with skins of pale terracotta, and they chattered merrily as they walked. Flavia wanted to know who they were, and she asked Orlinda on more than one occasion, but Orlinda always shook her head from side to side, shrugging her shoulders.

'I not know,' she would say. 'Where are girls?' and she

would peer out of the window, to left and right, as if unable to see the girls who would by then be fast disappearing.

In the end, Flavia gave up asking, deciding that she would find out from the Prince when next they met. But he did not visit her, nor did he send for her. Orlinda, when asked, just gave one of her perennial shrugs and said, 'Great Highness away,' making Flavia wish desperately that she had not left her own maid behind in London.

As the Prince had wished, she had travelled to Greece under the guardianship of one of his chief ministers, a dour man who had a speech impediment and sprayed her with saliva when he spoke. Thankfully, he was a man of few words. Arms crossed, he had stood over her wherever she went during the voyage, watching her as if she were a priceless *objet d'art* which might at any moment be stolen. At night, his servant had slept outside her cabin door on a rush mat – a habit which had startled her no end when she first discovered it.

Lizzie, her maid, even James the groom, had possessed a fund of sprightly tales, harmless gossip and anecdotes which had enlivened her days. Here, as she was finding out, people were solemn and took themselves seriously. As yet there was no way that she could attempt to make a joke with her limited knowledge of the language, although she did try. The result? Stony stares.

The fittings for her wedding gown were as tedious as dressing fittings always were. Orlinda spoke of the great numbers of guests who would be at the wedding, Turks and Greeks, a representative of the Grand Turk himself, who was coming all the way from Turkey. Everyone, said Orlinda solemnly, must witness this marvellous alliance, not only between Prince Zebukar and King George of England but also between the peoples of England and of Turkey.

'It is hardly that!' Flavia laughed. 'It really has nothing to do with King George, or England itself. It is the result of my father's friendship with the late Prince Bastan. Nothing political.'

Orlinda looked shocked. 'But it is a great alliance

between Turkey and England! Everyone is knowing this, but *everyone*.'

'They can think it, but it does not make it true, Orlinda. I have no right even to agree with such an inflated description of my marriage.' As far as Flavia knew, relations between Britain and the Turkish in Turkey were never very tranquil.

For some days, Flavia's every hour was filled with fittings and discussions concerning the ceremony, her part in it, and the future role she would play as a princess. The Kislar Agha, vast as a mobile mountain, visited her once a day to ensure that she knew exactly what the ceremony would consist of, what she must do and say, or not say, and how she would be presented to the Court. The Prince's religious adviser spent a day with her ensuring that she knew exactly what was entailed in marrying a Muslim; he wanted to find out how she felt about becoming a Muslim – what stage her instruction had reached, and if she was truly willing to become a convert.

'Absolutely!' Flavia smiled. 'My father would never have forced me to do anything that I did not want to do.'

The mullah stared at her piercingly for a long moment. His eyes were like nuggets of jet which glowed blue-black with an unnerving ferocity. After a few moments' talk with him, she realized that he was a zealot, and she knew that such men were capable of any act in the name of their religion. He was swathed in spotless robes, and he smelled of saffron and sweet oils; his skin was a very rich dark brown, the colour of sultanas.

'It is a father's duty to train his daughters in the ways of Allah.'

'In Islam, yes, but not in my homeland,' Flavia reminded gently.

'A father must ensure that his daughters are faithful, chaste and dutiful,' the man went on, his eyes bright black beams.

'There is much to be said for that, but often more can be achieved by love than by coercion.'

'A strange notion, His Grace.' Flavia had to suppress a smile. The mullah's English was really rather good, but for the occasional error. 'Allah loves all His faithful – it is a foregoing conclusion, so they in their turn must love and fear Him. So as you say, much can be done by love, but by no means all. What of the recalcitrant child who does not love his father? How would the father draw him to his side, then? Chastisement is imperative, greatly so. A severe punishment will drive out the evil from the child . . .'

'I do hope that I shall not have to chastise any child of mine. I do not like to think of my children being beaten.'

'The Crown Prince will be raised by myself and the Prince. We shall do what must be done, according to the laws of Allah.'

'I would hope that I shall have a say in his upbringing!'

'The boy shall be with his mother until he reaches that age when a woman's care is no longer needed,' the mullah intoned, as if he were reading a speech learned by heart.

'A mother's care is always needed!' Flavia stood up, feeling uneasy to say the least. Her son was not going to be taken from her and raised by fierce, arid zealots like this man! How much would the Prince listen to his religious adviser? Would he give him a free hand – a hand which might prove to be free with beatings, too? Coldness slithered along her skin. Some Muslims did not seem to feel secure until they had subjugated their women and their children. But of course her Prince was not like that. He was enlightened. If only he were here now, but she had not seen him for days . . . He was out hunting, she was told, or he was in council meetings.

'Before the ceremony, there will be an examination,' the mullah continued, as if she had not spoken.

'What sort of examination? I have studied many things in preparation for coming here . . .' – Would they want to know how much she had learned about her new country?

51

'Not an examination of the mind,' the mullah droned, 'but of the physicalness.'

'The physicalness? Oh, you mean a physical examination? But I am quite healthy, I do assure you. Please tell the Prince that—'

'Not for the health, His Grace. For the proof of the chasteness.'

'Ch –? I –' Flavia's mouth fell open. 'You mean, for the – the . . .' Colour burst into her cheeks, a surge of heat made her clothes feel thick and heavy.

'Such an one as the High Prince's chief Kadine must be proven to be of the greatmost chastity, pure, untouched . . .'

The mullah might have been reciting a shopping list.

'There is no doubt of that!' Flavia interrupted angrily. 'Please tell the Prince that I wish to see him immediately! He cannot know of this ridiculous, insulting examination!' Flavia strode to the far end of the room then back again, swinging her arms so that the rose silk of her caftan billowed like wings. 'There is no way that I shall agree to such a monstrous invasion of my privacy! It is unthinkable, disgraceful . . .'

'Allah ordains it. Allah ordains that all wives must be chaste. Especially the wife of the Most High, the Most Serene, the Most Beauteous, the Most Powerful Prince Zebukar.'

'And I am, I *am!*' Flavia cried.

'It must be proven. Allah has ordained it.'

'*I* prove it. I prove it by telling you that I am chaste – that there is no need for such an examination! I will not have anyone touching me in that way . . .'

'The women will be here at the middleday on the morrow. Four of them, so that there is proofing of the chastity,' the mullah droned, unperturbed.

Flavia glanced wildly at Lady Orlinda who was wearing a long-suffering expression. No help there, then. What should she do? This was outrageous.

'I wish to see the Prince at once, this instant, *now!*' Flavia cried, peridot eyes like twin gems of green flame.

The mullah looked taken aback at her vehemence. She could not help that. If he felt that way, then it was his right, but she was not going to be forced to do something so – so unBritish!

'The Prince is hunting, His Grace. It would be as well if you remained calm, sitting in the seat.'

'Tell the Prince that – that I wish to see him as soon as he returns. Tell him – tell him that I am deeply, deeply upset by this slur on my honour and reputation!'

'*Slur?*' the mullah could not comprehend her meaning, but he knew what honour and reputation were. 'The honour and reputation of His Serene Highness would be endangered if his chief Kadine was discovered not chaste. Must be no danger of the heir being not of the blood royal . . .' The mere thought caused the mullah to turn a sickly grey.

Flavia wanted to shriek out loud, to tear out of the tranquil, prison-like apartment to find her fiancé wherever he was, but she struggled to contain herself. It must be a misunderstanding of course. It had to be! If anyone in England got to hear of this . . . She shuddered at the thought.

'There is no danger. Tell the Prince that I wish to see him as soon as he returns, and that I am very *very* angry.'

The mullah nodded gravely, his saffron-scented robes coiling round his feet as he leaned forward to rise. His hands were greyish-brown, the fingers wrinkled and pouched, the knuckles like little dark-brown suede bags. His nails were dirty, however, which seemed out of order in a holy man. Muslims were also ordained by Allah to wash frequently, before prayer, three or four times a day or more – which was more than many of her countrymen did – yet this man's nails were ingrained with filth. She wanted to remind him of Allah's teachings on that subject, but she did not. Instead, she stayed silent until the door closed behind him.

Orlinda was silent too, busily sorting out jewels and ornaments from a scented coffer, her back to her mistress. So Flavia had shocked her too – well, that could not be helped, she was not a meek and biddable woman of Islam – and she would tell Zebukar so when she saw him! If he wanted a wife like that, then he must look for one in Turkey.

But Zebukar did not come. He sent a flowery message saying that he adored his Western Rose and could not wait to be beside her always, but that he had many council meetings and audiences to occupy him and time was short. With the letter came a trinket, a bracelet of knotted gold filigree work studded with amber, sapphires and cloisonné panels in pretty heart shapes.

'What comfort is a bracelet when I am about to be assaulted?' Flavia whispered as she clipped on the jewel. 'Oh, Zebukar, why do you not come to me?' She knew that just one look at him and she would feel so much happier. Nearly three weeks had passed now, and this apartment, which had looked so beautiful then, was now like a prison cell.

'We shall go into the gardens,' Flavia announced, for she must try to conquer her restlessness. She was putting on weight from too little exercise and too many rich and sugary meals. *Rahat Lokum* was piled high in a dozen dishes round the room and it was difficult to resist it.

'We go out?' Orlinda looked shocked.

'Why not?'

Orlinda shrugged, and would not meet her eye.

Flavia experienced a moment of acute annoyance. What was wrong with this girl? Sometimes she behaved in the strangest fashion.

'Answer me, Orlinda. Why on earth should we not go into the gardens?'

'The gardens of the harem, yes,' Orlinda muttered, still not meeting her mistress's eyes.

'All right then, the gardens of the harem. I did not know that they would still be in existence, after all these years.'

Orlinda looked at her with a sharp, darting glance, then flushed again. Having fetched voluminous cloaks, Orlinda opened the door for them both, saying something in rapid Turkish to the enormous, muscular eunuch standing outside on guard. The man grunted, and stepped to one side, his inscrutable slanting eyes revealing nothing of his feelings. As the two women walked past him and along the corridor, he padded behind them, his cocoa-brown bare feet making no sound. But they could hear him breathing. The noise was like that of a wild beast which had run for miles and desperately needed to rest. Listening to it, the hair on the back of Flavia's neck prickled.

She had felt like this only once before. Her Papa had taken her to a travelling circus when she was small, and the bellow of the wild animals there had made her skin tingle, but with excitement. What had scared her had been the sound of moans which issued from a roughly-built cabin. On its door was a notice which proclaimed that inside the cabin was the most frightening and ugly freak man who had ever been born. Flavia had longed to see him, but could not pluck up courage, and when her Papa had seen what she was reading, he had swept her away to the comparative safety of the animal cages.

For weeks, months, afterwards, she had longed to know what the monster had looked like and why he was moaning. His moans had sometimes intruded on her dreams, waking her with a pounding heart. Part of her had felt a terrible pity for him, the other part a swift curiosity which could not be quelled. There were mysteries and terrors in the world, but, however dreadful they were, she wanted to know them all. She imagined that the stertorous breathing behind her was that of the freak monster, that his paws would snap round her neck at any second, and crush her to a choking death.

The harem gardens were reached by a circuitous route, but they were worth the journey. In a pretty, sun-screened

55

court the air was languorous with the romantic scent of jasmine and carefully cultivated roses which looked as English as the ones in her father's gardens at home. Two marble fountains catapulted water into the air, and in the cool ripples encased in the carved marble, jewel-coloured fish swooped or dozed. The air was soporific, lulling, and Flavia felt refreshed. She sat on the steps of each fountain, seeing how many fish she could count, while the silent eunuch stood in the shadows, his arms folded like two great hams across his chest, and Orlinda waited, her eyes flicking uneasily from side to side.

Some time passed and then came the sound of high, chattering voices, young and female, which carried through the air like flutes. Flavia looked up, smiling. That would be the little girls she had seen out of her window. They must be daughters of the servants here, out for their daily jaunt. She would like to speak to them, and she said as much to Orlinda, who made a little sound, like a squeal of panic.

'We go back to rooms! No see children! Only servants, not for Lady Duchess to see. No, not possible – bad, bad!'

'Oh, Orlinda, this is stupid. Of course I can see them – why ever not? These are my future husband's people and I want to meet them, befriend them.'

Orlinda had gone deathly white, and she was pulling at Flavia's sleeve. 'Come, Lady! Come, now, must come,' she was almost sobbing, forgetting her careful English and lapsing into Turkish.

'I will not come!' Flavia said, quite angry now. 'I want to meet the children. Please have them brought to me, Orlinda. At once. If the Prince is angry, I will tell him that I ordered you to do this.'

'It must not be done!' Orlinda wailed, then clamped her hands to her mouth. 'Forbidden – forbidden by His Greatness . . .'

'Oh really, this is too silly!' Tugging her sleeve free, Flavia strode towards a wicket-fence in the trellis work, unlatched it and stepped out into the gardens beyond. Fig trees, heavy with plump, curvaceous brown fruit, bushes with blossoms

56

of every hue imaginable, a myriad scents of flowers and herbs awaited her. Smiling, she went towards the children, all girls, who stood in frozen silence as she approached.

Why did they look so scared of her? she wondered. She would soon show them that their new mistress need hold no fears for them. Closer now, she smiled broadly, looking at their sweet, creamy-brown faces and bright black hair. They were all little beauties, none of them over twelve, and she thought she recognized one – the dancer who had been entertaining the Prince's guests the night of the feast. She was the only child with bleached hair, for the others were very dark.

Flavia began to speak in Turkish, using a greeting suitable for children, and keeping the friendly smile on her face. Still they stood as if frozen, their eyes registering horror and disbelief. What was so awful about her speaking to servants' children? They were not even dressed like servants' families, but in silk and with rich ornamentation on their clothes. She spoke again, and again. No answer. At that point Orlinda stumbled towards her, begging her to come back into the smaller garden, telling her that the wrath of Allah the Most Powerful would descend upon them all if she did not obey.

At this, the children clustered together, wailing and clutching at one another. Then shouts were heard, and feet came thudding from another direction. Men with angry, savage faces and scimitars in their fists ran to the children and herded them together, away from Flavia, who watched, stunned at the turbulent scene.

Orlinda was nearly in tears, her shoulders shaking, her face ashen.

Turning to her, with suspicion lighting in her mind, Flavia said, 'Who were they, Orlinda? Tell me who they were. I want to know *now!*'

Orlinda seemed to crumple before her eyes. 'The Prince's daughters, they are the Prince's daughters, Allah forgive me, oh Allah have mercy on me!' Orlinda moaned, and then she collapsed to the ground in a heap.

CHAPTER FOUR

She could get used to the knowledge if she tried hard enough. After all, he was a man, was he not? And she could hardly have expected him to live the life of a monk all these years. All the same, it was a shock, a blow to her sweet, romantic dreams, and she felt unsettled.

Orlinda became ill that night, and the women took her away. When Flavia asked after her, no one would say how she was. Another woman replaced her, the Lady Zaba, and she did not like her half so much. Zaba was taciturn, monosyllabic and not nearly as careful about her duties as Orlinda had been. Questions fired at her by Flavia remained unanswered, and a bitter gloom descended upon Flavia's life. She wrote letters to the Prince, begging him to come to her, but he either failed to reply, or replied effusively, sending gifts, but not appearing in person. Flavia decided that the Turks were a law unto themselves and she would have to live with it or perish. It was a bitter moment.

Then came the letter which told her that her wedding day was only seven nights away, and that preparations were nearing completion. The ceremony would be in the mosque of St Zita, and there would be three thousand guests, including a representative of the Grand Turk, Sultan Mahmud II. Relief washed over Flavia at this news. She had been living in a hinterland, but soon she would be the Princess who would sit beside Prince Zebukar. She would have a title, a place and a right to do as she wished. Muslim wives had much more freedom than unmarried women, although there were still strict rules to be observed.

From then on, it was one event after the other. Final fittings for her wedding robes and nightrobes, which were translucent ivory silk, concealing little of her naked body beneath. On first donning them, she had blushed crimson, but after two more fittings, she was slightly more comfortable in them – but only slightly. Thankfully, there was a voluminous peignoir to throw over them.

Her wedding gown was a solid sea of diamonds and seed pearls, so stiff that it would stand up unsupported, the train being so long that it would need twelve bearers to carry it, and her jewelled slippers had one enormous, dazzlingly perfect diamond set into each tiny heel. Such riches, and yet they were nothing compared to the emptiness she was feeling after weeks of separation from Zebukar. How dearly she wanted to let him know her feelings, to pour out her heart to him. Over and over, she relived the way he had kissed and held her, the luxurious comfort of being in his arms. What diamonds could compare with that? They were cold, harsh lumps of glass beside true love. But after the wedding, she knew it would all be different. She would be Zebukar's wife, his Princess; she would have a place here, there would be no more of this isolated life shut away from people, away from the world.

She had grown up with more freedom than most Dukes' daughters, so she knew what she was missing. All the same, she knew that the average Muslim woman could never even comprehend life as a Western woman. To ride out freely, faces naked of the *yashmak* and of veiling, to walk in the streets and markets, similarly unveiled, with a chattering maidservant for company, these were her memories. One day, she hoped that she would be able to walk out freely in the streets of Greece. Why not? These were her husband's peoples. Maybe, to pacify Muslim laws she would have to be escorted by a guard or two, but that was a small price to pay. She had heard from her father that the Greeks were friendly, warm-hearted and hospitable, so she had no fears that they would be hostile or unpleasant to her. As they were naturally honest and open in their dealings, she had felt sure that she would be less likely to be attacked by footpads here than in the seething, unkempt heart of London.

She wanted no chilly barriers between herself and the people. She would offer her friendship, her support and aid, wherever she found it to be necessary – and if for some reason she could not go out to the people, then they must be brought to her. She would invite them to the Palace of the Silver Cicadas, listen to their troubles, and give them her assistance. She imagined that even a happy country · like Greece would have its problems, neighbourly squabbles, not enough money to pay physicians' fees, a sick child who needed special care, and so on.

The thought of distributing help in such cases was infinitely more satisfying than the anticipation of wearing priceless pearls and diamonds on her wedding day. Glittery trappings had never awed her.

To her relief no more had been said about the medical examination, and she was hoping that it was forgotten, that her protests had been noted. Then, a group of grim-faced matrons was announced. They had slept-in faces, baked a rusty brown by years of the sun, their eyes dark and dry, their brows thick as thatch, their mouths tight gashes. Few teeth remained in their heads, and their breath was redolent of rotting vegetation. Flavia spoke to them, but they did not respond, not even by a flicker of their arid eyes.

The Lady Zaba seemed to know why they were there, and she greeted them in rapid Turkish. The women advanced upon Flavia, while Zaba looked at her triumphantly, as if to say, 'Now you are at our mercy!'

What followed made Flavia's cheeks flame a scalding crimson, and her heart jerk violently. It was a physical assault, and even if it had been elsewhere on her body it would have been equally shocking. As it was, she was pressed towards a couch by the force of some twelve muscular, female arms, her skirts flung up over her head, and probing fingers thrust between her thighs. She had never been touched there before by anyone, let alone strangers, but one after the other these ancient crones reassured themselves that she was in full possession of a maidenhead, and only then did they step back and bow their heads deferentially.

'Duchess, it is over now,' Zaba said, her voice thick with what could only be delight, and then the gaggle of shrouded and sun-parched ancients was slapping away to the door, heads bowed, hands thrust into sleeves. It was like a scene from some age-old Greek tragedy. They, the punitive women of some Spartan tribe and she their helpless, unsuspecting victim. It was the first time that she had been humiliated by women, and she found it a disturbing, disorientating experience, as if her whole world had been tipped upside down. Betrayed by her own sex. Could anything be worse than that?

Hurt, she would not speak, nor eat for the rest of that day. When Zaba remonstrated with her, she cried, 'Stop calling me Duchess! I am not a duchess! I am Lady Flavia Audlington and you must call me Your Ladyship!' but Zaba's face went even tighter and she appeared not to understand.

Balling her fists, Flavia threw herself onto her couch and tried the deep, slow breathing that her old nurse had always sworn by. This time it would not work; there was no welcoming serenity sweeping through her veins and her pulses refused to slow down. Wild tides of passion and longing seared through her. She wanted to be back home with her father; she wanted to be a young and carefree girl again. She wanted to be anyone other than the daughter of a duke with all the weight of that responsibility upon her. If only she had been a son, there would have been none of this. She would have been in England, assured of her title, safe from such wretched difficulties and embarrassments, but she was a woman, a mere, helpless woman, and when her father died, – a moment which she dreaded – his cousin the Honourable Heatherly Hawthorne would inherit the dukedom, for it was passed down through the male line.

Humiliation heaped upon humiliation. If she had stayed in England, she would have had to see her father's title go to a strange eccentric who abhorred contact with those of his own class and who had seven mistresses, all of them adopted from the streets where he had found them, for the Honourable Heatherly Hawthorne had a predilection for whores of low birth. Men seemed to know nothing of the sufferings of women, or, if they suspected a little of it (which was rare) they imagined that gifts, a jewel, or a gewgaw, would pacify an entire battalion of seething, silent emotions.

Until that moment, Flavia had not realized how very much she hated the lot of women. Before, she had been favoured, indulged, pampered – certainly by comparison with others. Now, having been reduced to the mute, impotent helplessness of the lowest of women, she had become one of them, one of the sisterhood of silently suffering females.

Oh, she would complain to Zebukar when she saw him! She would tell him what she thought of such insulting tactics. How could he have allowed such an intimate intrusion of her body?

It was strange, but she was deeply depressed by what had happened. She was left feeling no better than a harem slave, a chattel, and she was very quiet for some time afterwards.

'Duchess,' Zaba's voice was like a distant bell summoning her back to life. 'His Serene Highness is here.'

'*The Prince?*' Flavia leaped to her feet, her hand to her mouth. 'The Prince is here?' Zaba nodded. It was like a dream, and yet more colourful than life itself. Zebukar had come to her at last. Now she knew how lonely concubines felt, after weeks of neglect, when their lord and master deigned to remember that they existed.

Her hair – she had not brushed it all day – and her kaftan was creased.

'Where is my silver robe – and fetch my brushes, and some attar of roses, quick, quick!'

Zaba obeyed, mute but competent, and within moments Flavia was flinging off her crushed robe and slipping into a silken one embroidered with silver cicadas, the Prince's emblem inherited from his father, and after which the palace was named. Attar of roses was always sweet, always refreshing and being headily scented had never yet failed to make her feel vigorously renewed, bright of mind.

When the door swung open to herald the Prince's arrival, Flavia made a deep and graceful curtsey, as she would have done to the King of England himself.

'My beloved Western Rose, all is well with you?' Zebukar's voice slipped along her senses like honeyed-wine, disseminating her fears, calming her agitation. All the accusations and complaints which she had been storing up for him evaporated. With his glowing, black-pearl eyes searing into her peridot ones, and his fingers lightly caging hers, a fluid fire coursed through her body, to the tip of every limb, to her heart, her soul.

'My Lord Prince, how I have missed you! Did you not get my letters? I have sent so many in the past weeks . . .'

'Letters? You have sent me letters? I do not think that they have been forwarded to me – Dazatan . . .' He turned to one of the eunuchs, a frown on his face. 'Dazatan, what happened to the letters which my future wife despatched to me?'

Dazatan looked perplexed. 'I not know, O Looker Upon The Stars. Not see letters, O Gazer Upon the Highest Moonbeams.'

Turning to Flavia, Zebukar gave a dazzling smile. 'Foolish servants, so careless, so disorganized. I will have the entire palace searched for your letters, my Western Rose, and be assured that they shall be found and the careless one severely, *most* severely punished.'

'Oh I do not want anyone in trouble because of them. Now you are here, My Lord Prince, I can tell you what was in them.'

A delicious twinkle sprang into the Prince's eyes. 'Dare I guess that you told me that you loved me, that you longed for me? If so, you were only echoing my own thoughts, O Fairest of the Heavenly Moonbeams upon which I gaze . . .' His eyes twinkled even more.

Flavia had been fully prepared for the hyperbole which the Turkish people used, but nonetheless she found it hard not to smile. She had heard of the Grand Turk's titles, which included Sultan of the Ottomans, Lord of the Lords of this World, King of Believers and Unbelievers, King of Kings, Emperor of the East and West, Prince and Lord of the most Happy Constellation, and Possessor of Men's Necks, so she was not unfamiliar with these flowery phrases.

'My Lord Prince, would you have me betray the modesty demanded of a Muslim bride?' she twinkled back, entering into the light-heartedness of the exchange. 'I think that you know my feelings are all that they should be – and more,' she blushed, lowering her eyes.

'Radiant dove, you are all that I would have wanted in a bride. Allah has been good to me.'

'And to me, Your Highness,' she blushed again, her humiliation and anger vanishing into the past.

'You are prepared for the ceremony? You have all that you want?'

'Yes, *now*, Your Highness, but I would wish to be allowed outside more. I love the sunlight and fresh air, and was accustomed to riding every day that the weather permitted.'

'Riding?' The Prince frowned.

'Yes, Your Highness – on horseback. I had to leave my favourite mare, Juno, at home. It has made me sad. I do miss her . . .'

'I did not realize. When it is safe to go outside again you shall have an Arab mare, one finer and sweeter than any you have ever known. I can think of one now, and she will soon be ready. Her name is Yali, it means shore of the sea . . .'

'She sounds beautiful! Thank you, Your Highness.' Then Flavia asked why she could not go outside now. 'Why is it not safe? We have guards to protect us.'

'Ah yes, Fair One, but I cannot risk your being damaged or, worse, assassinated. Our enemies surround us – some

64

smile and offer friendship with honeyed words and hypocritical gestures. Others swoop in the night armed with scimitars and garrottes . . .'

'Enemies?' Flavia felt a chill encircle her heart. 'You speak of the man they call the Pagan? Is he so powerful, then, that you go in fear of him?'

As soon as she had spoken she realized she had made a dreadful error.

'I fear no man!' Zebukar cried, his bright ebony eyes glittering with sudden rage.

Flavia swallowed, taken aback. Gone was the smooth-voiced, charming man who had been wooing her and in his place was a vehement, vociferous stranger.

'Forgive me, I did not mean to imply that you were afraid of this wretched traitor . . . Of course you are not. Only a fool would suggest such a monstrous thing. I have heard of him – he is a barbarian, coward, a rebel.' Her heart was thudding loudly, and she longed to sit down, but dared not in front of the Prince. She was not allowed to relax in his presence until she was his lawful Princess.

'That is the finest description of the traitor that I have ever heard. He is lowest of the low, a crawling, despicable worm, a gutter creeper. When he sees the foe he runs like a yellow-spined lizard. When he has helpless, vulnerable people at his mercy, he tortures and murders them, despoils their wives, their daughters, plunders their treasures, razes their homes to the ground. One day, I shall be avenged on him and you will watch him die as he deserves, in a public execution which will put the fear of Allah into all those who do not display total loyalty towards their Prince.'

Zebukar's face was flushed, a crimson stain beneath the rich brown skin, his eyes prominent with emotion, his voice choked. Flavia knew that he must be thinking of all the abominations committed by this rebel leader who had been nicknamed the Pagan because he behaved as brutally and violently as the pagans in ancient times. On the sea journey she had overheard conversations not meant for her ears, details of the Pagan's many atrocities, and she had been nauseated. Believing that a Turkish envoy was hiding in a peasant's cottage, this villain had burned the cottage to the ground, killing the peasant, his wife and their seven children. A daughter returning from the village had been pounced upon and raped repeatedly by the Pagan and his men. She had died of her injuries some days later. But for this vicious barbarian, there would have been continuing harmony and concord between the Greeks and their Turkish masters, just as there had been in the days of Prince Bastan. This rebel-leader, Zardos Alexandros, was brewing discontent, spreading lies about Zebukar and his countrymen – lies which had terrified the Greeks and caused them to rise up, led by Alexandros, whose major intention was not to 'free' his countrymen but to loot, plunder, and molest women. A full report of his atrocities had been sent to King George in England by his embassy.

'It is only right that you should punish such criminals,' Flavia said, her voice low. 'Deportation would not be too much for this man they call the Pagan.'

'Deportation? That is how your country deals with its villains. We Turkish have better ways. No monster must be allowed to breathe the same air as Allah's faithful . . .'

A fierce, brilliant light glowed in the Prince's eyes, yet there was a distant almost abstracted expression on his face. Flavia had been told that her future husband was deeply devout, a true believer, as the followers of Allah are called, and that, as soon as he had rid his domain of the Pagan, he planned to make a pilgrimage to Mecca. Flavia would be going with him – unless she were with child by then.

'As long as he is stopped, that is all I shall ask,' Flavia said.

'Ask? Ask? You will pray to Allah upon your knees!' Zebukar's steely brown hands gripped her wrists so tightly that the flesh felt scorched.

'Of course, Your Highness, as I do now . . .'

'Is it only when you choose, or at the designated times?'

'Both, Your Highness. I have always found prayer most restful and satisfying . . .'

'It is not for your own good, woman, but for the good of our peoples.'

'But of course, My Lord Prince! I never thought to use it for my own ends.'

The bright, glinting eyes seemed to relax their stare, the hands manacling hers dropping away. For a few moments the Prince did not speak. He seemed to be breathing deeply, collecting himself, and he did not meet her eye until some of the colour had ebbed from his cheeks.

'I was told that you were devout, that you were determined to become a true believer. Have I been correctly informed? You know what the word Islam means? Submission to God?'

'I do indeed, My Lord—'

'And dutiful obedience and submission to your lawful husband?'

'Of course, My Lord Prince.' Flavia bowed her head, sharply aware of a dozen things she wished to say, so many questions. There was also her urgent need for reassurance from this masterful, virile man she was to marry. Year after year they would be together, in bed, eating, sleeping, travelling, ruling, talking together, and yet she could not summon the courage to say what must be said to him. In his presence, she was overawed, virtually speechless. She knew why, of course. It was love.

She adored him. For as long as she could remember, he had been her fate, her destiny, what Islam called *kismet*. Her entire life had been a prologue to this moment, when she married Zebukar and became his Princess. Only now did she realize that she had been little more than half alive until she met him. He epitomized all she desired and needed: strength, love, power, the immortality which they would create with their children and their children's children. She had been a strangely lifeless creature, waiting for this moment when life would be given to her, poured into her body by her husband at the marriage ceremony.

Only after that would she be a real, living, breathing human being, capable of taking her part in Zebukar's domain.

Zebukar's metallic, black eyes were bright now, and his smile indulgent.

'I had been told that your hair was like living flame, but that description falls far short of the truth.' Lightly, he capped her head with his hard brown palm. 'Pulsing fire, regenerating itself on your spirit . . . My people will adore you. But you must remember this. At all times, you are my wife, my representative, and everything you do reflects upon me.'

She was mesmerized by the glinting black gaze, her heart shaking, her palms damp with passion and expectation. She worshipped him. She could not survive without him beside her. At the thought of their wedding night, she felt weak as an infant and barely able to support herself. It could not come soon enough for her . . .

The complexity of the ceremony was extraordinary. Ritual after ritual devoured the long hours before the actual moment when they became man and wife. Women in abundance waited upon Flavia. She was bathed in water so fulsomely softened with scented oils that it was like sitting in liquid silk, and her hair was washed five times, then liberally scented with fragrant, priceless oils.

She was given mouthwashes scented with attar of roses to freshen her breath, and when she stood sparklingly clean by the side of the gilt hipbath, the women set to with their tweezers to remove every hair from her body. It was agony after the first few hairs had been pulled, and her flesh burned a furious scarlet. Then there was a halt to the torture while soothing unguents were massaged into the inflamed areas. Flavia suppressed a smile as she saw herself on her wedding night – in so much pain that she could not bear to be caressed by her groom! But she said nothing, for to interrupt a Muslim ritual was to stand before the door of Allah Himself and shout insults.

The women were respectful, subservient and silent. Flavia, who found it extremely difficult to tolerate the first two, found it impossible to accept the third. Not speak? It was like being entombed alive! Even if she said something to the women in her smattering of Turkish, they would not reply. They would bow, and genuflect, crouch down, their heads touching the carpet, but nothing more. How much she wanted to ask them, how much she wanted to impart, but no it must all be silent and formal.

Words from the Koran flowed through her thoughts. 'Marry not idolatresses until they believe; a slave who believeth is better than an idolatress, though she please you more. And wed not your daughters to idolaters until they believe; for a slave who is a believer is better than an idolater though he please you. They invite to the Fire, but God invites to Paradise, and to pardon if He so will . . . Your wives are your field; go in therefore to your field as you will, but do first some act for your soul's good . . .'

'*They invite to the Fire, but God invites to Paradise . . .*' She felt disembodied, almost as if she were split into two, watching herself. She was a true believer, that she could never deny, but a true believer in what? Until her father had become enticed by Allah, the Audlingtons had been the staunchest Catholics in England. Jeremy Audlington had died at the stake in Elizabeth Tudor's day, his crime that of loving the Virgin Mary more than he loved the Virgin Queen. He had left a son who had fled into exile, who had sworn fealty to the Mother of Christ in a moving public ceremony in a tiny grotto in southern France. This ancestor of hers, Fulke Audlington, had dedicated his sons, their sons and their sons after them, into eternity, to the Virgin, saying that no man would ever be able to entice his descendants from fealty to Her.

Odd that she should recall that now, when she was about to marry a Muslim, and take her vows to both him and Islam. Submission to Allah. Would it be an invitation to the Fire, or to Paradise? Soon, she would know.

When the Lady Zaba approached her, face taut, she offered a smile, at which Zaba nodded curtly, and then brown suede hands were pinning something to her gown, beneath the jewelled neck. It was a *muska*, a charm to avert the evil eye. It was flat, triangular and made of solid gold. Blue stones were set into the gold and there was some intricate writing, a dedication to Allah and His Prophet, Mohammed. Fastened to the back of the *muska* was a minute piece of garlic. Flavia could smell it, and her nose wrinkled. She heard Zaba muttering some words beneath her breath – something about Allah the All-Merciful, the All-Powerful, and she echoed them in her heart.

It was customary for Muslim brides to be represented by a senior relative at their wedding. Flavia found this astonishing. Not to be present at one's own wedding! No one but a Muslim could have concocted that one, she had laughingly said to her father. Proxy weddings were of course not unknown in Christian lands, but these were always eventually followed by a proper Christian church ceremony. To appease the King of England (so Zebukar had said to her) he was allowing a Catholic priest to unite them after the Muslim priest had completed the ritual. He did not wish to offend King George, he said, by allowing the King to imagine that Prince Zebukar would take an Englishwoman to his bed without a proper English ceremony. This had all been arranged before Flavia could point out that it was she who was the Catholic. The King of England most certainly was not!

The silent, pallid-faced musician in the corner of the room suddenly ceased to move, the ude, the Eastern lute he was playing, falling from his fingers. The women around Flavia gasped out loud and Zaba rushed to the man, glancing frantically over her shoulder when she found that he was unconscious.

The man lay in a bundle of pale saffron robes on the floor, immobile, and Flavia knew that he was dead. Some strange seizure had suddenly deprived him of life. An omen? She swallowed hard, her fingers aching because she had clenched her hands so fiercely. No, no, she must not be like these superstitious Muslims who saw omens in everything, a feather in the breeze, a black bird appearing on the horizon, a birthmark with an unusual shape. But a man falling dead just before her marriage . . . Omen or not, Flavia rushed over to the musician, and lifted his wrist. She could feel no pulse, and his colour was yellow and waxen.

'No, not do it – not do it!' Zaba screamed hysterically as Flavia held the man's wrist. 'No touch – unclean, not to touch! No, *no!*'

'This poor man. Why should he suddenly die like this?' Tears glittered in Flavia's eyes. 'Fetch the physicians, and let them tend him.'

'Done, already sent for. Not touch, Lady Duchess not touch!'

Sighing, Flavia gently replaced the man's arm, and then she turned towards the waiting women.

'This man must be cared for – properly buried – his family informed. I request that this be done instantly.'

Her voice shook but they could see that she meant what she said.

Zaba glared. 'No family this man. None. Orphan. Slave. No family. Physicians come to him now. *Halaiks, Khalfas'*– Zaba ordered both young female attendants and older ones to return to what they had been doing. She looked outraged, ready to attack anyone who defied her. Flavia felt as shaken by her fury as by the fate of the poor wretch who had died so silently in his corner.

Within seconds, the musician's body had been removed and all was as before. A white-faced *halaik* scattered crumpled rose petals around the chamber as if that would cleanse the air, and their scent filled Flavia's nostrils. Roses, real roses, made into oils and unguents, made into *Rahat Lokum*, roses everywhere in this place, but none as fresh, sweet and cool as those in England.

Then the tiara was being placed upon her head, just as if nothing had happened. Death was to be swept away along with the wilting rose petals. She clenched her fists again, as if clamping down her fears. If it was an omen . . . No, no, put aside such medieval notions.

The tiara was tall and heavy and crushed into her scalp so that she winced. It blazed with enormous diamonds, like a chandelier, some set in thick gold, others suspended and gently swinging, making a tiny clinking noise when they touched one another. On either side of her face hung the long thick threads of gold which would later be broken off to be handed out to unmarried girls as souvenirs and good auguries for the future. The threads gleamed out of the corners of her eyes, like a sunburst, and she could not move her head suddenly or they rang noisily as they swung against one another nearly deafening her. The entire outfit, rich and sumptuous as it was, cloth of gold spider-fine embroidery on shimmering ivory silk, was restricting, so heavy that she wondered what was causing its great weight. Leadshot in the hems? she smiled to herself. She had sewn leadshot in her own hems in England so that the wind did not blow her skirts high when she was riding.

Plump white pearls mingled with diamonds round her neck and gold filigree chains were suspended from the blue, gold and ivory cloisonné belt, at the front of which was the enormous, blinding diamond called Allah's Teardrop, which had been given to Zebukar's great-grandfather by the Sultan of Turkey.

Now and again, Flavia's fingers caressed the diamond, as if to gain comfort from it, but it was cold comfort.

Nerves. Pre-wedding nerves, that was what she had. She must think of Zebukar, imagine him in her mind's eye, glorious and reassuring in his wedding robes. Soon, she would be standing beside him, soon she would be his wife. Soon . . .

At that moment, Zaba came to her again, and this time, she placed in her hand a tiny scroll of parchment. Frowning,

Flavia unrolled it and read what her new name was to be. Her Muslim name as Zebukar's wife.

Musbah. She was to be known henceforth as the Princess Musbah, 'the Light that Never Fails.' She whispered the name to herself. 'The Light that Never Fails.' Did she like it or not? Anyway, she hoped that it was true. She was glad that she would be called Princess, instead of the usual name for a wife, Kadine. This was another move to 'appease' King George, who had so many sisters and one daughter, all of them Princesses. Kadine, in its way, did mean princess but it did not command the same respect as the English title.

'Soon.' Zaba's sharp eyes caught hers. The sound of the crowds could faintly be heard outside the palace grounds, their voices a ringing hubbub of impatience. The Muslim custom allowed anyone who wished to enter into a home where a wedding was in progress. Flavia reflected that such a move would cause pandemonium in London, with the rabble gushing into the palace and snatching every treasure on which they could lay their hands. Here, there was such bonhomie, such devotion to their Turkish master, that no one feared for the safety of the Prince's possessions, or so she had been told.

Lord Graves, her father's oldest friend, would attend the wedding to represent King George. It was a small token to ensure that the ceremony, although considered eccentric and somewhat heretical (to say the least) was acknowledged and accepted by the British government. George IV had his hands full with the Irish problem and Daniel O'Connell. He did not wish to have anyone else on his heels. It was an excellent chance to make an ally of Zebukar, son of the idolized Prince Bastan, bosom pal of that old rogue, Audlington, whose eccentricity lived on in his daughter.

Lord Graves had bounced Flavia on his mountainous knee when she was an infant. She would be delighted to have him there during the strain and excitement of her wedding, but she would have much preferred her father.

Acteon had written, *'No words can describe my Happiness, my utter Joy at this great Moment. If only Bastan could have lived to see*

*it, but at least his wife will be There. Give her my Kindest Regards,
and my Felicitations on this radiant Event. And to you, my sweet
Child, all my love, all my Affection, all my care, all my Thoughts for
Ever More . . .'*

'Soon,' Zaba whispered again, summoning Flavia back
from her thoughts. Time had swept by since she had taken
up residence in the Palace of the Silver Cicadas, the hours
seemed to wear wings, bearing her along with them so that
she could not go back, could not return. There was no way to
go now but forward.

Ear-ripping trumpets sounded the arrival of yet another
dignitary, wheels churned up the dust in the streets of the
city of Bastani, people wept, roared their approval and their
welcome. Horses whinnied, hoofs cracked on the cobbles.

She was ready. The hand-mirrors which her attendants
held up to her showed a white-faced girl festooned in glittering silk, diamonds and golden sunbursts of filigree, her tiara
like a fairytale brought to life. The robes, the jewels, the tiara
were so heavy, so encrusted, that she could not move lightly.
Every gesture, every step would have to be gentle, cautious,
stately.

Suddenly her heart was hammering, her breath clamped
in her throat. Tonight – tonight – she would be in Zebukar's
arms, his embrace a golden manacle to chain her tenderly
for the rest of her days. Heat flooded her face. Her husband.
Soon, he would be her husband – and her lover. *Lover.* They
would sleep in one another's arms, his hands would touch
her where no other man had ever done, his lips, too, and his
lean, brown body would curve against her, scything deeply
into her to make her his. By the time dark fell, she would no
longer be a virgin. Eighteen years a virgin, and soon a
woman, a married woman. In his arms tonight! Some of it
she knew, some she had been told, but her informants had
skirted tentatively round the richer details. Tonight, she
would know the truth, every scrap of it, and she would
willingly lose her virginity to her beloved Prince.

'Princess Musbah,' Zaba whispered, tugging at her glittering, flowing sleeve. 'Princess Musbah, His Highness awaits you . . .'

The procession to the marriage chamber was so slow, so stately, that it seemed to take hours, yet she could not have moved quickly had she wanted to. After a few paces, her neck ached with the weight of the crown, the drag of the encrusted robes straining at her shoulders. The attendants who were following her, faces rapt, wore ivory brocade gemmed with seed-pearls, their veils covering all but their eyes. They were like dream figures, all white, silent, drifting slowly with her through the corridors, through the passage-ways, towards the marriage chamber at St Zita's.

What would Zebukar be wearing? Ripe yellow satin heavy with yellow diamonds? Scarlet satin festooned with rubies and emeralds? Whatever he wore, she would love him and could not wait to see him, to stand beside him. *Her wedding day*. This was her wedding day!

As she stepped into the marriage chamber she closed her eyes momentarily because of the piercing light from the thousands of lamps and tapers reflected on the jewels and silks worn by the wedding guests. A sigh rippled round the room as the guests took in her appearance. The light was so bright, the heat so intense that she could not gather her breath for some seconds. Where was the Prince?

He was smiling broadly when her eyes fell on him. How tall and powerful he looked, broad-shouldered, slim-hipped, in ice-blue satin dewed with sapphires, diamonds and ame-thysts. He was a magnificent figure, and she had to swallow hard at the sight of him. She knew with all her heart that there had never been such a handsome, splendid, noble prince in all the world before. And he was hers.

'Thanks be to Allah,' she whispered to herself. 'Thanks be to Allah for my beloved husband.'

Long forgotten now were the weeks of waiting and strange loneliness. Together they stood before the men of God, one Muslim, one Christian, and in a service which moved Flavia profoundly, she became the Princess Musbah, henceforth to be known at The Light of Zebukar Which Never Fails.

Afterwards, her veins seemed to be filled with molten silver, her heart a blazing star pulsing with an almost painful happiness.

Faces around them glowed with pleasure and delight. Lord Graves gave his congratulations on behalf of His Majesty King George and the British government and people, and then an ocean of glittering felicitations swept over Flavia, so that afterwards she could not recall any particular face or the identity of anyone who had spoken to her. She was wholly conscious of joy and happiness and of a sensation of relief – not her own, but coming from the Turkish dignitaries who had attended the ceremony. No doubt they were highly relieved to see the most eligible Prince securely married at last and able to put himself to the task of producing heirs.

Zebukar's strong brown hand was grasping hers, and a scintillating frisson was transmitted between them. It was all that Flavia could do not to blush scarlet and fall silent. Somehow, she managed to find her voice, but it was faint and anyone could have been forgiven for thinking that she was breathless.

Now came the *Koltuk*, the exciting climax to an Islamic wedding, and as the new Princess had no mother or aunt, she would be accompanied by Prince Zebukar's mother, the Lady Zaba and the Prince's cousin, the Lady Fatma, who had travelled to Greece for this very purpose.

In the *Koltuk* the bride was escorted to the entrance hall of the throne room by her mother, mother-in-law and aunt, where all the ladies of the harem would greet them rapturously. Here, led by the Kislar Agha, would come the bridegroom, to kiss the hands of his mother and mother-in-law, who would then reveal his bride to him. Normally, this was the first moment of meeting for the couple, and even then the bride would be heavily veiled. The groom could take his choice of giving the traditional greeting, the *salaam*, or kiss her hand, after which the Kislar Agha would put the bride's hand in that of her new husband and lead them through the bevy of noisy, excited women into the throne room, during

76

which procession they would be showered with specially-minted coins thrown by the older female relatives of the two families. Then would come a most unceremonious scene when the guests fought one another to pick up as many of the coins as possible, for they were considered enormously lucky.

Having placed his new bride upon the throne, the groom must tear aside her veil and look into her face. Normally, this would be the very first time he saw her. If she were cross-eyed or scarred, hook-nosed or bulbously misshapen, that was his misfortune.

Zebukar and Flavia kept closely to the ancient ritual, (which Flavia had rehearsed with the Lady Zaba) and tears came into Flavia's eyes when the Princess Fira, her new mother-in-law, took her by the hand to escort her to the entrance hall. The hand which held hers was small and it trembled violently, and Flavia knew then that the poor Princess had some terrible illness which had stricken her; this was why she remained heavily veiled and did not speak. No word of any kind escaped Fira's lips as she and the Ladies Fatma and Zaba led Flavia to the entrance hall. There, relatives and servants, all female, waited to cry their congratulations and make all the remarks that came to mind, cheerful, lewd or appreciative. Fortunately, Flavia could understand only something of what was said, although she could tell from the gleaming and flushed faces of the women, and the way the Princess Fira's hand shook even more violently that some of the remarks were *risqué*.

Now, led by the Kislar Agha, and behaving as if he had never met her before, arrived Prince Zebukar, wearing a cloak of silver cloth-of-tissue starred with diamonds and sapphires, and then the chief eunuch handed him a gauze veil of silver and gold weave which he placed over Flavia's head before taking her hand and leading her through the crowd of raucous women.

It seemed to take hours walking through the guests, and when the newly-minted coins started clattering around their heads, Flavia could not help but dart her head to left and right in a vain attempt to avoid them. Zebukar squeezed her hand more tightly and gave a soft little laugh.

'When you are in my arms you will not think of the pain from the coins landing on your head but only the pain from my manhood piercing your virginity,' he whispered so that only she could hear. Now she was scarlet, and fire was flooding through her body.

The throne came into view. Carved from solid gold and inlaid with pearls as big as fists, the throne was said to be over a thousand years old and had once belonged to Charlemagne the Great. Seated in it, Flavia felt as ageless as the pearl-studded gold, and when Zebukar swept off the shining gauze veil, his face appeared before her like a brilliant painting in brown, black and ice blue. She could not speak, but it did not matter. Next, he was kissing her hands so passionately that her legs turned to water and she could not get up. But there was no need, for he kept her there, while outside the closed doors of the throne room the bevy of excited women shouted for entry.

It was the custom for the groom to remain alone with the bride for only a few moments, and to give her a jewel. This Zebukar did, placing in her palm a ruby which was so enormous it concealed all but her fingertips.

'My heart – this is my heart, O Light That Never Fails,' Zebukar whispered, and then he was gone, and the chamber was thronging with noisy giggling women rushing to congratulate her all over again. She looked round for the Princess Fira, eager to strike up a friendship with her, but she had gone. Instead, the Lady Fatma, tall and gaunt-faced with eyes as blackly-bright as Zebukar's, pressed a dozen of the newly-minted coins into Flavia's hand.

'For good fortune, for the fortunes of love and life and the blessings of Allah and the blessings of many sons to fall upon you generously and ever more generously from Paradise,' Fatma said, her manner and voice solemn, and something akin to pity in her eyes. Yes, it was pity, Flavia decided. Poor Fatma, she has been unhappily married, Flavia decided, and she thinks that I will be too. How wrong she is!

Next came the marriage feast, which was to be held in the Western fashion with men and women eating together, the bride and groom seated side by side at the head of the main table. By now, Flavia could not find any appetite, but she was desperately thirsty and looked around for fresh fruit juices or the rather sickly sherbet. A goblet encrusted with rubies, emeralds and black pearls was placed in her hand by the Prince, who commanded her to drink. She did. The liquid which ran down her throat was sweet and pleasant like fresh dew mixed with wine and cream, but she knew it would not be real wine for that was against the custom of Islam. Thirstily she drank and Zebukar refilled her goblet, his eyes shining like black pearls. The faces of the wedding guests and the hum of their voices seemed to increase, at one and the same time. The noise became louder and yet more distant.

No time at all seemed to have passed, yet Zebukar was taking her by the hand and leading her from the dining chamber. She felt as if she weighed nothing at all, as if she were floating gently along beside him, and her body was flaming – especially that part which would receive most attention during the coming night.

How had they reached the bedchamber so quickly? She could not even recall having left the feast. Lights and stars danced in her head, and when Zebukar leapt towards her like a panther, she swayed into his arms. His mouth on hers was living flame, piercing into her soul, and her heart banged crazily, her breath jerked. Kiss after kiss stupefied her senses, and she was being pushed down onto the bed and her gown torn from her, its skirts thrust upwards impatiently. Next, through blurred vision, she saw the Prince kneeling over her, his desire having fully armed him, and then she knew how a man took a woman's maidenhead, which she had never understood properly before. Zebukar was pressing down on her, and her urgency was as desperate as his. She pulled him closer, arching up her hips to form a cradle for his thrusts. Passion and longing and aching love consumed her as he pushed open her thighs with rough, ardent hands and arched his back to drive himself into her.

'Beloved, beloved,' she whispered, and she could see his mouth open as he began to speak. But no words came and his muscles lost their steeliness, his arms flopping so that he fell across her heavily. Oh God, was he ill?

'*Zebukar!*' she cried his name, but he did not speak, and then she saw the ruby-encrusted handle of the dagger sticking out of his back. His own dagger used to stab him! She began to scream hysterically, and the men who had been hiding behind the heavy silk curtains around the bed stepped closer to see that the Prince was indeed dying. For good measure, their faces grim and vengeful, each of them plunged his own dagger into the Prince's back, so that blood began to spurt from the mesh of wounds, spattering out onto Flavia's face and breasts, into her hair and onto her hands while her screams went on and on and on.

The Convent of the
Miraculous Virgin

'Daughter, when you depart,
you will go up to the well,
to drink the last cup from my hand,
to say goodbye to the water of this village.
You will drink as your heart desires,
and what is left will be for your mother
who empties her whole heart with her
    tears.'

Angelos Sikelianos

CHAPTER FIVE

The convent of the Miraculous Virgin of Nauplinos was white-walled and awash with serenity. The Sisters were of an enclosed, contemplative order, that of the Sisters of the Miracle, women who had dedicated their entire lives to praying for peace, contentment and tranquillity throughout the world, amongst all mankind. Their convent was filled with paintings, statues and triptychs of the Virgin, her Son and the Holy Saints, ikons on every side.

In the chapel, which was cool and silent, stood the statue of the Miraculous Virgin from which the Order had acquired its name. She was black, and her eyes were pearls centred with ebony, her expression one of rapturous sweetness, mouth softly curving, brows high and gently scooped. If one gazed upon that face long enough, it looked as if it were about to speak, to say, 'I love you. I love you, my daughter.'

Only the most pious nuns experienced this, however, and the story was still told of one who, years ago, had lied, saying that the Virgin had spoken to her. She had been driven out of the convent to carve her own destiny. Afterwards, no one could have said how they knew that she was lying, but nonetheless everyone had known. But such harshness was rare in this hallowed place, where, for centuries the Sisters of the Miracle had led lives of exemplary dedication and selflessness.

Only the Mother Superior was allowed to discuss the original miracle which was connected with the statue (although there had been many since, of varying degrees). Eleven hundred years before, a blind sculptor had been given a set of tools with which he was commissioned to carve a statue of the Virgin for his local church. It was known that his loss of sight, which had grown steadily worse, had caused him much distress and grief, and the accompanying loss of spirit had shrivelled him so that he had little will to live. It was thought that the Virgin would protect him out of her gentle charity and sweetness, while he fumblingly carved what could only be an inept and artless statue of *her*.

The blind sculptor had begun his work, and within hours had severed a vein in his wrist with one of the sharp tools. Weeping, he was treated for the wound and he was sobbing that his life was over, that he would never work again, when suddenly, he was dazzled by a great white light before him.

Afterwards, he would laugh and say, 'I was blinded by that light, but how could I be blinded when I was *already* blind? God and His Blessed Mother alone know how they can blind a man into regaining his sight!'

For that was what happened. The sculptor's sight returned. He could see again. At once he went back to his work, praising the Virgin and completing a statue which could never have been called inept, and was most certainly not artless. Hearing of the miracle, people came to see the finished statue and pray before it for their own miracles. Gradually the village grew rich and famous, and lords and ladies, even princes and princesses came from all over the world to shower jewels and ornaments upon the statue so that soon all that could be seen of it was the beautiful black face, which now had real pearls for eyes. The rest of the statue from the neck down was encrusted with gems and ropes of pearls, silks and velvets and stiffly-embroidered brocade in gold, purple and silver. In the statue's arms sat a smiling Christ Child, dimpled, radiantly happy to be in His Mother's arms, and He too was laden with jewels and wore a solid gold crown studded with emeralds, while the Virgin herself wore a tiara of platinum hung with pear-shaped diamonds which sometimes twisted and glittered even when there was not the slightest breeze in the air. Why was the priceless statue still here, untouched by looters and pillagers?

The answer was simple. Having heard of the Miraculous Virgin, the cousin of the Grand Turk himself journeyed to Nauplinos to pray before the Virgin, and to offer her a gift: the Lion Rubies of Constantinople. The rubies would become the property of the convent if the Virgin gave one wish to the Princess Haitija, so the Princess bargained with the Virgin. She asked for a release from the barrenness which had hounded her for fifteen years. If she did not produce a son for her husband, within the year she was to be divorced, cast off in deepest disgrace. Her husband was a man of fierce and commanding passions. He wanted an heir, and such a necessity had now outweighed both his patience and his fading love.

For seven days the Princess Haitija prayed on her knees on the hard marble floor of the chapel, not leaving it for anything but necessity. She did not eat, she did not drink anything except for a few sips of water, and she did not lie down. When the week was over – what she would later call her 'holy week', – she left Greece and returned to Constantinople, knowing that she would face double disgrace if her people learned that she had not only prayed to a Christian idol, but had remained barren.

That was nearly three hundred years before; soon afterwards the Turks occupied Greece. One year after her pilgrimage to the Christian idol, the Princess Haitija bore twin sons, big, strong, healthy boys. One year after that she produced another son, then two daughters in quick succession, and then twin boys again. Nothing so astonishing had ever been known at her age. The Lion Rubies, said to fire their owner with the courage and defiance of the greatest heroes of Islamic history, were by then hanging round the Virgin's neck, glowing, pulsing with crimson fire, throbbing like the heart of the Madonna herself.

It is not recorded what became of the Princess Haitija, but it is recorded that her line continued and flourished, that her husband took her back into his favour, and that twin sons were born at regular intervals to her female descendants. And ever after that, the convent was under the direct protection of the Sultan himself, so that through-out the turbulent years of occupation, none dared harass, attack or besiege the building or its nuns, for fear of offending the Grand Turk. Haitija had seen to that herself, persuading her royal cousin to take the convent under his wing, and ensure that it remained under the protection of future Sultans. After all, one of the Ottoman Kadines might one day need to pray before the Miraculous Virgin for the very same reason as Haitija.

A short way from the convent the Aegean boomed and swished like Poseidon's seahorses, its colour changing from china blue to bottle green, then turquoise and bobbing amongst its waves were rippling jelly fish their streamers like sea fronds trailing beneath them. Black and spiky sea urchins clamped to rocks stabbed at the feet of children and fishermen who were foolhardy enough to tread barefoot on the shore. Fish, narrow and dynamic, flicked in and out of the rocks by the beach. Silver in colour, they were known locally as silversides. Squid and octopus were caught and eaten daily, their rubbery texture disguised by subtle methods of cooking.

The townsfolk who lived out their tranquil, seaside existence had only the slightest interchange with the convent which was, after all, an enclosed order. Each man and woman experienced a dart of warmth at the thought of the Miraculous Virgin and her proximity, and prayers were said to her daily, but no man and very few women were allowed inside the convent walls. On holy days, the statue of the Virgin was carried to the front entrance of the convent and the townsfolk and villagers from miles around would gather to pray to her and the Christ Child smiling in her arms, and gifts would be offered to the nuns: fish, fried squid, bread, eggs, tomatoes, vegetables, fruit and the local wines.

Sometimes, amongst the throng in their rough, hand-woven clothes and string sandals there would be a digni-tary, or a lord or lady who wished to plead for the Virgin's miraculous intercession. Often there would be children who could not see, speak or hear, and they would be carried to the statue to touch it, to kiss the hem of the rich brocade gown and caress the softly glowing jewels as if life itself sprang from them.

If a child shouted 'I can see! *I can see!*' there would be shared joy, intense delight, but no genuine astonishment. It would have surprised the people of Nauplinos more if the miracles had ceased.

The bay, some thirty minutes' walk from the village, was believed to have been a favourite meeting place of the old gods. There, it was said, Hera, Zeus and Apollo had frolicked with their companions, their lovers and children. Mount Olympus was famous as the home of the gods, but this was their holiday home.

The bay swept in a great and beautiful arc, carved out of whitish, dove-grey rock stretching down to the glossy, brilliant Aegean, dazzling in the summer sunshine. No one who has seen the Aegean could ever suggest that any other sea is half as beautiful. Its colours are vibrant and living, its sounds, the hissing and pounding, the booming and crashing, like the voices of the ancient gods themselves urgently crying out not to be forgotten. Now, sadly, their ancient language is understood by only a few. Elating, dizzying, heart-twisting, all of these things and more, the Aegean waits in the cove at Nauplinos for all those who can still understand.

That century, there was one, a girl, who spoke the forgotten language. In tune with the ancients, with time, with eternity, she stood on the rocky shore staring out to sea, her sombre grey robe made of a roughly-spun material little better than sacking. Her hood concealed her head completely, and was pulled across her mouth. Inside the heavy robe she was baking with the heat, but she would not change into a lighter outfit, a cotton blouse embroidered with zigzag thread, and a woven skirt, like the other women of the town and villages around. She had cast off the trappings of the world in preparation to become a nun, a member of the enclosed Order of the Miraculous Virgin,

and she was now in the eighteenth month of her postula-
tion. The time had dragged by, pulling at her like a boulder
strapped to her back and she had been sustained by one
thing only: her love for and dedication to the Virgin. The
first time she had seen the statue, something strange and
beautiful had happened to her. Even now, she could not
put it into sensible words, or try to describe it. She knew
that she had knelt before the Virgin, and that she had
been in a shocked and bemused state, half out of her mind,
wanting to die, and that the Virgin had seemed to smile at
her, the enamel and pearl eyes glowing with love. She had
been, as she later said, 'raised from the dead'.

That was it exactly. Raised from the dead.

She had known soon afterwards what her destiny was to
be. She must dedicate herself to the Virgin, become a nun,
devote herself to prayer, peace and solitude. How tempting
that thought was, and how she had leapt at it just as if it
were what she had always wanted. She had no living
relatives now. Her father was dead. He had died while she
was still shocked and grieving, not that she would have
been in a fit state to travel by sea to be with him at the end.
She had not been in a fit state for anything. She was a
widow in a country of strangers who, once she was
husbandless, seemed prepared to shrug her off. Before, she
had been Princess-apparent. After, she was an encumbrance.

Within days the Grand Turk had despatched a new
governor to take over from Zebukar. Prince Hassani's
despotism was already infamous. For a time, it had been
a possibility that he would make Flavia his fifth Kadine,
but she had been so outraged at the suggestion that it had
been dropped. She shuddered every time she remembered
her meeting with the vile and obese Hassani.

He had arrived in her suite unannounced, his guard –
two monstrously ugly eunuchs – shouldering open the door
for him. Flavia had gasped out loud, leaping to her feet.
She was not veiled, but for once she wished that she was.
Hassani ran his gaze over every curve of her body, his

eyeballs bulging, his tongue licking his flabby lower lip. He could speak very little English, and their exchange was limited – which relieved Flavia for she was sure that he was saying obscene things to her. He tried to touch her breasts, but she stepped back, startled. Hassani giggled like a little girl, pushing his hand down to his grotesque belly, and letting it slide over his groin. Flavia flushed scarlet and told him to go, at once. Grinning lasciviously, he asked her if she were a virgin.

'*How dare you!*' she cried, bunching her fists.

'Hassani marry only virgins,' the revolting man leered. 'Good to find barrier – much good. Exciting. No thrill without maidenhead.'

'How dare you speak to me like that, you fiend!' Flavia cried. 'Leave me at once! Go, *go!*'

'You no have Prince protect you now, woman,' Hassani had growled, touching himself again while his eyes rested acquisitively on her breasts.

'How dare you come here and insult me! I am in mourning! You can be sure that the Sultan will hear of this!'

'Ha, ha, the Sultan. He tell me put you in my bed if I like. You lush, pale skin, hair like flames burning in summer . . .' Out had come the hand again, but she reached for a cloak brought her by Zaba and was standing as far away from Hassani as the room allowed.

'Little Eengleesh virgin, you come into my bed, under me, yes? Show tricks, yes?'

'*Out!*' White and trembling, Flavia had pointed to the door and, surprisingly, Hassani obeyed.

Later she found out why. The Sultan had given him strict orders to placate the Princess Musbah because of her connections with the King of England. (What these connections were she never quite knew, but they served her well.) The Sultan was eager to improve the uneasy accord he was building with the British government and its monarch. He did not want to insult Flavia and thereby offend the King of England and the British government.

He had been working diligently to impress them, and his prince-pashas had been ordered to do likewise. The British navy was feared, although the Sultan would never have admitted it, and the last thing he wanted was a vast fleet descending on Greece.

Hassani had been carefully instructed. If the English Duke's daughter were agreeable to the idea of marriage with Hassani then she must be treated as respectfully as before, and Hassani must divorce his four chief Kadines, Mouma, Azata, Hasseta and Cazza, and make Flavia his one and only Kadine.

Hassani was most loath to do this, however beautiful, voluptuous and desirable Flavia proved to be. His four Kadines were all attractive and sensual women, knowing how to serve him expertly both in and out of bed, and while there was nothing quite so titillating as a new addition to his harem of concubines, he was not prepared to discard his four chief wives and replace them with one. To a Muslim, quantity is quality.

However he hoped that if he went about things as slyly and surreptitiously as he had gone about so many of his other underhand activities, he would succeed in keeping his four wives plus the English girl. As it turned out, the Sultan knew more about Hassani than he realized, and further instructions were despatched by the hand of a eunuch who stood seven feet tall and was notorious for his ability to behead a man with one sweep of his scimitar.

So, from being lewdly pursued Flavia was left in isolation to mourn as she had wished, and to recall and savour those few brief and poignant hours that she had spent with her dead husband, Zebukar, before his terrible assassination. She relived the murder in her dreams, over and over, as if it were a garish tableau of blinding colour. She would be lying on the nuptial bed in her new husband's arms and then would come the murderous figures leaping out from behind the bedhangings, daggers and scimitars like dazzling crescent moons falling from heaven to plunge into Zebukar's back until it was a bloody pulp.

Hassani set about removing all reference to Zebukar and his reign. Mourning for the late Prince was ended summarily, and only in the Princess's suite were there tears and wailings from the royal attendants and a thick and cloying sadness which lay upon her and her women like a surfeit of *Rahat Lokum* which time could never dispel.

Flavia's heart ached for hours as did her whole body with a throbbing and insistent pain. Waking in the mornings was to wake with the agony of death in her mind, and a sensation of morbid horror which struck her afresh at the break of each day.

Two months passed and an emissary arrived from Prince Hassani with a formal request for her hand in marriage. She replied that in her heart she was still married to Prince Zebukar and always would be, and that, another marriage being unthinkable, she wished to retire from the world.

Three days later the British ambassador arrived at her suite, asking for an audience with her. Delighted to see a fellow countryman, she received him in the rose-pink solar. His predecessor had retired and the new ambassador was a small man with a rigid spine, straight eyebrows and a nose which at some time in his life had been broken and badly set, giving him a pugilistic air. He was the most apologetic man she had ever met, begging her forgiveness after every few sentences he uttered. The gist of his message was that it would be most convenient for all concerned if she could bring herself to marry Prince Hassani so that the new and fragile peace between the Sultan and Great Britain could continue and strengthen.

'You have met Hassani?' Flavia's voice was faint.

The ambassador nodded, his bulbous cheeks wobbling.

'And would you want your daughter to marry him?'

At this the ambassador flushed an ugly puce colour, seeming at a loss for words. Which was how it should be, Flavia thought, with some satisfaction. She went on. 'Would you want your daughter to remarry within two months of the death of her husband?'

'Erm – um – naturally a decent mourning period . . .' the ambassador mumbled.

'Naturally.' Flavia said scathingly, but her hands shook. She had been through an immense ordeal, the repercussions of which continued to haunt her and would do so for some time, she knew. 'I had not envisaged myself as a political pawn, Sir Godfrey. This marriage with the late Prince Zebukar—' her voice cracked – 'was a private arrangement which took place as the result of my father's close friendship with Prince Zebukar's father. It was never intended to be political.'

'Erm, um. Benefit. Your, er, country is, er, that is, His Majesty the King particularly requests that you would look upon this matter with compassion, and see it in your heart to ally yourself with Prince Hassani. It is not expected that you should be the prince's erm, concubine, you know. He is instructed by the Sultan to divorce his four wives and make you his one and only wife . . .'

Flavia's cheeks went bright pink. 'I see.' She stood up in a swirl of black robes. 'How kind that the prince should do this for me – divorce his four wives and put me in their place. And these poor creatures, his wives . . . Where are they to go? What of their lives and their happiness? Even if I did not find it impossible to be the cause of such heartbreak, it would not be proper for me to step into the shoes of these poor women . . . Become any man's fifth wife . . .' She shuddered.

'I realize that it is most unusual, a considerable step for you.'

'How right you are! More like a leap over a cliff! I loved Prince Zebukar. I do *not* love Prince Hassani, and there the matter must end. I shall be leaving for England when I am more myself.'

'For England?' The ambassador's voice was a strangled cheep.

'Where else, Sir Godfrey?'

'But the terms of the will!'

'What will?' Flavia stopped her restless pacing and stared at the embarrassed man.

'I had hoped to spare you . . .' The cheep became a groan.

'Spare me? What on earth do you mean?'

'The late Prince, your husband. In his will he left all that he owned to the heirs of his body, providing that they were male and that you were their mother. His title, too. It was Prince Bastan's dying wish.'

'That would seem quite the usual way of going about it,' Flavia said, crisply.

'Yes, but you see. I wonder if I might have a drink – my throat.'

'Of course.'

Sir Godfrey sipped at his orange juice with the air of a man enjoying his final refreshment before going to the gallows. Finally, he had to be prompted into continuing by the impatient Flavia.

'In the event that the Prince had no sons conceived in marriage with yourself, Your Highness, his estates, possessions and titles were to pass to his nearest male relative, as is the custom also. There is of course a portion for your maintenance, but the rest goes to, well, it goes to his late Highness's nearest male relative, providing that, that . . . that he marries *you*, Your Highness.'

Flavia had gone cold, a misty, draining cold which robbed her of her senses and made her heart flicker.

'And who – who is Prince Zebukar's nearest male relative?'

The ambassador looked as if he were about to burst into tears. Water welled into his eyes and a sound like a sob hiccoughed from his throat.

'P-r-rince H-Hassani, Your Highness.'

'What happens to these estates and possessions if they do not pass to a man who must marry me?' Flavia's voice was a whisper.

'They revert to Prince Zebukar's next male relative, the

Sultan, Your Highness, but, but, only upon the death of Prince Hassani.'

'I see. So let them revert to the Sultan in due time!'

'Well, it is like this, Your Highness.' Sir Godfrey swallowed. 'The Sultan owes Prince Hassani a great debt. The Prince saved the life of his son – he actually uncovered an assassination plot, I believe. That is why he has been sent here to rule. His reward, you see, is your hand in marriage and part of the fortune left by Prince Zebukar.'

'But that is – is unthinkable, appalling, I will not have it! I will go back to England! No one can make me marry Prince Hassani!'

'I am afraid that if you did try to go back to England it would cause an international incident; war, even, between our country and the Sultan. I am so very sorry, Your Highness!'

'But that is stupid! Let the Sultan take the inheritance and give it to Hassani himself!'

'I am afraid that it cannot be done that way, Your Highness. The terms of the will are quite clear.' Sir Godfrey shrugged, looking desperately miserable.

'So, if I do not marry Hassani – and I shall not – he cannot inherit?'

'That is so. And, as a result, neither can the Sultan until Hassani's death. He is not an old man . . . Prince Zebukar's treasure will remain untouched for decades to come. The Sultan will be enraged. So will Hassani. Please, I beg of you, Your Highness . . .' Sir Godfrey was turning an unhealthy shade of yellow. 'International relations between our two countries will have a serious setback . . . the Russians will gain ground.'

Flavia did not reply. War. An international incident. A gross and loathesome, lecherous husband forced upon her. Her legs losing their strength, she sank down onto a silk padded stool, and stared unseeingly at the rose-pink and rich, cerise pattern of the luxuriant carpet at her feet. All she saw in her mind's eye were blood, death, and battle.

'There must be another way, surely . . .' she whispered, after silence had reigned for some moments.

'No, Your Highness. You are a very important personage now – even more so than when Prince Zebukar was alive, God rest his soul.' The ambassador halted there, colouring. Did one ask God to bring peace to a Muslim's soul? He hoped that he had not offended the Princess, but she seemed not to have noticed his error. 'It is – that is, our last hope, lies in you, Your Highness.'

Flavia looked at him with tortured eyes. 'You would have me spend my life with that vile man to ensure that there is peace? You would ask me to do that?'

'Not I, Your Highness, not I. His Majesty's government . . .'

'Sir Godfrey, it is well known in England that King George loathes his wife and will not reside with her. Will you give him a message from me? Tell him that if he will live with Queen Caroline, then I will marry Prince Hassani.'

Sir Godfrey's eyes bulged. His lower jaw looked as if it might well drop off.

'I could not possibly relay such a message to His Majesty, Your Highness! He would be most irate, *most* irate!'

'Understandably so. There is nothing more wretched than being forced into a union with someone who is not only thoroughly objectionable, but whom one does not love.'

Having spoken with a piercing acidity, Flavia felt calmer, and took pity on the poor little ambassador with the broken nose, wobbling cheeks and ineptitude in dealing with wilful women. No doubt he was accustomed to the 'Yes, my dear,' 'No, my dear' brigade. Well she was not one of those! Nonetheless, she could not live with the thought that her independence had caused vast political problems.

'Sir Godfrey, you may tell His Majesty the King, and

His Highness Prince Hassani – and of course Allah's Deputy on Earth that I am going into a nunnery.'

'A *nunnery*?' Sir Godfrey's voice seemed to erupt from the region of his scalp.

'Yes, you may tell them all that I am going into deepest mourning for my husband. As I cannot find the peace I need out here in the world, I am going to retire into a closed order of nuns. When a decent mourning period is over, then I will reconsider the Prince's proposal. That way, everyone's interests should be served.'

'How very clever, Your Highness, how very, very clever! If you would permit me to say how I admire your thinking up such an astute solution . . .?' Sir Godfrey beamed expansively, then frowned. 'But Your Highness, a convent? I thought, that is, I was told that Your Highness had embraced the Mohammedan religion . . .?'

'That is so. However, I am not taking the veil, only seeking the tranquillity of the cloisters, and if you know anything at all about the Dukes of Audlington and their ancestors, then you will know that they were staunch Catholics until this generation.'

'Ah yes, ahem, yes, of course. Staunch Catholics, yes indeed.' Sir Godfrey, a determined Protestant, could not boast of a predecessor who had been burnt at the stake for idolatry, but suddenly he wished that he could. Pride and dignity must come from such an inheritance, for this beautiful and regal young lady had both of these in generous abundance.

Bowing himself out, relief dancing in his veins, he tripped lightly towards Prince Hassani's audience chamber, a place which he had come to nickname the Lions' den, and himself Sir Daniel. This time he would be able to present a solution agreeable to all. He might even get out of this with his head still on his neck! But no, he must not jest about such serious considerations, he thought, as the Sultan's seven-foot headsman came into view. This gentleman always turned his blood to sherbet and his knees to lumps of *Rahat Lokum*. It needed all his tiny degree of courage for him to square his shoulders and walk past the headsman and into the first entrance chamber, where he must begin the long and complex procedure of begging an audience with the Prince who called himself Allah's Avenging Sword.

'Your Highness is happy to remain with us?' The Mother Superior asked, her voice gentle, like a palliative. Of mixed parentage, with a Greek father and a French mother, she had the stoicism of the former and the serenity of the latter.

'I am, Reverend Mother. Very happy. Indeed, these past few months have been amongst the happiest of my entire life.' Flavia meant every word she said.

'I know that it is not possible, but if you had not been meant for the world, I would have said that you had a very definite vocation. *Oui*, but very definite. Some who come here travail for many years to attain your serenity.' The nun smiled, but gently, as she did all things. 'If only you could transmit some of it to one or two of the others here . . . *Mes pauvres* unfortunates, who have such discontent seething in their veins. But not you, Your Highness, not you.'

Flavia waited, wondering what the Mother Superior was leading up to. As a rule, she said very little, choosing her words with great care as an example to the sisters.

'I was told when you came here that you would stay for only a short time, until you were recovered from your terrible loss. When you marry Prince Hassani I hope that you will not forget us. We need your prayers, and of course we shall pray for you, always.'

'Who told you that I would be marrying the Prince? His envoy, the man who brought me here? Yes, I thought so. That marriage is as far away to me as it ever was, Reverend Mother. I came here to get away from an intolerable burden, and here I shall remain. There is no way that I shall marry Prince Hassani and yet there is no way I can see of escaping that fate.'

Flavia told the Reverend Mother the terms of Zebukar's will, and as she spoke she realized something. In his will, Zebukar had viewed her in true Muslim light, as a pawn to be employed to the greatest advantage for his domain. At that thought, tears welled into her eyes but she let them roll down her cheeks. They were a cleansing balm. Of course, Zebukar had not seen her as a mere pawn! He had not expected to die until he was an old man, when he had adult sons to leave behind him. He could never have envisaged dying so young.

'It is part of the mourning process to feel resentment against the one who has died,' the Mother Superior said. 'Resentment for all sorts of reasons; for leaving his loved ones helpless and distressed, for not being there when he is most needed, for having perhaps left his affairs in a chaotic state. And feeling such resentment makes one guilty. But it is all a part of grief, not to be rejected out of hand, not to be experienced with self-disgust.'

'You are so wise, so very wise . . .'

'Ah, you would not think me so if you knew how my daughters spoke of me sometimes! I am human first and foremost and all humans make stupid mistakes. You loved your husband very deeply? From childhood, you said?'

'Oh yes. I did not meet him until a few weeks before the wedding, but we had corresponded for years and he sent me portraits of himself. He was so handsome, so kind . . .'

'Here we know little of the affairs of the world, and we are forbidden to listen to gossip from outside, but sometimes one or two snippets creep in to us.' The Reverend Mother then said something which puzzled Flavia. 'Sometimes, our idols have feet of clay, you know, my dear.' The broad, kindly face was loving as she spoke.

'To whom do you refer?'

'I can say no more, nor would I wish to. We shall be happy to have you here for as long as you wish to stay. You have made a niche for yourself already. You spread serenity and peace which are just what we need. God and

His Blessed Mother will let you know when the time is right for your next step.'

'I think they have already, Reverend Mother. For some time I have had a sort of inexorable pulling sensation, as if I am being drawn towards something very beautiful, very powerful, and altogether desirable. Something which I want more than anything else.'

'To stay with us? You know that we would never refuse you. If you wish to have more of your clothes and other possessions brought here so that you can make yourself properly at home, please feel free to do so, *ma chère*.'

Flavia looked down at her hands. They were rough from scrubbing vegetables and weeding the herb garden, from cleaning pans and dishes and sweeping out the convent chambers with an old, battered broom. Suddenly, her longing crystallized inside her like a great burning jewel, blazing with a fiery heat so great that she was sure the Reverend Mother could see it. Raising her face, she said, her voice a whisper:

'I want to become a nun, Reverend Mother. I want to take my vows and join your enclosed Order. I want to spend the rest of my days here in Nauplinos.'

CHAPTER SIX

Her postulant's robes were even coarser than the old roughly-woven robe she had worn during the past months, robes designed for the postulant's life of scrubbing floors, sweeping out rooms, washing dishes, weeding, digging, and polishing. Each day work began at the crack of dawn and did not end until late in the evening, interrupted only by prayers said at regular intervals. It was exhausting, repetitive, mundane, thankless, and it would have been humiliating, too, if Flavia had not entered into every action with enthusiasm and the beginnings of a joy which swelled rapidly once she had taken the final step.

She slept on a narrow, hard truckle bed in a tiny stone cell which was devoid of all ornament save for a crucifix. Sometimes, in the dark, she would stare at the crucifix and imagine that it was glowing with a silvery light, a comforting radiance which elevated her spirits.

There was no time for complaining, for aches and pains, for silly little ailments which really meant nothing whatsoever, and were meant to be ignored. Silence was the great quest, and there were hours of that, a stern rule that between certain times no one spoke save Reverend Mother and only then if there were a dire emergency. She herself had broken the rule only once in twenty-seven years, when an elderly sister had fallen down a flight of steps, in an accident that proved fatal.

Postulants had both more and yet less freedom than the Sisters. They could go to market, talk to the townsfolk, break the rule of silence once in a while if they were truly contrite afterwards; yet they must determinedly adapt themselves to a life which was rigorous, exacting, sterile in some respects, rich in others, and a total abnegation of their earlier lives. Gowns, slippers, stockings, frills and lace, pretty shawls and flowered fans, scent, nosegays and doting suitors all must be eradicated from the thoughts and memory of the postulant, even from her dreams at night. Banished, forbidden were all thoughts of worldliness. Hair must be swathed in white linen and over this a veil carefully arranged and kept in place, night and day. The bandaging must only be removed if it needed changing for fresh. Inside that bandage was the hair which would be removed when the postulant took her final vows. All of it would be cut off, in formal renunciation of the world and all its vanities.

Flavia had not seen her hair for weeks. Gone were the days when it was washed, scented and oiled by the tiring women of the harem. What a change there was in her life now, from immense riches to poverty, from wealth and abundance to living close to the earth in loving servitude to God and His Mother.

Most of all she loved to be alone in the chapel, kneeling before the miraculous statue of the Virgin. Here was her Mother, the Mother of all the world, a loving woman whose life was an example to all, and there was the Christ Child in her arms, the Child who was a son to every nun, the Child who had a hundred, a thousand mothers.

Flavia found a deep satisfaction in dedicating herself to this selfless life, understanding now that she had always been made for it. The blood of her ancestors was more powerful than she had guessed, and soon it seemed as if she had been a nun for an eternity. It was a timeless feeling, and one of rightness, of a deep contentment. She looked back on her life in the world with a strange detachment, as if it had not happened to her at all, but to another woman. Perhaps it was her mind's defence against ineluctable horror.

She was not the first to prostrate herself before the Virgin, to promise total commitment. What sweeter balm could there be? What greater joy and tranquillity? The mother she could not remember was here again, eternal, immortal. How could she have relished the Muslim religion with its concentration on man and man's authority, his power and influence? What Mohammedan woman had ever been allowed her say in public? The only happy Mohammedan woman was one who was content with being a mute. Her husband had been a beautiful vision for the future, her brilliant destiny, for as long as she could remember. Now he was a beautiful vision in her past; no longer her destiny, but in a strange way, her heritage.

As the nightmares of his death faded a little, becoming somewhat more bearable, Flavia tried to think of him as he had looked lying in state before his people. Remote, inert, he might have been sleeping but for his lifeless pallor. His robe had been of cloth of silver tissue inlaid with rubies and pearls, his bier swathed in amethyst silk fringed with purple, scarlet and gold. How noble he had looked, how serene, this man whom she had loved all her life, and whose life she was to have shared, whose sons she should have borne.

When the snake of crowds had gone, having paid their last respects, she had knelt by Zebukar's bier and spoken to him from her heart, yet she could not weep. The tears which had refused to come were the cause of her numbness, or so Zaba said later. A good Muslim woman would wail and sob and pluck out her hair over her husband's death, so said Zaba, curling her lip, but Flavia's quiet, stoic dignity had won even her stony heart in the end.

She had not cried yet, except in her dreams when she would wake, hearing the sound of her own sobbing in her ears, while her eyes remained dry.

'The soul may weep while the body cannot commit itself,' Reverend Mother had said wisely. 'To commit one's self is to accept a situation which cannot be tolerated. The mind is a strange vessel, and we shall never know all of its secrets. If the tears come out in dreams, then that is something.'

'The whole country mourns the death of my husband,' Flavia said softly. 'I have seen them in the town and the villages, and at market, with their faces dour and solemn.'

Reverend Mother said nothing, but felt the palms of her hands grow warmer as they frequently did when she was about to be called upon, when the forces of God were welling up in her. She remained silent, communicating only with Heaven. One day the child must know the truth, but she would not be the one to impart it. One day, there would be another with that mission. One day.

'I know I cannot speak the local dialect, but I am trying my hardest to pick it up. I know I shall not be able to do that once I have taken my final vows. There would be no reason to speak it then, Reverend Mother. The cloisters do not hold conversations . . .' Flavia managed a faint smile.

Reverend Mother said nothing, which was not unusual for mystics who have so much going on in their minds and souls that they are frequently silenced by it. The nuns would not have dreamed of disturbing their Mother Superior when she was communing with God, her expression rapt, her eyes fixed on distant, invisible scenes. How many mortals were like this? It was their great blessing to be her devoted nuns, her children but never childish, working hard to quell the little disobediences which plagued them.

Flavia looked at the Mother Superior. She was always very pale, with a translucent skin, and dark, iridescent eyes illuminated by her bright spirit. Her brows were sweetly arched, and thin as if they had been carefully plucked, which of course they had not. Her mouth was soft and beautifully etched, her dark lashes long and glossy. She looked like a young woman still, yet she was old enough to be a grandmother. If goodness kept one young, then that was a miracle in itself.

'She is ageless,' Flavia thought, and then Mother Marie Thérèse's eyes opened, their pearly lids lifting to show her soulful eyes, while a gentle smile swept across her mouth.

'You were meant for our Order, my daughter. You are so right for us, so very right. I have struggled with girls for years – and women too – and they have been as far from sanctity after it all as when they were postulants. But you

– you carry your own little Heaven inside you, and that is a rare gift. It comes from God.'

Colour flooded Flavia's cheeks. Such monumental praise from Mother Marie Thérèse whom she adored. She had never heard the Frenchwoman speak so warmly, yet so sadly.

'I fear that this Heaven you speak of has often been Hell,' Flavia confessed.

'There can be no good without bad, they are two sides of the same coin. Can you not see that, my daughter?'

'So evil must exist, whatever we do? It will always be there?'

'Yes.' The reply was uncompromising, almost harsh, yet it did not reflect Mother Marie Thérèse's nature. 'There is one who never fails to help us. Our Blessed Mother. St Anselm said that we may receive what we want more quickly by asking Our Lady than by asking Jesus. That would seem strange, yet it is because she is mercy only, not justice. Pray to her as you have been doing since you came here, and I know that she will answer soon.'

'She has answered, Reverend Mother – she has given me peace when I despaired of ever knowing it again.'

'Is that all you asked for, peace?'

'I do not think I really knew what I wanted when I first knelt before the Miraculous Virgin . . . My life had ended totally. I did not want to live.'

'And she revived you? Yes, she did that for me too when I first came here. You may have wondered what a Frenchwoman is doing here? Well, I will tell you.' And Mother Marie Thérèse broke her long years of silence about herself. 'When I was a child, I was very seriously ill – a mystery illness, a strange fever followed by a chill. The physicians were puzzled. They spoke of melancholia and brain fevers destroying my mind, and so on. For two years, I could not walk. We lived in a tiny, friendly little village near Annecy, such a pleasant place, yet I could not leave my bed. I did not have the strength. The fevers had robbed me of all vitality. My mother was very pious. She went to the village church and said that she would give up what she loved most in all the world if the Virgin would make me better.'

Mother Marie Thérèse gazed into space, her expression profound.

'You were made better? The Virgin gave your mother what she wanted?'

'Yes. I was cured. And a few months later my mother lost what she most loved – me, her only child. I realized that I had a vocation, that I wanted to join an enclosed order and dedicate myself to God.'

'So how did you come to be here in Greece?'

'The war of the Peninsula, have you heard of it? But yes, of course, being English you will know of Wellington and his men. Wellington is your country's hero, *non?*' Flavia nodded. 'Men at war can be brutal savages, philistines. English soldiers burned down our convent and . . .' There was silence while the nun composed herself. 'I was young – there were about six of us who were around my age. We, we were used – as soldiers will use young girls.'

Flavia could not believe what she was hearing. This serene and holy woman talking like this – what she must have suffered!

'I had a child – he was born dead. Can you imagine my shame, the disgrace and humiliation I felt? In the end we were rescued by men from our own side, but it was too late for some of my sisters. One had crept away during darkness and drowned herself. Another died of a terrible disease given her by the soldiers . . . One died in childbirth.'

'But you did not lose faith?'

'Never. Who says we are here to have a safe and joyous life? Who says that it will be easy? Why should hardships break one's faith? No truly loving, caring parent spoils his child, now does he? It was God's will that I should be treated like that. It was God who sent me the child, and I would have loved the child had he lived. Would God have expected me to abandon my own infant? No, no! Love is

105

what I send you, God says. *La Vierge* is called Queen of Martyrs. *She* suffered – why should I escape?

'But I am rambling, my daughter. I came here to this convent a shocked and distraught woman, with no hope for the future, tortured, confused. I had lost a child and I was grieving deeply, yet I was also torn because I knew that it was considered a grave sin for a nun who has taken the vows of chastity to bear a baby. They thought that Greece was sufficiently far away, so that I could hide here and lave my wounds! So I came here, and knelt before the Miraculous Virgin, just as you did, and She breathed life and hope into me. They could not keep me down for long, my daughter! As you see, I became *la mère supérieure* here!' The nun's eyes twinkled like French jet.

Flavia was overcome by what she had heard. Tears flooding her eyes, she knelt before the Frenchwoman, and, lifting the hem of her robe, kissed it.

'You are a saint,' she whispered.

'No! Simply a fortunate who has received the full abundance of Mary's mercy and grace. "I read in the Gospel that Mary stood by the cross, but I do not read that she wept." Those are the words of St Ambrose. I tried to model myself on Mary, that is all. If I had any courage or fortitude, it was hers, her gift to me.'

Weeks passed and Flavia prepared herself to take her final vows. Poverty. Chastity. Obedience. If she faltered, she thought of Mother Marie Thérèse's early life and it strengthened her, but, as time passed, any doubts evaporated. This was her home now; this was the place where she wished to remain until her death. Here, by the cerulean blue and shimmering jade-green of the Aegean, she would stay.

If she had one regret other than losing the man she had loved it was that she had never been able to befriend the Princess Fira, Zebukar's mother. She did not know what had become of the Princess, for she had not seen her at all in the weeks following Zebukar's murder. Zaba would never speak of her, and when Turkish people wish to remain mute on a subject they succeed admirably. She had sent messages to Fira via Zaba and others, messages of comfort and consolation, but she had never received any by return. She supposed that the Princess would be in deepest mourning still, or at least continuing her life of retirement from the world. It was tragic that they had never been allowed to become friends or to comfort one another in their shock and grief. Flavia had so longed for a mother . . .

She had begun to make her initiation robe. This bridal gown – for that was what it was – that she would wear when she became a Bride of Christ, could be as fine and lavish as a nun wished. It would be the very last time that she would wear worldly finery. Afterwards she must cast aside the gown as she cast aside her life in the world, and cut off all her hair. Flavia had brought some jewels to the convent with her – her own property – and had given them all to the Reverend Mother to be used for the nuns, for a nun was allowed no property of her own. She had no wish for a showy wedding dress. She had worn one of those in an entirely different ceremony which had been paradise leading to hell. Her robe this time would be simple and plain, and she would carry lilies to place at the foot of the Virgin's statue. A ruby which had been her mother's was now hanging round the Virgin's neck on a gold chain. Flavia had placed it there personally, whispering to the Virgin, 'This is my heart, and it is yours, Madonna.'

So her vows would be heartfelt, she knew. She would regret nothing. It was the only solution, the only way. If Hassani had heard what she intended, he gave no sign. There had been no message from him in all the time she had been there. She hoped that he had forgotten her completely. He was a depraved man, a sybarite, and she had no wish to have any connection with him whatsoever.

They say that it is summer all year round in Greece, and May that year was lyrical. The thyme and sage, vine and olive would be even more abundant that season, it was said, as would the lemons, the lush and fragrant figs, the sweet chestnuts of Lesbos, the carobs and juniper, pomegranates, quince, almonds and plums. Such a fertile land, a Paradise of fruit and flowers and shrubs, the air sensuous with the scent of jasmine at night, sweetly drifting, haunting the nostrils; the cypresses like muscular, hairy giants; the ugly, sprawling cacti, somehow vigorous and possessive in the way they dominated the rocks and clefts, thrusting thorny fists arrogantly towards the skies. Nowhere in the world were there such delicately-flavoured plums and prunes, which sang with aroma in the mouth. Nowhere were there more fish in the seas, coiling in silvered ribbons, twisting, turning, darting. After a hard day's cleaning and polishing it was bliss to sit down and drink goat's milk kept cool in an earthenware flask in a water hole, and eat sardines, freshly caught, boned, crushed, and fried with olive oil and garlic, followed by whatever lush fruit was in season. Flavia loved them all – except black olives which she could not bring herself to like. Life was idyllic, a scented heaven on earth. It would go on like this forever.

And then the barbarians came, riding out of the night, wielding swords and daggers, yelling curses at the moon, and there was no peace again for any of them.

CHAPTER SEVEN

As she heard their voices tearing at the convent's serenity, Flavia leapt to her feet in alarm. Who were they? Hassani's men come to abduct her by force, take her back to the Palace and force her into marriage with that repulsive acre of lard? Trembling, she waited for a few moments. Perhaps they would go past the convent. Yes, that would be it – they would be riding by, not stopping. She heard a scream, then another, and ice formed in her veins. They were not going past. They were coming here, to the convent!

Remembered horror stories about the barbarian Greeks surged into her mind. Those murdering fiends who had killed her husband were the Pagan's men. He had sent them to do their filthy work as part of his plan to overthrow Zebukar. Was he here now, the Pagan, to wreak more vengeance? On her? But how would he know that she was here? And would Hassani stand by and let her be harmed? She doubted it. He loved riches too well. She must hide.

The door to the chapel flew open and one of the postulants stood there. Her cap had fallen off and her black hair was wild about her white, pinched face. Her hands clawed at the air as if she were fighting off some invisible assailant.

'Men! Wild men! *Fire!* Oh Blessed Mother, save us!' The girl fell to her knees before the Virgin's statue, where she keeled over and lay still.

Having ascertained that it was nothing more serious than a faint, Flavia bit her lip. The noise was increasing. Fire, the girl had said. Would those barbarians stoop to burning a convent? With sinking heart, she knew that they would. Nothing she had ever heard about Zardos Alexandros had caused her to believe that he might have the slightest compassion in his nature. Zebukar had called him the Bloodletter, the Scourge of Allah. Breath stabbing in her throat, she padded to the door and stepped into the corridor. There she halted. Then she turned and went back into the chapel, where she fell to her knees before the Miraculous Virgin.

'Blessed Mother, if I should not see you again . . . If it is what I fear. If it is your will that – that I do not survive this night, then so be it. So be it, Holy Mother! Whatever you will, whatever you will, so be it.' Rising, she crossed herself, then hurried out into the corridor.

The gatehouse was a wild bush of scarlet and crimson limning the night. They had fired it – and were now standing in the inner court, shouting to the nuns to come out or they too would be burnt to death.

Courageously, Mother Marie Thérèse faced them, her voice stern. 'Desecrate God's holy place! Harm His Sisters, what manner of man are you?'

The leader of the barbarians laughed. He was huge, like a god from the ancient world, inhumanly tall, his shoulders like oak, his hair glossy and black, the colour of the olives which Flavia could not stomach. Nor could she stomach the arrogance of this man, whoever he was, sitting there on his huge horse like a mythical centaur. How dare he attack them. How dare he!

'A loyal Greek,' she heard the man reply, his voice rich and melodious. 'A man who has vowed to root out the violators of this land . . .'

'And *we* are violators?' Scorn thickened Mother Marie-Thérèse's voice.

'You conceal the violators – do not try to trick us. We have been told who is here.' The man's hand gentled his horse for it was frisky, side-stepping and swishing its ebony tail. Man and horse seemed to be one, indivisible, their cohesion powerful, almost unnatural. A trickling of icy cold tapped its way along Flavia's arms and down her spine. Was he human, or was he some god reborn, hewn out of oak and olive, bronze and marble, a monolith into which breath had been infused to bring him to pulsing, beating life?

Behind him and his companions-in-evil the gatehouse flamed, spitting gold, orange and cerise saliva, and Flavia knew that tonight she and the other Sisters would die, all of them. Burnt if they were lucky, kept alive for worse tortures if they were forsaken by God.

'Mother of Miracles, do not forsake us!' Flavia whispered, hands caged together like knotted bone from which all softness had evaporated.

'There is no one here but us. Women all of us – nuns!'

Flavia could not keep quiet any longer. Employing the Greek which she had learnt since coming to the convent, she called the man a savage and a barbarian, ordering him to return to the caverns beneath the earth from which he had come.

'*Devil!*' she cried, her eyes as fiery as the flames behind the man to whom she spoke. 'Leave us alone. Can you not see we hide no one here! No one!'

To her fury and consternation, the man roared with laughter. It was a demonic sound which made the hair on the nape of her neck prickle in the most painful way.

'Women are all the same, liars and cheats – we cannot wait here all night. If you do not send them out, or tell us where they are hiding, then we shall burn down your convent. With you in it if you wish . . .'

'Who do you want? *Who* is supposed to be hiding here?' she asked.

'Hassani's men – seven of them, murderers all.'

'They are not! What have they done to hurt you?'

'Not me, woman. The villagers over the hill beyond in Chia. It was a happy village, but now it is no more. Razed to the ground, the children beheaded and flung into the sea, the men castrated and left to bleed to death with their hands lashed behind their backs. And the women . . . do you really want to know what was done to them?'

She could not see his expression, for there was such

brightness behind him. His face, his eyes, were in shadow, and he seemed like shadow too, ancient, terrifying. She knew that he was lying, of course. Hassani's men would never do that. It was the men led by the Pagan who committed such atrocities. She forced back tears at the thought of the fate of Chia, then realized that if Hassani's men had not done the evil, then the men now standing before her most certainly had. It was this man's way of warning what would happen to them if they did not obey . . .

'No men like that are here, nor have we seen them,' Flavia cried. 'We do not harbour murderers.'

'We followed them. They came this way. If we do not catch them, you might be next on their list. If they are hiding here, and say that they will not harm you, then they are lying. *Lying.*' He repeated. 'Do you understand? You will be next!'

'They would not hurt me, I am—' Flavia stopped herself in time. Tell these men who she was, so that they could abduct her and hold her to ransom? Never!

'Why would they not hurt you, woman?' The monolith of black and bronze and gold leaped down from his stallion as lightly as an avenging angel, to plant himself in front of her, his eyes a glittering black. He smelt of leather, horses, sea, sun and wind. He seemed to be twice her height, but she did not flinch for her mind was racing. What if she told this man who she was, and made a pact with him? In exchange for leaving the nuns unharmed he could take her with him, hold her to ransom – or whatever he wished. Heart crashing against her ribs, she asked to speak to him alone.

'No!' Mother Marie-Thérèse cried, '*No!*' but Flavia did not heed her.

A few yards away in the isolation of the washhouse, dark, cool, but scented with the choking odour of burning wood from the gatehouse, Flavia spoke.

'You must not harm these women. They have done nothing to hurt you, nor would they. They are all loyal

Greeks save for the Reverend Mother who is French, but she has lived here for many years.' Her voice quavered, but she went on. 'Please, I beg of you not to harm them or their convent. You can search it – please do – you will find no men here save for yourselves.'

'Who are you?' The barbarian was close to her; she could smell the sun, the salty richness of the Aegean on him, in his hair, his breath. He wore leather, dark and comfortable with wear, and a Greek shirt in coarse ivory linen with a drawstring neck. He had leather breeches and thongs twisted round his calves in the manner beloved by Roman soldiers, but his eyes were redolent with all the mystery and legend of this land she had grown to love so deeply. There was mystery in his smile, too, evoking a thousand years of myth and fable. In truth what was real and what was imaginary about this country and its past? Would she ever know if this man was human or a god woken from his sleeping tomb?

'Who are you?' he repeated impatiently. 'You are no nun – nuns do not speak with such fury! Tell me, quickly, quickly!' Lashing out, he caged her wrist, manacling her so that she could not move, at which she kicked out with all her might, but she no longer wore riding boots as she had in England. Now her feet were bare, with soft thonged sandals and the blow hurt her far more than it could ever hurt him. His muscles seemed to be made of bronze.

There was a struggle, but it was as equal as a water nymph fighting off the almighty Zeus. With tears sharp from the pain of his grip, Flavia told him that he was a devil, a fiend and a monster.

'So all the more reason to fear me, to do as I say . . .' he grinned, infuriating her anew.

'I shall do nothing that you say – nothing! If you hurt these women – if you dare touch them – I shall have you punished by Prince Hassani! His men will pursue you throughout the land until you are caught and hanged. It will be only what you deserve!'

'Why should he do that for you? Are you – but no, you

are not a Turk, how can you be his kin? Your accent is strange – newly-learned, am I right? Come, tell me all I want to know, or those women out there . . .'

'You coward, you vile coward, warring on women, on nuns! May God forgive you, for I never shall!'

'Tell me who you are, or I shall have to hurt one of those women. I am sure the Reverend Mother knows your identity.'

'You despicable, foul . . .' Flavia slashed out with her free hand, crashing it against his cheek so that the corner of his mouth split open and blood welled like a ruby. He laughed, catching that hand too, and crushed her against him, pinioning her arms behind her back. Pressed against his muscular body, she could not struggle, nor even try to squirm herself free. It was hopeless. In the end, pain forced her to bow her head against his chest as if in supplication.

'Now tell me who you are, and I will not harm the women.'

'Princess Musbah – widow of Prince Zebukar . . . Soon to be married to Prince Hassani!' she flung that last at him defiantly. Now he would know that she was protected, that he could not harm her or the Sisters, or Hassani would come after him.

He released her instantly, so that she wavered on her feet, and when he next spoke it was in English. Impeccable and cultured English.

'His widow? *You* are his widow!' He seemed unable to believe what she had said. He stared at her as if in horror, his face aghast.

'Yes. What is wrong with that?' She cried in English, hands clenched.

'You look so fair, so innocent, so untouched by evil . . .' He seemed to be thinking aloud.

'Why should I look otherwise? I was to be a nun!'

'Yes, a nun,' he mused. 'His wife a nun . . . How ironic. Penance no doubt, but if you did penance for one hundred years you could not bring peace to his soul. He will squirm in hellfire for all eternity.'

'Hellfire? He was a Muslim, you forget.'

'Hellfire, I said. Burning, twisting, as do all evil men.'

'You, *you* can call him that, after the way you have behaved tonight? Burning down this convent . . . terrifying those poor defenceless woman . . .!'

'Don't worry. If it turns out that there are no villains hiding here, we shall recompense them.'

'Oh a fine gesture after you have nearly scared them to death! Here, take a few coins, go and build your gatehouse with your own bare hands!' Flavia fumed.

'My men will do the work. His widow, eh?' The man strode up and down, a monolith of muscle and power, authority and fearlessness. She wanted to run, but he was between her and the door and she had suffered enough of the indignity of being trapped in his brutal embrace.

'Hassani is to marry me – if you harm me . . .' she warned.

'That walking seaslug, eh? You are looking forward to being in his bed?'

'How dare you speak to me like that, how dare you! It is no business of yours!'

'You are very proud for a nun, for a woman of God. Some would say arrogant.'

'And what would they call *you*? Barbarian, savage?'

'Something like that.' He was amused again, his mouth tilting, his cheekbones filling out. 'They call me the Pagan, if you really wish to know my name.'

The eager retort faded from her tongue. She looked stricken. *The Pagan*. That soubriquet which had been dinned into her for something like ten years now. The cause of all Greece's woes, the greatest enemy of Prince Zebukar, the one man who stood between peace and contentment in this land. A murderer, a pillager, a rapist . . . All the terrible tales she had heard of him swirled round in her mind like fire.

'You have heard of me?'

'Who has not? They say your name in the same breath as the devil's!' she spat.

115

'Who does? The Turks you favoured? Who asked them here to Greece? Who welcomed them? Who wants them to stay? Call them devils for they have spawned hell in this country.'

'Lies, all lies! You are the monster who has done that, you with your savagery and greed, your ambition to become master in their place!' Not caring, she ran towards him, looping her fingers into the leather of his jerkin and tugging at it furiously. At that moment he was to blame for everything, for all her sufferings, her loss, her widowhood. It had been his men who had slaughtered her husband, her beautiful, loving Zebukar . . .

'Who better to rule Greece than a Greek?' he said, but his voice was grim now, his face cold.

'Zebukar was loved. The people loved him, and you killed him, you with your brutality and callousness!' The tears which had drowned her dreams now fell, streaming down her face, and a weakness slipped through her veins like a silken cord tightening, paralysing her. The tears hurt, they broke out of her like tiny pins threaded through the satin of her lids, their advent like blood ebbing from her very heart. But for this man, but for this foul, degenerate man . . .

Finally, drained, she could shout no more insults, weep no more tears. She was cleansed, yet powerless. A great lassitude overcame her; she would have slipped to the cold stone floor had the Pagan not caught her as she lost consciousness.

The Lost Fortress of Queen Atalanta

'It is terrible to desire and not possess, and terrible to possess and not desire.'

W. B. Yeats

'The voice of my beloved! He comes darting down from the mountains, leaping over the hills like a young hart . . . Until the day dawns and the shadows fade, turn again to me, my beloved.'

Song of Songs

CHAPTER EIGHT

She opened her eyes and was blinded by the ivory, sheeny satin of moonlight. A great fat camellia-coloured pearl glimmered way above her in the indigo skies, its rays blindingly fluorescent. Next, she realized that she was being carried. Huge bronze arms were carrying her. She was pressed against a matching chest. Looking up, she saw the face of the Pagan, stoic as that of an ancient Spartan, as beautifully-sculpted as a Greek god. He was staring upwards, to the path they were ascending – or was it a path? More like steps, carved stone steps snaking their way upwards far, far up a mountain. Fear bedazzled her, but by then his eyes had done the same. They were emerald jewels, incandescent and brilliant as the emeralds which Zebukar had sent her as a gift. A Greek with jewels for eyes . . . Lush black lashes shadowed the living emeralds, and above were strong black brows. It was a noble face, born of myth and legend, yet he was the most dangerous man in what would have been her husband's *pashalic* for decades to come.

'Where are you taking me?' she asked, her throat sore, her head aching, her eyes feeling puffed and bruised. He did not answer. 'What did you do to the nuns? Did you – did you – harm them? Are they still alive? Answer me that at least!' Dread filled her as she waited for his reply.

'They are alive and well. They have their gatehouse back. My men have worked through the night to rebuild it.'

'And why – *why* did you not leave me there?' Her heart pounded. She had never feared anyone before as she feared this enigmatic man.

'You, the Prince Hassani's betrothed? A prize as valuable as the Lion Rubies? Leave you in a nunnery?'

She winced. Yes, she had told him that, but she had not meant it. The thought of being Hassani's wife still sickened her. Yet would she not prefer the safety of the Cicada Palace to this maelstrom? What would this fiend do to her? She might never escape him. Even while she dreaded to think of his plans for her, some semblance of sense began to permeate her mind. If she was a hostage, then he would not be so foolish as to harm her. So she must play on that, stress that Hassani loved her, wanted her, and then she would not be hurt. She hoped.

'Hassani believed I was safe there – why should I not have been, but for you?'

'Muslim men are all the same. Only virgins please them.'

'I imagine that you are nowhere near as choosy!' she retorted. 'Any whore would meet with your favour I have no doubt!'

'Any whore? Yes, that is right,' he roared with laughter, and while his head tilted she saw past his shoulder the height to which they had ascended. Far, far down below was a little net of lights, some village or other, and a limitless purple-black expanse which must be the Aegean. This was a great mountain, and he was carrying her up it as if she weighed as lightly as a child's doll.

'How high have we come?' she asked, suddenly awed.

'There are nine hundred and ninety-nine steps up to my fortress,' he grinned, not in the least bit out of breath, not even flushed.

'Nine hundred!' She paused, stunned. Then, refusing to let him see how impressed she was at his strength, she snapped, 'Why could you not have made it one thousand? You Greeks are tricky as the devil!'

'So you would have me believe, Princess. So you would have me believe.'

He had not asked her what she was doing, the widow of one Muslim, the future wife of another, hiding in a convent. She hoped that he would not, although it was well known that Muslims did not mind choosing wives of other religions. She would tell him that she was still in mourning, which was true enough. Fleetingly, she thought of the Miraculous Virgin – they would have plundered her jewels, of course, the fiends, and as she thought of the statue stripped of its valuables, its beauty, the Lion Rubies, she wanted to weep again. Forgive them, Blessed Mother, she prayed silently, forgive them. And do not forget me, please!

The moonlight seemed to be growing more potent, as if they were now so near the silvery orb that they would be able to reach out and touch it. The light seemed to be forming a halo behind the Pagan's head, which was certainly not what God had intended, she thought. In the silence, she heard the murmuring swish and thump of the waves far below; they made a sound different from any other waves she had ever heard. It must be the shape of the cove, or the echo from caves nearby, perhaps.

Cicadas were carolling fervently, a riot of silvery cheepings, and this, mingling with the moonlight and the boom of the Aegean would have been magical – in any other situation. How could she feel thrilled to the soul when she was being carried up to the lair of a man whose infamy was rivalled only by men like Genghis Khan and Nero? Yet something was intruding into her fears and misgivings, ejecting them one after the other, despatching them like nine-pins and leaving room for . . . what? Shimmers of sensation were dancing along her skin, tingling and sparkling like moondust cascading down on her from the ripe, glowing pearl in the sky. For long, enchanting seconds such a feeling had her in its grip that she was powerless to fight it. This man's arms were hard and muscular like steel, and the chest against which she was crushed was the same. Was he human? Indeed, could any human be so stalwart, so indefatigable? They were half way up a mountain, he was carrying her in his arms, and yet he was not even slightly out of breath . . . How many hundreds of steps had he climbed, bearing her weight?

The swaying movement must have stupefied her, she

decided. The moon, the coruscating stars, the scent and sounds of the sea below, were a delicious manna which must have affected her senses. But what manner of woman would she be if she forgot that this was the monster who had ordered the assassination of her husband, who had dealt out death summarily in the land which she had come to consider her home?

In all the tales which she had heard of the Pagan and his misdeeds, she had never heard anyone call him an enchanter, or a magician, yet what if such nefarious talents were indeed his own and he had put her under his spell? This was the very same land from which had sprung the tales of Circe, who had turned Ulysses and his men into swine, and the Sirens, who lured sailors to their deaths by singing bewitching songs. Here, Zeus had metamorphosed into many different forms so that he could seduce young girls who took his fancy. Cyclops, Titans, the nine Muses, who had been produced in a marriage lasting nine nights, gods who could change themselves into swans, bulls, flames, rocks, clouds, satyrs. Who could deny that all things might be possible here?

'Who are you?' Her voice was little more than a whisper. 'Tell me who you really are . . . ?' She was thinking of the great king of the gods, Zeus, who had regularly carried off any maiden who inflamed his lusts. Perhaps she had been transported into another world, or was this all a dream?

He laughed, in place of a reply, which, she was to learn, was infuriatingly characteristic of him. Enraged, she knotted her fists and pounded them against his chest.

'Put me down, I demand that you put me down! Take me back to the convent, take me back! Now, *now*, I command you!'

His laughter was loud and genuine. 'Princess, your commands are not obeyed here, in *my* kingdom. Here, I am master, and you will do *my* bidding.'

Her cheeks burned. 'That is no way to speak to a princess. You are an arrogant and insolent peasant and you will be punished when Prince Hassani finds out what you have done! He will cut off your ears and pierce your nose. He will have you flogged, he will—'

'Always supposing that he can catch me.'

'Of course he will! He has men everywhere – soldiers, guards, spies . . .'

'Not in my mountains. No one has ever set foot here save for my friends, true Greeks, born in this land.'

'Then why am I here?' she cried.

'Have you not noticed that your feet are not on the ground, O Great Imperious, Commanding and Bossy Princess?'

The massive walls of the fortress palace loomed above them like a vision from Heaven. Its stones were smooth and bulbous. Yellowish-rust, coffee and silver-grey in colour, they appeared to have been fitted together in a fashion which was at one and the same time primitive yet highly efficient. The moonlight was even more brilliant up here, the stars seeming to be hovering on the tops of the palace walls like immortal diamonds.

Flavia, who had been silent for some time, was awed by the gigantic walls. Ancient fortresses must have been exactly like this, vast, impregnable, forbidding. For the last few yards the path was beaten earth, and then they were standing before a gateway tall enough to allow entry to the Cyclops himself. At the Pagan's shout, the gates began to swing open slowly, and men ran out, grinning and crying welcome.

As he stepped into the inner courtyard which was cobbled in the same smooth, greyish-white and rusty stones, the Pagan whispered in her ear, 'Welcome to the fortress-palace of Atalanta, queen-empress of the ancients . . .'

'The warrior-queen?' Flavia gasped. It was said that Atalanta had come from Atlantis, suddenly arriving in Greece out of nowhere, when the country most had need of her. Having crushed any would-be conquerors, Roman invaders and all, she had crowned herself queen-empress. Or so legend would have it, for some historians hotly denied her existence. Flavia could remember her father telling her about Atalanta, saying that the warrior queen-empress would rise again when Greece had most need of her.

Now here she was being carried into Atalanta's own palace, which was also thought to be a myth, or long-vanished if it had ever existed. She might have disbelieved the Pagan, but something about the antiquity of the fortress, its air of ancient, almost timeless brooding and its magnificence, told her that this might well be Atalanta's legendary home.

She remembered years ago, her father showing her the warrior-queen's coat of arms, which was the Atlantean symbol for eternal life: a glowing orb held in the palms of two cupped hands. Now, glancing over her shoulder she saw torchlight flaring like luminous blood on the fortress walls, lighting up the symbol carved above the gateway: cupped hands holding an orb.

A chill billowed through her veins, as if some long-dead spirit had risen up before her. Atalanta, dead yet not dead, myth yet suddenly reality. She was mute with amazement. If only her father could have seen this place.

A girl's cry came from a dark corner of the court, startling her, and then Flavia found herself unceremoniously plonked on the cobbles as the Pagan held out his arms to enfold the woman who had run towards him. She was as petite as a child but shapely as an odalisque, and wearing diaphanous peach-silk robes over Turkish harem trousers of cerulean blue gauze, caught at the ankles with beaded ribbons. Her hair was knee-length and black with rich indigo lights, her skin tawny-gold, her eyes coppery, her mouth bright as cherries and she was laughing delightedly to see that the Pagan had returned.

'Xinnia, this is the Princess Musbah. Your Royal Highness, this is Xinnia, a dear friend of mine.' His eyes were aglow with laughter as he introduced the two women, but Xinnia scowled, clinging possessively to the Pagan's arms and darting furious glances at Flavia, while Flavia remained silent, staring at the voluptuous, heavily-painted girl who was obviously far more to the rebel leader than just a friend.

Xinnia pulled down the Pagan's great ebony head and flourished kisses on his mouth and face, then glared at Flavia defiantly, as if to say, He is mine, keep away! Flavia, weary, and possessed of an emotion which was both confusing and uncomfortable, averted her eyes as if the scene displeased her.

'Show the Princess to the women's quarters,' the Pagan ordered Xinnia, who clung to him still more passionately, and had to be gently prised away. 'Do as I say, Xinnia. I will see you later.'

Jaw thrust out, Xinnia obeyed. Flavia followed the little curvy figure into the darkness, through an arch, into a corridor and up twisting stairs to the women's quarters. There, flambeaux lit the rooms like nocturnal suns, and all was colour and richness. It could have been a Turkish harem, worthy of a chief Kadine's own suite.

Xinnia began to mutter in what sounded like Turkish, as she showed Flavia into first one glowing chamber then another. Here, there were no bald stone walls to be seen but only a panoply of luxurious Turkey carpets and French tapestries covering the stonework. Ankle-massaging carpets concealed what were surely rough and chilly floors.

Flavia was silent. Such luxurious, sumptuous beauty and elegance, and for what? This petite and capricious Turkish girl? Why was the girl here, anyway? The Pagan was the Turks' greatest enemy, everyone knew that. He had said that only Greeks set foot on his territory. He decapitated Turkish girls for breakfast, and then went on to massacre their fathers, husbands and children. Flavia had so many questions to ask, but she was not going to put them to this girl. She was drained of energy and feeling; so much had happened, and the entire experience possessed the quality of a nightmare. Now she must sleep and break the waking dream.

Seeing that she was eliciting no response, Xinnia began to scowl, her fingers swaying backwards and forwards like seaweed fronds buffeted by the waves. They came to a plain but cosy chamber in which was a narrow bed spread with rugs and cushions which seemed to be begging Flavia to lie on them. She was so weary that when Xinnia gestured towards the comfortable bed, she flung herself down on it gratefully. She was asleep before Xinnia had crept out, grinning. She did not see the girl quietly close the heavy studded door, lock it, and pocket the key.

CHAPTER NINE

All Flavia wanted after her ordeal was peace and quiet in which to gather her tangled thoughts and to rest. It was not to be. Her head was barely on the pillow when her door was flung open and the chamber apparently filled with an almost supernatural presence. It was the man who had abducted her, the man they called the Pagan. Pulling the covers up to her chin, she stared at him in the gloomy light, fearful of what was to come next.

Silently, he lit tapers with a torch which he had brought in from the sconce on the wall outside. By their gilded-orange light he looked down at her, his eyes glittering with contempt.

'Let me see you clearly, Princess Musbah.' He sneered her name. 'Let me see my enemy as she really is, weak and trembling with fear.'

Stepping close, he tore the covers from her face and shoulders, making her gasp.

'Strange, I had expected to find you with horns, and scales on your body. They say female devils are the worst.'

'Why are you talking like this? What have I ever done to hurt you?' she stammered, perplexed by his hostility. Trying to pull back the covers she found them gripped in an iron fist. Where now was the laughing god who had carried her up the mountain?

'What have you done? What have you *not* done?' he growled. 'You, daughter of an English duke, supposedly an educated woman, agreeing to unite with a Turkish monster. Did you not see how it would affect our cause, how it would give respectability to the Turks?'

'Respectability? What do you mean? No, do not answer, for I shall not speak to you while you insult my husband so!' Tears threatened but she controlled them.

'Men have been dying here in their hundreds. Were you so sheltered in your English house that you heard nothing of our trials, of the oppression of Greece by the Turks? Do not ask me to believe that for one moment. London society rang with Lord Byron's work for our cause. Have you not read his epic poetry about our struggles? He died at Missolonghi for us, Princess. For us, the Greeks. Did you not read your newspapers?'

'Byron? He was a scandalous man. They say he had an *affaire* with his sister, that she bore him a daughter. He used women selfishly for his own ends.'

'His private life is not under discussion! What of our cause, for which he came to Greece and gave his all? Did you not hear of it, did it not give you pause to think? Where were your wits? Could you not see how your support would add weight to the Turkish rule here? You were used, Princess, used as a pawn!'

How she longed to be clothed properly so that she could leap out of the bed and rush away from this odious man. Instead, all she could do was try and twist the sheets round her in a vain semblance of decency.

'When I was a child, a very small child, I was betrothed to Prince Zebukar. It was the dearest wish of my father and of Prince Bastan that his son Zebukar and I be married.'

'When you were a small child, things were different. Bastan was alive; in this province he was beloved and had been for years. It did not take his son long to prove that he was bred from different blood and bone. What of the past few years when the Turkish oppressors massacred my people? Over and over again, villages and towns were decimated. Did that not reach you in your English newspapers? How could anyone with any intellect not know of it?'

'I had some misgivings, yes, but the King sent an embassy to Greece to meet with Zebukar, and they found everything to be as it should. They saw proof that the Greek people loved the Turks and had no argument with them. Besides, whatever the result of that embassy I would have come here. My father was dying. He had been ill for some time. For years he had anticipated my marriage to Zebukar. He had dreamed of the day and I had no intention of disappointing him. It *was* his dying wish.' Tears gemmed her lashes.

'For one man you would sacrifice my people? Is that what you are saying? You speak like a child who has been tempted with sweetmeats and believes that an ogre is really her fairy prince. I cannot believe that anyone could be so stupid, so gullible!'

Stung, she cried, 'Believe what you like! It is no business of yours what I think or do! *You* have behaved like an ogre, you and no one else! You abducted me, threatened the nuns, terrified us all. I certainly knew about *you* before I came to Greece, Zardos Alexandros! I know about all the women and children you raped and killed and all the villages you put to the flame. That was well known in my country. That was headline news in *The Times*!'

He was white, but whether with fury or dismay she could not tell. Both, she hoped.

'And you believed it all? All those lies, the smokescreen created to remove attention from what the Turks were really doing here?'

'A moment ago you asked me if I read the newspapers, and it was plain then that you thought I should believe what was in them. Now you expect me to know that certain items were lies? How could I do that if the editors of those newspapers could not? I am not an oracle! In England, it was hoped that an English marriage would help to keep out the Russian influence which is growing here. Presumably you know about that?' she said cuttingly. 'Did you know that the English government fear Russia will step into Greece, so that in place of the Turks you will have the Tsarists ruling you? They are not known for their gentleness!'

'We have never had any doubts about Russian support for our cause. It has already sustained our fight, weakening

129

the Turkish power where it would have become intolerable.'

'So not all of the Turkish rule here is intolerable, then? But according to what you said before, it is *all* vicious and depraved. It is you who is misguided and misled, Zardos Alexandros, not I!'

She cowered as she watched the rage blaze across his features, turning his eyes to dark tourmaline. Any second, she feared that he would lash out at her, beat her until she was a dapple of bruises. He was a bully, a monstrous bully who had never met a lady before and did not know how to treat one.

'You are not an oracle, you say, yet you speak as ambiguously as one! You expect me to believe that your wits fail you when you hear the news of Greece? From your behaviour since we met, I would say that your wits are far from failing. You wanted to be a princess, to revel in a luxurious wealth undreamed of in your homeland, and you did not care who it was you married to make your desires come true.'

'What contemptible rubbish! I am the daughter of one of England's great dukes. There were lords in plenty who would have married me, given the chance.'

'But did they possess the fabled wealth of Bastan's house? The gold and jewels and treasures?' he accused. 'That was what you were after, wasn't it? A title which England could not have given you, and the riches of Turkey to lavish upon yourself.'

'Get out of my bedroom!' she cried. 'You have no right to be in here! You're vile, a bully and a savage!'

'Tears now, eh? The fortress of the weak and selfish. Do not think that I shall be moved by them, Princess.'

'Will you go, *go*! I have not asked you to gloat over my distress!'

He sat down on the bed, his weight tearing the sheets from her breasts. Gasping, she tried to wrench them back, but failed. He leaned closer, his eyes tourmaline fire.

'You enjoyed being in Zebukar's harem and now you

can enjoy being in mine. You are what they call the spoils of war, did you know that?'

'But not yet spoiled.' She dared him with her eyes, but he stared straight back, unflinching. Finally, to her chagrin, it was she who was forced to turn her head away. By then she was trembling, a coldness creeping over her for she knew that he could do whatever he wanted to her. Anything. And who would save her? No one even knew where she was . . .

When his arms came round her like a trap, she wanted to faint, to shut out consciousness. Like iron cords, they clamped her tightly, while her heart banged crazily, painfully. All along, deep in her heart, from the first moment she had seen him, a black and bronze centaur, she had known that this was inevitable. In a terrible, terrifying way which she did not understand as yet, he was her fate, and, for all she knew, he would be the instrument of her death, if not her murderer.

'I have never taken a woman by force.' His voice was low but vibrant.

She flung back her fiery head in disdain, her scathing glance proclaiming that she did not believe him.

'Plainly you do not believe me?'

'Should I? You took me from the convent by force!'

'That is not what I meant, Princess, and you know it.'

'Let me guess what you mean. All your life you have had women falling over themselves to be noticed by you. Women fling themselves into your arms, into your bed, because you are so handsome and powerful and manly.' Her eyes were icy with a raging scorn.

Angrily, he increased the pressure of his grip, shaking her so that her hair whisked across her face like scarlet ribbons.

'You are the most incorrigible, wild and stubborn creature I have ever known,' he growled. 'One day your pride will cause your destruction, high and mighty one!'

'But not before I have caused yours!' she spat, digging

131

her nails deep into his shoulders. She could not have dug harder and yet he did not flinch.

'Then we shall be the cause of one another's destruction, Princess. Our own Greek tragedy brought forward to the nineteenth century, is that what you would have?'

'It will be a tragedy if you insist on keeping Greece divided! But for you, relations would be amicable between the Greeks and my husband's people. You have stirred up the ordinary folk, made them discontented and vengeful. Have you no compassion for their fate? Violence breeds violence. Hate spawns hate.'

In disgust, he flung her from him, leaping to his feet in one sinuous, effortless movement.

'A little time spent alone might well bring you to your senses. That is, if you have ever had any,' he growled. And with that, he left her, the door crashing shut behind him.

She had wound herself up into such a tight knot that his departure was like a slap in the face. Sinking down onto the bed, she dug her nails into the coverlet and wished with all her heart that it was his face.

She was left alone for the next two days, a virtual prisoner. Food was delivered to her on a tray, but the bearer never paused to chat. How easy it was to imagine a dozen terrible possibilities while she was immured. Alexandros might be plotting her death by starvation. That had been her first thought until the tray of luscious food was brought into her the next morning. Finding herself ravenous, she had eaten well, then wished she had left the food. He would laugh when he saw the empty dishes, thinking her weak and ruled by physical need. To refuse all food would have been far more effective, she felt, but too late. A thought drifted into her head before she slept. Hades, King of the Underworld, had carried off Persephone, the daughter of Ceres. Persephone had been free to leave his kingdom until she had eaten of his food. From that moment, she was his prisoner for six months of every year, unable to leave

Hades or go back to her heartbroken mother, who, in her grief, had plunged the earth into winter.

A prisoner of Hades. What an appalling thought. Shackled to a dark, mysterious god . . .

Turning her head into the pillow on the second night, she slept, but uneasily. She was woken by the door opening. For a moment she saw nothing but a pewter blur, then an outline took shape, and finally, a face with piercing, soul-stripping eyes and hair black as basalt.

'Have you come to persecute me again?' She sat up, forcing her mind awake.

'There are certain facts which I must know. If you care for the people of Greece then you will help me.'

'I would sooner keep a cobra for a pet!' she cried.

'So you care nothing for my fellow countrymen?'

'I did not say that. I said I would not help *you*. Do not twist my words. It is not my policy to trade with renegade leaders.' She emphasized the last two words, revelling in his furious expression.

'All I want to know is how many soldiers your late husband kept in his palace?'

'Now how would I know that? I hardly saw the rest of the palace, only my own suite, nor did I ever hear Prince Zebukar speak of such things. It is hardly the sort of conversation piece to discuss with one's bride, is it?' she added cuttingly.

'I suppose not,' he agreed, 'but one does pick up information like that, sometimes without knowing it.'

'Well, I did not, nor would I tell you if I knew the answer. Do you really think that I would inform on Prince Zebukar's fortifications? No doubt you plan to attack his palace.'

'Not yet, and do not forget that it is Hassani's palace now, Princess. Surely you are a little less protective towards Allah's-Vat-of-Blubber-on-Earth?'

She almost gaped at him. Was he jesting, being contemptuous, or both? If she happened to agree with his summing up of Hassani, she was not going to let him know. Allah's-Vat-of-Blubber-on-Earth, yes, how that suited the gross Hassani! Tightening her mouth to kill her laughter, her eyes twinkled, so she cast them down.

'I can only repeat to you what I said two days ago. I have nothing to tell you. I want to be left in peace. And I would much appreciate the chance to stretch my legs.' Now she stared straight into his eyes.

'That will not be possible, I am afraid. Security is too tight here. We cannot have a Turkish sympathizer strolling around like one of us, now can we?'

His words hurt. He made her sound like some sort of spy, a woman to be feared and avoided. She felt somehow tainted. It was not a pleasant feeling.

'One of your guards can accompany me. I ask only a little fresh air now and again. It will not be for long, I assure you. When Prince Hassani sends his men to rescue me, then you will not have this little problem any more, will you?' She managed a sweet and serene smile, but her throat felt dry.

'You are so sure that he will want you back?'

'Yes. He has good reason to rescue me. Without me, he will be unable to have something he desperately wants.' Having realized how ambiguous that sounded, she paused, her face flushing. 'And I do not mean what you are thinking, Alexandros!'

'I know about the terms of Zebukar's will, do not worry. No secret is safe in Greece.'

'You *do*?' she gasped.

'There is very little that I do not know on that score, Princess. I have my spies, too. And you can be sure that I do not have their heads cut off when they bring me news. It is such a self-defeating policy.' He almost grinned, but decided to look stern instead.

'In all the time I was at my husband's palace I never saw anyone executed, or mistreated in any way,' she reiterated.

'But then, on your own admission, you saw nothing beyond the doors of your suite, Princess. I am sure that you had plenty to occupy you while men were dying in agony elsewhere. Trying on your gowns and jewels, your silk robes and crowns encrusted with gems, bathing in priceless oils and being waited on by a score of respectful servants, am I right? If only we all had the chance to indulge ourselves in such luxury. I know many a Greek peasant girl with bare feet and one ragged dress who would do anything to spend an hour in such surroundings.'

She turned her back on him at that, but he twisted her round to face him, shocking her again with his familiarity. As a duke's daughter, she was accustomed to a distance between herself and others, unless she chose otherwise.

'*Agio partheno!*' he roared. 'What am I going to do with you, you stubborn, misguided woman? A day's work in the kitchens here would show you what real life is all about!'

'So you are one of those men who think the kitchen is a woman's place? It might be if she is without wealth or title, but certainly not in my case.'

'Brains come into it somewhere, I am sure,' he growled. 'How could a female cope with man's work, and the dangers he must face?'

'So now you say that a woman should spend her time on nothing more demanding than choosing gowns and jewels? A moment ago you spoke of such activities with the greatest scorn.'

'It does not take any brains to cook food, to make cordials, to set a table, or to bake bread.'

'I agree. I am sure that any idiot could do it,' she snapped. 'That is, any female idiot. Men never have less than the most brilliant minds, of course. That is *so* well known.'

'It is.' He grinned suddenly, infuriating her so much that she lashed out at him, putting all her strength behind the stinging blow which would have crashed against his cheek had he not moved neatly away.

'You – ig-ig . . . !' she could not finish her words.

'Iguana?' he prompted, grinning more broadly.

'Oh! You ig – *ignoramus*!' she cried, and then his arms

135

were round her and she was struggling to free herself, somehow managing to pull back and lash out with her arm so that she caught him a glorious blow on one cheek. Unperturbed, he clamped her into his arms so tightly that her breath was crushed from her lungs.

'Proud and arrogant Princess, it is long past the time when you were taught your lesson,' he growled through gritted teeth.

Then she knew what he planned to do, and wild laughter began deep within her. Everything she had ever heard about him was true. *Everything*. Now she was to be his next victim. Would they find her wrecked and lifeless body on this bed in the morning?'

'You can teach me nothing that I do not know already, you pig. You are a . . .'

'Yes I know, an iguana,' he drawled, the pressure of his mouth arcing her head backwards.

Infuriated and panic-stricken, she tried to reply, but his kisses devoured her breath, sweeping the power of speech from her. She still had her fists, however, and with these she pounded at his eyes and nose and temples, praying that she would kill him, praying that he would collapse dead at her feet. She had never wanted anything so much as to kill this vile traitor, this man who continued to breathe while her Zebukar was dead. How could it have been allowed to happen, that one so evil had survived, while one so good, so beloved, had been murdered?

He hardly seemed to notice her attack. Somehow, he managed to kiss her again, a kiss bright and fierce as one would expect from a pagan, but even as her senses were jolted into an intolerable reaction, her fists went on beating, grasping his hair and tugging at it. That was what she wanted most, to hurt him, to wound, to kill, but when she saw clumps of his black hair come out in her hands, she was dismayed. What was happening to her? She felt confused, unsure. He held her at arm's length now, staring at her, and she stared back, silently daring him to kiss her again – or worse. She vowed that nothing he did would affect her. Nothing. She would live through it, and somehow escape to bring Hassani's men to capture him. A proper retribution.

'When I look at you, I swear that I see intelligence in your eyes, and a warm heart, but I am wrong. I must be wrong.' He seemed to be musing aloud. 'How could anyone with intelligence marry a Turkish despot and draw a veil over his crimes? You were living in a dream world, Princess, like a child who refuses to grow up. It is a tragedy.'

'It is a tragedy that you are blind, Pagan!' she retorted. 'Thousands have died because of you, because of your dream, a dream born of greed and the lust for power. You were the child, wanting to throw off the yolk of a benevolent father, wanting his wealth and position for yourself.'

'Benevolent father!' he threw back his head and laughed, the sound tingling along her spine like cascading sequins. 'What benevolent father plots to massacre and destroy his children?'

Her face froze. She knew what he was going to say next. That her dear Zebukar had slaughtered hundreds, that he was a murderer. Lifting her hands, she clamped them over her ears and shut her eyes tightly. She did not remove her hands until she heard the door close, at which she opened her eyes, sighing with relief. But he had tricked her. He had opened and shut the door, but he was still in the room. Before she could scream, his palm caged her mouth, while she gazed up at him in terror, her eyes dilated. She could feel the bronze-brown hardness of his body against hers, and time seemed to float backwards. She was a wood nymph picking flowers in a field, when Zeus, the god of gods, saw her, desired her, and enveloped her in his potent and magical embrace. Zeus was infamous for such unfair tactics. He could steal a young girl's wits and enslave her in a few brief seconds, and all with one aim in view: to make love to her. After he had brutalized her, she would be abandoned like all the others, forgotten save in the pages of mythology. She shook herself mentally. What was

137

she thinking of? The pagan's hands had fallen to his sides, and he was looking at her as if he were wary of her instead of the other way round.

Finally, after a long, taut silence, she said, 'Why do you not leave me alone? There is nothing I can tell you, nor would I if I could, and if you mistreat me you will have Hassani to answer to.'

'It seems that we are back where we started, Princess.'

'If it is progress that you seek, then you go about it in the most offensive manner,' she hissed.

'You find my kisses offensive?'

'Such unwished-for advances are always offensive, to put it mildly!' she cried.

'Is there such a great difference between a Turk and a Greek?'

'They are as different as angels from Philistines!'

'For a postulant you have a fiery turn of phrase. What of your vows of meekness and obedience, Princess?'

'They do not include meekly obeying my abductor – especially when he is a vulgar brigand!' she cried.

'It is very sad that we cannot find some common ground.' His mouth was now against her temple, coaxingly velvet.

'No doubt you would like that to be the bed!' she snapped, rigidly resisting his ever-increasing closeness, every muscle taut, every sense strung out. 'Give me the name of any woman who has sought an amiable relationship with the man who has abducted her! It is hardly the best way to begin a friendship.'

He did not reply but she could feel the power of his thoughts, the vibrance of his emotions assaulting her. She had never known such a mesmeric man, but she was not going to admit that his personality might be more powerful than Zebukar's. Suddenly, without warning, she clamped her teeth into his wrist and bit deep until she tasted blood. If only she could kill him that way!

'*Bitch!*' he cried, and then stars were glittering like silvered tinsel past her eyes as he slapped her face.

Nothing like it had ever happened to her before. Touching the stinging, scarlet imprint on her cheek, she choked on a sob, tears blinding her.

This time, when the door closed, he was on the other side.

She got into bed again, pulling the sheets over her head, suddenly feeling crushingly alone. Everyone she loved was dead, her father, her mother, Zebukar. More than anything, at that moment, she needed loving, comforting arms around her. But where would she find them in this Hadean place, this cold, stony hell ruled by a cold, merciless pagan?

CHAPTER TEN

Twenty-four hours later, Flavia woke from a nightmare, breathing in air that tasted chill and hostile to her lungs. She sat up, her heart thudding unevenly. Where was she? She could feel the softness of woven rugs beneath her body, but the room was ebony-dark and devoid of sound. Then she remembered, but she could not tell whether it was night or day. This chamber was as black and soulless as an oubliette.

Getting up, she paced around, touching the walls, feeling for a concealed window which might lie behind the hangings, but failing to find one. Hunger now dominated her mind; she thought longingly of a fresh Greek salad with *feta* – goat's-milk cheese washed down with crystalline spring water. Absently, she realized that her only clothes were her nun's habit, though it was torn and dusty now. Tears flooded her eyes at the thought of what she had left behind, the serenity of the convent, the sweet, uplifting spirituality. She had other needs too and these were growing increasingly desperate. Having found the door, she banged her fists against it, crying out for someone to come and free her.

An hour passed and she felt sick with the urgency of her need. Her fists were aching and scarlet from hammering on the thick wood, and no one had come to release her.

She was furious now. How dare the Pagan, that traitor, have her locked up like this! When Prince Hassani heard what had happened he would send out his guards to arrest the Greek rebel leader and have him suitably punished. As soon as she had envisioned that solution, she saw the consequences: Hassani would have her brought to him and where would she end? As his wife – or his concubine.

Either way, she wanted nothing to do with that obese, lewd, and avaricious Turk.

Again she hammered on the door, shouting out in Turkish, in English, then French, then Greek.

'Where are you, Pagan, coward, traitor, kidnapper of nuns! Where are you? *Come here and let me out!*'

But no one came.

Prince Hassani, Gazer on the Heavens, Allah's Avenging Sword, Taker of Maidenheads, lounged on a scarlet silk couch studded with gold, watching, with gaping jaw, the dancing girl who was performing for him.

Alliya was thirteen years old, which was the age Hassani most preferred, both in girls and boys, although he had no objection to older women too, as long as they were beautiful, shapely, totally devoid of disease or malformation, and, of course, virgins. One could always be assured that a virgin carried no venereal disease, so pure young girls were brought to him from all parts of Greece. Some were abducted, some bought for gold or baubles, some had to watch their families being slaughtered if they objected to the removal of their daughter. Some of the girls were interfered with on the journey, but always in ways which left their hymens intact, so Hassani would never know. Sometimes, their tongues were cut out so that they could not tell the Prince what had been done to them. As he cared little whether his women could speak or not, that rarely mattered. He prized silence in a woman almost as much as he prized virginity.

Alliya had been subjected to the perversions of the three guards who had brought her to Hassani. She had been eleven at that time, and as innocent as a snowdrop. Now, she knew all that there was to know about men and their lusts. She knew how to excite Hassani when he was too tired to respond; she knew how to satisfy him in a dozen different ways. She had watched him performing with

141

other harem slaves, both male and female, and more than once she had participated in such acts.

At first, she had consoled herself with the hope that she might become a Kadine, but she had soon realized that Hassani, for all his grossness and lechery, shared a deep bond with his present wives – a bond which no one could sever. He did not wish to marry again, but only to burn, and burn he did, frequently; in fact, whenever he saw a virgin, a woman with full breasts and red lips, or a handsome female of any age who possessed hair of a shade other than the ubiquitous black. Fair hair, blonde, or red, excited him beyond measure, especially the colourful triangle between curvaceous thighs. The first time he had lain with a woman with golden hair, he had performed seven times within a few hours, then been forced to return to her later when he could not rid himself of his rigid and painful erection.

Alliya wore silvery *shalwar* – baggy transparent harem trousers gathered at the ankles – a tiny, crimson bodice jewelled with spangles, barely covering her tiny breasts, and silver bangles on her wrists. Her feet were bare, her toenails painted silver, and on her toes were silver and gold rings studded with rubies and diamonds. She was liberally doused in musk and attar of roses, and her bleached hair flew around her like the wings of a golden eagle as she danced.

If the Prince were pleased, he would give her a bag of coins, or a jewel. She had quite a large collection now, and she hoped to abscond with her treasure when the right moment came. When that would be, she did not know, because she, like all the women here, was a closely-guarded prisoner. She hoped all the same, for hope was nourishing. Not to hope would surely mean early death.

Hassani seemed to be enjoying her dance. His eyes were bright with lust. Spots of colour had formed in his cheeks. She saw him reach down and lift aside the wing of his silk cloak to reveal what lay beneath and she shuddered inwardly, for she knew of old how the monster ripped and tore at her insides. Surely nothing in the world could be as hideous, as grotesque, she thought, as she swirled lightly on her tiny jewelled feet.

Sometimes, when her mouth was round the monster, she needed all her self-control not to use her teeth, and she would experience such violent fantasies about it that she would feel faint with emotion. But if she harmed him, the devil, then she would be hacked to death and never ever be free of this place.

Watching him with the young boys was the worst of all, for he always hurt them, showing no tenderness or concern for their feelings. The youngest had been seven years old, and he had not survived the onslaught, bleeding to death from a haemorrhage within an hour of Hassani's attack. How she had wept for that child, who had been so like the brother she would never see again. The memory of Hassani's lustful, brutal rape would remain with her, night and day, in darkness and in light, for all time.

Until that horror she had thought herself as weak and frail as a willow branch, but afterwards she had known that she was as strong as steel compared to some. They called her Alliya the Comforter, for that was what she tried to do, comfort all the young victims who languished in Hassani's harem. She knew, too, that if she continued to entice and intrigue him, then she would divert his attentions from those weaker than herself.

'Alliya, come here,' Hassani commanded, and she obeyed, running to him on fleet feet, smiling broadly, adoringly (what an accomplished actress she had become). 'See this . . .' Hassani gestured, his thumb downthrust towards his lap. 'See this, it needs some attention. It wants feeding with your mouth, and then it will feed you in its turn.' Hassani threw back his head and guffawed. His great fist reached out, palming her head and pulling her face down into his lap. She thought that she would choke, and very nearly did. He was not a good Muslim for he rarely bathed, and that alone could be so offensive that she had to fight nausea. When he had been with a boy it was particularly bad. The monster seemed alive, devouring, although she was meant to devour it, gently, but skilfully, never touching it with her teeth but only with her lapping, caressing tongue and soft silky cheeks.

If she thought of her stored treasures and escaping from here, it was not too terrible. Lights spangled in her head, and dazzled her, tears pricked at her eyes, and her stomach heaved, but she continued. The longer she could do this, the longer she could keep him away from the little boy who was even now being bathed and scented in readiness for his first meeting with the Prince. She had heard the boy sobbing, screaming for his mother, and she had heard the slapping of palms against flesh as the harem attendants had tried to quieten him. Finally, they had drugged him, and that would be how he was brought to Hassani, as she had been, two years before. Little child sacrifices, one after the other, wounded, damaged, brutalized. A vale of tears. Oh, if she could summon the courage to bite now, he would never hurt a child again . . .

Hassani was looking down at the bleached blonde hair and imagining russet curls. Since arriving at the Palace of the Silver Cicadas, he had laboured to entrench himself in the place so abruptly vacated by Prince Zebukar. It had not been easy. Zebukar's harem had rebuffed him – something which he had never experienced before – and his young daughters had screamed loudly, refusing to listen to what he was saying. They all saw him as a usurper, which mystified him. For a time, he had panicked, deep inside himself. All this trouble, women hysterical and rejecting, no sight of Zebukar's fortune unless he married the English girl, and continual missives from the Sultan commanding him to do this, then that, then something else entirely.

'Marry the Englisher,' the Sultan had ordered. 'Marry her, and release Prince Zebukar's fortune. It is not as if she is ugly or diseased. What is your argument against this union?'

Hassani could not explain what he felt. For a start,

Zebukar had been slaughtered on his wedding night, and his murderers – the Pagan's men, of course – had been executed the instant that their crime was discovered. It seemed to Hassani that the Princess Musbah might be cursed in some way, perhaps carry death in her hands. Also, she might not be a virgin any longer, and he could not bring himself to bed with an impure female. Oh, he knew it was Muslim law that male relatives marry widows of the family so that they were protected and had a roof over their heads, but, all the same, he had never done it. He could not see it in his scheme of things.

His women were to him the dream women of the gardens of Paradise, the jewelled, scented and painted *houris* who were virgins, each one waiting for her husband with his name written upon her breast. Such women, pure and undefiled, were to him perfection, blessed, divine, for the rapture of Prince Hassani alone, and no other. For, in his dreams, all the *houris* in the gardens had his name emblazoned on their breasts, and his alone. A widow was soiled goods. He could not remove that phrase from his thoughts. Soiled goods.

It had suited him admirably that the Princess Musbah wished to hide herself from the world while she mourned. Had she remained here in the harem, he would have suffered a multitude of conflicting emotions. As it was, he had time to get over the barrier which stood between him and Zebukar's fortune. He had been the Sultan's man all his life, and no one had been more startled and dismayed than he when he found that he could not automatically obey his master's orders, as he had always done before. Prejudice, bigotry, such feelings were alien to the Mohammedan religion and yet here he was wallowing in them, whether he liked it or not. Of course, at the back of his mind was the knowledge that the day would soon come when he would have to capitulate, to bring the English girl back from her sanctuary, and marry her. No doubt the Sultan would insist on his envoy watching while the marriage was consummated, so that the Lord of the Lords of this World could be assured that his command was fully carried out.

A delicate shade of vermilion crept up the back of Hassani's thick knot of neck. If only the Princess Musbah had been younger, say, eleven or twelve, then how much easier it would have been for him. Increasingly, he was turning to children to satiate his desires. There was no fear of contracting a loathsome disease from them; they were fresh, wholesome, sweet-scented, their slim and tender little bodies like rosebuds waiting to be torn open.

He groaned as Alliya's ministrations increased in fervour. She was expert at this, his little yellow-haired odalisque. All the same, he was tiring of her. She was putting on weight – too many sweetmeats and sherbets no doubt – and her breasts were advanced for her age. In a week or two he would give her to Zabat Al Hahr, his chief of the guard and he and his men could sport with her.

At the rear of the palace there was a new graveyard with freshly-turned earth. No doubt after the guard had pleasured the chit to their satisfaction, they would bury her there, along with the others who had not survived their sport.

CHAPTER ELEVEN

Flavia was asleep, exhausted, when the door opened three days later. The light, muffled as it was, striking at her eyes like darts, she flung her hands up to her face.

Xinnia stood in the doorway grinning hugely. A silver engraved platter was in her hands, and on this reposed a graceful flask of wine, a loaf of fresh bread, goat's milk and butter and cheese – the *feta* which Flavia loved – olives, dull green and salty as seaweed, fresh figs and grapes. Before Flavia could gather her wits, the platter was flung at her and then Xinnia withdrew, her laugh grating, her cheeks flushed with evil delight.

'Wait – wait!' Flavia called hoarsely, but the girl had slammed the door, locked it and run off, all within the space of a few seconds.

Flavia snatched at the wine, gulping every drop, then crammed the delicious fruit into her mouth. Heaven. Paradise. Manna. She had not been given food for three days. She trembled with emotion after she had done this, for she had behaved like a crazed animal, and it had shaken her. Was this their aim? If so, it substantiated all that she had heard of the Pagan's savagery towards women. He wanted to break her, to destroy her health and courage, to reduce her to a trembling, wailing mouse, but he would not succeed! Oh no, he would not. She had prayed, she had begged for strength and endurance. She had not crouched there full of terror and submission, far from it. She had prayed so hard that she had almost been able to see in front of her the glittering, angelic figure of the Miraculous Virgin holding out her arms to her, and, shining on each palm like an infant sun, was a ruby-coloured heart from which light pulsed in ever-increasing streams.

So intense and beautiful had been her vision that she had been able to endure the last three days of physical torment in the blackness. She had felt a deep sorrow that she had once forsaken the Virgin for the Muslim religion. Naturally Muslims paid no homage to the Madonna, although they did look upon her son as one of Allah's prophets.

The food devoured, Flavia slept. She no longer knew what time of day it was, but she found a quiet strength in believing that this ordeal was for a purpose, although what purpose remained a mystery, unless it was to be her forty days in the wilderness.

The worst of it was the humiliation of having to relieve herself like an animal, in one corner, and without soap and water to cleanse herself afterwards. That brought bitter tears to her eyes, which she would wipe carefully from her cheeks to put into her parched mouth.

After that, food arrived once a day, which assured her that the Pagan did not wish her to be starved to death, after all. He wanted her spirit to be broken, but even if he kept her shut away here for a lifetime, he would never succeed in doing that. She had placed her spirit in the loving hands of the Miraculous Virgin, where it was safe.

She could not calculate how long she had been in the darkness, seven days, eight, perhaps even twelve, when the door flew open and Xinnia, helped by another woman, hauled her to her feet. Blinded, weak, unsure, she stumbled out into the corridor, the second woman, an ancient crone, mashing her gums together and muttering in some unintelligible language.

Eyes aching as if bruised, Flavia was half pushed, half dragged to one of the sumptuous chambers. It had brilliantly-coloured tapestries depicting Noah and his ark, all the animals, birds and beasts, in scarlet, emerald, and gold with flowers and trees behind them. The carpet was emerald and scarlet, rich and thick, and like soothing unguents beneath her feet. A hip bath was brought, filled with steaming, rose-scented water, and into this she was pushed, while Xinnia and the old crone rubbed her all over in the most cursory way with rose-scented soaps and oils. Her hair was washed, soap trickling into her eyes which began to smart agonizingly. Why were they doing this? To confuse her? To show her what she had been missing? As if she did not know that!

Then it came to her, and she did not know which caused her the most agony, the soap in her eyes, or what was to come. Of course, having broken her – as they no doubt thought they had – they were taking her to the Pagan so that he could use her for his pleasure.

'*No!*' she cried leaping from the water and swinging out with her arms. 'No, you will not take me to him!'

Roaring with rage, Xinnia pushed at Flavia so hard that her weak legs buckled. She clung to a chair for support, and struck back at the vicious girl. Xinnia howled, lashing out with a clenched fist, and Flavia saw a myriad silver stars flashing past her vision, then all went black.

When she came round, the two women were trying to rinse her soapy hair and body where she lay on the carpet. The crone was cursing and looking heavenwards, and Xinnia was nearly in tears with frustration. From outside the fortress palace came the sound of some kind of horn, a distant, haunting noise like that in a dream. On hearing it, Xinnia wept more tears and poked at the crone's chest viciously, snarling, 'Hurry! Hurry! He comes!'

At this point Flavia began to strike out again, enraged. They were late preparing her for their master's delectation. Well, that was just too unfortunate. Getting to her feet, swaying dizzily, Flavia fought off the women while clutching a swathe of linen around her nakedness.

'Leave me alone, leave me alone, *get away!*' she cried. 'I am not going to be taken anywhere! You leave me alone or you will rue the day you came near me!' Seeing a massive hour-glass-shaped copper vase, she lifted it above her head and aimed it at the two women, who backed away, cursing.

149

Suddenly Xinnia made off, dragging the crone with her. Flavia realized that they were going for help. Soon they would return with guards who would lash her hands behind her back and carry her to the Pagan . . . Fury made her cheeks scarlet as she rushed to the door to search for the locks. She could not see one, but there were metal props jutting out from the panels, props into which a bar could be placed to ensure no one could enter, but where was the bar? Panicking, she ran round the room in search of it. She could hear footfalls and shouts as the guards approached, and then she saw the bar. It had fallen sideways behind the tapestry. Sobbing with relief, she heaved at it. In her normal state of health she would have lifted it quite easily, but she was weak and growing dizzier by the minute. Panting, she pulled and heaved it into place, her neck and shoulders screaming with pain.

When it was done, and the door securely barred, she collapsed in a heap, tears of relief pouring down her face. Now the Pagan could do nothing to her. She was safe. For the moment anyway.

A little recovered, she dried her hair and towelled her body, rubbing unguents into her skin to soothe it. A selection of robes lay over the back of a carved chair: her presentation outfit for the Pagan, no doubt. Selecting one of hyacinth-blue silk starred with spangles, she slipped it on and sank down onto the velvet couch to rest. Outside, there were shouts, screams and anguished thuddings against the door, but she ignored them all. She was safe, and they would have to burn the door down to get at her.

They did just that. To her horror, a twist of smoke gyrated its way beneath the door, like a questing snake in search of her. The room was large, however, and had a tiny balcony. When the smoke grew choking, she would step out onto the balcony to inhale fresh air. If the door had not collapsed by then, of course.

Clenching her hands together, she stared at the smoke as if mesmerized, watching it undulate, thrusting and eddying its way into the room gaining strength with terrifying speed. She thought of plugging the base of the door with tapestries pulled down from the walls, but they would burn even quicker than the thick wood.

Unable to bear watching the insidious smoke, she went out onto the little stone balcony with its carvings of Atalanta's cupped hands holding the orb, the eternal circle of life. Brushing her fingers over one of the carvings, she thought of that famous warrior-queen. What would Atalanta have done in such a situation as this? Set her armies upon the Pagan, despatching him and his rebel traitors to death by the sword? If only she had an army with which to . . . Flavia caught her breath.

A small *cortège* was galloping towards the fortress palace, hurtling towards it at great speed. The riders looked like miniature dolls far below on the shrubby plain. There were about two dozen of them and at their head was a man who looked as lofty as a god even when seated in the saddle. The Pagan. So he had been away and was now returning. She shrank back against the stone, but even so she felt naked, exposed. Maybe those infallible emerald eyes could see her at this distance, even though she was on top of a mountain and he was on the plains below? With him, anything was possible. After her ordeal, he would expect to find her cowed, trembling, weak as straw in his hands. Then, like lace in the hands of a savage, he would rip her apart.

The sky was dark suddenly, the sun icy, and she shivered, visualizing her fate, raped, rended, torn by the Pagan, brutalized, possibly even tortured, and then . . . Swallowing, she pressed against the stonework, finding her way back into the room where she saw flames greedily devouring the door, while an urgent hacking noise proclaimed that axes were now being used to gain access.

Above the crackling, she heard Xinnia's screeching. 'Hurry, *hurry*, he is nearly home. He will kill us if he finds out what has happened!'

Flavia's mouth tilted. Single-handed, she had defeated them, wrecked their plans, flung them into a dilemma the like of which it was obvious they had never suffered before. Too bad. She smiled widely. There was nothing she could not do with God and the Miraculous Virgin on her side . . .

When the door finally caved in, attacked by fire, axes and a battering ram (which would have been the more sensible first choice), Flavia stood before her enemies with her back straight and strong as steel, her face impassive, courage etched on her features. She was ready for what she knew must come next, but whatever he did to her, she would not submit her soul. Her spirit would remain inviolate to the end.

CHAPTER TWELVE

They were like a screaming mob rioting around her, faces contorted with hatred and fury, fingers jabbing at her stomach and breasts. Her kaftan tore; someone snatched at the shreds of cloth and pulled them hard. Furious, she tugged back, only just managing to conceal her nakedness from the assembled gaggle.

Elbowing her way through the crowd of servants, guards and women, Xinnia stamped her feet hard on the ground, staring at Flavia with a triumphant look.

'*Stupid!*' she spat. 'Behave like ape, crazy ape. Oh how I love to put you back in room and leave you there to rot!'

'Then why don't you?' Flavia spat back. 'Go on, lock me up again and see if I complain!' It would be infinitely safer for her in that room than out here. 'Go on, lock me up, and see if I complain.' She started for the door, pushing her way through the staring gaggle of watchers.

Head down, she was within a few feet of the door and it seemed as if they would not stop her. At her outburst, no one had moved, nor protested, not even the raucous-voiced Xinnia. Then, coming to the door, she knew why. It was blocked. Standing amidst the wreckage of panels and wood stood the Pagan, arms folded, face inscrutable, eyes glittering like freshly-polished jewels. She halted, and it took an effort for her not to let her jaw drop open in surprise. How could she have forgotten his immense height, the statuesque power and strength of him? Like a bronzed god, Zeus and Mars rolled into one, he surveyed her quizzically.

'What would you like for your journey, Princess? A rope ladder? A loaf, some *feta*, a bag of olives, a flask of wine?'

Blushing hotly, she went to turn away, but he was not having that. Clamping his palms on her shoulders, he pulled her round to face him. Behind them, the crowd gaped, but made not a sound.

'Well? Do you want to be locked up? Do you really think that you can escape from a locked cell? We have them down in the dungeons you know. In ancient times, dozens of men starved to death or were tortured down there.'

'And not only in your dungeons! What about your prisons upstairs? It was iniquitous of you to have me shut away and starved like that. How could you, you fiend?'

She had the satisfaction of seeing his jaw drop now. Then, his eyes narrowing, he lunged past her into the room and took Xinnia by the arm. Scarlet with rage and embarrassment, fear, too, she began to whimper.

'Master, you said lock her away! Lock her away, you said, so I did. I was only obeying you, only obeying *you*!' Sobbing, she crouched on her knees before the Pagan, but as Flavia noticed wryly, the Turkish girl's eyes were quite dry.

'I told you, as you well know, to put her in the chamber of the warrior-queen, the most comfortable we possess. I told you to treat her gently, and give her all that she required. And you know full well that I did this. Xinnia, I think the time has come when you must leave us . . .'

'L-leave you! Oh no, beloved master, no, please, *please* no! I shall die! I cannot live without you! *I shall die!*' To illustrate this threat, Xinnia rolled onto her side and lay still as if she had suffered a seizure.

The Pagan sighed, unperturbed, then he said, his voice low:

'Tonight you will prepare your things and Marcos will take you down the mountain.'

Stepping over the girl's inert form, the Pagan strode back to Flavia.

'Princess I must offer my heartfelt apologies for what this poor girl has done. She suffered terrible cruelties – her family were put to the sword by Prince Zebukar's soldiers – and she was mistreated by them. It turned her mind, sad to say, but she was warned that if she transgressed again,

154

she would have to leave us. We have given her every possible care for three years now, and other than locking her away, I cannot see . . .'

'My husband? My *husband*, Prince Zebukar did this? That is a vicious lie! Hassani perhaps – I can believe anything of him – but not my husband! He was a kind and gentle man, a lawbringer, a father to his people—' Flavia interrupted angrily.

'A father to his many bastards, yes, but never to his people, whether they were Turkish or Greek, Princess!' the Pagan rasped. 'Do you know what he was called? The Headsman. And do you know why?' His voice split. He seemed to be struggling to speak. 'Beheading people – men, women, children, he did not care what they were – that was what he loved. My sisters—' He could not go on. Turning away, he stood as silent as a bronze statue, but before he had turned Flavia had seen the tears glinting like facets in his jewel-green eyes.

'Whatever you say, you will not make me believe such horrors of my husband,' Flavia said quietly. 'I am truly sorry if your sisters have been harmed, but it was not Prince Zebukar who did it, of that I can assure you.'

Facing her again, the tears quelled, the Pagan said, 'Time will prove that I am right and not you, Princess. Time will tell and soon. When we have rid our land of these infidel—'

'Oh no, it is not *they* who are the infidel,' Flavia cried. 'It is you, *you* who are that! Traitor, rebel, unbeliever – you are all these and more. How dare you criticize your betters!'

They were half way down the corridor before she could draw breath. He had snatched her by the wrist and propelled her along at breakneck speed. She did not have time even to think of struggling.

Along another corridor, and another, up stairs, and into a circular tower room he took her.

'Call me anything you like, but never unbeliever!' he roared, pushing her towards a hollowed-out niche in the

155

wall – something like a medieval fireplace except that the recess was not so deep. She could not believe what she saw there. It was some kind of illusion, a trick. Then the full horror of it dawned on her.

'You devil – you've stolen it! You've stolen it from the nuns! May God curse you for all time, Pagan!'

'Allah may curse a man, but not the God of the Christians, Princess. At times, I think that you are torn between the two. No, she is not stolen. She is mine.'

'How can she be yours?' Flavia touched the hem of the pearl-scattered robe with tender fingers, tears forming like pearls in her eyes so that she seemed to be looking in a mirror. 'She belongs to the nuns of the Miraculous Virgin in Nauplinos. She is not for unbelievers to possess. You must take her back, take her back now! They say that if she is moved, then Greece will perish. Is that why you brought her here? You would do anything to bring about Greece's downfall, wouldn't you?' Tears slipped down her cheeks, but she did not trouble to brush them away.

'This is not the statue which you left behind. That is still safe in the convent. Many would wish to have that, but I would rather die than steal it. This statue here is the replica which a Turkish princess had made to take back with her to her homeland. Have you heard of her? She was barren and after praying before the Virgin she conceived again and again. When the princess died, she gave the replica back to the people of Greece, to do with as they wished.'

'And you stole it! How can you deny *that*?' Fists clenched, Flavia faced the Pagan angrily.

'Yes, I stole it – but not from my countrymen. Prince Zebukar misappropriated it. He had a fancy to behead the statue, and then to burn its remains in a public ceremony, to instil fear in the hearts of the Greeks who would be forced to watch the desecration.'

'You are mad! Behead a statue? Who would dream of such a crazy act? Oh, that is witless.'

'Yes, you said it, Princess. Witless. He was, you know,

156

in a way. We Greeks would have given him something that he never had if he had troubled to earn it, but he never did. All he wanted was to destroy. The Headsman of Allah – I do not expect that he ever told you of that title, did he? He gave it to himself, out of pride. He would feast while women and children were beheaded in front of him, one after the other. That was how my sisters died. They were all under eleven years of age, three of them, sweet young girls, innocent. Before they were executed, they were forced to suffer certain indignities – I do not think that I have to explain what I mean in detail.'

'Stop! I cannot listen to these lies. If your sisters died then I am truly sorry, but it was not my husband who caused their deaths. Nor would he have allowed them to be – be assaulted.'

Flavia turned to the statue. It was true that, although sumptuously attired and scattered with fake jewels, this statue had a cold, carved face and none of the warmth and luminous tenderness of the Miraculous Virgin. Oh, how she would love to gaze upon that loving face again, to forget this nightmare, and return to the serenity of the convent.

The Pagan's voice droned on, but the meaning of his words floated over her. It had all been too much. If he thought to persuade her that he was a religious man then he had failed. He worshipped false idols, if he worshipped at all.

'You do not listen.' Suddenly his voice was like fire, scorching her ears. 'What did they do to you in Zebukar's harem? Torture you? Subject you to all manner of horrors so that you believed all that they told you?'

'What nonsense!' she retorted hotly. 'They treated me with great honour and indulgence. I had everything I wanted – I was to rule beside my husband. It was the wish of our fathers . . .' Tears pearled her eyes again as she remembered her father dying alone, far off in England. Now, he would never have his dearest wish. 'As for this harem you speak of – there was no such thing. I was the Prince's only wife, his *only* wife.'

The Pagan looked away, staring into the corner of the room as if he were staring into a great, empty distance. Once he opened his mouth as if to speak, but did not. Flavia waited, suddenly desperate to know what he had wanted to say, but he seemed to have had second thoughts. Finally he shrugged, his voice low.

'There is nothing more that I am prepared to say. We could wrangle over this from sun-up to moon-break and get nowhere at all. You are wrong. You are stubborn and intractable in your beliefs, and it is obvious that I am wasting my time with you. The sooner you are back with the Turks you revere, the better for all of us.'

And with that, he flung away, and was out of sight and hearing within seconds. Flavia stood, unsure, clenching her hands together, bereft in a way totally new to her. He had cheated and tricked her, told her unspeakable lies about her beloved husband, and yet when he left her she felt as if she had no support, no sustenance in the world. It was idiotic. Oh yes, that was the word, but then everything was strange in this place. Xinnia was deranged, the Pagan was like some mythical god – or beast! – risen from the ashes of ancient Greece. This palace was reputed to have belonged to a woman from Atlantis . . . It was like seeing one's reflection in a mirror, weird and unbalanced, distorted, everything right to left instead of left to right. She would need time to adjust to it – yet she did not want time. She wanted to escape, and return to the convent, to be free again, to sustain herself on peace and piety, not rage and damnation.

Why had he brought her here if not to rape and kill her? *Why?* Was she forced to stay here, like Xinnia, until she too lost her wits? Fearful, she knelt before the replica of the Virgin, wishing that she could resurrect the tumult of blinding spiritual passion which the real statue always evoked in her. Yet it was not the statue which she worshipped, for that was idolatry. It was like having a painting of a loved one on which to centre one's thoughts. If she could do it with the real statue, then why not with this one? Close to, the jewels were brash and glassy, the face ineptly painted in harsh colours, but the kaftan-like robe was a brilliant blue silk embroidered with silver lilies. That at least was worthy of the real statue. If she tried very hard, focussed her full attention on the sumptuous robe, she might be able to imagine that the softly beautiful face of the Miraculous Virgin herself was there . . .

'Blessed Mother, I do not mean to find fault with you – God prevent me ever doing that! – but it seems that you have brought me here for some purpose which I cannot fathom, however hard I try. Being in the dark is painful – anguish – I don't know what to do or say. People here are strange, as if from another world, and they believe all kinds of outlandish things. Mother, what do I do? Oh help me, please help me!'

Tears beaded her hands, but no answer came. It was night by the time she ceased praying and then she had to find her way back to the living quarters.

As she fumbled her way along the chilly stone walls, she felt as if she were lost in time, totally disorientated. She could not see behind her; she could not see ahead – and that was worst of all. If she had asked for an ordeal of the soul to strengthen her, then this would have been an excellent beginning.

She fell into the open doorway with a small scream of shock, and great, hard arms enclosed her, crushing her, trapping her so that she could barely breathe or struggle.

CHAPTER THIRTEEN

When she screamed, a powerful steely palm clamped across her mouth, so she kicked out backwards, bringing up her heel in the man's most sensitive spot. Whoever was holding her did not so much as wince. When she was drained of energy, the arms fell away, but by then he had kicked the door shut and was standing in front of it, barring the way.

'How dare you frighten me like that!' she raged, thumping out with a balled fist in the area of the man's jaw, or what she guessed to be his jaw for it was pitch black in this place. 'You monster! When your master hears of this, he will split you from end to end!'

'Oh those barbaric Muslim curses, Princess, how mellifluously they slide off your tongue!' The Pagan, for it was he, chuckled, but coldly. 'Perhaps I am wrong to try to convince you that your late husband was a savage and a murderer, for it may well have been that you supported his barbarity . . . Did you repent and enter a nunnery, thinking that God would forgive you for that?'

'You are the most insulting, despicable wretch I have ever had the misfortune to meet!' Flavia raged, thumping out with both fists clenched, striking at his throat, at his nose – but missing, for he was too tall. Her blows landed somewhere in the region of his bronze chest which was as hard and indestructible as the metal cuirass on a cavalryman. Her reward was to have such aching hands that she could not move them for a few seconds; she was sure that they were broken.

'You have said as much before, but that gets us nowhere. 'You see, I was right. We argue like lovers. Can we not be civil for once?'

'Civil, when you call my husband a murderer and accuse

me of being his accomplice? Civil, when you drag me through corridors as if I am a hound, and pounce on me in dark corners!'

His laughter rumbled again, and this time, because her fists were aching so much, she kicked him hard with her feet, one after the other, until her toes twinged with pain and tears came to her eyes. Never before in her whole life had she wanted to swear and curse at anyone, but now the expletives were biting at her tongue and she wanted to scream them all out at him. Only with the greatest effort did she manage to hold them back. Nonetheless, the words hammering in her head and at her lips had shocked her. Where had she heard words like that?

'You think you are god of all you survey, don't you! You think you can do anything you want, use women, kill, burn, loot and pillage, abduct princesses, insult them and trap them in dark corners like harlots!'

'Not dark any more,' he grinned, stepping away to light a lamp which stood on a circular carved table.

'So, light then! Does that alter the truth about you? If you have any sense you will take me back to the convent tonight!'

'So you want to be shut away in Hassani's harem, eh?'

'The convent I said, not Hassani's harem!' How stupid and slow-witted this man could be.

'Hassani knows where you are, and he is on the verge of sending for you to marry him. Or should I say, sending his guards to kidnap you. Or would you go willingly? I would have thought from your air of haughtiness and self-esteem that you would not relish being one of dozens of faceless pleasure women.'

'I, haughty? The way that you behave one would think you claimed descent from Alexander himself!'

'And what if I did?' He grinned at her, the sparkling emerald eyes intoxicating her with their brightness.

'*You?*' She could not keep the contempt from her voice. 'More like direct descent from the Cyclops!'

'So you think I eat people, do you?' He lunged towards

161

her, making her cry out, and then he was crushing her to him, his mouth travelling over her face and throat so violently that she did indeed think that he meant to devour her. Shivering with an icy fire, she tried to pull away, wrenching her head from left to right, desperate yet excited beyond belief. His lips were wild silk, his arms fiery steel, and she was being enmeshed, chained, imprisoned by them . . . She must get free, she must, she must!

When he released her, she felt as if she had been dropped into an icy pool. Staggering, she fought to collect herself, aware that her hair was wild, and that her torn kaftan was revealing far more than she wanted. Her breath caught in her throat as she struggled to pull the torn segments of cloth together.

'You can go now,' he said, his tone icily dismissive. 'Your chamber is ready for you, the fourth door along on the left. The key is in the door, so you can lock yourself in if you feel safer. No one will disturb you tonight, I promise.'

'Thank you, *Alexander the Great*,' she snapped, and then stepped past him swiftly, but she had forgotten that the bottom of her kaftan was narrow and as her legs stretched out in her hurry to escape, they tugged at the silk so hard that it went taut, acting like a vice on her ankles, bringing her to a sudden and unceremonious halt, her hair flinging past her face in a wild flurry. Fortunately, there was a sturdy chair nearby, which she used to prevent herself from falling.

'More haste, less speed, O Great and High Princess Musbah,' the Pagan taunted softly, his laughter billowing out into the corridor behind her as she rushed away, cheeks aflame.

Of course she would lock her door! As soon as she was inside the chamber, she turned the key with frantic fingers, grinning broadly in delight. So much for the presumptuous and overbearing Greek who thought himself her master!

The room was magnificent. Airy, with high, arched

windows, it had tapestries in amethyst, gold and a rich, dark blue, with a matching carpet. In one corner was a gilded, carved table which looked French, and beside it was a heavy, lumpy looking high-backed bench. A bronze bowl filled with wild flowers stood on a table beside the vast bed. How had they carried such a huge bed up here, she wondered? Then she remembered that the Elizabethans had taken their favourite beds with them everywhere they went, and that to be left such a bed in someone's will was a sign of deep affection or excessive gratitude. They had carved their huge tester beds in pieces, so that they could be dismantled for travelling. Even so, carrying sections of such heavy, ornate oak must have taken some doing.

She caressed the carvings. French, probably Louis XIII, the bed was inlaid with a design of *fleurs de lys*, lilies, marguerites and roses. Her home had been generously furnished with French furniture and she knew all the periods by heart. Their artwork and craftmanship was always so much more ornate, imaginative and beautiful, as if they breathed life and movement into their pieces. Her own bed was Louis XIV, carved with rosebuds, unicorns and crescent moons, as befitted a maiden . . . Tears smarted in her eyes. Home, father, childhood. All eradicated as if they had never been.

She was in the hands of a madman, a savage who imagined that he was descended from Alexander the Great, who behaved every bit as if he were a god-king, sovereign of all he surveyed, master of all women, lord of all men . . . And what was he in truth? Certainly there was no royal blood in his veins. They said that he was the son of a peasant, that his father had been the proud owner of a goat, a cow, and one ramshackle hovel. Then again she had heard it said that he was the son of a Greek woman whose beauty had deprived men of their speech, and of a Venetian Prince who had come at the request of the inhabitants, to govern the Ionian Islands, then occupied by Venice. The islands had been besieged by pirates in past centuries and needed the protection of the Venetian fleet. There was yet another story, that the Pagan was a pirate himself, half Greek, half Berber. Probably the latter, she thought, for Greece had been plagued by pirates for centuries, and was the Pagan not the greatest plague of all?

She tried to put all thoughts of her gaoler from her mind. There was a shelf piled high with food, goat's milk, *feta*, olives, grapes tiny and lime green in colour and sweet as honey on the tongue, the coarse off-white bread of Greece which she loved, and the creamy butter with its bright, mellow flavour. The next few minutes were divine as she sat in comfort on the bed, lace-edged pillows propped against her back, and devoured the feast.

The wine being red, which she had never liked, she drank only the milk, then she lay back replete, allowing sleepiness to trickle through her veins while her mind went over the extraordinary events of the past few hours.

She had not expected to survive the day. She had anticipated rape, brutality, torture, possibly even death, yet here she was, strong, alive and settled in a comfortable French bed and the Pagan had not laid more than a few fingers and his lips upon her. In that dark, strange room back there he could have done anything he desired to her and no one would have come to her aid. Why had he left her unharmed?

She was still puzzling over it when she slipped into sleep, knowing no more until the butter-bright sun streamed in through the high, arched windows to announce that it was morning. Rising, she was about to slip into the torn kaftan, when she noticed a cupboard which was flush with the wall. Opening its door, she was faced by rows of clothes. Beautiful silks in jade colours, beaded and fringed with gold and silver, embroidered with pearls and coral, inlaid with mother of pearl and glossy abalone. It was like something out of a fairytale, a wardrobe made for a mermaid princess perhaps, for the motifs and themes were all of the sea, the brilliant jewel-blue and bottle-green

Aegean. The gowns had trains shaped into fishtails edged with seedpearls and glittering stones which she could not identify. The lace trimmings were as fragile and flowing as delicate plants undulating beneath the water; the slippers had silver and gold scales and looked as a mermaid's foot might have done had she possessed feet. The clothes seemed to belong to no particular period. They were ageless.

One more of the many mysteries about this palace, and probably every bit as unfathomable as the others, Flavia thought, as she slipped into one of the sky-blue robes, its hem glittering with silvery stones which shone blue, then silver, then green. If only there were a cheval glass here so that she could see what she looked like. Inside the cupboard door was a shelf which held a comb, hairpins, ribbons and a silk scarf, but no mirror. Having combed her hair and arranged it loosely about her shoulders, she went to one of the windows to look outside.

What she saw swept the breath from her body. The sea, barbaric yet radiant, its colours rich and ever-changing, was pounding at the base of the cliff. There was no land on this side, just the Aegean thrusting and lashing against the jagged rocks far below. They were the sort of rocks on which a mermaid might have sat, staring dreamily out to sea while she combed her long gold tresses with a coral comb.

'The sea intrigues you, O Great, High and Mighty Princess Musbah?'

The voice behind her made her gasp with shock. Swirling, she saw the Pagan standing behind her, just as if he had materialized out of the naked air.

'Where did you come from?' she cried, recalling how carefully and triumphantly she had locked her door the night before.

'Did you sleep well?' he asked, ignoring her question.

'Yes, but—'

'And was the food to your satisfaction? I prepared it myself.'

'You – you did what?' The Pagan, rebel and raider, preparing a meal for her!

'I said that I prepared it for you myself. Why not? A man who cannot put a meal together is in danger of starving himself to death . . .' His eyes twinkled.

'With all the women you have here – or should I say slaves – there seems no likelihood of that!'

'We all take our share. When I am away, they do the work and when I am here, I help out. That is only fair, would you not say?'

'Fair! What has fairness got to do with you?' she cried. 'Is it fair to keep me a prisoner here? Was it fair to abduct me? Was it fair to burn down the gatehouse of the convent?'

'Ah, now that was a misunderstanding, I told you that. My men have reconstructed it far better than it was before, I assure you.'

'Which does not explain why you carried me off! Do you want to hold me to ransom? Do you know about . . .' she stopped, she had been about to tell him of the fortune Zebukar had left, the diamond called Allah's Teardrop, the emeralds, rubies, black and pink pearls and other priceless gems which could not be touched while she remained unmarried. The Pagan had said that he knew the terms of the will, but he might have been bluffing, or he might know only a part of it. On the other hand, the reason for her presence here might be because he wanted the treasure for himself. His plan might well be to exchange her for Allah's Teardrop . . . Her heart jolted. He would get the largest diamond in the world, and Hassani would get her . . . Horror of horrors!

'Carried you off?' he seemed to be musing, staring past her at the chopping waves. 'Shall we say a whim? There you were, not a nun at all, but a princess trying to look merely mortal in her plain robe. That beautiful, sharply-intelligent face, those pale Aegean-green eyes which refuse to show submission, which blaze with pride and indignation. I would have been a fool not to have abducted you!'

'But why? What *for*?'

'I told you, a whim. I have always loved beautiful things. Can you not tell that from this room? Who would expect a goatherd's son to possess a French bed, let alone a legendary palace?'

'So it is true that you are a goatherd's son? That is somewhat different from being descended from Alexander the Great!'

'Now did I say that I was a goatherd's son? No, I did not. Do not jump to assumptions all the time. Your mind is like a rapier, sharp and bright as steel, but if you let it run away with you, then it will wound you.'

'I am not accustomed to being lectured on my behaviour!' Flavia retorted hotly.

'You will get used to it.' He dared her with his eyes which were the colour of the deepest, most mysterious places in the Aegean.

'Why should I? I am not going to be here much longer!'

Ignoring her, he pointed to the wardrobe with its treasure of silks and sea jewels.

'It is two years since this room was occupied.'

'Oh surely Atalanta was just a little older than that!' she retorted acidly.

'Not Atalanta, no. A lady called Cassandra.'

'Not *the* Cassandra, the seer?' she said sarcastically.

'The dancer. She was half-Greek, half-English. She toured Europe performing for kings, queens, princes, presidents and dignitaries.'

'But I have heard of her! She danced for the Tzar, and he fell in love with her – is that the one?'

'Yes. She did not return his love. She returned to Greece and was to dance at a religious festival in the capital. Just before the performance began, she vanished. I was in the audience and so I headed the search for her. It was I who found her three days later, wandering in a vineyard. Her mind had gone; she did not even know her name.'

'What had happened to her?'

'She had been abducted by some Turkish soldiers as she was on the way to the temple. They took her into the hills and raped her until she went mad. That was a particularly bad period – constant attacks, women being carried off and never seen again. It is said that the Grand Turk's harem in Constantinople is full of Greek women. Houses were burned down if men resisted.'

'I do not want to hear about that! Tell me what happened to Cassandra.'

'I brought her here, hoping that the mountain air would help restore her, but it was useless. The terrible thing is that she became like the woman whose name she had assumed for she spoke only such nonsense afterwards that no one could possibly believe her.'

'And she lived in this room?'

'Yes, for six months. These are her clothes – the gowns she wore for the stage. She was famous for her mermaid's dance. She was so graceful, lithe and beautiful that no one noticed she had feet instead of a silvery tail.'

'So that is why these gorgeous dresses have fishtails like this . . . What a tragic story. Poor Cassandra.'

'Her story was more tragic than that. One morning, just when I had believed that she was showing signs of recovery, she put on one of her gowns, dressed herself as if she were going to dance for a king, and then threw herself out of this window, onto the rocks below.' Tears sparkled in the Pagan's eyes, but they were gone so swiftly that Flavia thought she must have imagined them.

'You – you loved her?'

'Who could not? She was the most beautiful, ethereal creature imaginable, with hair bright as marigolds which rippled down to her ankles, and eyes dark as Greek coffee . . .'

'I heard only that she had vanished. It was in *The Times*, our English newspaper.'

'Of course. All news from here is doctored before it is released. The Turks want as many allies as they can get; they want Britain to think they are benevolent rulers now, and no longer the despots of old . . .'

'I always thought they were! My husband . . .'

'Oh yes, your sainted husband. The kindest, gentlest most honourable mass murderer there has ever been . . .' His voice was suddenly grim but his face was grimmer.

The almost tender moment was shattered. Flavia pointed to the door. 'Please go, now!'

Bowing coldly, he obeyed.

She stood in the window, noticing now that there were sturdy nails hammered into the framework so that the window could not be opened. She had gone strangely cold. When she had looked down at the sea before, when she was alone, she had half imagined a gilt-haired mermaid sitting on the rocks below, combing her long, rippling hair . . .

She would pray for the soul of poor, unhappy Cassandra, for she was sure that the dancer was not resting in peace, whatever had caused her to lose her mind.

How ready the Pagan was to believe ill of the Turks. He was a man of primitive suspicions. She had never heard Zebukar say a word against the Greeks. He had always referred to them as 'my people', and he had promised that she would help him rule them . . . Quite suddenly there were tears in her own eyes.

'Zebukar, my love,' she whispered, 'rest in peace, too.' And she recited some lines from the Islamic Book of the Dead, which had been part of her childhood education.

'In the Name of Allah, the Merciful, the Compassionate . . .' then she paused, for that name sounded out of place here. 'In the gardens of Paradise, the roots of the trees are of silver, and some of their leaves are of silver and some of gold. If the root of the tree is of gold, its branches are silver, and if its root is silver, its branches are gold. The earth of their ground is musk, amber and camphor. Their rivers are milk, honey, wine and pure water. When the wind blows, the leaves of the trees strike each other and a sound comes from them, the sound of whose beauty has not been heard. There are winged horses with saddles inlaid with ruby and pearl, and they are ridden by the *awliya*, the friends of Allah. Those who are lower than they will say, "O Lord, for what reason have you given these servants of Yours this miracle?" And Allah will reply, "These are the ones who prayed while you were sleeping, who fasted while you ate, who fought Jihad while you were sitting with your women, and who were spending their wealth in the way of Allah while you were miserly . . ." '

Her words faded. She had received some small contentment from imagining Zebukar in the Paradise of the Mohammedans, riding jewelled, flying horses and drinking heavenly wine while sitting beneath gold and silver trees . . . For the faithful, there were the *houris*, with faces coloured white, or green, yellow or red, with bodies of saffron, musk, amber and camphor, and hair of raw silk, and on their breasts were written the name of the pious man to whom they would belong when he arrived in Paradise. It was said of these women that, 'their clay was kneaded with the water of life, and all the *houris* love their husbands, and had one of them spat into the sea it would have sweetened. Written on her breast is: Whoever wishes to have the like of me, let him work with obedience to his Lord . . .'

Flavia had not minded the thought of a beautiful *houri* comforting Zebukar, when she could not.

She had been through many phases in her grief, stupefaction, shock, tears, nightmares, waking to think that he lay beside her, then sobbing when she found herself alone; imagining that she saw him in the distance, his broad back and glossy dark head, only to see the face of a gnarled Greek villager when the man turned. There had been self-pity too, and over and over again she had asked herself why, *why* had it happened to her? A whole lifetime's preparation, her father and Bastan's great dream, and all ruined by the knives of the Pagan's men . . .

Or so she had been told, but the seeds of doubt had been planted. The assassins had been slaughtered on the spot, before they could speak. Perhaps they had not been the Pagan's rebels, the *Kleftes* as they were called? But if not, then who were they?

CHAPTER FOURTEEN

When she woke, there was a bronze tray by her bed on which was fresh bread and butter, the ubiquitous olives and grapes, and a large slab of rich plum and fruit cake, a recipe known to the locals of Corfu as 'kek', their pronunciation of the British word cake. There were wild strawberries, too, and frothing goat's milk in a white jug.

But who had brought them while she slept? She had locked the door again and the key was under her pillow.

As she ate, she could hear movement in the palace, voices, loud and badgering, as the members of the household urged one another on with the morning's tasks, the bleat of goats, the indignant bray of a donkey, the slapping of rope-slippered feet on stone floors. All so normal, so everyday, yet they were in a palace which was thousands of years old, ruled by a man who looked and behaved like Zeus and Mars rolled into one (well, not quite – he had not yet turned himself into a swan to try and seduce her!) and she was sleeping in a haunted chamber furnished with Louis-Quatorze pieces.

If she had clicked her fingers, and tried to conjure up a stranger, more colourful, more spectacular setting, she could not have done it. Nor could she have imagined a more extraordinary master for it.

She had wept herself to sleep, and now felt cleansed, her mind bright, yet why she should feel so cheerful she could not say. She was a prisoner in a madman's castle, and no one knew where she was. She might die of old age in this eyrie of a fortress . . . A few minutes later, a tap came at her door and a girlish voice begged entry.

'Who is it?' Flavia called.

'Ezta. I have brought your washing water, O Great Princess. Our lord says that I am to serve you, to do whatever you wish, to look after you in all ways and consider you to be my mistress.'

As Flavia could not find fault with this earnest-sounding announcement, she unlocked the door and Ezta came in, beaming. She was aged about fourteen, with gleaming black hair in two long plaits down her back and she wore a working version of the national costume of Crete. It comprised a waist-length black jacket with scooped neck and long straight sleeves with a dash of embroidery at the cuffs, a white blouse, and cream, ruffled trousers, rather Turkish in style but narrower, over which was a narrow cream skirt ending about six inches above the ankles so that the gathered anklets could be seen. At the front there was a long cream apron of coarse homespun linen whose edge was colourfully embroidered in royal blue and scarlet lozenges, daisies and zigzags. A red scarf completed this bright ensemble, and it was wound round Ezta's head.

Having digested all this, Flavia said: 'Your lord?'

'Yes, Lord Alexandros, our master.'

'So he is a lord now, is he?'

Ezta wrinkled her brow. 'Now? He has always been our lord, O Great Princess.'

'You do not need to call me by that title, Ezta. Your Highness will suffice.'

'I do it, Your Highness,' Ezta said solemnly, then set about fetching the jugs of hot water and the hip bath, which was borne in by two small boys with dark skins and enormous gleaming eyes.

The water had come rather a long way and could not be called hot, but it would be heavenly to bathe again so soon, after the days locked up in the dark. Rose and violet unguents were provided, and soft little spheres of soap liberally mixed with oils. When the wide-eyed boys had gone, Flavia threw off her robe and stepped into the hip bath, Ezta standing over her and pouring in nearly a whole flask full of rose oil.

'Not too much, Ezta, or I shall slither out of the room instead of walk!'

'No, not too much, O Great Your Highness,' Ezta grinned, only briefly chastened.

'Just Your Highness will do, Ezta, thank you. Now would you please pass me the soap. Thank you.'

Afterwards, wrapped in fluffy linen, Flavia sipped mint tea, offering a dish of it to Ezta who would not drink. It was over a year since she had tasted this light, refreshing beverage and the scent and taste were exquisitely nostalgic. Zebukar came back to her, a dazzling wraith, as did the solemn ritual of her wedding day, with him beside her. A bright prince, whose light was now extinguished for ever . . . Sighing, she replaced the dish on the tray. These days, it was as if she visualized him from an immense distance, as though all eternity were between them, the acute poignancy of the early days of her bereavement becoming dimmed.

She was surprised to find the wound healing, and it startled her; she felt almost guilty and a little uneasy. How could she have forgotten the anguish of those early months? It was like forgetting him . . . Like betraying his memory.

'Ezta, have you lost someone you love?' she asked, then wondered why she had said that. What would a young girl like this, so smiling, so contented, know of grief?

Instantly, Ezta's face crumpled, and tears flooded her cheeks.

Flavia reached out, touched her shoulder. 'Ezta, what is the matter?'

'You r-remind me. Oh, such sadness, and I try to forget. Not easy.'

'Who did you lose?' Flavia took her hand and squeezed it.

'My mother. She was bearing child again. My little brother. My aunt, my uncle, their five children . . .' Tears gushed.

'What happened? Was it an accident?'

'Aiyee, no! The men of Pasha Alafa did it. They like wild beast. Kill, burn, steal.'

173

Flavia had the feeling that what would follow would be an all too familiar tale of tragedy 'caused' by the Turks.

'Who is Pasha Alafa?'

'One of Sultan's generals come here, to our country, to teach us lesson. We not ask for it, not ask for them to come, but they come and we die, we burn, we starve . . . Some Greeks make army, but they killed, too. Some run off . . .'

'But, Ezta, surely they, the Turks, I mean, look after you all properly?'

'You call killing, burning, stealing looking after us properly, O Highness? No, it is not, not, *not*! You bride of Turk. *You* know truth.' Ezta's eyes were almost accusing.

'I did not mean that – I meant – Oh, whatever happened, I am very very sorry, Ezta, it must have been dreadful for you. As for my knowing the truth, well, can you believe that I might not?'

'I only survivor. I think my papa lives, but I hear he killed in fight with guards. So me only now, none other. When I have babe, I call it after my mother and father and brother, all names rolled into one, I not care if some man, some woman names. I not care!' Shoulders shaking, Ezta bent over, sobbing.

Flavia cradled the girl in her arms while tears came into her own eyes. The girl had suffered terribly, of that there was no doubt, but who had caused it was a different matter. At first, she thought the Pagan might have put the girl up to this, but she could see now that Ezta had gone through an appalling ordeal. She did not feel that the girl was lying, but there were bad generals in all armies, and Pasha Alafa was obviously one of those.

'Our lord, he is to find me a husband, a good husband, in two year when I sixteen. And he will give us home, safe home away from the Turk. I could stay here, but it better if I get 'way to safe country. English, perhaps. No one ever die in English.'

'Well, that is not exactly true, Ezta, although England is certainly a very safe country. But you would be strangers

174

there – with no money, no work. Life can be very hard for immigrants . . . That is, people who go from their homeland to make their homes in a strange country.'

'The husband our lord choose for me be so good, so strong, that I never poor, never troubled.'

'You obviously think that your master can work miracles . . .' Flavia managed a wry smile.

'We know he can. He do, alway. Many times. He have great power, great strengthness, like old gods.'

Flavia smiled again. This girl had been well schooled in eulogizing her master! Had he taught her all this himself? Knowing his great vanity, he probably had done just that.

'It is good that you are loyal to your master, but I doubt if what you say can possibly be true, Ezta. When we are young, we are prepared to hero-worship anyone who crosses our path . . .'

'Not such a thing I do. Lord Alexandros is prince among men, our great brave leader, like god of the old ages. He has worked miracles – I have seen.'

Seeing that the girl was adamant and that her tears were drying, Flavia encouraged her to talk. And talk she did. Apparently, Alexandros had once walked into a burning monastery and, single-handed, had rescued all the monks.

'Strange, but I think of him setting fire to convents, not rescuing their inmates . . .' Flavia commented wryly.

Ezta went on. Alexandros had heard of a healing spring in the mountains and he had carried a young crippled child for many miles to reach it, so that she could bathe in the waters. He had returned her to her parents with the power back in her limbs and no sign of their former deformity, and yet, when questioned, the child had said that there was no spring, that she had not bathed in any waters, but had been held in Lord Alexandros's arms all the time. The strength had come back to her limbs from the warmth of his heart, she had said.

Only with the greatest difficulty could Flavia keep quiet, allowing Ezta to go on, which she did with ever increasing enthusiasm.

A small earthquake had partially destroyed one of the islands and its inhabitants were facing certain drowning, when Alexandros had rowed out to them and rescued them all, in twos and threes, although a savage storm had been raging, with waves reaching more than thirty feet high. Had he not acted, the entire island and its people would have been washed away and lost.

'So he is very strong, Ezta, but not a miracle-worker. The child must have experienced what they call a natural remission, that has been known to happen.'

'But I saw the child, O Highness. She had the twisting of legs—' Ezta wove her hands through the air to demonstrate how twisted the limbs had been – 'yet when she came back from the mountains, she was walking, as never before, and with the straightening of legs.' Ezta swept her hands down in two straight lines.

'Tell me about the people who live here in this palace, Ezta. Who are they?'

'Kios, aide to our lord, he is good in the looking, kind, but merciless with knife to enemy. He has killed many enemies. Our lord save him from funeral pyre – he being burned alive for helping womens escape the Turk. Our lord ride into square on horseback and carry off Kios before he harmed. He carry off sister of Kios, too, but she overcome by smoke and die. We all cry much at that time.'

Flavia jumped to her feet, her eyes sparking with anger. 'Why should the Turk want to burn anyone like that, Ezta? *Why?* It is just too improbable, too far-fetched . . . all these ridiculous stories! I have no reason to believe any of them. They are Greek propaganda!'

Ezta looked shocked. 'But they all true, so true, I am swearing it by Our Lady of the Miracles.'

'You mean that effigy in the tower room? Do not be misled by that, Ezta, it is false, like everything else around here. The real Virgin is in a convent near Nauplinos – or was, if she has not been carried away by – by looters.'

Ezta's eyes were dark with pain, yet at heart she was a

warm and generous Cretan girl. The moment Flavia had berated her, she felt ashamed, yet what else could she do?

In the weeks that followed, Flavia reflected upon how she had exchanged one prison for another. For all the freedom she now had, she might have been reliving the days of limbo before her wedding, save that now there was nothing to look forward to.

Ezta served her well, as instructed by her master, but it was obvious that the young girl was puzzled by her new mistress's moods. Sometimes Flavia was talkative, sometimes she was uncommunicative or acid-tongued. It was not surprising after all she had been through, and considering the instability of her present position, for no one would tell her how long she had to stay there, or what was planned for her future. Two or three times daily she wrote messages to the Pagan and sent Ezta to deliver them, but no replies ever came back.

'Why, why am I here?' she would write, anger darkening her script. 'Tell me when I can go free! I am a princess of the Turkish royal line, and you have no right to keep me caged here like an animal! Return me to my people. Write to Prince Hassani and he will send his men to take me home. I do not belong here.'

There were limits to the amount of entertainment one could derive from sequestration in a fortress. Narrow, dark corridors which led nowhere, or to eerie, exposed battlements where the wind blundered into her hair and against her face in the most threatening manner. It took courage to step out onto these battlements, where air pockets flourished, and even more courage to stare down the sheer, stony walls to the plains below, plains which stretched for mile after mile into the distance.

What she would have given to have been able to escape, to gallop off into that distance on the back of some fleet-footed stallion taking her to freedom . . .

The battlements were gargantuan, built of rocks whose colours were pale sand, dove grey, ginger, coffee, white and cream. They were timeless, so ancient that one could guess at their having been built during the Roman occupation of Greece, or even before. She could not see the sea except from her window, and she longed to be able to stand out in the open air with the speedwell-blue and peacock-green of the Aegean pounding way below her vision, a watery demi-god.

To one side were levels of land, one above the other, on which grew gnarled and twisting dull-green olive trees, and a handful of steeple-shaped cypresses, almost black against the sandy coloured earth. Sometimes, she would hear the weirdest sound – a breathless, almost deafening buzzing whose origins she could not guess at, nor did Ezta know what it was, and so Flavia christened it the puzzle bird, and waited for the puzzle to be solved, but it never was.

There was a limit to the enjoyment in trying on beautiful shimmering gowns with fishtail hems, even though they were a delight to wear. And although she was kept generously supplied with scented soaps, unguents and oils, and could bathe daily, she was very soon desperate for intelligent conversation, with anyone – even the Pagan. But he did not come. Had he lost interest in her? She had been expecting a continual siege. Increasingly, she would spend time in the tower room, thinking of the original statue of the Miraculous Virgin, and wishing that it stood before her and not the replica with its empty, overpainted face, somewhat petulant, and not a little haughty.

She sent more notes to her jailer, longer and more pertinent, but still he remained silent.

'This is no way to treat a princess of the Turkish royal line! You will pay dearly for keeping me incarcerated here like a felon! Traitor, rebel, assassin, abductor of women! There is no insult too vile to fling at you! You know that you have gone too far in this – and that you will be brought to justice. By marriage, I am related to the Sultan of Turkey, ruler of the Ottomans, and he will not brook this insult to one of his family, you can be sure of that. He will send his

armies to deal with you, and I shall not speak one word in your
defence, Pagan! Murderer, coward, thief, savage, devil . . .'

She had been shaking when she finished writing that, but she was not sorry for the insults she was hurling at him. They were all true and she meant every one, in triplicate.

One evening, she had two visitors, Ezta and Kios. Kios was in his mid-twenties, dark as a Turk but most definitely Greek. He had a handsome, bold, light-filled face, chocolate-brown eyes which glinted with humour, and deep dimples in his noble cheeks. His hair was wild and very black, and always looked as if it had just suffered a long and victorious skirmish with a comb. He had visited Flavia once or twice before, brief, formal calls to ascertain that she was being fed properly and had all that she wanted. She had cried, 'Of course I do not have what I want! I want to be free!' and Kios had withdrawn, somewhat red in the face, but bowing courteously. Now here he was, and so late at night, with Ezta pink-faced beside him.

She was to be taken to another room, to meet someone. They would not tell her who or why, and she would have felt distinctly uneasy had this summons come during her first days in the palace, for example when Xinnia held sway. As it was, she shrugged, pulled on the nearest kaftan, which was of rich gold silk snaked with twists of gold beading, ran a comb through her hair and announced that she was ready.

Where were they going? Neither would tell her. She was now more or less accustomed to the dark, eerie and wayward corridors of the palace, and Kios led the way, a flambeau in his hand, its leaping, darting flame lacquering the walls with vivid light. Was she being led to the sacrificial pyre? Had Hassani sent his men for her and she was being surrendered to them? A veil of ice swept over her at the thought, her veins turning to icicles. Delivered into the slimy palms of that gross monster . . .

179

A door clanged shut in the distance, and Kios chuckled quietly to himself. What was going on? She glanced at Ezta. The girl's face was devoid of expression but her cheeks were scarlet. She wanted to cry, 'Will no one tell me what is going on?' but she stayed silent.

Air billowed along the corridor like invisible hands tapping and pleating at her gown, and she wrapped her arms round herself. Someone had been standing out on one of the parapets, and when they had stepped inside, a gush of night air had come with them. One of the guards maybe, for lately there had been a restlessness as if attack were expected. She had been surprised that, living such a wild and daredevil existence, they were not constantly under siege.

They arrived at a door, huge, heavy thick oak studded with metal nails. Before Kios could knock, the door swung open. Kios gestured to Flavia to enter, which she did, then the door crashed shut behind her. She had half expected lions to leap at her, to tear at her limbs, for she was no Daniel, but there was no wild beast in the room, nor a human one. It was sumptuously furnished, rich, resplendent and kingly, amethysts and purples mingling blissfully with emeralds and sapphires. Priceless carpets lined the floor and the walls, and the scent of roses, jasmine and white-necked lilies was pungent on the air. From some undetectable corner came the plaintive yet romantic sound of a lyra being played.

She felt out of place standing there. What was she meant to do now? Wait? Why? For how long? An aching sensation of forlorn isolation gripped her; a brightly piercing feeling of irreplaceable loss. The music had something to do with it, she knew. The lyra player was direct from Mount Olympus, a veritable Orpheus, and the notes of the song undulated coaxingly, cajolingly, around her heart.

'Who is there?' she called, not expecting a reply and not getting one. Turning, she tried the handle of the door but found that it was now locked. Sighing, she sat on a stool and let the music evaporate her tensions. She looked at the tall, flute-like lilies with their graceful ivory necks, remembering the days when she had placed such flowers before the Miraculous Virgin in the convent. Purity, chastity, perfection, the lilies were all these, and . . .

A twist of night air had billowed over her, but there had been no sound of a door opening. Someone was close by; she could sense it.

Then, standing before her was a woman she had not seen before. A Greek woman with a haggard, life-beaten face and dull, olive eyes.

'This Princess's chamber now,' she said, her voice husky. 'Princess sleep here. Food is brought now.' The old eyes were hostile.

A wicker basket was placed before Flavia who saw a luscious selection of fruits for her delectation. There was wine too, and it sang down her throat. How thirsty she was; she could not help but drink. The woman went, silently, and Flavia glanced at the bed. If this was to be her room now, then the least she could do was use the bed.

It was comfortable, welcoming, and she stretched languorously, then curled up in a cosy ball. Within seconds, she was asleep. In her dream, she was lying in a scented garden. It was paradise and yet it was also earth. A man was standing over her, his dark, blatantly handsome face alight, his eyes dazzlingly black. It was Zebukar. Yet there was something frightening about him, almost devilish.

'Welcome to the Garden of a Thousand Caresses,' he said to her, eyes slumbrous, and then his mouth was on hers, his hands palming her breasts and she was roused, oh so fiercely, wildly roused that her soul lifted from her body in its urgency to join itself to him. Then, as they were about to merge, his body into hers, his hand swooped down, avenging, merciless, and she saw the savage glint of a scimitar, felt the steel slice through her neck in one deadly stroke.

She woke with a cry, sweat beading her body. The Garden of a Thousand Caresses – where had she heard that before? She knew that there was something in the recesses of her mind, but she could not recall it. Knowing that to search for it would spoil her chance of sleep, she settled down again, cosily, and soon was drifting into dreams.

Zebukar greeted her again, brilliant, vigorous, demanding. His powerful arms were scooping her up as if she were a lush, ripe fig – that fruit which, when fresh, is said to resemble the most secret place of a woman, soft, moist, inviting. She knew full well that only the briefest of seconds lay between herself and the moment of consummation, and she could not wait. She could not . . .

A tug of the sheets woke her as urgently as a flare of lightning. The chamber was in blackness. She could see nothing, but there was movement, someone was sliding into the bed beside her, curving their body close. A mouth was clamped over hers, arms like serpents entwining, so that she could not move however hard she tried and the scream was slaughtered in her throat.

While her mind cried out, 'Who is it? Who is there?' her arms thrashed and her legs kicked, all to no avail. She was weak as a child in her captor's embrace, and crazy with terror.

Then he spoke, his words soft and lulling, mellifluous, sensual, so that they soared along her veins to flower in her heart. She was still dreaming, after all.

'Let me welcome you to the Garden of a Thousand Caresses, my Princess. You have heard of it? Young maidens are taken there when they enter the harem of their new lord, and they are instructed in the arts of love, from the very beginning to the very beautiful finale . . .'

Then, as he clamped her body to his, she knew who it was and that it was no dream. 'I shall not stay here while you do this!' Flavia found her voice. 'How dare you come into my bedroom like this? How dare you take advantage of me in this way! It is shameful and loathsome! Loathsome, do you hear me?'

For answer, he threw back his glossy black head and roared with laughter like the lion that he was.

'Princess, I thought you professed to love the ways of the Turks? You say that I am a heathen, a philistine, while they are possessed of all the virtues and nobility in the world . . .'

'Rape is heathen behaviour, yes! You are famous for it the length and breadth of Greece!' Her heart was hammering, causing a pain like broken glass between her ribs. Her face was crimson, her breath choked.

'I fear that you have been misinformed again, Your Highness, Rose of the West.'

'How did you know of that name? Who told you that?' That had been Zebukar's pet name for her – how could this man know of it?

'Zebukar was boastful. There were few he did not tell about his Rose of the West and his plans for her, of the great alliance he was to make with the King of England, thereby gaining himself immense power to attack his enemies. Do not forget what a famous navy your England has. He would have given anything to gain its support.'

'Against his enemies, maybe – and that would include you, of course.' Her lip curled. 'No wonder you hated him. No wonder you've caged me here, you low, vile coward! That fleet can still sail against you. My godfather . . .'

'When England knows the true state of affairs, that fleet will rise against Greece's enemies not its protectors,' the Pagan said grimly.

'Yes, yes, against *you*, I said against *you*!' She was almost sobbing. How powerful he was, this man whose verdant jewel eyes could not be discerned in the darkness but whose spearing glance was raking her nonetheless. She could feel its beam searing into her.

'The Princess Musbah is very confused, but her confusion can be treated. A woman's frustrations are common knowledge, and any man who is worth more than a fig knows how to deal with them.'

'Why, you arrogant, overweening, bumptious . . .'

His mouth was flesh and flame against hers, so that her senses twisted wildly and she forgot her own name. Who was she? Flavia, the English daughter of a duke, or the Princess Musbah, wife to Zebukar? Would she ever know again?

Carved bronze hands were gripping her wrists like manacles, and his breath was hot as the Greek sun, fiery on her face, fiery as his passions. During their verbal sparring he had seemed so remote, so emotionless, and yet here he was, behaving as voluptuously as any Sultan . . . What was he trying to prove? That he was a man, after all? In case she doubted it? Nothing that he said or did could ever persuade her he was also a gentleman. He was a coward, a rapist, a persecutor of women and children, a . . .

Zebukar's kisses evaporated from her memory, shown up for the passionless, artless attempts that they were, made when she was very young, very innocent and naive and thinking that she was in love with her dream Prince. Such a long time ago, when she had been little more than a child, and had believed, with a child's presumption, that she knew all that there was to know. Now she was an adult, a grown woman and could see the truth for what it was. Her will had returned, like a beam of ice-cold light penetrating her mind. She must have been mesmerized all those years. When the Pagan's mouth seared against hers, she was as malleable as silvered water from a stream, scooped up into his palms to slake his thirst. She was the moon and he the sun; she was nectar to his ambrosia, silver to his gold. Had a statue of Zeus stirred and moved and breathed, taken her in his marble arms, she could not have been more electrified. His flesh touching hers was like a trillion tiny bolts of lightning coruscating through her entire body. She could not bear it; the pain, the bewilderment, the searing joy was too much. She wanted to beat him away, make fists and pound them into his face, but all she could do was shudder like a hart which had been pursued and now is finally caught, a hart seeing its fate staring it squarely in the eyes and knowing that it is trapped. His kisses were fire on her lips, the heat of his body was passion, consolation and delight. There was no time for puzzlement, for questions and wondering, although she was mystified as to why he was here, holding her, making love to her.

The pungent scent of lilies was like a mist in the air, and the scintillating strumming of the lyra from its invisible corner was eerily strange. Lilies and music. Would she ever be able to think of them again without remembering this exotic, fiery moment, this strange and perplexing man? Time fled and she was back in Zebukar's arms, thrilling to his very first kiss, melting in his embrace, then, suddenly, sharply, she did not want it to be Zebukar. She did not want all that frustration and agony revived. Let it go; let it die, as he had done. Please God let her forget that time of terror and pain and how near she had come to marrying that grotesque and debauched Hassani.

The tinkling notes of the lyra undulated to a halt, the scent of lilies evaporated, and she was in her right mind again. No man would ever rule her with a kiss, not ever again. Snatching back her arms, she fought to get free of the Pagan's hold, slamming her forearms at his chest and shoulders, scratching her nails across his neck, his cheek. All he did was laugh, loudly.

'You would not dare touch me!' she cried. 'You will be punished, imprisoned, executed, shot . . . Traitors are always shot!' Tears forming like hard beads behind her lids, she clamped her mouth shut in an effort to hold them back. They were weakness and she would die before she showed weakness to this man.

'But I am no traitor, Princess. I am Greece and Greece is me. We are indivisible, inseparable. We are one, this country and I. Hewn from the same rock, coloured with the same sky and sun and foliage; our blood is the same blood and we have the same heart which beats in unison. Remember how powerful Greece was in ancient times, when the pagans ruled. That is why they call me the Pagan because they know that Greece can be strong and free again with my aid.'

'And you are not called that because you are a philistine, a brutal, unschooled peasant? I rather thought you were.' Flavia's cheeks were scarlet. He had released her and she was standing, facing him across the room.

'If it would free my land then I would behave as savagely as any unschooled peasant, but it would not.'

'Then why are you here in my room? Why are you holding me, kissing me?' she cried, part of her enraged, bewildered, and part desperate to be back in his arms again.

By way of reply he quoted some lines which sang in her ears and moved her to silence.

' "Snatch from the ashes of your sires The embers of their former fires; And he who in the strife expires Will add to theirs a name of fear That Tyranny shall quake to hear, And leave his sons a hope, a fame. They too will rather die than shame: For freedom's battle once begun, Bequeathed by bleeding sire to son, Though baffled oft is ever won. Bear witness, Greece, thy living page, Attest it many a deathless age." '

'Who wrote that?'

'The Lord Byron of whom I spoke earlier. Your own countryman who was willing to die for our cause. There were no doubts in his mind, as to its rightness. Have you forgotten how we spoke of him?'

'Of course not. Byron, the lecher and libertine. I know him.'

'As to that, I cannot say. He and I went to college together in England.'

'You went to college in England?' Her brows rose.

'I did. Trinity, Cambridge.'

'So that is why you speak such excellent English.'

'Praise at last from the fair lips of the Princess!'

'Not praise but a factual comment,' Flavia said primly, wanting to know what he had been doing in her homeland, and why. Could it be true that he was the son of a Venetian aristocrat? 'Why did you quote those lines? Do you want me to weep for the crimes that you have committed?'

'*I?* How obdurate you are, Princess Musbah. Always accusing, never accepting any of the guilt for yourself. I do not suppose that it has ever entered your head that you might be in the wrong . . .'

'These continual arguments are so petty! I know what I have been told about you, and it was not pleasant. Now I am your prisoner and that is not pleasant either . . .'

'Would you rather be Hassani's?' he interrupted coldly, his eyes emerald ice.

'I would have been his wife, not his prisoner.'

'You had a taste of Muslim life. How long could you have survived purdah and the imprisonment of the harem?'

'It was never intended that I should be a concubine. I was Prince Zebukar's only wife . . .' She said it proudly, holding her shoulder squarely.

'How deceived we are, but never more than when we choose to believe all that we are told.' He sighed, turned from her, and she was suddenly cold, alone.

'I tell you I was his *only* wife, his chief wife.' The hard pearls that were her tears were dangerously near to falling down her cheeks.

'It was better that you should think so at the time.'

'Better for whom?'

'For you. What independent, proudly reared English daughter would accept that she was one of many? There would have been mayhem, a great scandal. Would you have come willingly to marry a man who already had half-a-dozen wives?'

She could not help but laugh for what he said was so asinine. 'Six wives? Muslims are allowed only four.'

'But he had six. Some were dead, some still alive. He had a desperate lust to sire an heir. Surely you knew of it?'

'A longing for an heir? But of course. What prince does not?'

'He had many daughters, eight or more. All young, of course, and perfect, but no son. If a wife gave him girlchildren he rid himself of her in the quickest way – death.'

187

'It is not difficult to divorce the Muslim way. Why should murder be involved?'

'And have the country filled with ex-wives who will spill the truth about the activities in the Palace of the Silver Cicada? He could not have that. They were publicly divorced, then taken away to die a natural death – if starvation can be called natural.'

She shuddered despite herself. The stories this Pagan told were always so numbingly, horrifyingly real. She must not believe them, of course.

'You have me here a prisoner in your fortress. You can tell me any lies you wish and who will gainsay them?' Her voice bitter, she turned away, clenching her hands, forcing back the painful tears, and then, to her surprise, his hard, warm palms were like velvet caps on her shoulders and he was pulling her round to face him.

'If I could make it all untrue and have you back with your Zebukar, happy and content, then do you not think that I would do it this instant? Do you think that I delight in seeing your misery? But I cannot have you dreaming in a paradise where fools tread, for then you would be a prisoner for all time. You would end your days a lonely, bitter widow, believing only good of the man you married, thinking yourself the saddest, most bereft woman ever born. I could not have that, could not bear it. I have loved and lost – ah, how I lost. My dancing mermaid with the sea-green eyes and the silver-foam hair . . . How I grieved for her until I was twisted ice inside, a hard, tight knot of pain. I would not wish to see you suffer that way, become like that.'

She stared up at him, wanting to deny the compassion in his voice, the tenderness in his eyes. The light in the room had changed dramatically in the last few minutes. Gone was the peach and rose of sunset and now there was the last silvered cry of the sun before it died. The silver glimmered behind the Pagan like an aureole and she could hardly see the dark, carved shape of his features. But she could feel the sympathy emanating from him. Behind that craggy, iron-like façade was a heart overflowing with kindness.

Taken by surprise, she hung her head. It had been so much easier when she had thought him callous and unfeeling. What was she to do now, with this new knowledge?

'Princess Musbah, do not become twisted with grief for a man who never existed.'

'Oh, but he did! He did!' she cried and then the tears came, pearl after pearl, white-hot, agonizing, tearing at her lungs and throat so that she could not hold herself up straight. Gently he caught her in his arms, lifting her up, placing her on the bed so delicately that she hardly knew when she was safely there. Sobbing, her arms round his neck, she clung to him, her tears a flood at the base of his throat as she emptied herself of the pain that had been like a hard iron fist inside her.

The light changed again as she sobbed, becoming a soft misty pewter, then a sudden blackness, the velvet black of the Aegean night, and the lyra player crept away on silent feet, the scent of the flowers died and the cicadas throbbed out their passionate, eternal song.

When she woke, close to dawn, the light had changed again to lemon and tangerine pleated with gold, and his arms were waiting for her when she turned into them. Now his kisses were sharp white flames flickering at her mouth and neck and breasts and she was his willing captive. Her tears had dried, her heart was free, and this beautiful Greek rebel had worked the miracle. Returning his kisses with an ardour to equal his own, she felt such an exquisite lightness of spirit that she wanted to laugh out loud. Her Pagan was all she had ever dreamed of in a man, passionate, tender, loving, comforting. It was he who had healed her inner wounds and made her strong enough to face life again. Now she was ready for his love, ready and oh, so willing, wanting him, knowing that he would heal and revive her, as she would him. Kiss after kiss, until her senses reeled, and then his fingers were curving against her breasts and thighs as if he were admiring the finest marble, as if he were in awe of her beauty and fragility. She tingled and sang inside as he touched her, silent laughter bubbling, a spring of joy, and she clasped him to her like a long-lost lover, brother and father all rolled into one and the tears of joy when they came were soft, tender pearls which cleansed, and were pain free.

The dream they were sharing was a magical scene from the greatest love story ever told. She was Sleeping Beauty being woken by her prince after a century of sleeping, or Beauty who kissed her Beast and found him to be the most handsome, kind and gentle lord in the world. She had dreamed about love and now here it was spilling into her like an ocean, her own Aegean of love, wave after wave, and he was the source, the sun, the light, the heat. There were no words for what she was feeling. The greatest pedants in the universe could not provide a fitting description. It was ambrosia and nectar, manna, the first radiance felt on seeing that love is eternal, an eternal joy which spans the centuries.

Their lovemaking was melodious and sweet, entrancing music, mesmeric as a pied piper's, and wherever that music commanded, they would go together, hand in hand, inseparable, as *kismet* ordained. Their kisses were fragrant fruits ripening as they caressed, glossy and filled with nectar, and their eyes were founts of adoration and wonder, their hands vessels with which to revere and fondle. They were gods coming together in an ancient, mystical rite from which would be born love and yet more love, on and on into eternity.

Completely oblivious to her surroundings now, Flavia clung to the man whose arms were breathing new life into her – the first real, true life that she had ever known, totally apart from the old, rigid existence with its hidebound strictures, its rôle-playing. In the Pagan's arms, she became a fully-fledged woman, bright as a goddess, and, like

Athena springing from the head of her father, fully armed. She provided no defence when he slipped onto her body, for it felt as if that place were made for him. There was no clumsiness, no moment of embarrassment but a blissful knowledge that this was her destiny, to be here in this man's arms. Sweet seconds danced by, then he was thrusting against her maidenhead, pushing, driving. She felt curiously numb yet at the same time a white-hot heat was stealing throughout her body, then he was through the entrance, just a little, about an inch or so, and instantly she was desperate for more, for all that she could have, for him to be deep, deep within her, as far as he could go. They had to be one, they must be one! Crying out, she curved herself up to meet him as forcefully as possible, feeling herself being torn open, rent apart, split, wider, wider . . . Then they were joined, fitting together perfectly, created for this moment, a rhapsody for two.

She heard again the strange music, the eerie, lilting notes from an ancient lyra, this time being plucked by long-dead fingers. Then came the heady scent of lilies, the most exotic and unearthly lilies ever grown, and yet so familiar to Flavia that she greeted them both with a rapturous delight, a feeling of coming home at last after lifetimes spent in exile. Laughter broke from her lips, then her lover's mouth was caging hers again and he was scything deeper and more fiercely inside her, so that she was turning into flame, bright, sharp, searing flame which would never be extinguished. There was nothing above them but the cerulean dawn sky, the last pallid vestiges of ivory moon and incandescent stars, yet they were bathed in ghostly silver white light, as if a thousand full moons shone down on them. Flavia was dazzled, mystified. It was as if she had entered into the most secret temple on earth to be initiated into the greatest mysteries of all, and now she was reborn, stronger, wiser, free of the shackles of her old life.

'Are you human?' she whispered to her Pagan, who grinned, his jewel eyes spangled with lights. 'Are you really human, or a god from Olympus? Are you Zeus in one of your many disguises?'

'Do I look like a shower of gold, or a swan, or a bull? I am afraid that you will have to take me as I am: a mortal man, all too frail and human.'

Flavia did not reply. Yes, she did want to take him – as many times and for as long as he wanted to give himself to her. As for his being frail, well, from what she had seen of him he had incredible, inhuman strength. How hard he was now; hard and beautifully big. Yes, she would take him, for he had cast a spell on her which she had no intention of fighting any longer. The only thing that worried her was what he would do, her beautiful, emerald-eyed god, when he found out that she was no goddess, that she was not one of the favoured immortals like himself. Would he reject her then? Cast her off as easily as he had cast the spell on her? What weapons would she have then to get him back? She shivered, as if envisaging that moment of alienation from him, and it was as if he knew what she was thinking.

'Sweet Princess,' he whispered, 'forget your sorrows, put all that aside and enjoy this moment. Stolen hours are all the richer for their swiftness.'

'I do not want them to be swift,' she whispered back. 'Why should this pass? Why can it not last?'

'All good things pass; it is enough that we have known them and can remember.'

'What comfort are memories? They have not soothed me!'

'Perhaps your memories were colourless? From now on, they will be brighter, I promise you that.'

'Is that all I shall have then? Memories?'

'Tomorrow I leave here – we go into battle against the Sultan's army. They are on the march again, burning and looting. They have only recently arrived from Constantinople, and they are crack troops, fresh, superbly disciplined. How could I do anything else but promise you memories of this night? What else is in my power to give you? Within a few hours, I might be dead.'

She could not reply. What could she say in answer to that? Her throat felt as if it were choked with ashes; her heart had stopped; her blood was draining from her limbs. If he died, then she would die too. She knew that she would be able to tell the exact moment of his death wherever he was, for her heart would register it as if it were her own dying.

He kissed the tears from her eyes and cheeks, licked them from her neck and breasts, but still they gushed. Finding her voice, she begged him to make love to her again, and again, for if she was going to have memories alone to support her, then they must be unforgettable ones.

She wanted his love inside her, thrusting into her, oceans of it nourishing and feeding her. She wanted his kisses imprinted on her lips for eternity, and the memory of his face engraved in her mind, his glossy black hair and the iridescent emerald eyes, the strong, charismatic features, the flashing, adorable grin which made her heart leap. She told him her thoughts and he laughed, but gently, and she knew that even while she held him in her arms and was filled with his passion, he was insubstantial as moondust in her embrace.

She did not have to plead with him to make love to her a third time, for he was ready, urgent to plunge into her, to mark her as his very own, and when he poured his love gift deep inside her, she wept again, curving against him as he crushed her in his arms, their cheeks pressed close, her legs coiled round his thighs to anchor him to her.

Later, he said, 'Whatever happens, you must not mourn for me. Remember the stories you have heard of me, and hate me, hate me as you never hated me before. Remember me as I am: arrogant, cold, heartless, destroyed by a love affair which left my emotions paralysed two years before you met me. Think of what I would be like had we been able to stay together. I would have caused you nothing but pain and anguish.'

Flavia stared at him, bemused, stricken. What was he saying? How could he mean such words after their loving hours together? Protests gathered on her tongue, but she could not straighten them into any sense for some moments. When she did, she felt old, weary, as if she had suffered decades of grief.

'We – If you would tell me that you – you love me before you go. Give me something to remember, *please*.'

'I told you, little princess – remember me as I really am, cold and unfeeling, arrogant, and all those other words you have called me for they are all true. I am not fit to be your lover, what joy could I possibly bring you? In a few hours I go into battle. I loved my sea-green mermaid, loved her with all my heart, and what good did I do her? I can never love again like that.'

'I need you to tell me that you love me!' she pleaded, her breath a sob. How could she bear another loss?

'You have mourned one dead love. I do not want to burden you with another. You are young, and you will find another man to share your life. All is arranged so that if anything happens to me you will be taken to a ship on the coast and returned to your homeland.'

The starkness of his words, his presumption that he would die, hit her like a physical blow. 'I shall not go! I am staying her! You will not die – I shall not let you!'

'Will you pray to your Miraculous Virgin for me?' There was a gaunt twinkle in his eyes. 'Only she can save me now – unless God has ordained that it is time for me to die. Return to your dreams now, little one, and forget me.'

Kissing her goodbye, he was silent, while she could not speak for her misery. Burying her face in the pillow, she sobbed heartbrokenly. When she glanced up through her tears, he was gone. She knew then that she would never see him again. That she had found him too late.

PART TWO

General of the Death's Head

'Man is like the Basilisk. He dies if he sees his inner self.'

Hebbel

"Oh, thy voice is bewitching, beloved,
This wound of my heart it makes whole;
Ah, when thou art coming, and thee I
    behold,
Thou art bread and sweet wine to my
    soul.'

Verse of Egyptian love song, 3000 years old

CHAPTER FIFTEEN

Muhammad Baswar was the Sultan's most dreaded General. Six feet, two inches in height, he had thick ebony hair with one ivory streak above his ear, and it was said that he had never shown fear, never been defeated, nor ever been so much as scratched in battle. Allah was his lord and master and rode beside him to war, or so it was believed.

Baswar was freshly arrived in Greece. It was his mission to slaughter the Pagan, to hack off his head, his limbs and his sexual organs and display them publicly for all to see what happened to the enemies of Mahmud II. He was commanded to be speedy, however, for, as Mahmud's most loyal general he was much in demand in Constantinople. The Janissaries were turbulent these days, and Mahmud expected another revolt any day. However, much as he wanted the Janissaries put down, he also wanted the Pagan dead, Greece back under the sole command of his Pashas, and the Princess Musbah safely married to Prince Hassani, so that Zebukar's fortune could be released. Hassani would have some of it, of course, but certain items were preordained for Mahmud. For example, the world's largest diamond, Allah's Teardrop. This was to be obtained by Hassani and given to Baswar who would take it to Mahmud, who would then place it round the neck of his beloved concubine, Besma, who was pregnant with his child.

Baswar was confident that he would be as successful as ever in this, his double mission. His master's humiliation had been his humiliation. He would find this Pagan and hack him into miniscule pieces the size and shape of *Rahat Lokum*. A few years before, during an uprising in the Morea, when Greek peasants had rebelled against their Turkish overlords, the slaughter had been horrifying, the carnage in towns such as Tripolitza and Navarino beyond belief. Years of misery, persecution and suffering had fired the Greeks to revolt, but what was accepted as everyday behaviour in the vituperative Turks, could not be condoned in their subjects. Despite his ignorance of the entire affair, the Greek Patriarch in Constantinople had been hanged on Easter Day along with other Greeks, including four Bishops and thousands of the Greek populace. Retribution was still continuing, for the Sultan could not forget or forgive. Mahmud had vowed that he would not rest until Greece was entirely his again.

Later events had proved that Zardos Alexandros, the man known as the Pagan, had masterminded the revolt. Soon, it had become obvious that he and he alone could do what no other Greek Kleftsman had managed. He had united the various Greek factions, which were splendidly unruly, stubborn-headed and independent, and formed them into a formidable and amazingly successful guerilla force. Between his own turbulent and avaricious Janissaries, and the steady onslaught of the Pagan and his Kleftsmen, Mahmud slept little, and, when the Sultan could not sleep, neither could Baswar. The general considered his master divine and wished to emulate him in as many things as possible, as if he were Allah. If his master could not rest then nor could he; if his master's favourite concubine was pregnant, then so must Baswar's be; if his master had a son, then he must have one, too. In secret, his men mocked him, calling him Lord-Mighty-Baswar, Sultan of Noland, but even if he had known of this, he would have continued to despise them as much as ever.

In Constantinople, unknown to his enemies, Mahmud II had assembled a massive army of some fourteen thousand men, who were at this very moment being drilled and trained by Baswar's second-in-command, Abdul Akim. As soon as Baswar returned to Turkey he would take command of the army, ensure that it was skilled, competent and programmed to murder the Sultan's foes, and then he would annihilate the Janissaries.

Before that, he would hand over Allah's Teardrop to Mahmud, and watch, beaming, as the Sultan placed it round the neck of the voluptuous and fertile Besma.

Mahmud was half-French, his mother being a relative of the Empress Josephine, wife of Napoleon. Aimée had been abducted by pirates and had become the favourite Kadine of Hamid I, an elderly and morose man whose life she had proceeded to brighten beyond the dreams of angels. Everyone knew how romantic the French were, besotted with love. Mahmud was no different. He worshipped Besma, honouring no other woman, when he could have had a thousand concubines at his bidding. Being a man of cunning and foresight, besides being genuinely devoted to Mahmud, Baswar knew that to ascend one must support the inclinations of the most powerful. He who gave the largest diamond in the world into the hands of the Sultan so that he might place it round the neck of his beloved, would be a man with ever-increasing dominions.

A life of achievement upon achievement stretched enticingly before Baswar, he whom men were already calling the Lord-Mighty. Soon, he would be rich, and immensely powerful. If he were infamous, too, that would be nothing more than he had anticipated. Any Turk worth his salt could behead a man with one sweep of his scimitar, or creep up on his enemies and strangle them silently with a cord.

One thing he missed here, on this treacherous and barren, shrubby plain was his favourite drink, *khoshab*, Agreeable Water, which was made from peaches grown in Turkey, mixed with various other fruits, and delicately flavoured with rosewater, amber and musk. This fragrant, thick liquid was eaten with a sandalwood spoon, and Baswar devoured it compulsively. He had even been known to interrupt the act of love with one of his concubines so that he could fill his belly with *khoshab*. The girl, an Armenian belly dancer had solved this problem by smearing herself in the fragrant nectar and letting Baswar lick it off her breasts and thighs. He had become so roused that he had injured her internally with the violence of his love-making and she had lost the child she was carrying. It would have been the son that Beswar wanted more than anything else. Enraged, he had taken a leaf out of the books of the Sultans of old and ordered his dancer to be tied in a sack and thrown into the Bosphorus.

He had his new favourite with him now, waiting for him in his tent. She was heavily-veiled, forbidden to speak to anyone but him and her serving woman, and her name was Medisha. She was fifteen, plump and heavily-breasted with pale-blue eyes and silvery-peach hair the exact shade of *khoshab*. Unfortunately, she was a little unbalanced. She had strange dreams from which she woke screaming, saying that she saw what she called 'rivers of blood', but Baswar wisely ignored this female nonsense. A woman's mind could be completely deranged and not prevent her from bearing healthy sons.

The plain of Argos stretched out before him like the crater-filled landscape of some strange extraterrestrial land. He cherished the scents and dust and chaos of his home city, finding Greece pallid and sterile by comparison. The people here crept round like ghosts, shoulders hunched, eyes averted. That he liked, for it showed that they knew the Turks were their overlords, but it also robbed his life of some of its colour and richness. He grinned spectrally. Where now were the famous ancient Greeks who had conquered the world? Where now was the omnipotent Alexander the Great whose legions had marched for thousands of miles without hindrance?

Baswar the Lord-Mighty returned his sharp and steady gaze to his men who were camped around him, eating the oily pilaf that they loved, cramming stuffed cucumbers into their mouths, or the dry, crumbling mixture of mutton and spices, which, safe in its bladder, could be carried for miles and heated up on the portable stoves they carried with them. The Turkish armies were renowned for their ruthlessness, their savagery and their penchant for rape and slaughter. Mingling with the ordinary men-at-arms were numbers of Janissaries in their striking costumes. Astonishingly, these crack troops had originally been Christians, captured as small boys and raised in Constantinople. It was not necessary for them to exhibit intelligence, as physical prowess was the prerequisite for entry into this élite corps. They wore dark-blue uniforms and eye-catching white hats made out of felt, from which sprang the glowing and multi-hued plumes of the bird of Paradise. In previous centuries, they had taken oaths of celibacy, keeping to their rigid code of rules, but now they were more like tigers who had gauged their own strength for the first time. Proud, cunning, ruthlessly ambitious and, at times, intransigent, they demanded more and yet more privileges. In the summer of 1807, they had openly revolted against Sultan Selim, behaving in the traditional manner when they had a grievance, overturning the large kettles in which they heated their food, and refusing to eat the pilaf sent to them by the Sultan. That revolt had been solved by Selim voluntarily abdicating, having acknowledged his half-brother Mustafa as the new Sultan. Selim's allies had then risen against the Janissaries, and forced their way into the palace demanding to see Selim. Mustafa, realizing that he could never be safe while Selim lived, had immediately ordered his half-brother, and his heir, Mahmud, to be strangled. In a frantic and fearless action, Selim had saved Mahmud who had fled with his mother, Sultana Aimée, while Selim had paid with his own life.

Mustafa's death was demanded, but instead Mahmud had consigned him to the Cage, the prison where royal heirs and rebels were confined for safety's sake. Years of turbulence had followed, with Mahmud never being allowed to forget that the Janissaries were no longer the ardently-loyal troops of old. Civil war and mutiny, all bred by the Janissaries, had forced Mahmud to order Mustafa's death so that he might rule supreme as the last surviving male of the Ottoman line. In response, the Janissaries had snatched all power from Mahmud, forcing him to concede to their wishes, and for the next few years they had dominated the Sultan. Now, when Mahmud had regained some of his power, was the time to wipe out the Janissaries, but it could not be done while they were needed to conquer Greece.

'Master.' Medisha's silky voice, and the touch of her small, soft hand brought Baswar's thoughts back to the present. 'Master, come with me.' All he could see were her eyes, harebell-blue and slanting like almonds, as she gestured to his jade silk tent. Taking her hand, he led her back inside its steamy, scented warmth, kicking out his slave boy, Guttab, who sometimes took the place of Medisha when she was indisposed.

Tearing off his cloak and *shalwar* and the robe which he wore over them, Baswar displayed a magnificent erection. Grinning, Medisha tugged down her *yashmak* and pressed her face into his groin in silent worship. His hands were fierce and brutal as they ripped at her silken robes, pulling out her heavy snowdrop-coloured breasts with their tearose nipples. Clamping his mouth on them, he bit first one and then the other while Medisha groaned in frenzied delight. Arching her back, she begged him to enter her, for she could feel his iron hardness thrusting into her soft thighs.

'Not yet, tigress,' he laughed, cupping her ivory buttocks and pulling her upwards so that her knees were on either side of his face and he could sink his mouth into her dewy warmth. She writhed as his tongue slid along her flesh, dipping into her, then out again, while his own passion trebled within those few brief seconds and her silky palm, curving tightly round his manhood, made him jerk and almost spill his offering onto the bed.

'My love, my god,' Medisha whispered, her voice hoarse as she pulled him back towards her so that he could fill her mouth, moving in and out frantically, her teeth never so much as grazing him, for in this she was an expert. When his orgasm bolted through him, searing along his manhood like an electric charge, she revelled in it, taking all that he had to give and loving it.

202

With no sign of needing to rest, Baswar moved down and plunged between her soft, snowdrop-silk thighs, scything in and out some half dozen times before he was hard as steel once more. Medisha sighed, fingering her breasts and nipples, thrusting against him, harder and harder until she had her own multiple orgasm, and threshed about, crying out his name repeatedly.

Neither of them saw Guttab who had insinuated himself in one of the tent folds. He knew what he would like to be doing at this moment, but his master had not asked for that today, so all he could do was clamp his lips closed to stifle his groans as he brought himself to a frenzied crisis while spying on the love-making inside the tent. Then, knees weak, he sagged a little, his senses whirling, before creeping away until he was summoned again. It was his dream to make love to his master while his master was making love to his woman, but Baswar had told him that he was not yet big enough for such activities.

Showing Guttab his own massive erection, he had said, 'When you are big as this, you can do what you wish with me.' Then he had grinned, knowing that few if any ever achieved that size. Knowing this too, Guttab had experienced a particularly acute sense of frustration. As he loved his master, he directed his animosity at Medisha, believing that if she were not there, he would gain all that he wished. It was the selfish, egotistical belief of a child.

The sun, round and bright as a polished apricot, drifted slowly down to rest, allowing dusk to fall like pewter ashes. Soon it was black, densely, richly black, with only the urgent cry of the cicadas betokening life outside the perimeters of the camp. Men snored after their rich and oily meal of pilaf and haggis, while the look-outs prowled, their eyes straining to pierce the ebony night. In their tent, Baswar and Medisha dozed, woke, locked together in another embrace, then dozed again. Baswar could trust his own men, who would keep their eyes on the Janissaries as well as on the darkness.

Dawn danced down from the skies, a lilting young girl

wrapped in a silver-gilt shawl, her hair golden, and still there was no sign of the approach of the Pagan and his army. Showing no sign of weariness after his night of passion, Baswar strode from his tent to view the day. The weather was fresh, warm and sweet, like liquidized honey against the skin. His men were waking, faces split by ape-like yawns. The cooks were stoking up the camp fires and placing kettles of food to heat. Boys had fetched the great cactus leaves from a distant hillside and were tearing open the leathery outer skin to release the nectar within. Horses neighed and stamped, swished vibrant tails. Men who had eaten began to polish their scimitars and daggers with studied expressions. None knew what the day might bring, for so far all they had heard of was the Pagan's challenge. Zardos Alexandros had warned that if Baswar brought his army into the heart of Greece, he would not rest until the enemy was dead.

On hearing this, Baswar had vowed the same. He would not rest until the rebel insurgent, Zardos Alexandros, was dead, cut into pieces the size and shape of *Rahat Lokum*, or, better still, kebabs. He would skewer Alexandros on a spit. Skewer him and hang him over a great, blazing fire, watch his flesh melt and the fat drip down in spluttering streams, see his skin turn brown and crisp, listen to his screams of agony. Thinking of it, Baswar laughed out loud, uproariously, slapping his steel-muscled thigh. His laugh woke Medisha, who called to him to return to her bed where she had a new delight awaiting him.

The Pagan was on fire with restlessness. Greece, his beloved country, was like a jewel which too many men desired to possess. He knew that if a man truly loved a country he would never wish to damage it or lay it waste. Like the mother of the baby which had been brought to King Solomon, he would sacrifice his own needs, his own love, to keep the object of his love intact. Greece was the infant, and the Turks would divide it and strip it bare to retain their hold on it, while he would die before he let them do that, as would his army of loyal and fearless *Kleftes*. Drilled, trained and ready for battle, they waited for him to give them the sign.

He knew what they would face that day. He had heard of all the exploits of the man called Baswar, Allah's General, who wore terrifying black and white armour, painted like a skeleton, with a death's head glaring on his visor. Baswar's god was a vicious, bloodthirsty deity, for his faithful were frequently men of violence and mayhem. Nonetheless, despite their comparative poverty and lack of weapons, he and his men, helped by their loyal companions had ensured that the Turks were not allowed to relax. Ever since the massive revolt which had begun in the Morea in 1821, the Turks had been fighting to keep their foothold in his homeland. Zardos Alexandros was well aware that Prince Zebukar had married the Duke of Acteon's daughter in order to ally himself with the British government in the hope of winning the military and naval assistance which would be needed to conquer the Greek 'rebels'. With this aim in mind, a thousand foul lies had been spread about the Pagan and his men, his name blackened, his reputation destroyed. The truth had been hidden from the British embassy sent to the Morea. They were allowed to see only a carefully-staged display of amicable opulence.

Men and women had been bribed to tell horror stories about the Pagan and the atrocities he had supposedly committed. Afterwards, the tale-tellers had been taken privately to Zebukar, who had beheaded them himself. Zebukar had been assassinated by a group of *Kleftes* whose sisters, wives or mothers had all been raped and murdered by Turkish devils. Everyone of those men who had volunteered to do the deed had known it could mean their own deaths, yet they had been more than willing to avenge their womenfolk. Zardos clenched his jaw as he thought of his own sisters, dimpled, laughing girls, the children of his mother's second marriage. After his father had died in Venice, she had grown homesick for Greece and returned there. Three years later, she had married the man with whom she had enjoyed a childhood friendship, and Zardos had become a brother for the first time. Now they were all dead, his mother, his stepfather, his sisters, because his stepfather had dared to defend their home against Mahmdi Ahdi, one of Zebukar's captains.

Zardos had begged his family to leave Greece. He had arranged everything for them, the journey, the home where they would live safely in northern Italy, well away from the Islamic hordes, and then his youngest sister had contracted a fever which had left her very weak and unable to travel. Valuable time was lost, and although Zardos had concealed his true parentage at all times, fearing retribution against his family, Mahmdi Ahdi had descended on their mountain village during a routine reconnoitring of the area. It was automatic for the Turks to burn, pillage, loot, murder and rape and they had behaved true to form that day.

Zardos clenched his fists so that his knuckles gleamed like polished china. In a way, he could not blame the Princess Musbah for refusing to believe the stories of Zebukar's atrocities. Who, not having experienced them at first hand, could believe such monstrous tales?

His dazzling eyes scanned the horizon. Was that a cloud of dust coming into view, raised by thousands of pounding hoofs? No, it was his imagination overworking. All the same, it could not be much longer before Baswar and his men arrived.

Zardos had survived a pantheon of tribulations and vicissitudes. Skirmishes, routs, three assassination attempts by the Sultan's hired killers. An epidemic of typhus, and one of cholera had swept by him as if he were truly invincible, just as legend said he was. Yet, for some time, he had been filled with foreboding. It was useless now to tell himself that he was protected by the Miraculous Virgin, as he had long believed. Since he had so foolishly allowed his men to attack the gatehouse of the Virgin's convent and he himself had abducted one of her novices, he believed that she had forsaken him. What else could have caused the strange gloominess in his heart? Serving her, assured of his holy mission to free his homeland from the rule of Islam, he had been indefatigable for over a decade, ever since completing his education in England. Now, since his entanglement with the proud and fiery Princess Musbah, he felt uneasy, not so sure of himself. Was she Hassani's spy? For all he knew, her presence in the convent had been a trap, the story of the Turkish pillagers hiding in that convent a lie to bring him to its doors. When he looked back, he saw how soon she had brought herself to his attention. Then that melodramatic faint, after she had revealed her identity. Hassani had revolting sexual habits, but he was no fool. Even he could see what a marvellous weapon an English girl could be against Zardos.

All the same, she had appeared so genuine in her outrage, her distress. He had gone over and over it repeatedly, part of him wanting to trust her, part of him insisting that she must be a spy, that she would betray him given half the chance. Why had he allowed her to attract him? Male weakness! She was simply the most beautiful and intelligent woman he had ever known, an irresistible combination.

But if she had genuinely found herself to have a vocation to the Virgin, then he had abducted a girl who had dedicated herself to God, and, if that were true, it would account for his uneasiness now. Yet if he had not taken her, Hassani would have done, and after that she would have found out the truth about the Turk, in all its vile reality. If she were Muslim in truth, and Hassani's spy, however loyal to him she had been, a few weeks spent in his bed would have cured her of her gullibility. The Pasha wanted her for her late husband's fortune, nothing else. He would use her cruelly, as he had used so many others, male and female, and then she would be discarded, hidden away in his harem, an eternal prisoner.

But should Zardos die in battle this day, it would not be

the end for the Princess Musbah, Christian or Muslim, even if it proved to be the end for his beloved Greece. Her escape to England was planned down to the last detail, whether she wanted to go or not, and his men knew exactly what to do should he fail to return from the battlefield.

Glancing round him one last time, he sent up a silent prayer for his men.

'Blessed Virgin, whatever I have done to offend you, and for that I am truly penitent, please protect these good men in the battle to come and help them rid Greece of the Turkish yoke so that your faithful can live as free men once more . . .'

His men, all so dear to him, who could be quarrelsome and foolish as children without the right leader to unite them. He was the one who had succeeded where all others had failed. *Kleftes* from every mountain region, villagers, townsmen, citizens, men from the islands, from the mainland, all were faithful to him, putting aside personal squabbles and vendettas. These disputes had been the cause of the Turks holding sway for so long, for a people divided are a people dominated by any overlord who wishes to exert his power.

Believing that he would not survive this day, and fully aware that Greece could not survive without him, Zardos Alexandros stepped back into his tent to prepare for battle.

CHAPTER SIXTEEN

A mist had risen like angels' veiling, swirling up high and twisting round the fortress palace. Beyond it, the cicadas carolled as jubilantly and persistently as ever, but inside the fortress the air was damp and filled with gloom. Faces were taut and sad, people were jumpy and nervous. Out there, somewhere, their beloved master was battling with the Sultan's cohorts so that they could be liberated. The burden on the ones left behind, the ones who were too young, too old, or too infirm for battle, was immense. Never believe that the ones left behind do not go into battle too, for they do. Things had not been helped by old Zea, the fortune teller, who had looked into her scrying glass – an old cracked handmirror from which she would not be parted – and cried out that she had seen their master dead, pierced by a dozen spears.

Flavia was eating in the vast and chilly kitchens with the rest of the fortress's inhabitants when Zea gave her cry and told what she had seen. Flavia's hands turned to lumps of ice so that her cup fell from her grasp, while a pain like the lash of a whip sliced through her heart. Zardos, dead! Oh, if he were dead, then so was she! Weeping tears of ice, while her body shuddered uncontrollably, Flavia thought of all the curses she had directed at him, how she had longed for his destruction, his death. She put her face in her arms, and cried out silently, 'I did not mean it, I did not mean it! Oh, beloved Mother, let him be alive!'

Days passed and no word was brought back to them. The youths who bore messages on swift, tireless feet did not do so this time. It all confirmed Zea's terrible prediction. Misery enfolded the fortress and as spirits crumbled, Zardos' people took out their fears and anger on Flavia, widow of a Turk, and bride-to-be of another. Ezta had been comforted by Flavia the first day that they had met, and it was she who spoke up for the stranger in their midst, who was now hated as the enemy.

'*Spy!*'

'*Traitor!*'

Flavia would hear the insults hissed at her as she walked by, yet when she turned, she could never tell who had spoken.

'She not spy!' Ezta cried after one of these outbursts. 'She good, kind, can you not see? She not know truth when she came to Greece to marry Turk. She not know!' She spoke first in English so that Flavia would be sure to know that she was defending her, and then in Greek.

But Ezta's defence had little effect, or did not seem to at the time. With no word of their beloved Zardos, the palace inmates had to take out their resentment on someone and on whom better than Flavia?

She wanted to cry out that she was their friend, that she had come to Greece to help care for them, but she knew what their reply would have been, for she knew what they thought of Zebukar. These were men, women and children who had endured purgatory before Zardos had rescued them from their private horrors. Her tears were shed in the loneliness of the mermaid chamber, but never in public. Before them, she was proud, and that was her mistake. That well-controlled expression spoke to them of contempt and coldness. So warm and laughing when times were good, they saw her as heartless.

It was not surprising that she dreamed wild and disjointed dreams. Sometimes they were filled with the clash and dust of battle, the shivering smash of steel, with the silvery suns of shields carried high for protection, with the whinny of plunging warhorses, and the screams of the dying. Then she would wake, flinging herself into consciousness, sitting up suddenly, her heart thudding, while pictures of the battle floated across her vision. Strange, antiquated weapons and armour, chariots pulled by horses, gleaming bronze helmets like those worn by the ancient Greeks in her father's books. Why did she dream of ancient battles and not the present-day one? Sometimes, she would catch a dream-glimpse of a woman steering her chariot single-handed through the chaos. She was tall and slender, but strong, and her ivory robes flared around her like albionic wings, as did the flares of her crimson-russet hair. On her head, carved from some ancient, precious metal there was a coronal which rose at the centre of her forehead into two cupped hands clasping an orb which was studded with jewels.

Flavia woke with the woman's name on her lips, but when she tried to recall it, she found that it had vanished. Accustomed as she was to the atmosphere of this beautiful but *triste* chamber, where the mermaid dancer had thrown herself to her death on the rocks below, Flavia did not become alarmed by the vividness of her dreams. Frightening, realistic and haunting they might be, but, in some inexplicable way, they also seemed to give her courage. Day by day, she grew in stature, strength and determination. She would care for the Pagan's people. She would see that they survived even if he had not. She would be their leader and their mother now. Somehow, she would defend them and care for them whatever happened – and however much they hated her at the present time, she would change their minds, convince them that they could trust her.

Dawn was striping the sky in flamingo pink, peach and silver when the lone messenger arrived. He was on foot, half-starved, his face blotched by sweat and dust, his feet bloody and blistered. White, and gripping her trembling hands tightly together, Flavia heard what the messenger had to say. Bathed, fed, feet smeared with healing unguents, he was so overcome that he wept when he told his tale. Soon, Flavia was weeping with him, a fact which did not go unnoticed by the others. Heartbrokenly, she sobbed, and in that moment, she was one of them and they knew it.

'The fight – the fight went well for us at first,' the boy

stammered, colour sweeping over his face and vanishing so that he looked as pale and shiny as porcelain. 'Then, when it looked as if we would win, word passed round that our leader was dead. It was not true, but the damage had been done. The men lost heart, some panicked, fled, then realized how they had been tricked and were massacred as they tried to reform their ranks. Baswar had reinforcements waiting behind a hill to fall on all those who tried to flee.'

The boy paused to sob, unable to speak for some moments. To still her juddering heart, Flavia found herself counting the tears as they rolled down his cheeks, until they were coming so fast that they became an uncheckable flood.

'My companions, all of them – my brothers-in-arms – all dead. *Dead!*' He lapsed into a gabble of Greek which Flavia could not decipher.

'And – Zardos?' she managed to whisper through a wooden throat. 'Is he – is he dead, too?' When she spoke, every face turned in her direction.

The boy shook his head. 'Not dead, but he should be! Oh better that he were!'

'What happened to him? Oh tell me, *tell me!*' she cried.

'Baswar took him prisoner. It was what he wanted, what he came to our land to do. They – they captured him as he was fighting single-handed to keep them away from Kios, who was badly wounded. Dozens of them, their faces black like devils, fell on him and wrapped him in chains. Then they stood him to watch while they hacked Kios's arms and legs off and smeared his blood on our master's face . . . They laughed all the time, wildly, like ones who are moonfevered.'

'So they have him a prisoner?' Flavia fought back nausea and the pain which was jabbing at her temples with piercing fingers.

'It would be better he had died. He will be made into an example. They will commit atrocities on him publicly to show our people what will happen to them if they continue to resist. For ten years the Sultan, Zebukar, now Baswar and Hassani, have yearned to get their hands on him. Now they have. Oh it would be better if he had died in battle!'

Later, alone, Flavia tried to collect herself, but it was impossible. She shivered with cold then was suffused with warmth. She felt sick, then empty in turns. She wanted to weep again but was curiously hollow and arid inside, wracked by pains which made her feel old and feeble. If she had held on to any of her romantic notions about the Turks, they had all been finally dispelled by the messenger's words. Brutal, merciless, homicidal, those were the adjectives which now sprang into her mind when she thought of Zebukar's countrymen, although she continued to believe that Zebukar himself had been different, a good, just man like his father, who had been judged on the sins of his fellow Turks. That was the past now, however, and she must put it aside. There were people here who would need a leader in the coming days and she must be that to them, whatever her own heartbreak. Her brief, sweet and beautiful hours with the Pagan before his departure hung around her like a protective cloak of bright velvet which she could pull closely around herself for comfort. Oh, if only they could have had more time together.

Ezta was at the door, her face pinched and wan. She fell into Flavia's arms and sobbed, saying Kios's name over and over again, and as Flavia held her, stroking her head, she wanted with all her heart to cry out, 'Zardos, Zardos!' as Ezta was crying out, 'Kios!'

Where her strength came from, Flavia never knew, but whenever she came face to face with the people Zardos had left behind, even though they were distrustful of her still, she found herself revived, invigorated. They were like her children, even the old men and women, even Zea who was more than a little mad these days. When she heard that Zardos was taken prisoner, she plunged her scrying mirror into the fire, forgetting to let go of it, and badly burned her hand and arm in the process. The burns were not healing and Ezta had to cleanse and bind them daily.

Then there were the men ordered by Zardos to collect Flavia and despatch her on her journey to England and freedom.

'I am not a parcel!' she cried in their astonished faces. 'You will *not* take me anywhere! I am staying here. What would happen to all these poor people if I left them?'

'Our lord gave his orders, Highness. You are to be taken to Kifa and put on a ship for—'

'I shall not go! I am staying here.' Flavia glared at the men who stared at her, aghast.

That she should refuse had never occurred to them, nor indeed to their master. They had no instructions as to what they must do if the English lady would not go with them. Treat the Princess with the utmost gentleness and care, respect her as if she were your sister, their master had told them. He had not said, bundle her up like a prisoner, fling her over your horse, and carry her away against her will.

The men protested. They argued forcefully with Flavia that she must do as they said, but she just became more obdurate. Finally, they had to give in, for the ship which was to carry her to freedom was carrying some hundred or so other persecuted Greeks and their families, and the longer they waited in port the more dangerous it would be for them.

As the three men rode off, Flavia sighed out loud with relief. Coming up to her, Ezta slipped her hand into hers.

'You are one of us now, Highness. You are Greek freedom-fighter like Zardos, for you fight for your own freedom and you win.' Then Ezta's tinkling laughter rang out for the first time in weeks.

Later Flavia knelt in front of the replica of the Miraculous Virgin, her hands clasped tightly together.

'I do not ask much, beloved Mother. All I need is unlimited reserves of energy and strength, the wisdom of Solomon, and a man's ability to defend myself should it come to that . . .' She crossed herself, realizing for the first time what she had done in sending her rescuers away. After Zardos, she must be the most wanted person in Greece, yet she had stayed here of her own free will. And as she knelt there, mulling over this, she thought back to the years of her childhood when she had looked forward so enthusiastically to helping the people of this land. That had been one of the most attractive things about becoming a princess, to have a free hand to help and succour Zebukar's subjects. How could she have foreseen that she would get what she wanted but in such a very different fashion? No wonder she had found herself taking up the reins here so swiftly.

Ah, if only the replica would make her feel as the genuine Miraculous statue did, reborn, revived, invigorated. Kneeling before the original statue, she had been healed, her will to live had returned. Here, in this curious and alien fortress on its mount, where time had stopped centuries ago, how could she practise her religion as wholeheartedly as she had done in the convent? When the ancient Greeks had flourished, there had been no Christ and Madonna.

'Blessed Mother, you know what is in my heart. If my Pagan is suffering, then comfort him, send my love to him so that he knows I think of him all the hours of the day and night. Restore him with your love and with mine, Blessed Mother. And if you will, let these people here learn that I shall not betray their trust . . .'

Hearing a sound, she turned, Ezta was clinging to the door, tears like waves down her cheeks.

'Ezta, what is it!'

'Highness, I must tell you. Kios, he, I – we loved! I am carrying his child.'

Getting to her feet, Flavia rushed to take the girl in her arms.

'Oh Ezta, why did you not tell me before? You poor mite.'

'He is dead now, my Kios is dead. I have none now.

215

None in the world.' The Cretan girl slumped in Flavia's arms, unable to support herself.

'You have me, Ezta. I am here to take care of you, and you have all your friends here in the fortress. Everyone loves you. I love you, too.'

A mere few years divided the two girls, but at that moment Flavia felt old enough to be Ezta's mother. She was thankful that she had not left with the men, running away from her troubles, leaving Ezta and the others to cope alone, putting her love for Zardos behind her as if it had never been. That would have been the coward's way out and she was no coward. She would lead these people; she would guide them as best she could, as their master would have done were he still free. In time, surely, they must see that she was on their side now?

'Ezta, who will be your master's second-in-command now?' she asked.

'It – it would have been Kios, but, but, now that – he is – is dead, I do not know.'

'From what I have learned of your master he would not go into battle without preparing for every eventuality. I should have asked those men who came to take me to the ship. They might have known.'

'Not be them, Highness. They not soldiers of our master but men who owe him favour. They know nothing of his secret plannings.'

'Then who will? Surely there must be someone?'

Through muffled sobs, Ezta said again that she could not think. Then after a short time of silence, broken only by sniffs, she said, 'There is Constantin Tiarchos. He not go to battle, for he break leg in riding accident.'

'Where is he? Here in the fortress?'

'No, Highness. Now I recall. Our lord say Constantin not live with him, ever, for safety. If one taken, the other still free.'

'So where does this Constantin live?'

'In one of mountain villages, Highness, very far up, high near skies, with others who fight with our lord.'

'Then I must talk to this Constantin and find out what his plans are. Surely the *Kleftes* will not stand by and allow Hassani and his men to take control?'

'You are different now, Highness.' Ezta looked up at her with round, pink-rimmed eyes. 'When you come here, you say Turkish overlords like saints and our master like devil. Now you say opposite, now you speak truth.' Despite her tear-drenched gaze, Ezta's eyes shone.

A blush of heat rose in Flavia's cheeks. There was still much inner conflict within her. She knew that Hassani was a gross and loathsome monster, and that the Sultan's terrible general, Baswar, had decimated the *Kleftes* and taken her lover captive. But she had loved Zebukar for most of her life. Perhaps she always would love him to a certain extent – or at least the dream of him. There was nothing fickle or shallow about her; she had given her heart to her prince and he had always treated her with tenderness and indulgence. She was sure that the indignities she had suffered while in the Palace of the Silver Cicadas would not have been allowed to happen had he known of them. Yet even so, a tiny voice at the back of her mind would prompt her. What manner of prince did not know what his own servants were doing with his bride?

Now there was Zardos in a Turkish prison, the Greek rebel leader of whom Zebukar had spoken with such hatred and lust for vengeance. She had no rosy dreams about what the Turks would do to the man who had infuriated and eluded them for a decade. They were past masters at vengeance and retribution. Their treatment of their enemies was legendary and infamous. What would they do to the man who had infuriated them for so long?

'Truth, Ezta? I know that there are some things which I fear more than death itself, and that is the truth.'

'Highness is sad because she does not carry our lord's child,' Ezta said authoritatively. 'I weep because my Kios will never see his son. You weep because you do not carry the son of Zardos Alexandros.'

Flavia turned away, a twist of pain spiking her heart. A

son. *His* son. She had never even considered that she might be with child from their night of love, or had she? Chills slipped down her spine, one after the other, to branch out through her body. If she could have got word to him in his Turkish prison that she would bear his child, she knew that he would be strengthened. Greek men adored their children, especially sons.

She felt a hand on her arm. 'Highness is not alone. Highness be mother of God to my babe when he is born, please?'

Flavia's eyes twinkled briefly.

'I think you mean godmother, Ezta. I would not think of assuming the personage of the other one you mentioned.'

'You will say yes, Highness, even though I am having great cheek to ask you?'

'Of course I will say yes, Ezta. Now tell me more about this Constantin. We do not have any time to lose.'

What had possessed her to make this journey? Constantin's village could not have been more inaccessible had it been on Mount Olympus itself. She had been trekking through the foothills for two days now, and she was aching, bruised, and footsore. All the time, she was dreading that they would come upon one of the bands of Turkish soldiers who roamed the area, or even the dreaded Baswar himself. Cut off from information as she now was, she could only imagine what was happening to Zardos and the *Kleftes* who had survived the battle. Behind her in the fortress, she had left a household which had been given firm orders, and a plan of action which they were to follow to the letter should Hassani's or Baswar's troops attack them. She knew that some had believed she was escaping back to Hassani, but others, following Ezta's lead, had been filled with admiration for her idea.

She wished that her mission were not so desperate; that she was with Zardos enjoying a sojourn in the beautiful Greek countryside. The weather was divine; it seemed to be eternal summer in this land, and the skies were a translucent china-blue pearled with pirouetting white clouds, but the ground was uneven and rough, stony in places and bone-breaking if one did not take care. She was dressed as a goat boy, her legs entwined in light skins, her feet bandaged inside the chamois slip-on shoes which were little more than slippers. Her baggy, coarse linen shirt was devoid of ornament or embroidery and hung loosely over equally baggy, rough linen breeches. Her hair was pinned flat to her head and over it was pulled a floppy, stained and shabby leather hat which had belonged to one of the men working at the fortress. A red corded sash was twisted round the brim of the hat and tied in a bulky knot, the ends of which dangled over her face, screening it from view.

Princess-goatboy, she had thought to herself wryly as she looked in the mirror before leaving. Accompanying her were two equally shabby and rough-looking men, Giorg and Stephan, who knew the way to Constantin's village, for they had been raised there. They were carrying old-fashioned flintlock rifles over their shoulders, and pistols and daggers were tucked in their sashes. She, too, carried a pistol and a dagger, but as she had never used either, she felt no safer for possessing them.

They had been travelling for nearly three days now and the men, who were courteous and kind, had shown her how to take aim and fire at wild animals, which they then would skin and cook over a fire. She found out that standing face on to her prey when she fired meant that she could maintain a stronger balance and thus have a better chance of killing her dinner. At first, she had flinched at the thought of killing small furry beasts, but as the hours passed and she grew more ravenous (for she had at first refused to eat the meat cooked by the men) she felt so weak that eating became imperative. When she shot her first rabbit, her heart went into spasms and nausea filled her throat, but when Giorg held out the luscious, tender meat, steaming from the spit, she fell on it.

There were numerous bright crystal streams; Greece seemed to be a land of springs and natural waterfalls. The water was always fresh, sparkling and pure, so they were hardly ever thirsty for long. Sometimes, when her feet were burning and throbbing with pain, and her blisters a fiery agony, Flavia would plunge her feet into the cool waters, bandages and all. Then, peeling off the bloody wrappings underwater, she would wash them and put them to dry on a rock. The baking sun soon dried them out.

She and Stephan were lying asleep in the sun one day, with Giorg on the alert for anyone approaching, when they heard the sound of distant gunshots. Fear danced along Flavia's limbs as she woke with a jolt, every muscle and nerve tensing. The firing continued, bullet after bullet whining through the air, some ricocheting off rocks, some finding their target.

'Those men not after rabbit,' Stephan growled, his jaw clenching.

'What will it be?' Flavia asked.

'Kostas village in that direction. Small, but Turk not say no to destroy, whether small or big. Turk greedy, always wish for more.'

'Do you know any of the villagers from Kostas?'

'No, we not. Fortunate, else we bound to avenge our kin. Man of revenge must have one, lone mind, think of nothing else but dead kin.'

The firing stopped, and the ensuing silence was eerie. In her mind's eye Flavia imagined a pile of dead bodies, bloody and broken, heaped in the village square while the Turks looted and burned their village. Would they have kept the women separate so that they could rape them when their men were dead? She shuddered. Men who wished to prove that they were masters had to be masters over all. She felt heavy inside; weighted down with helplessness. She had come to Greece to do all she could to help its people and instead she had no power, no authority. Where would it all end? They continued with their journey.

Night was black and dense in the open, the stars glistening like many-faceted teardrops high above, the moon a pale, curving hand to cradle them. Looking up, imagining that she could see fingers clasping the moon, holding it securely, she thought of Atalanta, the warrior-queen, and the symbol of eternal life which she had displayed as her emblem. Eternal life? Who would want to exist for eternity in this moribund, heart-breaking life that she was now living, not knowing what had happened to her lover; fully aware that she might never see him again, and with no friend but Ezta in the world?

A sudden chill sweeping over her, she huddled down into the goatskins which were wrapped round her like a sack. These days, she thought of Atalanta more and more. It might have been because the warrior-queen had endured similar hardships; or it might have been because Flavia could closely identify with a woman who had been forced to fight and rule as a man. If only she were a man, how different things might be. Then, she would not have to go searching for Constantin Tiarchos. If she were a man, she could don her own fighting gear and sit astride a war-horse to lead the remaining *Kleftes* into battle herself. Her heart soared at the idea. Leading men into battle against the cruel Turks, killing them, and rescuing Zardos from his foul prison! If only she could. Where would he be imprisoned? She had no idea, but she was hoping that Tiarchos would know; and that he would already have some plan to free her lover.

Her lover. The teardrop stars bubbled and scintillated above her, the moon radiated an unearthly, soul-stirring light; it streamed down onto her as if investing her with some strange and eerie power force, tingling along her bones and invigorating her blood. Perhaps Atalanta herself was looking down at her from the stars, urging her on, sending out her support and inspiration? She could certainly do with it now.

In the distance a sheep gave its tremulous bleat, then there was total silence. Here, the nights were blacker and more silent than anything she had ever known. Only if the cicadas were carolling could she throw off the oppressive feelings evoked by the extreme blackness and stillness.

She thought longingly of the bedlam and clatter of the city streets in England, of London with its seething, twisting alleys and backwaters. People thronging all day and during early evening, before the respectable citizens locked themselves up in their homes by the fireside, with servants to wait upon them, while the footpads, highwaymen and vagabonds reigned. There was a court of thieves in London; she remembered her father telling her about it. A woman had ruled there for some years, a notorious creature called Abella Swynford, who boasted of the men she had strangled. She had a posse of infants, and almost as many lovers, and the beagle and his men had failed dismally in all their efforts to catch her. Even the vagabonds had trembled when she held sway.

Women could be forces for good or evil, she thought, before closing her eyes to sleep on the uneven, rocky ground with the company of a great burly cactus looming over her. Somehow, when a woman was bad she appeared to be far worse than her male counterparts; and when she was good, she appeared to be far better. Mother Marie-Thérèse's words drifted back to her.

'*La Vierge* is the mother of mercy, not justice, that is why she will answer your prayers, smile upon you, prove benevolent. She is not involved with what is right and what is wrong, but with the distress and sadness in your heart and your great need of her. Her heart is sweet and she is filled with compassion for her children. Be one of her children, my daughter, and know what it is to be loved as Christ Himself was loved.'

She started to pray to the Miraculous Virgin, but she fell asleep, exhausted and aching. The goatskins were crumpled beneath her back and she would wake feeling bruised, but for the moment she felt nothing, only sleep's deep unconsciousness. Giorg was on guard, so there was nothing to fear. He was sitting with his rifle across his knee, his currant-black eyes staring piercingly into the gloom.

Thirty minutes passed, then forty. Giorg got to his feet, silently so as not to wake the two sleepers. Stretching his stiff limbs, he gripped the rifle in his right hand, then, looking cautiously to left and right, he crept away, disappearing into the cave of night.

him, his intense black eyes staring vacantly into the
gloom.

Thirty minutes passed. Dchesterry Unity got to his feet
... it to work like two shapes. Troubling for
still limbs, he gripped the rifle in his right hand, then
looking cautiously to left and right, he crept away, disappearing into the cool night.

The Demon Pasha

'Through the new wound that fate had opened in me
I felt the setting sun flood my heart . . .
and the rock I found rooted at the roadside seemed
    like a throne
long predestined for me. And as I sat
I folded my hands over my knees, forgetting if
it was today that I'd set out or if
I'd taken this same road centuries before.'

Sikelianos

'Every anxiety is the fear of one's self.'

Dr W. Stekel

Prince Hassani was feeling thoroughly delighted with life. He was wearing a robe of buttercup-yellow samite, a rich silky brocade, trimmed with topaz, pearls and jade, and fringed with silver. On his head was a convoluted turban of jade silk stuck with emeralds, and on his forefinger was a cabochon emerald which thrilled him afresh every time that he looked at it. These were his anniversary gifts from Sultan Mahmud, and he was enraptured with them. It did not matter that when the Sultan had his anniversary, he would have to send gifts which far outweighed these in value. What was important was that the Sultan had not ignored Hassani's name day feast.

There had been a message with the gifts, of course. Mahmud wanted action, and he wanted it immediately. The Princess Musbah must be married instantly. Allah's Teardrop, the world's largest diamond, continued to lie in Zebukar's vaults and Mahmud would not rest until it hung round the neck of his beloved Besma. There was much more to it, of course. Pride. Masculine pride – and vanity; the reputation of the Ottoman line, the Ottoman Empire. If others heard that a mere girl had outwitted Hassani, and, by inference, the Lord of the Lords of this World, Mahmud himself, then shame would descend upon him and the Sultan, a greater shame and humiliation than any known before. How could they control the Janissaries if they could not control a mere slip of a girl?

Hassani assimilated the message, scowling, but saying nothing. He had not been lethargic. His men were scouring Greece for the Princess, but she had vanished from her convent, and no one knew where she was. Hassani would have liked to torture the nuns, who professed to know nothing of her whereabouts, but he was too cunning to do that. For one thing the convent had been under Ottoman protection for decades; for another, the Miraculous Virgin was there, and although he was a faithful Muslim, he had a healthy fear of idols which were reputed to work miracles. Christ was one of Mohammed's prophets. Who knew how it would displease Allah to see the statue of his prophet's mother profaned?

Hassani rubbed the emerald on his blubbery chest and smirked at its gleam. He was skilled at procrastination. He could summon a myriad excuses why he could not, or need not move on a matter. Sometimes he astonished even himself at the sound reasons which he could invent so that he need do nothing except continue to indulge in his hedonistic round of sensual delights. If the worst came to the worst (which it had been known to do more than once), then he could just about muster his wits to bark a few commands and set in motion whatever activity was vital. Thus far, Hassani believed, he had outwitted the Sultan, even if only by concealing from him the fact that he was the laziest sybarite under his rule.

He knew what he would do tonight. Have his little dancing girl brought to him, and that new boy – the very young one with the fair hair. It was most unusual for a Greek boy to be fair like that. It was some sort of disorder, a lack of colouring in the tissues, his Arab physician had said. What matter? The boy was clean and healthy, and his pale hair would be highly stimulating. As for Alliya, she could watch him deflower the boy and then he would tell her what he had in mind. He giggled to himself, a husky, obscene giggle.

The boy was brought in, bathed and scented with violets. He was ten years old, small for his age, and he wore nothing except a gold-tissue loin cloth. He looked somewhat dazed, which well he might, for he had been fed a mixture of drugs to inflame his senses. Leaning towards him, Hassani stroked his flat, hairless chest, then let his fingers slip downwards. The boy did not give any sign that he knew what was happening. He did not even flinch.

Hassani's questing fingers slipped inside the loincloth and found the soft little implement tucked away there. It was like velvet, warm and malleable. Hassani nipped and tweaked at it, stroked the silky little sacs which hung beneath it, and felt an answering response in his own loins. Still the boy did not move, or look at him. They had fed the boy too much of the drug! Hassani clenched his jaw. Now he would get no pleasure when the boy squealed and tried to fight him off, nor, it seemed, would he respond ardently as some had been known to do, even the first time.

Raging, Hassani continued to stroke, caress and knead the boy, his other hand doing the same to himself. Where was that witch-child Alliya? She was late, the little bitch! Wait until she got here, he would whip her and then . . .

'Master,' Alliya knelt before him, her bleached hair cascading like corn ready for harvesting. He blinked. He had forgotten how big she was now; far too big for his own taste. Her breasts were swelling like sweet pears and her shoulders were square. Involuntarily, he shivered. It was time for him to get rid of her.

Watching the foul and bloated Hassani, Alliya was barely able to control herself. In the two weeks during which she had been caring for Natuk, the ten-year-old boy, she had grown very fond of him. Her maternal instincts were increasing all the time; she would have dearly loved to be settling down to marriage now and the bearing of her own family. Instead, these poor, gentle boys were her children. It was she, who, knowing what Natuk would be forced to face, had fed him more than double the correct quantity of drugs. Half that quantity inflamed the senses; double ensured that nothing was felt at all, everything being observed as if in a waking dream, with no memory remaining afterwards. She knew, because she had experimented on herself with the boys in mind. Glancing at Natuk, she could see that his eyes were glazed, his spirit far away. He would recall none of this, all blessings be to Allah.

'Is the boy sick, or have you overdosed him, you incompetent bitch?'

'Master, he says little at the best of times. He is not a great talker. I have told him how great and powerful you are and how greatly fortunate he is. Perhaps he is overwhelmed by your marvellous presence, master? It could be so. Who would not be, master?' Alliya gazed at Hassani, her eyes wide with awe and reverence, her tiny jewelled hands, their palms painted terracotta with henna, clasped together in front of her breasts.

Hassani grunted. 'Then fetch me another boy, you stupid, ass-brained chit!' he growled.

Weak with relief, Alliya led away the bemused and mindless Natuk, giving orders to the eunuchs at the door to bring Marmari, one of Hassani's favourites. He was an older boy who had taken to his life here with enthusiasm, being no little innocent.

Having put Natuk into his little bed, leaving one of the harem attendants to care for him, Alliya returned to her master's bedchamber. Slipping in silently, she tiptoed towards Hassani, who was leaning into Marmari's lap, his tongue busy.

Padding across the ivory and peach-tiled floor, Alliya went to the *cloisonné* chest which contained all the implements and aids used by Hassani during his feasts of love. Having taken out what Hassani would want, Alliya replaced the lid of the chest and returned to her master's bed. Gently she climbed on to it, leaning against the pillows until Hassani gestured to her to begin work on him. Leaning forwards, she opened her mouth in the customary manner, making the noises of awe and admiration which Hassani relished so highly. Then, having him fully inside her mouth, and fighting fiercely to quell the desire to vomit, she began to move her head up and down.

It was midnight a few days later, while Alliya was asleep, that the guards came for Natuk. He was returned to his bed the next morning, white and cold, bleeding internally from massive injuries, breathing in stertorous gasps which wrenched at his little lungs. Alliya nursed him as lovingly as she could until he died, then she set about finding out what had happened. Having used the boy and found him not to his liking, Hassani had handed him over to his army commanders who had taken turns with him during the night. Alliya did not weep, nor did she say one word to anyone of what she was feeling. Next time she was summoned to Hassani's bed, she knew exactly what she would do.

The storm was barbaric and terrifying. Bright spears of silver lightning hurtled across the basalt sky, while sharp, drenching rain catapulted to the earth. Shivering, Flavia huddled beneath a rocky outcrop, her goatskin cloak clutched round her. The temperature had dropped at least ten degrees, and she was reminded of the weather in her homeland, of how the rain waited carefully for people having picnics and then pole-vaulted onto them with extravagant delight, then, when they were housebound for one reason or another, the sun would burst out, shining with relish. No British storm could ever be like this, however. This was savagery as she had never seen it before, Heaven breaking its heart so tempestuously that the sound and fury of it dominated everything. She felt that if she did not tense herself to shut it out, then the storm would invade her very being and she would die.

Beside her, Stephan squatted unperturbed. He had seen it all before, including the Cretan squalls, and after having lived through one of those, all else was temperate, even this blast from the stars. She looked at him sideways, marvelling at his pacific expression. He was chewing something, the juicy pulp from inside the flabby leaf of one of the monstrous mountain cactuses. Since Giorg had vanished in the night, Stephan had been a rock. He was not a gregarious man by nature, and to be left stranded in the foothills with a greenhorn would have thrown most men into a panic, but he was coping with it very well. It was true that Flavia was learning fast, and could hardly be called an encumbrance even though her feet were covered in septic blisters and her back felt as if she had been kicked by an ass. But for this storm, they would have reached Constantin's village by now.

An hour passed, two hours, and still the rain did not abate. Acute boredom and a chilly feeling of imminent disaster trickled along Flavia's bones. The hearty beating of the rain was making her ears ache, her temples pound.

Suddenly Stephan's arm was pushing her back into the dank hollow beneath the rock, making her leap with alarm. Horsemen were galloping by, their cloaks black and leaden with rainwater, their heads bowed. It was doubtful if they could have seen through the trellis of rain even if they had looked up towards the rocks.

'Turks,' Stephan whispered, and spat on the ground with a violent loathing.

Once they were out of sight, Flavia relaxed, huddling into her cloak and trying to sleep while Stephan kept watch. For a moment or two before she collapsed into exhausted slumber, she wondered why Giorg had deserted them. He had seemed as stalwart and loyal as Stephan, at the start.

Prince Hassani's face went bright scarlet and bulged with rage so that it looked as if his flesh and bones would burst out of his skin. The man kneeling before him had needed a translator to tell Hassani what he knew, but the telling was over now and the man was awaiting his pouch of gold.

Hassani got up, fists bunched, and strutted round his audience chamber his face puce, his head bobbing up and down. Time passed and it did not look as if his temper was fading. The kneeling man spoke again, through the translator, who repeated his words to the Prince. Hassani swirled on one fat heel, his mouth curved down at its corners like an inverted crescent moon, showing his crooked yellow lower teeth. Then he rattled out something in Turkish, and two of the mountainous black eunuchs stepped forward to grip the man by his elbows. He yelled and screamed as they dragged him away, but that was customary behaviour in one who was going to be beheaded by the Prince's order. Had Prince Zebukar still been alive, he would have beheaded the man with his own hand.

Hassani's eyes rolled, his cheeks quivered, and he let out a roar of fury resembling a great, shuddering sob. The English girl had been with the Pagan! Allah alone knew what the man had told her. Now she was on her way to the village of Constantin in the mountains and no doubt they would be recruiting soldiers to come and free their so-called hero. Hassani well knew how turbulent and quarrelsome the *Kleftes* were when left to their own devices. Not even to free their country of their invaders could they have banded together without the Pagan's help. He and he alone had united them; they would follow him to the ends of the earth, but no one else. The man, Giorg, who had brought the news was one of the *Kleftes*, but a man with a grudge, who wanted his revenge on Zardos Alexandros for Allah alone knew what. Hassani did not care. All he had wanted was information as to the whereabouts of the Princess Musbah and now he had it. Dressed as a goatboy, she was travelling on foot towards this man Constantin's village. Hassani's heart felt like a lump of clay and a seething sherbet drink by turns. When he could find his voice, he would order out his men. They were devoted to him – did he not give them fresh young boys to sport with as they chose? None of them would ever betray him as had the Pagan's man. On horseback, they would soon catch up with the Princess and in no time at all she would be back here in the Palace of the Silver Cicadas, standing before him. No, better still, kneeling, and awaiting his commands. How could he have been such a cretin? Why had he not forced her into marriage immediately and bedded her the moment that the ceremony was over?

The Sultan was in an ungovernable rage because he had been kept waiting for Allah's Teardrop, and Hassani was in disgrace for putting personal whims before the desires of his royal master. Had it not been for the capture of the Pagan, which had elevated Hassani's reputation overnight, he was well aware that he might have lost his own head by now. What had he been thinking of? He loved his life of sybaritic indolence! In Allah's name, was he not the greatest hedonist ever born? Why then had he not done the easy thing when it was open to him, instead of letting the Princess elude him? It would not happen again! When the Princess was brought to him, even if she were in her goatboy's clothes, he would consummate their marriage on the spot. This entire affair had taught him how to arrange his priorities, if nothing else.

Squelching through the quagmire left by the storm, Flavia reflected that mud was known to be good for the complexion and if her anguished feet were anything to go by, then mud would soothe them too. The time had passed when the pain had cut through her; she was numb now, longing only for the sight of the village they were seeking. Stephan had not spoken for some time, but his broad, hard hand was always there when she needed to be hauled up an incline or pulled over a rock. She hoped the village had comfortable beds. Straw would be better than nothing, but feather would be even better. To sink into the softness of a downy mattress and sleep, sleep, sleep for days! But first a delicious bath, steaming hot water to bring her bones back to life. She wasn't hungry. Their pouches were crammed with black olives and tiny, shrivelled grapes which they had found growing wild. But she would donate them all for a big chunk of fresh bread dripping with butter, some *feta* and the creamy goatsmilk yoghourt beloved by the mountain folk. She had been warned that it was an acquired taste and indeed she had found it to be so, for she had acquired it immediately on tasting it.

Mountains the colour of silver birch bark were ahead of them. Stephan had called them the Three Graces, at which she had given a little smile. Everything in this land had to be romantic, allegorical or mythical, and how she loved it all. Who would want to call a mountain range Snowdon or Ben Nevis, or the three Peaks – such prosaic names – when they could call them the Three Graces?

The track was as rocky, uneven and treacherous as ever, but at least the next few yards were flat before they began to ascend again. Now Stephan unrolled the huge, heavy rope from around his shoulder and circled it round her waist, securely knotting the rope so that if she slipped, he would support her weight. She felt rather like an ox, but anything was better than plunging down into the ever-deepening gorge behind them. The mountain air was making her feel a little dizzy and out of the corner of her eyes she imagined that she could see the Three Graces dancing gently in the distance, their ferny, heathery skirts swirling, their snowy crowns gleaming. How cold it was up here, and how silent. They could die here and no one would ever know.

Turning to her, and grinning, Stephan made a throat-cutting gesture.

'No Turk ever up here, or else our look-outs do this . . .' he made the throat-slitting gesture again, hugely amused. 'No Turk ever see look-outs, too clever. But they see us long ago, watching us now.'

Thankfully, the village was within sight shortly afterwards. Men and woman ran towards them, gathering them into their arms and hugging them, shouting greetings in their ears. Food was brought, and wine, milk, water; all that they could possibly desire, and, after eating ravenously, and drinking until they could drink no more, they were taken to Constantin.

Flavia had pictured a rugged Greek of mature years, with a bushy beard, perhaps, and ham-like hands with broken, black nails, not a nineteen-year-old boy with burning eyes, and a splendid command of five languages.

Constantin was filled with mercurial energy, yet he rarely smiled. He was, it transpired as they talked, consumed with a fiery desire to rid his homeland of Islam, and he worshipped Zardos like a god. Tears glimmered in his eyes when he spoke of Zardos's capture and imprisonment.

'We do not know yet where they hold him. It is terrible. I wake during the night thinking of his plight. Their ways are vile; they are fiends without souls, without consciences. You cannot know how I have suffered since my leg injury. If I had been there, this would not have happened. They would not have taken him. I would have died first!'

'I believe that many did die protecting him,' Flavia said, her voice low with sadness.

'No one can use a sword like me. I learned how to fence from Master Juan of Cordoba. Zardos sent me for lessons as soon as I was old enough. It was intended that I learn everything there is to know about bearing arms and fighting hand to hand, then that I return to Greece to teach our army. And what do I do after being back here only a few months? This stupid leg!' Constantin slapped his leg, which was firmly strapped to splints and swathed with bandages. 'I came to visit my mother and my horse threw me – can you imagine the humiliation?' His thin cheeks pulsed with heat.

'I am sorry – sorry about everything,' Flavia sighed, feeling exhausted, and longing for sleep. 'We came to find out what is to happen, what is to be arranged. No one seems to know anything now that Zardos is taken prisoner. There is no unity any more, or so it seems. If things continue like this, the Turks will regain all their lost footholds and you will be back exactly where you started.'

Constantin's eyes sparkled. 'Do you think I do not know this? Of course I know this. I have done my best from this wretched bed! Messages have gone to the mercenaries who promised to aid us if we needed it, and Master Juan of Cordoba is recruiting soldiers at this very minute. All the Greek exiles are returning to help or finance us. Juan is an old man now, but he has taught hundreds of men during his lifetime and many of them will come to aid us. All good Christians will want to free us, you can be sure of that.'

'My country too, if they knew all of the truth,' Flavia put in.

'Maybe. Although not Catholic, great supporters of the free man are you peoples of the islands of Britain.'

At that moment two women came into Constantin's room, a young slender girl with a bright, sweet face and eyes black as olives, and an older female version of Constantin himself. It was his mother and his sweetheart, Kita. The latter was carrying a message which she handed to Constantin, who read it, then shouted out loud.

'A consignment of muskets is on its way – and pistols! From a Turkish galley which has been pirated. Is that not excellent news? If only I could find out where Zardos is, I would go and free him myself!'

'Do not be so impetuous, Constantin,' his mother abjured, hands on hips. 'How would you walk with that leg?'

'I would hop all the way!' Constantin retaliated. Then, knowing that he had spoken foolishly, he sighed. 'I suppose that I must put this in the hands of others. It will break my heart to do so. What will posterity say of Constantin Tiarchos? They will say that he lay in bed while his companions fought to the death.' Obviously the thought of this was more than he could bear.

Kita flung her arms round her sweetheart and stroked his brow, making soothing noises, but the tragic emptiness remained in his eyes.

Overcome by mind-numbing exhaustion, Flavia begged leave to go and sleep. Curling up in the comfortable bed provided by Constantin's mother, she was too tired even to weep.

The bleating of goats woke her. It was dawn, and the air was bright as cut-glass and spangled as if newly-polished. How long had she slept? She felt totally revived. Kita entered with a tray, a broad smile, and a cheery greeting. The hospitality of Greek mountain folk was marvellous to experience. On the roughly-carved wooden tray was a flask of goat's milk, musky and fresh, a selection of seasonal fruits, the coarse Greek bread she loved, a dish of honey made from mountain flowers, and the sweet, tasty almonds of the area. While Kita sat on her bed smiling and chattering, Flavia dined handsomely.

The room was bare and white-washed, the floor baked earth packed down hard. The bed and chair were carved from local wood, of a pale golden colour. A small window looked out onto a vegetable garden. Beside it were the goats, a nanny, a billy, and their two sons. They were sturdy, bad-tempered looking beasts, yet their bleating was mild and temperate. The mountain air was fresh and invigorating. It might have been spring.

'Fresh after the great storm,' Kita said. 'Now for two or three day or more we shall have clement weather, sweet air, then the cold again. That is how it goes.'

'You need iron lungs up here in winter,' Flavia said, sipping the frothy milk.

'Iron lungs? Oh yes, that is a good thought. We are strong. Raised to this like goats. Nothing keeps us in bed save a broken limb.' She made a face, thinking of her sweetheart.

'When are you and Constantin going to get married?'

'When he drives out Islam. That is what he says and so that is what I say. It is not right that we go on being slaves. We must throw off the Turkish yoke!' Kita's eyes glowed as she repeated the words which she was accustomed to hearing from her lover. 'I have prepared my gown. It is ready. So, too, are my shoes and other garments. But none shall be donned until the Turks are chased out. Then we shall be free, beautifully, beautifully free!'

When the lively village-girl had gone, Flavia dressed in the clothes which had been brought for her. A straight dress of unbleached cotton, coarsely-woven, with loose sleeves without cuffs, which had blue-striped oversleeves hanging to just below the elbow. The bodice had a drawstring neck, and the blue overblouse was fastened at the waist with two large circular buckles of some cheap silvery metal. Below the buckles was a sash of dull orange, and there was also an apron to wear, of a deep yellow colour, but Flavia dispensed with this. It was an article of clothing which she had never worn in her life. There was a sleeveless jerkin which went down to the knees and which was a dull grey edged with orange stripes, a round red cap edged with blue, and a pale yellow veil to wear over the cap and throw round the neck, the rest hanging down the back. The slippers were orange and very like those she had worn in fashionable drawing-rooms in England, except that those had been silk and these were roughly-sewn leather. It did not matter. She could not have continued in the goatboy outfit for it was caked in dried mud, damp and uncomfortable. Soon enough to disguise herself again for the return journey.

Constantin was in excellent spirits. He was propped up on hassocks and sipping ouzo when Flavia was brought in to see him.

'There has been news,' he announced, grinning hugely. 'We have heard where Zardos is imprisoned. Men arrived during the night, while you slept.'

'Where? Tell me where he is!' Flavia cried.

Constantin's high black brows trembled slightly, but he gained control of his expression rapidly.

'In the – the main Turkish prison in the country.'

'Where is that?'

'Roughly half way between the palace where you married your Muslim and the convent where you took your vows.'

'You know a great deal about me, but you are wrong in one matter. I did not take my vows.'

Constantin placed his palm over his mouth and trapped a cough. It was a curiously polite gesture in one whose origin was a mountain village. She did not know it but it was the gesture of the consumptive Master Juan of Cordoba. What she did notice was that the cough was hoarse, rather like a dry bark. She had heard a sound like that before: in a family who had come to work on her

239

father's estates and who had lost two children from consumption. They had coughed like that. Constantin looked so healthy, though. His cheeks were rosy, and his eyes bright.

'What is the name of this prison?'

'It has no name,' the youth shrugged. 'It is just a prison, like so many built by the Turks.'

Despite his words. Flavia felt sure that he was hiding something, but what she could not say. He would not have looked so happy had word reached him of Zardos's illness or death (she shivered) so what could be wrong?

'What are you going to do now? At what stage are your preparations?' she asked him.

His long thin fingers tapped the bedsheet. 'Orders have been sent out to all our followers wherever they are, in Greece, or abroad. As I told you, they are mustering now. Word of Zardos's capture has spread like the wind and the world is shocked.'

'So everyone knows? Even the government in England?' Flavia leaned forward eagerly.

'Oh yes, they know, but of course they have been led to believe that he is a vile fiend, a devil. And some have believed it.' His gaze pierced hers until she looked away. 'But not all. Some will help us.'

'Can you not get word to the non-believers? Convince them of what is really happening here?'

'I? Why should they believe me, a Greek peasant? Besides, how do I get to them?'

'You are no ordinary Greek,' Flavia insisted.

'All the same, I am a crippled one for the moment.' He coughed again, palming his face as before, and Flavia thought she saw a speck of blood ease its way out between his first and second fingers. Icy shock trickled down her back, and, for one dreadful, sickening moment she succumbed to despair. Where was it all going to end?

'*You* could change their minds, tell them the truth,' Constantin said, his eyes boring into her, the blood-specked hand discreetly wiped so that not even Kita knew

240

of it. 'You have friends in the government in Britain, or your father did.'

'Do you not think that I would if I could!'

'Then why did you not go on the ship?'

'That was not taking me to London, but to a strange country. How did I know what would happen then? How could I have run away?'

'Why should you not run away, Your Highness?' Constantin stressed the last two words. 'Raised in luxury, married to a powerful prince, a splendid future before you. Why did you throw in your lot with us? We are a lost cause, can you not see it? A lost cause . . .' A fit of coughing strangled his lungs, at which Kita rushed towards him, crying out his name. Pushing her away, he swallowed hard. 'A lost cause! We are a lost cause I tell you!'

Flavia turned away from the pitiful sight of the sick, despairing boy, while Kita, tears rolling down her cheeks, tended to him. Hearing her cry out, she turned, to see that the linen square which the girl had passed to her sweetheart was drenched with blood.

The next few minutes were terrifying. There was blood everywhere and Flavia had no idea what to do. Kita was just as helpless, and it seemed hours before the boy's mother arrived. They held him in turn while he writhed and coughed. Kita mopped up the blood which spilled from his mouth and Flavia wrung out cold cloths and placed them on his burning forehead. The quilt was kicked off and Flavia replaced it only to see the long, sound leg kick it off again while the broken limb, heavy in its splint and bandages, moved to left and right.

'Hold him!' his mother instructed, before running down to her herbal cabinet to make up a pain-killing brew which would enable her son to sleep. She did not know what else could be done and there was no physician in the village. Even if there had been, she could not have afforded him. If only Zardos had been here, everything would have been all right. He had been their symbol for hope, for freedom, for casting off the Turkish shackles. Sobbing beneath her breath, she ran back to her son's room. He was a ghastly colour, lying flat on his back, drained of strength and of blood. Gently, his mother eased some of the tincture between his lips, while Flavia propped up his head. Kita sat in a corner, ashen-faced and shuddering from head to foot.

When the boy slept, and they were seated in the kitchen, his mother apologized to Flavia, but Flavia would not hear of such courtesy.

'The poor boy! If only I had some money to give you, but I have nothing. It is I who should apologize to you for not being able to help.'

Constantin's mother looked at her with wild eyes as if such a thought was anathema. She had put a guest to great inconvenience and frightened her, and that was unforgivable. Greek hospitality was warm and genuine and guests were treated like revered members of the family, never more so than in the mountains and the islands.

Kita came into the kitchen, her step wooden. Sinking down onto a stool, she put her head in her hands.

'Why did we not know?' she whispered. 'Why did he not tell us?'

'He hoped to keep it secret. He did not want to upset us. Perhaps he thought he would be cured in time?'

'But it is incurable! Always incurable! So many have this sickness now, and they all die. They waste away to bones.'

'We have it, too, in my homeland,' Flavia said, her voice shaky. 'They say that it is connected with the great consumption of sugar which has increased so much in the last century.'

'Oh, how can that be?' Constantin's mother gasped. 'We never have sugar up here, only mountain honey.'

'Yes, that is true!' Kita said sharply, her eyes almost accusing.

'Yes, but Constantin lived in other countries for years, and in cities there is not the natural honey so easily available,' Flavia said, her chin trembling. She felt like some sort of criminal because of Kita's reaction, but she knew it was because the girl was frightened.

'That too is true.' Constantin's mother gripped the edge of the rough wooden table where she had prepared meals for her family for over a quarter of a century. 'They say that city life kills . . . now I know it to be so. The worst that happens up here is a broken limb.'

Going to the sad-eyed woman, Flavia put her arm round her. The body was rigid and tense. It would not weaken, nor admit weakness. She thought of the disciples of the philosopher Zeno, who had gathered in Athens to hear his teachings. They were called Stoics after the Stoa, where they had gathered, and it was plain that their blood lived on.

Flavia stayed for one week in Constantin's village and then she began her return journey to the fortress. Again she was dressed as a boy, as a poor, roughly-garbed peasant, but this time she was on the back of a donkey for part of the journey to the lower regions. A village youth came with her to take back the donkey, and of course there was the indomitable Stephan beside her. She had done all that she could for Constantin and his family, but it seemed obvious that the boy would not survive for many more months. She felt heart-heavy as she left them, for she could do nothing to make their lot easier. She had come all this way to be given hope, and instead she had found a fresh despair.

What of the reinforcements alerted by the boy before his illness? She could only hope that the messages had reached them safely and that they were massing in readiness to retaliate. As for freeing Zardos, she knew nothing save for the rough geographical location of his prison in the Morea. All the way back to the fortress, she thought of him in the days of his freedom. How big and handsome, and vibrant with life he had been. Tough, brave, bold and invincible, a leader, an inspiration. Touching him had been like linking herself to a spirit force which would never fade, never die. Tears were like sequins on her lashes. She wanted him back, oh, she wanted him back! If only she had loved him more and reviled him less while she had him! Now what could she do, one mere, small frail woman against the force of Islam? Nothing. Nothing.

Alliya had swallowed the required dose of the drug which would take her life. She knew exactly how long she would need to accomplish her task before the drug took its effect. Dressed in her most seductive outfit, she danced for Prince Hassani, who seemed restless and bored by her display. A small yellow-haired boy was sitting in his lap and now and again he would fondle him and pry at his body with hard fingers, so that the boy groaned and wept a little. Alliya wanted to stab the Prince, mutilate him horribly and fling his private parts out of the palace window for the hounds. She had considered poisoning him, but his death would have been too swift. It was only right that he should suffer as he had made so many others suffer.

Having danced, she approached the Prince, who gestured to her to join him on the great silken bed. Throwing open his robe, he revealed the sight which was all too horribly familiar to Alliya. Bending her head, she began to minister to her master's needs, swiftly bringing him to a peak of frenzy. Then, when he was at his most vulnerable, she clamped her teeth together, biting deep. His screams woke the palace, but she did not release her grip. She could not, for she was dead, the drugs having taken effect. Writhing in agony, Hassani begged his guards to free him of the pain, which they did eventually but only with much difficulty, and not before he had well and truly received his just deserts.

The Warrior-Princess

'Oh, when my lady cometh,
　　And I with love behold her,
I take her to my beating heart
　　And in mine arms enfold her;
My heart is filled with joy divine
　　For I am hers and she is mine.

Oh, when her soft embraces
　　Do give my love completeness,
The perfumes of Arabia
　　Anoint me with their sweetness;
And when her lips are pressed to mine
　　I am made drunk and need not wine.'

Ancient Egyptian love song.

CHAPTER EIGHTEEN

Time. It was the most precious possession in the world. With time, all could be accomplished. Without it, nothing.

Flavia, safely back in the fortress of Atalanta, had the unenviable task of telling its residents that she had gained little by her journey. She did tell them that extra recruits had been rallied, and were now forming, but they would not be led by the brilliantly-trained Constantin, who was seriously ill.

'Who will lead them, then, Highness?' she was asked, at which she could only shrug, the enquirer going on to say that the *Kleftes* in the main were unruly, fierce and turbulent, given to tempestuous disputes amongst themselves. Only Zardos had been able to unite them.

'I know it,' Flavia said. 'How many people have told me that since I came here?'

'What will become of us then, Highness?' Ezta said, her face pale, her arms wrapped round her slightly swollen stomach.

'We are safe here for the moment . . . After that, I just do not know,' Flavia confessed. 'Constantin will send messengers to us. We shall be told what is happening, do not fear on that score.'

'What if the Turks come here, what if they try to kill us?' Ezta shivered.

'Then we shall hold them off!' Flavia looked round from face to face. They were all ages, mostly Greek, but some were of other nationalities. They all had one thing in common: they had been badly treated by their overlords. That in itself was a prime motivation for unity. Here, yes, but what of those wild, freedom-besotted *Kleftes* and their allies? Fire raged in their blood, along with pride, honour and aggression. Even in the eyes of the dying Constantin she had seen more spirit than in the average Englishman in his prime. Originally brigands, their very name coming from the ancient Greek word for thief, the *Kleftes* had been the only ones who could steal Greece back from the Turks. But she did not know how many had survived the battle with Muhammad Baswar, nor did she know how many still lurked in their mountain hideouts; not even Constantin had known that.

There were something like fifty or sixty people living in the fortress now, not a few of them aged or disabled in some way, or young girls or children. What she would have given to have had an army of vigorous young men here, men whom she could equip and instruct, sending them out to slaughter the Infidel . . . She brought herself up with a start. She equip and instruct young soldiers? Send them out to conquer the Turks? What was she thinking of?

Ezta caught her hand. 'Highness, what is that I see in your eye? Such a look of fire, of determination! What was it that pass through your mind?'

Flavia looked down at the sweet-faced young girl, and somehow managed to smile. 'If I knew that, I would have the answer to all life's secrets,' she said.

Was patriotism catching? Certainly something was firing her. Every morning, she woke with a new resolve. A whole household of people was dependent on her now; they looked to her for their comfort, their inspiration, their security. She had returned to them, not fled to Hassani, and for that they were grateful, even though still unwilling to forget her connection with the enemy. Yet she was a mere woman, little more than a girl, one who had come here to fulfil all the most beautiful, misty romantic dreams of her childhood and instead was finding her life filled with war, shock and tragedy. At night she dreamed of Zardos. He was always as she had first seen him, bronzed, immortal, invincible, all the passion and fearlessness of ancient Greece glowing from his emerald eyes. In her dreams, he was close to her, warm, protective, doting, and she would fling herself into his arms and lay her head on his breast. The first time that she had dreamed this, she had woken in pain and distress to realize that he had not come back and that it was indeed a figment of her imagination. As the weeks wended their way by, she learned to live with this, too; it was amazing what one could become inured to.

Sometimes she found Ezta looking at her curiously, as if the girl could not recognize her as the Princess Musbah who had first come to the fortress all those months ago. Secretly, she, too, could no longer recognize herself. These days, she was tough, hardy, self-reliant; on the surface anyway. Could she continue like this indefinitely? She did not think so. Now, all that she did had a beautiful purpose. They were going to free Zardos from his foul prison, free Greece of the Turks, live happily together again, in peace.

One night, messengers arrived from Constantin. One thousand mercenaries had landed in a cove near the tiny fishing village of Hersonikos, and they were awaiting instructions.

'Has Constantin not given them orders?' Flavia asked, puzzled.

'He know they come. He know they here, but he sick, much sick. Life going quickly,' the gruff-voiced Greek messenger told her, his darkly-tanned face wrinkled with concern.

'So bad?' Her hand went to her mouth. 'But has he not found someone to take his place? Surely there is another who can step in and do what Constantin would have done?'

'All dead. Baswar the devil see to that. Dead or prisoner. Constantin say we come here, to you. You know what to do, he say.'

'*I* know?' Flavia almost laughed out loud. 'How could I possibly know where these men are to go, what they are to do? I am sure that you have misunderstood the message.'

'No.' The man sounded emphatic. There was trust and hope in his bright-brown eyes.

Flavia spread out her hands like fans. 'I'm sorry, but I

do not know what to do. I have no orders from anyone, and these mercenaries will be accustomed to a male leader. Do they not have a captain with them?'

'Yes. He will listen to you,' the man said stubbornly. 'All mercenaries are Greek, of Greek birth or married to Greek women. No trouble there. All want the same as us.'

'I cannot see a captain accepting orders from a mere woman,' Flavia protested.

'You are not mere woman.' The man's rocky jaw jutted. 'You are Pagan's woman.'

That certainly took her by surprise. Had they known all along? How had they found out? She was silent, but her flaming cheeks spoke volumes.

Eventually, having collected herself, she said. 'What am I expected to do?'

'Come with me to Hersonikos where men wait you. All will be well, you see. I, Marios Andrakos vow this!' He touched the amulet at his neck, raising it to his lips to kiss it fervently.

It was marvellous to be riding again, and on a horse which was as fleet as her own pet horse in England. Black, defiant and spirited, her mount, brought for her by Marios, seemed to be able to see in the dark. Sure-footed and reckless, it thundered along the track without hesitation, neck and neck with Marios and his companions. The journey was something like ten miles, and they travelled non-stop. With muscles aching and back sore, Flavia was guided to the cove where the mercenaries awaited her. They were squatting round fires, roasting whatever birds or small creatures they had been able to catch. They were silent, aware of the dangers of revealing their presence, but when Marios rode into their midst to present Flavia to them, they gave a roar of appreciation and greeting.

It all seemed like a dream as Flavia dismounted. Their captain came forward, bending his knee to kiss her hand, then food and wine was brought to her and a comfortable seat prepared for her to sit on. The captain was young and wiry with a broad face and grinning mouth. He was half-

Greek, half-French, so he said, but totally committed to helping his countrymen in their fight. He called her Princess, or Highness, and it was only then that she began to realize that something of a legend had been built up around her name. Why and by whom she did not know, but people seemed to know of her wherever she went, whoever she met. After exchanging small talk, and introducing themselves, she asked the captain, whose name was Jacques-Pierre Trakakios, how he had come to know of her.

'For years, we were told of the coming of the beautiful princess from London, England. She would marry the son of Prince Bastan, who was greatly loved. Mind you, this was before Bastan's son showed his true colours. In all the years the Turks have occupied Greece, Bastan was one of the few who was revered. His nature was excellent; he might well have been a Christian and a Catholic at that. We were taken by surprise when the son proved to be the very opposite of the father. There has been much misery, death and bloodshed over the past decade or so, Highness. We thought that our beautiful English princess would hear of it and not come, for the English delight in freedom and free-thinking. How could she ally herself with a cruel despot? we thought, sure that she would not come now. And if she did marry him, we feared for her treatment at his hands. Men tried to warn the ambassadors of your king, but all of them were murdered. A façade of peace and happiness was presented for those ambassadors. Everyone they saw and spoke to was bribed to lie, on pain of death, or the death of his or her loved ones.'

Flavia listened to all this in silence. It no longer cut through her to hear these things. So many said them that there must be truth in them. The man went on.

'When you did come, we did not know what to think.' The captain shrugged apologetically. 'Had you heard of the horrors and decided that you did not care? Or had you been misled? If you were innocent, we knew that you would not long remain so. When Zebukar was murdered, we feared for you, but we breathed again when you entered the convent of the Miraculous Virgin. There, we knew you would be safe. It was known by then that you were to be married to Hassani, whether you wished it or not. Your rescue by Lord Zardos was surely superintended by the angels. We prayed that all would go well for you, for both of you together.' Jacques-Pierre grinned meaningfully, while tears misted Flavia's eyes as she remembered the days she had spent with Zardos, and their night of love.

'There is a legend which we hold dear,' the captain went on. 'Constantin spoke of it often, and believed in it. Now, he says it is our final hope. You have heard of Atalanta, the warrior-queen in whose fortress you now live?' Flavia nodded. 'We have believed for centuries that she would return to deliver us in our greatest hour of need, and that hour is come, Highness. Constantin bid me tell you this, from him.'

Jacques-Pierre, his expression now deadly serious, almost reverent, fell to his knees before Flavia, taking her hand to kiss it for the second time. 'He – and all of us – believe that you are she, our saviour, returned to free us of the Turkish servitude. At first, I must admit that we did have doubts about your reasons, and for that we humbly beg forgiveness, but Constantin was convinced that your motives were of the truest. He says that you are the one we awaited, and his word is more than good enough for us.'

No protestation she made would change their minds, so she fell silent, all the time feeling a hypocrite. They had created a myth out of reality, invented a persona for her which she had never possessed, and now they were expecting her to perform miracles. She almost wished that they were distrustful of her again. Then, at least, she had not been expected to move mountains.

That night, she slept beneath the glittering firmament, the stars perpetual diamonds embroidered on basalt silk; the sharp, scythe-shaped moon painted silver. All around her was the gentle, steady breathing of dozens of men, men who looked upon her as some variety of miracle worker, a form of female King Arthur, if they knew of that British legend. It was all so preposterous, crazy, yet she was helpless to convince them otherwise, and, indeed, if she did, would it not strip them of what little hope they had left? With hope, they were bright and happy people, childlike in their trusting optimism. How could she deny them that? They had suffered enough, one way and another. Tonight she had heard some of their experiences and while she listened she had been thinking that there was only one story in this land, for the Greeks who lived there, and that was one of death and pillage, rape and destruction. Beautiful Greek women, sisters, mothers, daughters, had been despoiled. Cottages and homesteads had been burned to the ground, livelihoods ruined when farm animals were slaughtered or flung over cliffs. They said that it was retribution for Tripolitza and Navarino, but none of these people had been involved in the uprising there, an uprising which had, after all, been caused by the intolerable cruelty of their foreign overlords. Some Greek merchants had allied with the Turks in the cities, and grown rich, but they were considered beneath contempt.

She closed her eyes and bowed her head when Zebukar was mentioned, and finally she had to tell them not to talk of him. They had understood, or at least she thought they had. Husbands were gods in this land, after all, even when they were the Infidel.

The stars seemed to be coruscating just for her, with a friendly pulsing glitter. The night air was kind, and she was warmly wrapped in sheepskins, but she dearly wished they were Zardos's arms around her. For dinner they had given her roast meat of some kind, enveloped in dark green, slightly bitter vine leaves which had been cooked in the ashes of the fire. There was goat's milk from out of leathern flasks, and retsina, the wine which gained its unique taste from the resin of the pine needles which were soaked in it. She did not like it at first, but when Jacques-

Pierre told her that it was a man's drink, she narrowed her eyes and drank more deeply.

Grinning, he then told her how to tell a good retsina from a bad.

'Pour some of the wine in your cup, put your hand over the top and shake it. If it is good retsina, then the distinctive scent of wine and pine will be there just as strongly as before. If it is bad retsina, then it will smell acrid, like *vin aigre*. Even the best does not keep for long. They say it must be drunk during the year it is made, but I have drunk some which was seven or more years old and it was good.' He licked his lips at the memory.

After emptying the first cupful, Flavia began on a second. The wine was already growing on her. Its heady scent was so evocative of the beautiful Greek pine woods which she loved that she could hardly dislike the wine. After a time, she would find that it was like drinking the very air of Greece itself. Never again would she be able to drink it without thinking of this night.

Many of the men had been draining their flasks of ouzo, the anise-flavoured drink which becomes milky when water is added. It was deceptively flavoured, Jacques-Pierre told her, and he would not recommend that to a man, let alone a lady.

'If Your Highness has a stomach-lining of steel and a liver of the same matching metal, then drink it by all means but not of course tonight, for no man in his right senses would mix his wines.'

Jacques-Pierre was asleep now, but the guards were prowling round the camp which was sheltered by high rocks. The ships which had brought the men had bobbed away on the tide, but they would not be far. They planned to anchor in different coves around the coastline, evading the Turks and waiting in readiness for a rapid departure should the need arise.

Jacques-Pierre's ship, *La Vierge*, had been dedicated to the Miraculous Virgin, he had told her proudly. He said that while his craft was under her protection, it would never sink, at which Flavia had thought of Mother Marie-Thérèse's words, about Mary being the mother of mercy, not judgement. The faith of these Greeks was profound; she hoped that hers would prove the same.

Dawn was ushered in gently, its lighting a pallid rose-pink edged with translucent apricot. This deepened to crimson and gold as the sun billowed out from behind the horizon in a burst of egocentric glory, glad to be back and assured of its welcome. The men were waking, lighting their fires, filling their pots with food to break their fast. Some were eating pilaf in the Turkish fashion, for even though one can hate one's invaders it is hard not to absorb something of their culture in the course of nearly four hundred years. Goat's milk and *feta* cheese were brought to Flavia, and a hunk of the coarse creamy-beige bread which she loved, plus a wooden bowl filled with velvet-textured yoghourt mixed with sweet almonds and black, succulent raisins. On a rock nearby, a dazed lizard struggled to cast off sleep, swishing its rubbery tail and staring at her while she ate as if she were an interloper in his house, which indeed she might well be.

'He is a Turkish spy!' joked Jacques-Pierre, pointing at the lizard, at which she laughed out loud, despite a mouthful of bread. 'See those cold, staring eyes? They are Turkish, there is no doubt on it. And the way he watches you, so acquisitively. That is the way of the Turkish, too. Be off, you knave!' Jacques-Pierre made one or two very rude comments in French, and the lizard scampered into a dark crevice in the rock. 'He must have more brains than a Turk for he can understand French!' Jacques-Pierre raised his brows.

'So can I,' Flavia grinned, and this time it was the young captain who blushed.

The sea was busily eating up the sandy shore, smacking the little rocks and pebbles and retreating swiftly before they could retaliate. Birds gyrated overhead, screeching as they searched for fish. The sky was a soft and misty-powder blue, the water iron-grey but beginning to flaunt some jewel shades, jade, turquoise, lime, silver. She would have loved to tear off her clothes and run naked into the sea like a nereid, laughing into the sunlight, but that she could only have done with her Pagan beside her. There could be no such exultant joy until he was free. She looked about her. What was she to say to these men? Strangers all of them, although their captain had such a warm and easy manner that she felt as if she had known him for years. Gregarious and charming though he was, however, she sensed that his persona was not the stuff of which brilliant strategists and generals are made. He was too happy-go-lucky. If only he had possessed something of Constantin's fierce and single-minded fervour . . .

'Highness, the men will be ready for your inspection soon,' Jacques-Pierre told her later on.

'What am I to do?'

'They will make ranks and you will ride along, looking at each one in turn. It is very simple.'

'I may speak if I wish?'

'Of course, Highness. These are your men, they will do whatever you say!'

Will they die if I tell them to do so? she thought, sick at heart for their future. Could I ask them to die if the need arose and I had to send them into battle? She could not answer that question. How did generals overcome these problems? Perhaps they never had qualms about ordering their men into battle, yet surely a general loved his men? She did not think that she could watch these men die, or know that they were dying because of her, even if she loathed them heartily. Lives cast into the whirlwind of time because of her . . .

Riding along, looking into each man's face, she thought of the warrior-queen who must have inspected her men so often. Atalanta had believed in the rebirth of the soul, through generation after generation, into infinity. Flavia did not see how such a phenomenon could take place and yet it had a ring about it, a conviction which she found pleasing.

Strange how the Greek sun could suddenly become blinding, the air dry as ancient, baked dust, the throat tight and parched, light glinting off a sword so that it struck her eyes painfully. So many dazzling swords, inflamed by the sun's rays, and breastplates glittering like molten silver, bright metal helmets with their nodding feather plumes, horses caparisoned in scarlet and white leather, inlaid with shining studs. Beautiful, high-necked beasts like the small-headed horses in ancient Greek paintings. So many men-at-arms, thousands of them, and all under her command, willing and eager to die for her. Such love surrounded her, their love, and she returned it a hundredfold. That love in itself was more protective than any breastplate, than any shield.

'Highness! – Is the sun too bright for you?'

She came back to the present with a jolt, to see that she was staring sightlessly into a mercenary's face, her hands clenching the reins. No breastplates and shields glittering; no plumed helmets bright and fiercesome, just roughly-clad but vigorous men with sturdy limbs and square, peasant features. Where had she been? Her throat felt like pine bark and her head was throbbing. Touching her stomach, she felt the softness of her gown with its high waist in the Napoleonic style. It was woven from local cloth and she had sketched the design for it herself, being nostalgic to wear a modish outfit again. What had she been expecting to feel, a breastplate and the heavy burden of a surcoat of metallic mesh? Closing her eyes, she sought for equilibrium while Jacques-Pierre galloped off to fetch watered wine for her to sip. He was sure that she had been overcome by the glare of the sun.

It was nearly midday, and there was every reason for his fear. Her gown was of a heavy cloth to keep her warm while riding at night, but a loose white blouse and peasant skirt would be more appropriate now. That was what she usually wore these days. Having quenched her thirst, she handed back the flask to the young captain.

'Highness, if you are weary there is no need to go on. The men will understand.'

'I go on,' said Flavia, clenching her jaw. Go on they did, despite the heat, despite the mosquitoes buzzing round their ears. Her inspection was a triumph. She won every heart with her steadfastness, and by the cheery way she conversed with the sturdy soldiers. I wonder what they will call me now, she thought to herself? General Flavia? Somehow it did not sound right.

They had given her a title, as she was to find out later. As she was being served her midday meal sitting on the rocks with the emerald swish of the waves in her ears, Jacques-Pierre told her what the men called her. Warrior-princess.

'Warrior-princess? But that makes me sound like an old warhorse! I have never been to war. I have never so much as held a sword!'

'You will. It is ordained.' Jacques-Pierre nodded his dark, shaggy head. 'History always repeats itself, always.'

Flavia went on munching. Really, what could she say to these determined people? Acquiescence seemed to be the wisest course, on the surface at least, so she turned her attention to the food. The cucumber was crunchy and sweet, the tomatoes a rich blood-red and tasty enough to be a fruit. As usual, she discarded the black olives whose salty, bitter flavour she could not tolerate, but the accompanying *souvlaki*, chunks of lamb in a rich, herby sauce, was very appetizing.

'The more meat that the Princess eats, then the more will she become a warrior-princess,' Jacques-Pierre grinned, piling more of the juicy chunks onto her platter. 'It is well known that the beast transmits its strength to the eater.'

Flavia stopped eating for a moment, her eyes twinkling as brightly green as the sea.

'Let's hope it is the strength only and not the physical appearance!' she said wryly.

After it was all over, it seemed like a mysterious and

elusive dream. Had she really been down to the sea to inspect the mercenaries, to speak to their leader and talk about war as if she were a soldier, too? Back in the quiet confines of the fortress, falling into the easy, natural routine there, she would have found it easy to forget that other life. It was lived by a girl who often seemed to have little connection with the Flavia she knew of old. In England she had thought herself daring, galloping alone on horseback on the heaths, striding along in the countryside with her father's hounds, walking on town and city streets after dusk when cutpurses and footpads came out of their lairs. Those had been nursery days compared to this! In a few days' time, Jacques-Pierre and a selected band of his men would be arriving at the fortress while the remainder continued to ride round the country gathering their forces.

'We kill the Turks and make you *pringipisa* in Hassani's place,' the half-French captain had said. 'Then, when we free our Lord Zardos, you rule beside him, as it was meant to be.'

But he had not appeared to know how her lover was to be freed. They had no concrete plan, yet they seemed to experience none of the doubts which she was trying to quell within herself. The thought of failure never entered their heads. She did not want it to enter hers either, but how did she keep it out? She had lived with both sides and she knew that the Turks considered themselves invincible, the chosen ones of Allah the All-powerful. As she had learned, they could be ruthless, barbarous, and pitiless overlords; they massacred with a cold and cruel delight, while, basically, the Greek temperament was one of cheerful and trusting friendliness, and was almost childlike at times. That was why the Turks had gained dominion over them so easily. Over the millennia, so many races had invaded Greece and Crete. For example, the Dorians, who had walked into Crete and been accepted as friends with very little commotion. The Minoans had become Crete itself, their true name being the Keftiu, the people who come from Crete. Arabs, Venetians, Turks, all had marched into Greece and enslaved it. Under the Saracens, Heraklion had been the slave centre of the Mediterranean. Greeks were not new to invasion, to turmoil and to foreign overlords, but they had borne it for far too long, and times were changing – as were the people. Freedom and liberty were the passwords now. There was a limit to what even the warmest and friendliest of people would tolerate.

If only Queen Atalanta were here and she could consult her. What would she say? Gripping the stone window-ledge and staring out into the amethyst and dark-honey haze which quilted the hills, Flavia tried to put herself into the shoes of a woman whose philosophy and beliefs were thousands of years behind hers. What would she have said to her men in this situation? How would she have acted?

Get Zardos out of prison, Atalanta would say. But how? Turkish prisons were fortresses in themselves, and guarded by the barbarous servants of Hassani who would execute anyone who failed him. She had nearly been his wife. Her fingers gripped the stone more tightly so that her bones ached with the coldness of it. She had almost been Hassani's wife . . .

Her hands falling to her sides, she turned away from the romantic hills which were balm to the heart, for the last thing she wanted at this moment was to be soothed.

CHAPTER NINETEEN

A cloud of grey dust in the distance always caused panic in the fortress, but the women and older children were as good at being scouts as any trained soldier, and word was brought to Flavia instantly. She went to stand at the most advantageous viewpoint until the blue scarf fluttering on Jacques-Pierre's lance became visible and she was able to relax. They were friends, she told the Greek women standing beside her and they hurried off to spread the word that the mercenaries had come. In that moment she realized what a difference had taken place in their treatment of her. Now, they trusted her. She had come back to them with Stephan.

The approach of men who were also allies and saviours had the same effect as a strong draught of *raki*, the firewater which the Cretans brewed from grapes. The women and children ran around with scarlet cheeks and made preparations for their visitors. Blankets were shaken, mattresses turned over, their lumps pummelled flat; two goats were slaughtered and their meat prepared for roasting, lemons picked from the rustic trees which grew behind the mountain, and, from the thriving fortress gardens, fruits and vegetables were plucked. Bread had already been freshly baked, so that did not need to be done. They would have to eat four days' supplies in one.

Ezta had been lying down, but, on hearing the news she rose to her feet, her face shining.

'They have come,' she said, 'oh, they have truly come!'

Sitting in a comfortable chair, she chopped cucumbers and tomatoes, shared out black and green olives onto little dishes, sliced up the huge, creamy-coloured loaves, and sliced green capsicums into rings, smiling all the time she worked. It had seemed like a lifetime since her Kios had died, and as his child grew inside her, she had become increasingly lethargic and depressed. She did not want to birth a child which her lover could never see. She did not want to hold their baby in her arms if Kios could not do the same. Not for one second had she entertained thoughts of vengeance for Kios's death; that was not it at all. Rather, she craved release from the pain of what had gone before. She wanted to forget the death of her lover and the fact that it would make their child a bastard. If it would help that child, she wanted it to be taken away when it was born, so that she need never see the face which would surely be the exact replica of Kios's. It could be placed in a loving home where a man and a woman of kindness would raise it as their own, then she would be content. But as for raising it herself? That she would never do. Never.

'Those steps are no way to greet welcome visitors!' Jacques-Pierre threw off his Greek-style tasselled cap and looked round the kitchens of the fortress-palace. 'You must bury more friends than you feed! Ah, that smells good.' Catching sight of the petite dark-eyed Ezta in her chair, a dish on her knee, he grinned. 'That is how I like to see a woman: preparing food. And is this one not a beauty?'

Leaning over Ezta, he reached out to chuck her under the chin, but she twisted her head away nervously, making a strange little sound almost like a strangled scream. Whatever the Frenchman had seen in her eyes was enough to stop him in his tracks. Turning back to Flavia and the group who accompanied her, he grinned broadly. 'We eat now, I hope, Princess?'

How very Greek he was, she smiled to herself. In a Greek kitchen, whether she be a peasant or a princess, a woman was meant to provide food.

'The dinner will be a few minutes more. May I show you round our home?' Flavia walked out of the kitchens, into the chilly stone corridor which led to the upper floors. She did not want Ezta upset by this charming and boldly dashing young man. The *esprit* which he so confidently

262

exuded was not unlike Kios's own high spirits, and would surely remind the Cretan girl of all that she had lost.

'You have quite some château here,' Jacques-Pierre looked about him admiringly. 'Such fortifications, such strong stone, and sturdy walls. You could survive a year-long siege here!'

'I hope we never have to!' Flavia spoke with feeling.

'There would be the problem of water, of course. You have a cistern?'

'We have a well to the rear of the fortress. It is essential, of course. Otherwise we would spend all our time carrying water up and down the hillside. It is fed by a mountain stream.'

'A well, eh? That is good fortune. So if the worst comes to the worst, you will not mind a few hundred mercenaries joining you in here?'

'You mean if the Turks are after you? It would be an excellent idea!' Flavia cast him a look which seemed to say, Don't you dare put us at such risk! but her smile belied it. 'Have you got any further with your plans to free Lord Zardos?' She waited for his reply, her body taut.

'Yes and no, Princess.'

'What sort of an answer is that?'

'We know where he is now. The exact place. The most notorious prison in the land, and I include Turkey in that. Its nickname is Hades, that is the old name for the Underworld, the world of the dead from which no one returns. It is as bad as that. They do not want anyone to survive their stay there. Why should they? Now and again they let someone out who would have been better off dead, but that is only so that he can spread the word as to how vile and hideous the prison is. The last man to be released from there was horribly mutilated, a cripple. His legs had been broken and reset, some three or four times, and each time the resetting was planned so that he would become more deformed. He had his hands hacked off, and then he was carried out and dumped at the edge of the nearest village.'

263

Feeling giddy, Flavia reached out to touch the cold stones so that she would not fall. Crying out that he should not have told her so much grisly detail, the Frenchman helped her to a seat. It seemed to take her hours to reach it, and she wanted to faint, but, to her chagrin, could not.

'I am sorry, Princess. It us just that I am so used to reviling the Turks in great detail. How insensitive of me to tell you these harrowing details. I am a dolt, an imbecile, a vast and bungling fool!' He banged his temple with his fist.

Slowly her weakness passed, but it had taught her something quite startling. When Jacques-Pierre had spoken of the tortured prisoner, she had seen him with Zardos's face, imagining him being flung out of the gaol with his legs shattered and twisted, his mind destroyed with the pain, for all she knew. She had hated Zardos Alexandros for as long as she could recall; she had been tutored to loathe and despise him, according to her late husband's politics. On meeting him, she had found him arrogant and insufferable, learning nothing to alter her opinion – at first. But time had passed, as it is wont to do, and her feelings had undergone the most unexpected metamorphosis, aided by the time they had spent in one another's arms. War made everything more acute, more intense, speeding up feelings and emotions. When she visualized Zardos tortured and half dead, she realized that she no longer feared him. Now her feelings were very different: food for thought in the days to come. How long would the fierce and vengeful Turks allow Zardos to live?

Tears like hot little pearls jabbed at her eyes and quickly she brushed them away.

'So you have no plans to free him?'

'I am a military man, not an intriguer, Princess. I obey orders and the one who would have given them is dead.'

'Kios, you mean?'

'Him, too, but the one I meant was Constantin.'

'So he has died?' More tears trickled down her cheeks. 'Poor, brave boy. He so wanted to be a hero.'

'He has gone down in the annals of our land as one of the greatest heroes. His heart broke because he could not fight beside Lord Zardos, and he had no resistance to his disease.'

'Yes, I know it. There is nothing sadder than a man of action who cannot act. With Lord Zardos, do you think they will have – have chained him in his cell? Or – or tortured him?' Her face was pearl-white now, her eyes red-rimmed.

'We must not think on it. Who knows what they plan? They have said nothing. They have not released any message, but there is still plenty of time for them to do so. The Turks love making pompous pronouncements. They speak as if they think they are Allah personified, as if none but they have the right of life or the authority to act.'

'I have an idea, Captain, tell me what you think of this?' And Flavia told the Frenchman of her plan to free the Pagan, and while she spoke, relating the idea which had been formulating in her mind for days, Jacques-Pierre's dark brows arched higher and higher and an expression of admiring amazement spread over his features.

The litter and its *cortège* wound its way along the dusty, rutted track. Here, it had not rained for seven months and the land was shroud-dry, parched, the rocks like powder, the playful wind thrusting dust and grit into the faces of the weary travellers.

At the centre of the *cortège*, which was obviously that of a rich and worthy person, there was a litter hung with sumptuous violet silk tasselled with gold, and, now and again, a jewelled hand pulled back the silken curtain slightly to peer outside for a few seconds before the curtain dropped back into place. Guards on horseback accompanied the litter, and serving women, pages and squires, with two female attendants riding on horseback within a few feet of their mistress's litter.

Inside it, Flavia's heart was doing the most alarming

contortions. Word had been sent ahead of them that the Princess Musbah, widow of Prince Zebukar, had decided that she would marry Prince Hassani, and was now on her way to join him. She would like her arrival to be a delightful surprise for the Prince, so she had requested that no advance warning be given. All the same, convincing as that might sound, they did not know how well informed the prison governor was. It was true that the prison was in an unsociable spot, but the roads between Hassani's palace and other main towns in the Morea bypassed this area. Although she and the Greeks had acted with the utmost secrecy, one never knew if word had been spread.

Flavia knew that she risked everything by taking part in this charade. In a very short time, she might find herself a prisoner, the sacrificial lamb, locked in some bleak room until Hassani himself came to claim her. Icy spangles danced along her spine at the thought. The child that she had been might have felt a frisson of excitement at the notion of becoming a princess again, and living the life of a royal bride, but she was no longer a child. Now, she was a woman, and her determination and strength were growing deeper every day. She had a debt to pay for her childish ignorance and the blindness which she had entertained in earlier years. Since then, she had tasted the bright reality of freedom, of thinking for herself, of making her own decisions in a manner which was not encouraged even in English girls of her own class. In the hours to come, she might see that brightness dimmed forever. If Hassani had found out what they were planning, if he was called here despite her request for secrecy . . . Her pulses thudded. She could almost feel the pounding of blood in her veins, and her throat was dry as parchment. God alone knew what lay ahead. It might be the beginning, but it might also be the end.

By now the guard should have reached Nekros Prison, to relay the news that the princess had been taken ill during the journey and would need to rest, to break her journey to Hassani's palace. She would of course need a chamber of opulence, befitting her rank, and there must be no disturbance to wake her. At the prison, there were apartments for visiting dignitaries, and one of these must be prepared for her.

A comfortable suite, or a gaol where she would be locked until Hassani came for her? The iciness was spreading across her back, down her arms and legs. Her fingers were like icicles as they knotted themselves together in her lap. Sudden terror convulsed her body, and she wanted to cry out, '*Let me out! Let me out! Go back, we must turn back!*' but instead, she clamped her mouth shut and prayed for courage.

The governor of Nekros Prison was astonished to find that he was about to become host to the highest lady in Greece, but, fully aware of how precious she was to Prince Hassani's heart and pocket, he barked out orders for the tower apartments to be made ready with all speed. The prison was in a building which had been erected as a palace two hundred years before by the Venetians, before the Turks had driven them out of this area. Solid, grim and forbidding, it smelt of pestilence and death. Its very name meant Dead Prison. However, in the tower rooms, far from the cells, there was comfort and the sweet, stifling scents so beloved by the Turks, violets and attar of roses, ambergris, and the drifting smell of incense as fragrant barks were burnt in braziers. The governor was determined that the Princess would speak well of him to her future husband, and servants bustled about in frantic preparations.

When the prison came in sight, brooding, dark and threatening in the dusk, Flavia trembled violently. In God's name what had possessed her to conjure up this insane idea? She was making an offering of herself, of her freedom, putting herself into the power of the Turks . . . If Hassani had been told, he might have hurried here, he might be waiting now in the room made ready for her . . .

When she was helped out of her litter, her legs felt soft and shimmery as silk, and she could not support herself.

Helped by her two heavily-veiled attendants, and pulling her own veil across her face, she half walked, half staggered, towards the prison entrance. Walking through its stone archway was one of the hardest things she had ever done. Had lions waited for her in the courtyard, she could not have felt worse. A feeling of imminent doom washing over her, she leaned more heavily on her attendants. They seemed to know what she was suffering and she could see a new respect in their eyes, and sense it in the way they supported her. But what a way to earn her spurs, she thought wryly!

Watching, the governor was stricken with panic. What if the Princess were dangerously ill? She certainly looked it. What if she died here in his prison, without the aid of a competent physician? The wrath of Prince Hassani was like the wrath of Allah Himself. A cold sweat was making his clothes stick to him; he gave thanks that he did not have to entertain the Princess himself.

Flavia would never know how she succeeded in climbing the twisting tower steps to her lavishly-scented suite. Behind her was dread, but ahead of her lay the unknown. At any moment, she expected Hassani to lurch out at her from the shadows, grasp her with his acquisitive hands and plant his slobbery mouth on hers. Then it would all be over, her companions taken prisoner, herself forced into marriage, and she would never know freedom again. A veil would literally fall between her and the outside world. She could not bear it!

Think of Zardos, she told herself silently. He is in this place somewhere, suffering horribly, believing that we have forgotten him, that all his dreams are finished. Think of him, think of him *hard*, she told herself.

The wind was rising, howling and whistling round the tower, and now the rain began, drumming against the stonework, hammering for access, lashing out of the sky like steel whips. Soon the deep, dusty tracks along which they had travelled were a quagmire of sticky, oozing clay mud.

'The rains have really arrived,' Angela, one of her attendants whispered as they paused at the door of the suite. 'Travelling will be difficult now . . .'

'Ssh,' Flavia said, her eyes bright with warning. Who knew what lay on the other side of this door?

A servant hurried forward to open the door for them and usher them in, bowing extravagantly. The scent of oils and burning barks billowed out to greet them. Heart pounding, Flavia stepped into the room, every nerve expecting a trap.

The room was empty. She was so relieved that she collapsed onto the nearest couch. Her attendants bent over her solicitously.

'Her Highness must not be disturbed,' Angela said, frowning at the servant and those who stood outside not too sure what to do now that all the excitement was over for the moment. Bowing, they withdrew, palms pressed together before their mouths in the Muslim way, and Angela was able to shut the heavy door behind them and bolt it, satisfaction bringing a grim smile to her face.

Flavia, seemingly miraculously strong again, was soon stripping off her voluminous Turkish-style clothes and the hated *yashmak* and pulling on soldier's breeches, shirt, and a tough leather jerkin which Angela had pulled out of one of their bags. Having pinned her hair flat, and tugged on a clumsy, turban-like cap, she rubbed wood dust onto her face and hands, thinking how fortunate that there were braziers in the room.

Time passed and Flavia grew impatient. Striding up and down the room, she went over and over the rescue plans in her mind. Everything was arranged in great detail, from start to finish. There should be no panic, bungling, or alarms. Thirty minutes passed, then forty, then sixty and still Jacques-Pierre did not arrive. What if his disguise had been spotted and he was now in one of the cells? She shivered. If that were so, then she and her companions would be next to be investigated.

'Holy Mother protect us!' she whispered, almost leaping out of her skin when the tap came at the door.

'Do I open it?' Angela whispered, eyes wide.

'Wait.' Flavia tiptoed to the door and whispered, 'Who is there?' As arranged, back came the reply, 'A Frenchman.' Had Jacques-Pierre been taken prisoner, he would have replied with his name.

Once he was inside, they spoke in whispers, eyes gleaming. Very soon the plan would be into its final stages, the most dangerous time of all. If it went well, then they would escape from here with Zardos, the darkness hiding their flight. If they failed, then it would mean terrible torture for them all, from which death would be a blessed deliverance.

The *cortège* wound its way clumsily through the quagmire while Prince Hassani screamed out for his men to go faster. They were all soaked, their clothes, the curtains of his litter, the horses, drenched, wallowing in rain. It was not easy to move in such conditions with the horses' hooves sticking in the glutinous mud, making the beasts lurch from side to side and whinny out in their distress.

'Cretins! Dolts! I'll have you all cut into little pieces and your blubber fed to the hounds!' Hassani roared, leaning out of the litter so that it heaved dangerously to one side. 'We are late! Late, d'you hear? Get a move on, you lazy louts!'

Withdrawing from the lashing rain, dabbing at the trickles which were cascading down his puce face, Hassani scowled and cursed obscenely to himself. This was the first time he had ventured so far since the shocking attack by Alliya. It had shaken him to the core and he had been very ill with a fever, though whether that was a direct result of her assault, he did not know. He had insisted that it was all hushed up, of course. Broadcast that a Turkish prince's concubine had turned against him, and become violent?

Such a thing was unthinkable. Yes, people could be told of the fever – why not? – but not the rest.

A Greek surgeon had done what was necessary, and now all was almost as good as new once more. He had been told that the next few weeks would make all the difference. Meanwhile, his desires were hardly diminished at all, and he had found an ingenious way of enjoying himself without putting a strain on his injury. Riding beside his litter was a handsome, yellow-haired Dorian boy, with blue eyes and a beautiful body. He was an expert in the arts of love-making and the giving of pleasure.

Ah, praise be to Allah, there was the Nekros Prison ahead of them. He could just make out its outline against the dark night sky. Within a few hours, the Pagan would be dead, for that was why Hassani was here, to watch his execution, and then life could return to normal again, or as normal as it could ever be after the last few months. He would find the widowed Princess and shut her in his harem, after he had swived her a good many times to show her who was master, and then he need not even see her again unless she bore his son. In which case, he would perhaps find a little tenderness in his heart for her. At that very moment, his soldiers were on their way to the Convent of the Miraculous Virgin in Nauplinos, to force the nuns into telling him where the Princess was.

In the Convent of the Miraculous Virgin, Mother Marie-Thérèse knelt in prayer before the statue after which the convent was named. Prince Hassani now knew that his intended bride was no longer within the cloisters of Nauplinos. His guards had just left, after searching the building from top to toe, in case the Princess had returned to hide there, to trick them. They had not believed her when she had said that she did not know the whereabouts of the Princess Musbah. Growling and cursing, they had flung her aside and begun their search. Now the convent was in chaos, pallets ripped open. Did they think the

Princess was hiding inside the mattresses? Cupboards were wrenched from their fittings, drawers were torn out and their contents strewn everywhere; the nuns were searched in such a way that they either became hysterical, or crimson with mortification, or both.

When Mother Marie-Thérèse had reminded the captain of the guard that the convent was under the protection of the Sultan himself, the man had spat in her face. But there was much to be thankful for. None of them had been raped or murdered. Now the men had gone, although for a few moments towards the end she had believed that they were going to set the building alight. She had prayed, silently and fervently to the Blessed Virgin, and eventually the men had jumped astride their horses and gone. She prayed that they would not return, but she had a terrible feeling that they might. Nothing was sacred these days, and their eyes had bulged when they had seen the Miraculous Virgin's jewelled statue

'Wherever the Princess is now, guard and protect her, beloved Madonna,' prayed Mother Marie-Thérèse. 'Hassani will scour the land 'til she is found. And then, poor girl . . .' The nun crossed herself. Months ago, a message had been left for her, a few words scrawled on dusty, splitting parchment telling her that Flavia was safe and well and in good hands. She thought back to the darkness of the night when Zardos Alexandros had arrived at the convent, and taken the Princess with him. For all his arrogance and blatant male vigour, she knew that he was a good man at heart, and that he was the only one who could unite the disputatious Greek factions. In unity was strength, and the Greeks had played into their foreign masters' hands by remaining divided with petty quarrels all these years. She had been told when Zardos was captured after the battle, and she had longed to know what had become of the Princess. Gone into hiding in the mountains, possibly. It was said that the mountains of Greece could conceal anything, and that was no overstatement. Millennia ago, a range of mountains in Crete had hidden Zeus himself until he was ready to face the world – or so legend would have it. Well, Zeus was needed now, as never before, but the man who was his peer in every way was languishing in Nekros Prison, and only the dead, the mindless and the crippled came out of there.

She was stricken by a feeling of cloying heaviness, and it was some time before she recognized it for what it was: a lack of faith. All these years and she had never suffered such a crisis before. The darkness of the soul. Lessons that she had been taught as a postulant crept through her mind like shy little creatures. '*He who comes to God must believe that God exists and is a rewarder to those who seek Him.*' '*Without faith it is impossible to please God.*' Jesus himself had said that those who did not believe would be condemned.

'Blessed is she who has believed, because the things promised her by the Lord shall be accomplished.' Saint Elizabeth had said that of the Virgin.

As a young woman, freshly initiated, how she had wanted to emulate the saints! Recently news had come of a girl in Paris who had been blessed with the apparition of the Blessed Virgin under her title of the Immaculate Conception. The Virgin had held out her hands, and glowing golden rays had poured from them, symbols of the graces that Mary obtained for man, so the girl was told. Mother Marie-Thérèse had known a bitter moment on hearing this. All her life, she had wanted to be the instrument through which would come some form of Divine hope or blessing which would help the world. She had ached to have a vision, prayed and yearned for such a joy, but it had not come. It was easy, all too easy, to look back on her life now and consider it to have been an arid emptiness. What had she achieved? How had she changed the world? Yes, she had quelled her sinful soul. Yes, she had prayed for hour upon long hour, but what active, positive thing had she ever done? A waste of life, hers. A waste of breath and brain and heart! Shut-away, hiding from what? Something which she did not understand. Where was it leading? Nowhere. Too late now to consider what her future might bring, for her future was gone. Age and weariness had conquered her bones.

'I wanted to be your saint,' she whispered to the Miraculous Virgin. 'I wanted to be blessed by you, see you and receive your love, but it is too late now, I can see that. Others younger and better than I have been blessed. Yet why should I need a visitation when I have your beloved effigy here before me? I ask too much; yes, I know it. I am greedy and vain. I wanted to become special in the eyes of the world, and that is arrogance.'

'I can hear my daughters sobbing and yet here I am thinking of myself when they need me. Forgive me, Mother!' She crossed herself again, but could not throw off the chilling void which had seated itself so firmly in her soul. 'Again I pray for the Princess, wherever she is, and for Greece and Zardos Alexandros. If he dies, then all is lost. We need a miracle, beloved Mother, and yet I am ashamed to ask it of you. All you ever hear are requests from all over the world, people wanting, begging, pleading, but how many are truly grateful?'

The jewelled effigy gazed down, seeming coolly detached; its face glitteringly exquisite, fragile, unforgettable, yet remote. There was no miraculous vision. Nothing but an inanimate, aloof and strangely-disinterested statue, and her own heart-stopping feeling of bereftness. She had lost faith. It had gone, and she had not even known until this moment. Well, she had wanted to be a saint and in this she was like them. Trials, temporary loss of faith, they knew all there was to know about that. Now she did too. Unfamiliar tears were like hard gritty beads behind her lids. Greece was lost and so was she. There would be no miracle this time.

The stench of filth and pestilence was choking in the labyrinthine corridors of Nekros Prison. Now and again, as if borne on some unfelt breeze, would come a blood-freezing groan or a whimper of pain. Flavia had heard about people being so terrified that the hair on the napes of their necks stood erect and now she was experiencing it for herself. Clad in her boy's concealing clothes, her face grimy with dust, and her flamboyant hair tightly coiled away, she crept along the passageways with Jacques-Pierre and the men whom he had carefully selected for this moment. It was bone-numbingly cold down here in the snaking intestines of the Venetian gaol, and difficult not to remember those old tales of the terrible Minotaur who lurked in a Greek labyrinth not unlike this. Any moment, such a heart-stopping beast might leap out from the shadows, stamping its hooves and snorting fiery breath over them.

Before arriving there, they had pored over an old crumpled sketch of the gaol which Jacques-Pierre had bought from a Turkish thief turned spy, a man who had been viciously punished for his crimes, by having his ears cut off. Now, unable to do enough to revenge himself for his sufferings, he had used his underworld contacts to obtain the gaol plan for the French mercenary. To ensure that no one would get the truth from the Turk, Jacques-Pierre had then knifed him, a fact of which Flavia remained unaware. From that same source, he had learned which cells were most likely to cage the Pagan. Intending to try each one in turn, they prayed that they could free their leader and escape with him into the night.

The first cell was empty, its door hanging off the hinges. No one was in there, not even a skulking rat. All the same, the stench was acrid, almost palpable in the air. The second cell was empty, too, or so they thought at first; then a man emerged from the straw, stumbling on legs which were as twisted as candy-sugar sticks. A face swung into their vision through the grille, a nightmare mask, both haunting and haunted. Muffled words came from the mouth, but none made sense. Sickened, her heart juddering, Flavia moved on past that hellish place. Time was passing and they seemed no nearer their objective. Soon after that, surprised by a guard, Flavia turned her head away as the man was despatched abruptly and silently. Then a little way along, yet another, quietly strangled by the expert mercenaries, but still they did not find the Pagan's cell.

Flavia wanted to weep. They were going to fail. Soon it would be dawn and they would have to flee without her lover. Oh, she could not leave here without him!

'What if he is not here after all?' she whispered to the French captain. 'What if they have taken him somewhere else?'

'We would have heard. We have our spies, you know. He is here. I tell you he is here, Princess,' he whispered back.

The dimness and the chill were clamped round her bones, biting into her heart. How many months had her lover been in this fiendish place, and what had they done to him? She had tried not to think of his being injured, perhaps tortured so cruelly that he could not walk, but they had brought a makeshift stretcher in case.

They went on as silently as worms undulating through the earth, and now it was almost as if the Pagan no longer existed; as if he were as much a myth as Zeus and Apollo and Poseidon; as if they had invented him out of their need and had been dreaming about him all this time. Possibly it was something to do with the icy cold, but certainly the stygian atmosphere helped.

Suddenly there was a gutter under their feet, running along the centre of the passageway, filled with sewage and rubbish. Bold and arrogant rats cavorted without fear while the stink increased with every step they took. Then, ahead of them in the flickering light of a flambeau, they saw what looked like an open midden, a great hillock of sewage and effluent piled almost to the ceiling of a room which was carved out of a rocky wall beneath the gaol. To her horror, Flavia saw that men were staked in the mire, chained by the ankles, unable to rise or move away. Pulling her neckerchief across her face like a mask, she walked slowly towards the midden. The first man she looked at was dead, she was sure, and had been for some time. The others looked near death. Thank God none of them was Zardos. How could anyone survive for long in this icy yet foetid air? They had not been fed or given water, and she wanted to do this for them, but Jacques-Pierre would not let her.

'We must make haste. Come, Princess.' He pulled her bodily away. Tears were in her eyes and, silently praying for the chained men, Flavia stumbled on past the midden.

'Only five more cells to go,' the Frenchman whispered, and she heard him as if from a great distance. The cruelty of man had never sickened her more than on this night. Animals were kinder to their own! Why did men have to vilify and torture one another? They always made such excellent excuses: colour, race, creed, religion, but, after all, what were these differences? They meant nothing, nothing. Take a Muslim from his parents when he was an infant and raise him as a Christian and he would be a Christian, knowing nothing else, adhering to nothing else. Flavia had never felt further from God and His Mother as in this Hadean hell.

The five cells were all empty, comparatively clean and bare. It was then that Flavia felt the great bursting in her breast as tears demanded to be loosed. Dizzy, she fell to her knees, hands covering her mouth to stifle her sobs. 'He is not here! He is dead, oh, he is dead! We are too late!'

For once Jacques-Pierre had nothing to say. The men with them, whose wits and courage had not failed them before, were uneasy, too, biting on their lips and shifting from foot to foot. They had come this far, so sure of finding their leader, yet he was not here. After a few minutes of tortured inactivity, their thoughts racing, Flavia said, 'Could he be elsewhere? In the rooms above?'

'That is unlikely. They are living rooms for the governor and his family and officers, comfortable, well-furnished rooms.'

'Would he be with the garrison in their part of the fortress?'

277

'I cannot see why he should be there. This is the gaol. This is where they put the prisoners.'

'If they look on Lord Alexandros as a political prisoner, might they not have put him somewhere else, in more comfortable surroundings?'

'What, the man they hate and fear most in the world? I had expected to find him ill, tortured . . .' Jacques-Pierre clamped his lips shut as the Princess's face twisted. God, but he was a clumsy fool!

Collecting herself, Flavia cried, 'We do not go from here until we have found him! We search every room, every floor!'

'Dawn is not far away. If we are discovered . . .'

Flavia glared at the Frenchman. Her spirits were suddenly fully recovered.

'If we are discovered, then we die fighting, that is what you were going to say, is it not, Captain?'

Jacques-Pierre nodded, swallowing. She had put him to shame, but he deserved it.

'Then we waste no more time, we go on. Follow me!' And with that Flavia marched on ahead into the murky dimness of the corridor.

Any one of the chambers might contain armed men and so all were approached with the utmost caution. If a door was not bolted from the outside then they tiptoed away. In this way, they covered the ground floor and then the floor above. It seemed that the Venetians were as skilled as Daedalus at building labyrinths and the twisting passages were like a maze. Inside, it was dark and gloomy but they knew that dawn must be emerging, and that her light would be a silvery-tangerine streaked with rose and gold. How would they escape in such a brightness? Each of them in his or her own heart was preparing for certain death.

'Hail Holy Queen, Sweet Madonna of Miracles,' Flavia whispered beneath her breath as another sequence of rooms failed to deliver Zardos to them. 'Let him be here, Blessed Mother, please, *please*, let us find him! I know you can perform miracles, sweet, sweet Virgin . . .'

They came upon the four guards suddenly, without warning. They had heard no sound, nor realized what lay round the corner. It was fight or die and fight they did, with the searing savagery of desperation. Flavia stood to the back, where Jacques-Pierre had thrust her on seeing the guards, but she was fully armed with a dagger in each hand. Strangely, she felt cool and fearless, but as one of the mercenaries was stabbed to death, she became uncomfortably hot and her heart began to fibrillate.

Groans, thuds and the clatter of dropped weapons echoed along the corridor and she dreaded that someone would hear and an avalanche of murderous Turks descend on them. Clamping her eyes shut, she held her breath.

'You can open them now.' Jacques-Pierre's voice was in her ear and she obeyed instantly. 'They are all dead. See what we have found.' Her eyes followed his pointing arm.

She saw a barred room, which had been heavily-guarded, multiple locked and bolted. What else could it contain but her lover? With a cry she leapt to the bars.

There he was, her darling Zardos, but he was not in some vile and foetid cell. This chamber was well furnished, possessing all that was necessary for comfort, including a massive four-poster bed of French workmanship. There, chained to the bed, lay the Pagan, not in filthy rags as they had expected, with his body deformed by torture, but dressed in soft leather and a silky shirt, with breeches of beige kid. He was even wearing glossy black knee boots . . . She could not understand it, but she urged the men to break open the locks, which they did after finding that none of the dead guards carried a key which fitted. The bolts were easy. As they were drawn back, Flavia felt life returning to her, flooding back into her heart and mind and veins. Soon, soon she would be in this arms again . . .

The door was heaved open. She ran into the room and flung herself on the bed.

'Zardos! My darling, darling Zardos! Are you alive? Oh God, is he still alive?' She turned to Jacques-Pierre in anguish when Zardos did not respond. She curved her hands round her lover's head and wept over his beautiful, unmarked face, his night-dark hair, the closed eyes which she ached to see open and looking up at her with love and joy. Were they too late? Was he dead?

Having felt his pulse and the heat of his forehead, Jacques-Pierre said, 'He is drugged. I do not know what they have used. Thank God it is only that, and not some fiendish torture. Thank the Virgin he'll be able to walk if only we can rouse him. *Hurry!*' He and the other men smashed away the chains which bound their leader to the bedposts and then they half pulled, half dragged him to a sitting position and then to his feet. He moaned, as if he were about to revive, but his eyes stayed shut.

'Zardos, Zardos! Wake, oh please wake!' Flavia cried as loud as she dare while she pummelled his chest and arms to try to rouse him. 'Water, is there no water in the room?' She looked round her.

A *cloisonné* jug and bowl stood in one corner beside a low-burning scented brazier which filled the chamber with the delicate, romantic aroma of violets. After the cold water was dashed in his face, he stirred, and began to blink, then he opened his eyes to see Flavia's anxious face in front of him. To their astonishment, he began to laugh.

'What have you done to me now? I wanted to see her face and now I can. What have you done to make a miracle possible, Alrhashid?'

As Flavia turned a perplexed face to the French Captain, he whispered, 'That is the name of the Turkish torturer here. So . . .' He looked increasingly miserable.

'So they have tortured him, but we cannot see what they have done! The fiends! The vile, vile fiends!' Turning to her lover, Flavia spoke to him, with tears streaming down her face. 'Beloved, it is really me, not a dream. I am really here, and so are your loyal men to help free you. We have to get out now, before we are caught. We have lingered too long as it is.'

Zardos shook his head as if to cast out mirages. Then, realizing that she was truly there, he snatched her into his embrace and crushed her to him with all the energy of desperation and months of aching yearning. For her part, just being in his arms again was a miracle. How had she endured their separation?

'My Princess, oh my brave, sweet Princess!' His tears wet her hair, amazing her. The Pagan weeping! Her beloved, how they must have tortured him to weaken him thus.

He was dizzy, and his vision kept blurring, but within minutes they had him out of the room which reeked of violets. Never again would Flavia be able to enjoy that scent; from that moment on it was always to sicken her. Torture and barbarous cruelty mingling with the scents of violets and attar of roses, rich unguents and fragile silks, that was the Turks personified.

The next minutes seemed to stretch out interminably as they sped silently along corridors and up to ground level where their companions guarded the small door through which they had gained entry from the guest suite. The women who had volunteered to act as Flavia's attendants would be well on their way to safety, and they, too, had soldiers to protect them. Now she and Zardos and their companions must make haste, escape from the fortress prison and find the horses which were waiting for them.

Hearts hammering, sweat beading foreheads, they made their way silently round the edges of courtyards and beneath arches, past the stables where there appeared to be no guards on duty at all, unless they were asleep and on to the final few yards of cobbled path which would take them to freedom. Now and again, Flavia looked in alarm at her lover whose face was deathly white and shiny with sweat, yet he would not stop to rest, although his breath was rasping. What had the Turkish torturer done to him while he was a captive?

'*Sacrée Vièrge*, I can hear horses!' Jacques-Pierre hissed. Turning, they saw in the far-off distance a twisting *cortège* of men, and horses bearing a great litter. In this light, like a dark snake wending in their direction, they could not see who it was, but they were not going to stop to sightsee. Having found the horses waiting for them, they leapt on their backs and thundered away in the opposite direction, as if chased by devils.

Afterwards, it would seem like the figment of a drugged nightmare to Flavia. The search for her lover in the hideous bowels of the gaol; the guards being garrotted and stabbed one by one, and then finally finding where Zardos was and freeing him; creeping out into the night to make their escape with the velvet-black Greek sky above them like a rich surcoat padded with stars. Then the approaching *cortège* and all its dangers, and the final wild gallop away as the first silver, pink and peach embroidery skeins of dawn threaded their way across the heavens.

Flavia had to tell herself over and over again that her lover was beside her. That she had done it, really done it, braved the Turks and rescued the Pagan. Frequently, she glanced at him sideways, as if he were a mirage in the rocky terrain, and joy would bubble inside her; she would want to burst out laughing. They could not speak. There was no time and they were riding too fast anyway. Not until the horses were drained would they pause, and then they would be at the village of Deloykos, where new horses and refreshment were arranged for them. No time to rest or sleep there but only to snatch food and drink and take fresh mounts, and then they would be heading for the second stage of their journey back to the mountain fortress.

During it all, Zardos was pale in the way that only agony can cause, yet he said nothing, not one word of complaint, wrapping himself in the warm cloak that they had brought him and exchanging adoring glances with Flavia whenever opportunity allowed.

After, when they were safely back in the fortress and Zardos's people were sobbing with joy to have him returned to them, it was all revealed. They learned why the Turks had imprisoned him in a such a pleasant room.

'Only for these final days,' Zardos told them. 'Before, I was in as stinking a cell as anyone could wish for. They did not want to drag me out for execution in rags, a broken and humbled wreck, for what glory could they gain from bringing a weakling to his knees? No, after they had taken their revenge, they put me in a luxurious room, and I was fed properly and bathed, and every care was taken of my health.'

'And when was your ex-execution to have been?' Flavia whispered, clinging to his arm.

'Sunrise this morning, my Princess. Hassani was coming especially to see it. They could not take the risk of letting in my men amongst the hundreds who would come to see the Pagan die, so the execution was to be held a few miles from the prison in a deserted village. They told me that more than two thousand people waited there to see me being tortured and then hacked to death. My head was to have been taken to the Sultan.'

'Oh do not speak of it, my love!' Flavia was white to the cheekbones, nausea rising in her breast. As she leaned against him, he winced, and it was then that she pulled away the cloak which he had kept so securely wrapped round him. What she saw made her scream hysterically. From waist to ankles, his clothes were drenched in blood.

'The torture of a thousand cuts,' he explained almost apologetically. 'They began a few weeks ago, but advanced slowly because they wanted me to stride out to the scaffold looking fit and healthy, for the reasons I told you.' A spasm of pain danced across his face and Flavia remembered the arduous journey they had just completed and the way he had climbed the hundreds of steps to the fortress without one grimace of agony. She wanted to scream and sob and tear at her hair, but instead she hurried everyone out of the room and ordered hot water, herbs and unguents to be brought, and then, with his help, she began the heart-rending work of undressing him and bathing his wounds.

She could not pull off his clothes; that was too painful; she had to cut them off and what she saw as the cloth and leather fell away brought her heart into her throat. The entire surface of his legs and thighs, his lower back and stomach was an open wound, lashed with dozens and dozens of cuts which had been allowed to heal partially but which had broken open during the rigours of the journey. Slowly, she bathed him, as tenderly as she could manage, and wincing more than he did when she hurt him unintentionally. Bowl after bowl of bloody water was taken away and fresh ones brought, and still she had not finished.

He was silent while she worked, but the eloquence of his emerald eyes said all she needed and wanted to know. Her lord was back with her. They were together again. Nothing must come between them again. Nothing.

She had reckoned without the fever. It might have been caused by his long ordeal, the torture and the exhausting journey, she did not know. Next morning, he was burning like fire to her touch nor did he recognize her when she spoke to him. Terror, dagger-sharp sliced through her. She was going to lose him after all! He was going to die! What did she know of nursing a fever as virulent as this?

He had slept well, or so she thought. Bathed and with unguents massaged into his wounds, he had fallen asleep instantly, a cool clean sheet protecting him from chafing. Even at dawn he had seemed to be sleeping serenely when she woke to examine his progress. Now this. After the first panic came a gritty determination to nurse him back to health. It would be weakness to bow to fate, and she was no longer the submissive young girl who had lived on a folly of dreams. They said that death was a great leveller, but that was to suggest that it brought people down. It could raise them in stature, too; strengthen them, give them courage and constancy. Death could be an awakening, and if some small, youthful and tenderly romantic part of her had died with Zebukar, then the rest of her had grown a thousandfold.

Leaving one of the women to watch over Zardos, she ran down to the kitchens which were the centre of the fortress where the inhabitants chose to gather, to chatter and exchanged gossip as the Greeks loved to do. She wanted to find old Zea the fortune-teller who had foretold

Kios's death and the disastrous battle with the Turks. The old woman was said to be skilled in the use of herbs and medicines. The Greeks of old had been the world's leading doctors and physicians. For centuries, Europe had accepted their teachings as gospel, and, in the fourth or fifth century BC, Hippocrates had drawn up his famous oath which all doctors must take before becoming practitioners. It had saddened Flavia to find that so little of this brilliant talent remained. Where had it gone? Was it lost for ever, like the skills of the ancient Greeks who had built such fabulous temples for their pantheon of gods? When she had mentioned this to Ezta, the girl had said that her Cretan people were so strong and healthy on their diet of natural honey, raw fruits and vegetables, goats' milk and cheese, that they did not need physicians.

Zea was not well, she was told. They said that the seer was over a hundred years old and that advancing senility had caught up with her after the shock of hearing that the Pagan had been taken by the Turks.

'Does she know that he is freed now? Has she been told?' Flavia said.

'Oh yes, Highness. We told her when you got back. She smiled and has not moved since; nor will she drink, although we have tried to tempt her.'

'Is she too weak to speak to me, do you think?'

The women shrugged. 'If you wish it, Highness, you do it.'

Zea was comfortably tucked up on a pallet with soft blankets, and a young girl was watching over her, murmuring prayers. Flavia sat down on a stool by the old woman and looked into her face. It was the colour of dove-grey kid, its shadows and hollows purple, the lids deeply sunken, the eyes closed, but the mouth, thin though it was, curved gently as if she were happy.

'Zea,' Flavia said the old woman's name gently, then again, but there was no answer. Taking the nerveless hand, she pressed it gently. 'God and His Blessed Mother be with you,' she whispered and then she got to her feet.

'She go to the arms of God very soon,' whispered the girl, and Flavia nodded agreement.

Back in the kitchens, aware of time passing by, she questioned the women as to their knowledge of medicine, learning that there was an ample supply of health-giving herbs, brews and potions, ointments and unguents and so on, kept in a cupboard at the back of the cold room where dairy foods were stored. Going to the place, she found that everything was neatly arranged and in good order, but nothing was labelled.

'Does anyone here know what all these things are?' she asked, but the women shrugged and said no.

'Who put them here, then?' Hearing the name of the old seer, she experienced a moment of sharp desolation. How could she give any of these to her lover when some might heal and some might exacerbate his condition? 'Surely someone can recognize these herbs by their colour and smell?'

Two or three women came forward to examine the bunches of greenery, and eventually half a dozen or so names were proffered. Then one of the women confided that none of them wanted to be responsible for the death of their great leader.

'It would help a great deal if one of you could tell me which are the most dangerous things here, so that I can put them out of harm's way,' Flavia said, her voice impatient now. This remark bore some fruit, for digitalis was removed as a potential killer if used in the wrong conditions, and so were another four or five tinctures.

'One of you must have used something for a fever at one time,' Flavia insisted. 'Do none of you recall a cure?'

Two names were hesitantly put forward, but these could not be identified with any of the bottles, so she was back where she started. Heaving a sigh, she left the women and ran back to Zardos, dreading that he might be worse.

The woman sitting with him looked askance as she entered, and when Flavia looked at her lover she saw why.

A rash had broken out on his chest, and his breathing was rasping.

Her heart lurched. She knew of a terrible illness which haunted London and which had symptoms very like this. She had never seen a victim but she had heard the symptoms being discussed. Terror broke into her mind. Typhus. She knew its nickname too: gaol fever, because that was where it often broke out, being carried by lice.

'Typhus is usually fatal, and God help those who recover, for they are but ghosts of their former selves.' Those words came back to her like a curse. An old physician, a friend of her father's, had said them, years ago. And she knew nothing, absolutely nothing of how to treat it.

Impotence was like a disease of its own, flooding through her veins and stupefying her wits. What must she do? Words rang through her head. Fever. Intense heat. Lice. Bites. Rash. He was fiery with fever to her touch. Should he not be cooled in some way or would that make him worse? Oh God, if only she knew what to do!

Perhaps she had not cleaned him properly the night before and some of those vile lice still lingered on him? Having no notion as to what other course she could take, she began to bathe him again, even more thoroughly than the previous time, lathering soap and hot water on a sponge and wincing if she was rough and broke open one of the cuts. These seemed to be healing well, thankfully, but they would become infected if she broke the scabs. The closest of examinations revealed no lice, and she had no way of knowing how the Turks had washed him before putting on his new finery. A loop of rope had been put round his neck and beneath his arms, and he had been lowered into a vat of some foul fluid, his head being dipped beneath the surface some half dozen times until he nearly choked. Thus all the lice had been removed, but his long months of hell in the foul and stinking dungeon had done their work. When a prisoner died, the lice leapt off him to lie in wait in the fouled straw for the next meal to be ushered in to them. The man who had occupied Zardos's cell before him had died of typhus, but of course neither of them knew this.

The washing over, and fresh unguents gently massaged into his wounds, Flavia sat beside her lover, knowing that if he were to die, then she wanted to die with him.

At regular intervals, she managed to get some watered wine down his throat, and every time his linen felt damp to the touch, she took if off, bathed him in cool water scented with roses and dressed him in a fresh shirt. The fever was now so great that he was delirious. In England, the physicians would have been cupping and bleeding him, trying out their brutal methods for saving life which more often than not hastened death. Slithering black leeches would have been applied to his veins at regular intervals, and now and then a vein cut so that blood could flow copiously into a bowl, for it was believed that this reduction in vital fluids greatly aided the patient.

If only she knew all the symptoms of typhus. If only she could identify the fever, and yet what more could she do, even if she knew what it was?

Zardos was now in a stupor. He could not respond to her coaxing words nor move himself unaided. His ebony hair was slick with sweat and the rash seemed to become brighter even as Flavia looked at it. His flesh was bruised and blue as if he had been beaten and she wondered if his blood was poisoned in some way. Hours dragged by, growing into days and she could no longer force even a drop of water down his throat, for his jaw was clamped shut.

Ezta, who had been forbidden to come near the sick room because of her pregnancy, sent a message that Flavia must take some rest. She must bathe and eat a strengthening meal which Ezta had prepared for her.

'How can I leave him?' Flavia sent her message back.

'Just for a short time, and after you will feel so much better,' Ezta replied.

'I am sorry. I would love to eat your meal, in different

circumstances, but how can I now? Pray for us, Ezta.'
Flavia sent back.

Three days, then four, drifted by and Flavia had become so weak that she could not countenance the thought of food. So it might have gone on until she died beside her lover if he had not stirred, opened his eyes and whispered her name. A sob catching in her throat, she leaned over him, gazing adoringly into his eyes.

'My darling, how are you feeling?'

He said her name again, but she could see that it caused him agony to swallow. Clasping his hands, she told him that she loved him, that he must get well, for she could not live without him. At this, an almost bemused expression filled his eyes, to be followed by a frown as if of alarm.

'Do you think you can drink something? Water, or wine? Some milk?'

Holding his head, she helped him to sip some goat's milk, after which he sank down into a fitful sleep. She prayed that the fever had turned, that the crisis was past, but he was too weak even to lift his arms or support his own head. Tomorrow he would have been like this for six days. It seemed a lifetime.

Turning away, tears jewelling her eyes, she clamped her lips shut on her sobs. She did not want to see her god-like hero wasting away, growing feebler by the hour, the flesh and the muscles evaporating from his very bones. If she was forced to watch this happen, then she would put the blame entirely upon herself. She was incompetent, ignorant, useless. It was a woman's job to nurse and nurture, to cure the sick, and soothe them, yet what had she done beside bathe and watch over him? Anyone could have done that! Anyone. She worshipped him, so that by rights she should be able to help him more than others, yet she could not. Clenching her fists, she crept from the room and ran down the corridor to weep where he could not hear her. There, she had to clutch at the cold, rough stone, for dizziness swept through her head. She could not remember when she had eaten last; her stomach seemed to have closed in upon itself. Holding shaking hands to her mouth, and trembling from head to foot, she slumped against the jagged wall.

'*Highness!*' Ezta's voice floated into her ears like a ghostly whisper, and then strong arms were supporting her, and she was being carried down into the kitchens where warmth, gossip and bustling activity were halted at the sight of her ashen face.

'*Pringipisa!*' the women cried, rushing to help her as Elisavet and Athanasia bore her to a bench.

'Food, bring her food,' Ezta ordered, chafing Flavia's hands. 'That heated milk with honey, and some *feta* – Her Highness loves *feta*.'

Their voices came from a vast distance, like faint echoes eddying back at her from a mountain, and as Flavia struggled for composure she saw Ezta's face.

'Stay away, the contagion!' she cried, but Ezta would hear none of it.

'Me no go 'way,' she said firmly. 'Stay with you!'

The milk was as fragrant as the nectar of the gods and she sipped it avidly. How stupid of her to think that she was not hungry. Now suddenly she was violently so. They gave her minced meat cooked with herbs and onions, and then one of the dark-red juicy tomatoes which tasted like no others in the world. The women planned to take it in turns to watch over their leader while she rested, they said, and this time she did not refuse their offer, but she did say that she would sleep for only a very short time.

She slept the clock round, and was totally disorientated when she awoke. Dark fearful shadows gyrated on the wall; she felt sticky and very stiff. What was more, she was ravenous. Leaping up, she flung off her clothes, washed, donned a peasant blouse and embroidered skirt, and a little woollen bodice which Ezta had decorated with flowers for her.

It was late evening, and she thought that she must have been asleep for about seven hours. Later, to her disbelief, she would find that she had lost a day. Rushing into

Zardos's room, she found him propped up on a pillow. Slowly and painfully, he was eating *tiropitakia*, flaky pastry triangles stuffed with hot cheese, and sipping watered wine. Beside him stood an empty cup. As she glanced at that, she caught the eye of Elisavet who was watching Zardos eat, her face shining. Later she would find out what was in that cup. For now, she went to her lover's side, smiling broadly. He still looked desperately pale and his eyes were dull, but he managed a smile for her.

'You should have gone away sooner, then I could have cured him all the quicker,' Elisavet grumbled, and it was hard to tell how serious she was. A stocky, very dark woman with more than a hint of Turkish blood in her fierce eyes, she was also very superstitious, believing emphatically in charms and lucky omens.

'How did you cure him, Elisavet?'

'Olive oil in boiled water. I knelt before the Virgin's statue and offered the mixture to her for her blessing. It saved my son's life many years ago when he had a fever.'

'What a splendid idea.' Flavia looked into Zardos's eyes, which were almost black with twinkling humour. 'We must give thanks to the Virgin.'

The next few hours were blissful, sweet with tenderness. Hands linked, they gazed adoringly into each other's eyes.

When it was time to sleep, Flavia curled up on the trestle bed in the corner of the sick room after she had settled Zardos for the night. Lying in the darkness, hearing the soft sigh of his breathing was heaven. The fever was over. Her lover was safely returned to her.

CHAPTER TWENTY

She had reckoned without the pugnacity of the man whose name was a legend throughout Greece. Lie in bed like a woman who had given birth and be waited on? *Never!* First, Zardos insisted on sitting up, and then by the end of the second day he got out of bed and staggered to a chair. When Flavia returned with his dinner, she was shocked.

'Zardos, you must not get up yet! You have been so ill for over a week. You have hardly eaten . . .'

'Lying down for so long will turn my muscles to water and make my mind weak. Would you have me staggering about on a stick like a *papous*?'

'There are many grandfathers hale and upright because they have cared for themselves,' Flavia protested. 'We do not even know what the fever was. How do we know . . .'

He cut her off. 'Whatever it was, it has gone. What is for dinner? It smells divine.'

'Roasted fish, and *mezzes* of liver and garlic, with moussaka cooked to Ezta's recipe, and of course salad.'

Zardos fell on the food, Flavia watching with a deep pleasure as he ate. She imagined that she could see him filling out before her eyes, and the healthy colour flooding back into his cheeks, but she foresaw a time when he might become fractious, for it was well known that strong and active men made the worst invalids. She did not know how she would get round it. As his nurse, he should do what she told him but if he refused, how could she argue with the man whom she adored?

Having eaten, they sat holding hands and talked of the long months of loneliness which were now behind them. Flavia gave Zardos all the news which he had missed, and was moved to see tears fill his eyes when he heard of Constantin's death.

'He was a valiant youth. His dreams were my dreams and his hopes were my hopes. Had he lived, he would have been a worthy successor to me.'

'Before he died, he arranged for the mercenaries to come, including Jacques-Pierre. Because of them, we were able to set you free.'

'That was what Constantin most wanted to do: to set men free.'

'In helping to free you, he would count it as freeing the whole of Greece. He knew you were the only man who could lead all these different factions, the *Kleftes* and the mountain men, the ones who have lived in the hills and become vagabonds and bandits. Under you, they can turn all their energies to expelling the Turks.'

'I can see that you have been changing your mind on one or two matters,' Zardos's eyes twinkled. 'Where now is the haughty girl who called me by every insulting name, while believing that the Turks were angels?'

'She is dead,' Flavia whispered, blushing a little. 'Youth must be allowed its fantasies. I have grown up now.'

He gripped her wrist lovingly. 'I can see that. When Captain Trakakios came to see me this morning, he spoke of you as if you were one of the warrior-goddesses. Artemis, or the embodiment of the Panayia herself.'

'What is the Panayia?'

'The Virgin of Battle, a Christian warrior goddess. You will find temples to her in the places where once stood temples to Artemis/Diana, the Virgin of the Hunt and young maidens. The Madonna has many guises.'

'I prefer her as the Miraculous Virgin. Does she need to be known as anything else?'

'I suppose not.'

They looked at one another. How strange it was to be lovers and friends while they were still strangers, and, so recently, enemies. How could she ever have considered him an enemy, she thought? Was he not the dearest friend she would ever have? Her heart trembled with joy at the mere thought of him.

Next day when she brought his breakfast of dried figs, grapes and goat's milk with honey, she found him walking round the room, gripping onto the furniture for support, his face ashen, and sweat running in streams down his face.

'Zardos! Get back into bed at once! You must not strain yourself like this!'

For a moment he was mighty Zeus, enraged at her temerity in rebuking him, a spasm of anger searing across his face and then vanishing. He did not do as he was told. Instead, he went on struggling to walk, forcing his weakened muscles to work, while she stood in the doorway watching, tears in her eyes.

Only when he had completed his exercise did he get back into bed, falling onto the pillows, the breath scouring his lungs cruelly so that she feared for him. He tried to hide his discomfort, but she could see by his pallor how distressed he was.

'If I am to nurse you back to health, then you must do as I say,' she insisted gently.

'I have never taken orders from a woman and I do not plan that I should begin now!' he gasped, 'I have work to do. I cannot lie around like a woman when Greece needs me.'

'Greece has need of women too, but it is insulting them to say that they lie around. The women of Greece work every bit as hard as their men.'

'It takes no strength to wash vegetables and stir the cooking pot,' Zardos growled.

'Is that how you see a woman? Some have good minds, you know, keen minds.'

'Ah yes. Jacques-Pierre is greatly impressed with yours. He calls you the great battle princess. He said that you commanded his men while I was in prison, and that they all loved you for it.'

She felt herself blushing. 'I – I was coerced into it. I did not see how I could get out of doing it. Anyway, I didn't command them. I went to inspect them, to welcome them to Greece.'

There was a strange feverish glitter in his eyes, and she was frightened by it for she could not see what he was thinking. He was angry, yes, but why?

'It is exciting to be the centre of attention, to imagine that you are still as important as if Zebukar had lived.'

'Oh!' Now she understood – or thought she did. 'I did not do it for that. Jacques-Pierre asked me and I complied, that is all.'

'And who is this Jacques-Pierre?' His face was grim.

'Who is – ? But you know that, he is a mercenary captain hired in your name by Constantin . . .' She was puzzled.

'Yes, *hired*! Do not forget that, hired! Yet you do as he commands as if you are his servant and he is your master.'

'It was not like that at all. Oh, you are incorrigible!' She whirled on her heel to leave the room, but he summoned her back, imperiously.

'Princess Musbah, bride of the Headsman of Allah. Do you think any of us will ever forget why you came here to Greece? To marry our Turkish overlord, a foreigner who invaded our land and defiled it with his barbarous savagery! How can we ever overlook that? We would as soon forget our own mothers!'

'Then do not forget it, do not!' she cried, crushing back her tears. His face was strained and twisted; she wanted to run to him and cradle him in her arms but the almost ferocious look in his eyes kept her away. Turning, she ran in the opposite direction, her legs as soft as tissue.

She found one of the small balconies, and even though the rain was crashing down in bright, soaking arrows, she stood in the fresh air and fought for control. How had it happened? One minute they had been sweetly loving, the next he was raging at her. The things he had said . . . Did he really have such a low opinion of women, of her? After all she had done for him? Greek men were worshipped by their wives, that she knew. They had dominion over them, as the Turks had dominion over Greece. Lords and masters

295

in their own home, Greek husbands were waited on and revered. Living a simple, agrarian life, it was easy to do that. There was no gay social round for the women; when time was available, it was the men who socialized. Women were present at weddings and birth festivities and deaths, but apart from that they usually stayed at home cleaning and cooking while the men gossiped and drank *raki* and *ouzo* beneath the sun, or so Ezta had assured her. With the Turks lurking everywhere now it was difficult to relax. Sensible people kept to their homes as much as possible. They would work in the fields and on the vines before sun up, then enjoy the long afternoon of rest or sleep, then more work until the evening, with a late dinner. That was how it was in Crete, Ezta assured her.

She was oblivious to the arrows of rain which dashed themselves madly against the stonework, just missing her head. How very dearly she wanted to understand these Greeks, her lover's people. Think of the men gossiping and sipping their potent wines as if they were men in the coffee houses in London, she told herself. Yet she knew that the women who were married or related to the Londoners would be enjoying company of their own, meeting for tea or hot chocolate, to exchange news and discuss the latest fashions. She had relished that life, and the freedom of a privileged English girl, daughter of the aristocracy. Would Zardos expect her to be cowed and meek? To think of nothing but food and washing his shirts, of bearing his children and then cleaning, washing and cooking for them too? Could she stand that, for it smacked of a subjugation which was little better than slavery.

A coldness knifed through her. New dreams are as brittle as dried herbs. The slightest friction and they turn into powder for the breeze to carry away. Whatever had happened between them those long months ago had been potent magic. Once, a witch's spells had been called glamours and casting a glamour on someone was the equivalent of casting a spell. From that had sprung the word glamorous. She thought of that now. With Zardos, it had been so glamorous, rich and delicate, romantic and heady, a delicious fantasy which she had craved desperately after the shock and bewilderment of the weeks before. In his arms she had been reborn, refreshed, revived. Her life had begun anew, and, like a chrysalis she had broken out of her constricting cocoon to unfurl her wings in his sunlight.

'I am alone,' she whispered. 'I must not think of myself in any other way but alone. It is weakness to depend on another for my happiness. Weak, and foolish too. If he leaves me . . .' She corrected herself. 'When he leaves me, what shall I do if I cannot live without him?'

The drumming of the rain continued, day after day. Ezta said that it was always like this in December and January. 'How else would the grapes and the vines grow?' she shrugged. 'Sometimes, we have seven, or eight months, even, without rain, so we need this.'

A message was brought downstairs to Flavia. Zardos told her to come to him at once. Smiling, she told Elisavet that she was busy.

'Tell Lord Alexandros that I am fully occupied stirring soup and washing vegetables,' she said to the puzzled Greek woman, who raised her brows, but did as she was asked.

The message came back that Zardos hoped that the soup and vegetables were for his dinner, at which Flavia's mouth fell open in disgust. Did he think she was his slave?

'Tell him – Tell him it is for the French captain's dinner,' she instructed Elisavet, whose eyes bulged quite frighteningly at this. She pulled urgently at Flavia's sleeve and asked her to repeat the message, which Flavia did. Shuffling away to relay it, Elisavet's eyes remained as blank as if she had been stunned. Well, if the great and almighty Zardos Alexandros took offence, then it was too bad, thought Flavia, but she trembled all the same. What had she done?

Flavia told no one how empty and vapid her days seemed now. Routine tasks could never occupy her lively mind, her questing intellect. Jacques-Pierre and his men went off on a sortie, leaving a skeleton command to protect the fortress and its occupants. Dull was the word which sprang to mind without the noisy, rustic mercenaries about the place, drilling and gossiping, swilling *retsina* and *ouzo* and gobbling their meals like ravenous beasts. Furthermore, it was not considered seemly by any of the women that their Princess should wait on common men-at-arms and so there was no work to take up Flavia's time in the kitchens. If only she and Zardos were still speaking . . . She knew that lovers had quarrels; she knew that he had been through a terrible ordeal, yet he had said such cruel, decimating things to her. Did he still think of her like that, even though she had risked her life to rescue him from prison?

She went for long walks round the ramparts and across the courtyards, peering out through the stone arrow slits to the countryside beyond. Brush and scrub, flat plains stretching for mile after mile, olive trees, ancient and majestic, some of them a hundred years old and more but still bearing fruit. If Icarus had flown over Greece dropping trillions of mixed seeds, then the result would have been exactly like this. She had looked out on this scenery too often, she knew; such a pastime was more suited to the aged and housebound. Such a delicious taste of adventure she had experienced while Zardos was away . . . The warrior-princess revered by her troops, indefatigable, triumphant in battle after battle, the blood of Atlantis in her veins. But now she was getting herself confused with Atalanta again. No man would ever have told *her* what to do!

It was back to the dreary, aimless days of her early stay in the fortress, and it seemed as if there was nothing she could do about it. She would rather die than go into his room and beg apology. He should be apologizing to her yet it was plain that he had no intention of doing that. Lord Alexandros the Almighty was back on his throne . . .

'*Pringipisa, pringipisa*, come quickly!' Elisavet's terrified voice shrilled against her ears. The stocky woman, scarlet for want of breath and the speed of movement, almost fell on Flavia. '*Pringipisa*, Lord Zardos, he, he, please, *please* to come quickly!'

He was dead! She knew he was dead! He had got up too soon and strained himself, exhausted his energies and had a fatal relapse. There was always the danger of that after a high fever. Shock dried her eyes and lent mercurial speed to her feet. With Elisavet panting behind her, muttering disjointed *Hail Marys* when she could gasp them out, she arrived in the sick room.

CHAPTER TWENTY-ONE

He was on the floor, and for a moment she thought he was dead, that his heart had given out after the severity of the fever and the long months of torture and malnutrition. She glanced at Elisavet, hoping for clarification of what had happened, but the Greek woman was gibbering, her fingers stuffed in her mouth. In one stride, Flavia was across the room and kneeling by him. She knew that if she had paused to think she would have collapsed, or run away.

Her palms on his back, she could feel the feverish beat of his heart. He was still alive!

'Help me, Elisavet!'

The woman continued to gibber, her feet rooted to the ground. Gritting her teeth, Flavia struggled to turn Zardos onto his back. His skin had a yellowish, translucent tinge and sweat poured from him. The feverish rigours were growing stronger.

'If you cannot help me, then find someone who can!' she shouted at the petrified woman, and was rewarded by Elisavet turning on her stumpy heels and vanishing. 'Dear God, let me not be too late,' she prayed as she waited, a rug thrown over her lover. 'If he dies, God, I go too and nothing can stop me. If he dies, then Allah will take all of Greece and your Mother will be forsaken for all time . . . Miraculous Virgin, give me strength to make him well!'

Two squat and burly soldiers appeared, took one look, and within seconds Zardos was back on the bed. Having thanked them, Flavia asked them to bring bowls of hot and cold water, fresh linen and a clean shirt for their master. They bowed low before walking out of the room backwards, as if she were an empress. Not that such refinements bothered her now. Turning to her lover, she wiped his streaming brow and spoke to him.

'My darling, you are going to get well, I vow it. Whatever this wretched fever is, we shall conquer it together, you and I.' She held his hands. They were ragingly hot. His eyes looked bruised and sunken, his face was grey. Was this the final stage of the illness, whatever it was? Some strange variety of lapsing fever which allowed the sufferer to rally before he died? Her heart felt as if all the blood had dried up inside it, and her veins were tightening, like cords crushing away her life. She knew that she was feeling what he was feeling; they were so close that her body was emulating his symptoms. And when he died, so would she.

The rigours were now so violent that his entire diaphragm rose up with each one, and the bed shook. The men-at-arms came back in double quick time to bring what she had ordered, and at once she began to bathe Zardos, first in hot water and soap, and then in cold. Afterwards, she dressed him in the clean shirt and changed the soaking sheets as best she could with the weight of his body on them. Still the rigours continued, and he became blue round the mouth and so pinched that his face looked small and frightened like a child's. She knew then what she must do. Stripping off her own clothes, she climbed into the bed with him, and wrapped herself round him like a heat-giving tourniquet. For a long time he went on shivering painfully, his body like a torch, then she moved around to his other side to ensure that she warmed every part of him. Not once did she think of contagion or of the risk to herself. Even if she had done, she would not have cared.

Night imprisoned them like a shroud and the hours dragged by, an interminable burden.

Reluctantly she drifted into unnerving and crazy dreams. A woman rigged out in glittering armour was galloping by on a superb stallion, ranks of men following behind. There was a banner fluttering at the head of the army, and it was bright blue, with the symbol of eternal life embroidered on it in scarlet and gold, the cupped hands holding the orb. Was it an orb or her heart, for she could feel that beating pugnaciously in her ears? Then again it might be the beat of a thousand horses' hooves . . . What delight to ride into battle knowing that you possess the secret of eternal life; that you can never die or be killed. Atalanta was invincible, while she was alone, ah, how she was alone.

'*Princess!*'

His voice thundered in her ears and she thought he was well again. Turning, she went to enclose him in her arms and found that he was a black, rotting skeleton which dissolved into a choking grey dust when she touched him. She screamed, but no sound came. Next she saw him being buried, and she was standing at his graveside weeping tears of blood, her own blood gushing from her until she was lifeless. For they were not tears but the flow from her throat where she had cut herself, to die with him, like the Indian women who sacrificed themselves on their husband's burial pyres . . .

She woke with a terrifying jolt. The room was black and she could not recall anything for long moments. How close was death? Never far away. Too near, sometimes. Why had she been dreaming about a funeral? Hopes buried? Then she remembered and reached out for her lover. He was still shivering, but slightly now, and nothing like the earlier rigours. His clothes were soaked. Should she disturb him to make him more comfortable? She decided against it, for the night was chill. The rain had brought the temperature down, and even here it could sometimes be as cool and damp as an English autumn, as she had found out. Getting up, she bathed his face and hands and then climbed back in beside him. The terrible blue had gone from round his lips and they were almost pink again. She had forgotten to douse the taper and she examined his face closely before she got out of bed again. Her lover, her prince, yet she knew as little about him now as before. No, that was not true. She now knew that he was as staunchly Greek as his fellow countrymen who liked to see their womenfolk gainfully occupied in lowly female tasks. Perhaps they had learned this attitude from the Turks? They would not like anyone to suggest that, but it was true that the Turks had held sway in Greece since the sixteenth century, and such things had a habit of being assimilated.

Only two years ago she had been eager to be subordinate to a man, to adopt her husband's religion and change her way of life to that of a Muslim princess. In theory, English women were supposed to be beneath their husband's rule, but it was rare all the same, unless they chose it themselves. True, some men were despots but it was not a matter of course. No doubt in an English farmer's home, his wife went about her daily tasks exactly as did a Greek farmer's wife, or a Greek peasant's wife, but in the English upper classes a married woman was often free to live her own life as she pleased and many did — unless they happened to love their husbands and to be loved back.

Could she be subservient, a glorified cook and cleaner for this enigmatic, autocratic man? It might mean spending the rest of her life in some kitchen, and then, later, a nursery . . .

'Andrea,' he sighed, while she felt the snowy chill of shock. He had said a woman's name! Did he have another lover then? But surely not. Everyone treated her as his woman. Perhaps this Andrea was some light of love? Well, that was to be expected in a man of such passionate sensuality. Andrea may well be one of many in his past. And if they stayed in his past then it would not concern her, nor would she fret. She did not want to think of his having been too lonely before he met her, although she knew that he had grieved deeply for the mermaid dancer.

She fell asleep without dousing the taper, and when dawn silvered her face, she woke with alarm, but all was well. Zardos was sleeping gently, his breathing light and easy. His cheeks were healthy with a slight colour and his fever was dying. Offering up thanks to God and His Mother, she opened her eyes to find Zardos staring at her.

'Forgive me, sweetheart, did I fall asleep while we were

making love? That is unforgivable of me. This wretched weakness . . .'

She wanted to laugh out loud, to dance round the room and shout out that he was well and she loved him, but instead, she whispered, 'Go back to sleep, my darling. You were ill again, and I was keeping you warm.'

Within seconds, he was doing just that. She stared into his face adoringly before she too drifted off to sleep again.

A Greek sunrise is like the birth of Apollo and Aurora. Hands linked, bright, gilded hair flowing, dressed in silvery-orange robes, they rise upwards into the skies with laughing mouths, while their radiance grows ever stronger and more dazzling, the flood of their power shimmering and vibrating so that the sun appears to move and tremble, to vibrate with life. Flavia could well understand how the ancients had worshipped the sun as a deity, the giver of all life. Blinded by pure, shimmering gold, she turned back towards her lover who was still sleeping. If only she could take some of the strength from the sun and pour it back into his limbs, fleshing him out like a young god fashioned from gold dust and the breath of Zeus himself. But she could not. He was going to take some time to recover from this relapse, but next time he was not going to be allowed to dominate her. She would keep him in bed until she decided he was fit enough to walk. When a man was truly strong, he did not become weak while proving his strength.

Breakfast was brought for them, and yet Zardos was too weak to eat. He managed to swallow some honeyed milk and then slept again. Elisavet whispered to Flavia that the entire household had spent the night praying at the foot of the replica of the Miraculous Virgin.

'Then she has performed yet another miracle,' Flavia whispered back. 'Tell them so. Tell them their prayers cured him. And tell them to keep praying! He is not over the worst yet.'

He slept for two more days while Flavia washed and tended to his needs. How she welcomed this healing sleep, for it meant that she could care for him without argument, without being flung out of his room. Yet after a while, she longed for the old Zardos back with all his fire and spirit. This was a ghost, and she knew how close he had been to becoming that permanently.

When Jacques-Pierre returned from his sortie he begged to see her. Not understanding what he wanted, she agreed to meet him in the small hall. There, he bowed very low and stared at her with serious eyes. She could never have guessed what was to come next.

'Highness, we need a leader,' he began, an almost pleading look in his eyes. 'With Contantin dead, and Lord Alexandros ill for so long, we do not know what to do, where to go. The men talk of you, of how you rode to meet them when they landed. They remember it with joy. They speak of the old legend which says that when Greece most has need of her, the warrior-queen, Atalanta, will rise again and cast out our adversaries.'

Flavia was genuinely puzzled. 'But what has that to do with me?'

'Highness, they think that you are she, that the legend has become fact before their eyes. They have no doubt of it, none at all.'

'They think that I . . .' she almost smiled. 'I cannot imagine anyone less like a warrior-queen than myself! Are you serious? You are telling me that those tough men want a woman to lead them?'

'It happened in the ancient days, Highness. There were many warrior-queens then, of your country too, but none as successful and feared as Atalanta. She came from nowhere with her armies and drove out the foe who were crushing our land, and she ruled here until peace reigned as powerfully as did she. Then she vanished exactly as she had come. They say that the gods bore her body away in the night, and that it is buried on Mount Olympus.'

For some reason, Flavia felt a flicker of anger. 'Well, if she is dead and buried, how can we be the same woman? Really, I cannot talk of such things while Lord Alexandros is so ill. It is, well, it is almost like treachery.'

'Treachery talking of a leader for our beleaguered soldiers? *Non*, Highness, it is not that! Lord Alexandros must have a second-in-command who is as trusted and respected as Constantin was.'

'And *I* am? A foreigner who was married to one of your hated overlords? You are saying that they trust and respect me?' Thinking of Zardos's words, she said, 'How do you know that I am not a spy?'

Jacques-Pierre grinned disarmingly. 'The day that olives can be eaten straight from the tree then will you be a spy, Highness. In love, you are one with our leader. You came here as mysteriously as Queen Atalanta did, and you have won our hearts. We know that you are to marry Lord Alexandros one day and bear his sons. They will be future leaders of our land, a land which shall be free and glorious when the enemy has been driven out.'

Flavia turned away with tears in her eyes. If only she could share his optimism, but he had not seen her drained and enervated lover who was barely able to sip milk. As for marriage, well, he had never mentioned it. And as for sons . . .

Turning back, her voice choked, she said, 'I truly hope that day will come. I want it as much as you and all your fellow countrymen but if a second-in-command is needed, then you must go out and choose him yourself, or find someone who has the authority to do so.'

'I do not think that you understand, Highness. If you will forgive me for being the audacious one and explaining: we wish *you* to be that person.'

Flavia sighed heavily. 'I have told you that it is not possible. How can I do that? Would you have me wearing armour and bearing arms? Riding out to battle with you? I know nothing of such things. I can ride a horse, but that is all. Besides, I cannot think that there would be much of me left to marry your leader if I went into battle knowing as little about its tactics as I do!'

'We would die before we let you be harmed, Highness!' Jacques-Pierre looked outraged that she could think anything else. 'You are our lady of good fortune. With you, we shall not ever lose a battle, just as it was with Atalanta herself. She is still spoken of as if she still lives, as if she will return any day.'

'If your men wish to put me in her place, then I do not suppose I can do anything about it, but you must have a man to take over while Lord Alexandros is ill. I beg you to choose one soon so that valuable time is not lost, and morale is maintained.'

'He is badly ill then?' His eyes burned with a basalt sadness.

'Very badly ill. I do my best to care for him, but he got up too soon, and now he is weaker than before. If only we had a physician. I think of how famous the Greek doctors were thousands of years ago.'

'It was so, but now our leading physicians are in prisons or fled, or in bondage to the Turks.'

'Look for a new temporary general, and tell the men to keep praying for their leader, if they love him.'

Dropping to his knees, Jacques-Pierre took her hand, kissing it ardently, but it was the ardour of a devoted servant with more worship in it than passion. Surprised, she said nothing.

When he had gone, she returned to the sick room to ponder over what he had said. It sounded so improbable. In a country where women were revered in the kitchen and the bed, they wanted her to be their leader . . . Really, these Greeks were as unfathomable today as they had been in ancient times! She could only hope that it would be forgotten, and that they would find a suitable male general.

She was not to be left in peace, however. The young captain was back again in a few days, begging for further news of their leader and asking if she had changed her mind. No, she told him, she had not changed her mind, nor was she likely to.

Two days later he was back again. She told him that Lord Alexandros was slightly better, and that she had no intention of changing her mind whatever the captain said, however much he begged her. It was not women's work, she said, and Lord Zardos would be the first to agree.

It was a chilly day and the rain had lifted for a few hours. The bow and arrow was heavy, heavier than anything she had imagined. How did men carry these and march into battle in heavy armour and chain mail as they had done when the bowmen of England were feared throughout Christendom? When she stretched the bowstring ready to fire, her breast muscles ached furiously. The first arrow went completely wide of its target and slumped into a bale of straw. So did the second, but this time the bale of straw was three yards to the left. The third arrow dropped to the ground at her feet with a dull twanging noise. Despite herself she giggled. She was hopeless.

Staring the target straight in the eye, she clenched her jaw. This time she would do it!

The bowstring twanged and the arrow made as if to leave and then dangled on the string in the most embarrassing fashion.

'I shall never do it!' she cried. 'This whole thing is a farce!'

'Highness, please be patient,' Jacques-Pierre pleaded. 'No one can become an expert overnight. You have days in which to practise. It needed only one arrow to kill King Rufus and King Harold, do not forget that. Soon you will be adept.'

She shuddered at the thought of firing an arrow which killed anything, let alone a human being, but, the mercenaries apart, they were desperately short of weapons, and short of food too. Scouts had reported that the Turks were everywhere. A messenger had returned to tell them that Hassani was mad with rage at losing the Pagan only hours before his execution, and he had begun to wreak a fearful vengeance on the Greeks. He was giving orders that whole villages be burnt to the ground, the women and young girls despatched to Turkey for the Sultan's harem or any

308

harems in which he chose to place them, while the men were either treated to whippings or the bastinado, the terrible torture so beloved by the Turks. For this, victims were hung upside down and their feet beaten savagely until they fainted – or died – from the agony.

Some homeless youngsters had been brought to the fortress, and now there were two dozen able-bodied girls and boys who needed feeding along with the rest. The boys had begun drilling, and the girls sewing coats for the mercenaries.

Soon after this, Flavia had told Jacques-Pierre that she wanted to learn how to handle a gun. He told her that they did not have many and that most of the ones they had were old or dangerous, or both.

'Then what else can I learn to use?' she had said. Jacques-Pierre, eyes gleaming, had told her that a bow and arrow was a deadly weapon in the right hands.

'Most of the other weapons we have are of the bludgeoning variety which require brute strength, Highness. Cudgels, staves, daggers and so on.'

'Swords?'

'We have those, but not as many as we need. A shipment is on its way – if it gets through.'

'Then I shall begin with the bow and arrow. After all, it was good enough for my forebears.'

And so here she was, out on the ramparts. A hastily-fashioned target had been made from charcoal sketched on a block of pale wood, with bales of straw as protection around it. Here the men practised too, along with the youngsters who had recently arrived.

'What better weapon for fighting off besiegers?' Jacques-Pierre comforted as Flavia's fifth arrow vanished into eternity over the fortress wall.

'So you think we are in for a siege?'

He looked uncomfortable, flinging his arms in a colourful Greek gesture while at the same time managing a very Gallic shrug.

'Who knows? Yes.' Now he looked shame-faced.

'What else did the messenger say? I thought he told me everything.'

'He did. Well, almost, Highness. The, er, the Turks are closer than we thought. Their general is on his way – Muhammad Baswar. You know the name?'

She had gone white. 'Of course I know him! He captured Lord Alexandros! Come, tell me it all, Captain. There is more, is there not? Oh, how could you keep this from me?'

'Hassani has vowed to kill our leader with his own hands – but he is a greasy coward, everyone knows that. He will never risk his own life. Not until Baswar has incapacitated our leader will he stick in the knife.'

Flavia swallowed. There was a ringing in her ears.

'He will never do that! *Never!*'

'Decidedly *non*, Highness. However, now that Hassani knows how you helped our leader to escape, he guesses that you are here with him. Unfortunately, one of our men was captured and under the torture of the bastinado he gave away our position.'

Flavia could not speak. Moments ago, she had been grinning at her ineptitude with this huge and cumbersome weapon, wondering if she could ever bring herself to aim it at a rabbit or a hare, let alone a man, and now . . . In her mind's eye, she saw Hassani's vast, grotesque belly bulging over his groin and then she saw herself taking aim at it with her bow and arrow. Next moment, the arrow was arcing through the air and thudding into the shivering tumulus of lard. Yes, she could shoot *him*!

'Why did you wait until now to tell me?'

'When the messenger came Lord Alexandros was still so weak. He is stronger now. Yesterday, you said that he was going to get well. So you are stronger now – strong enough to take this news.'

'That is true.' A blast of damp wind gusted against her back and she shivered. Zardos would be waking soon and he would expect to see her sitting serenely at his bedside with his supper. He had no idea what she got up to while he slept.

310

He managed a pale smile as she came into the room.

'I am told that you saved my life, yet you would not tell me that yourself.'

'It would be boasting. All I did was keep you warm when you became ill again.'

'How many others would have done it?'

'Every woman in Greece if she had been given the chance!' she teased.

'Ah so you say, but would they have been willing to risk contracting a virulent fever?'

'Elisavet was quite happy to watch over you while I rested.'

'Somehow I do not think that I would have enjoyed Elisavet in bed with me naked as you were, Princess . . .' His eyes sparkled.

'Who told you that I was, was . . .' she blushed furiously.

'That you were naked in bed with me, pressing your body against mine to keep me warm when I shook with fever? Perhaps I was only pretending to be sick, so that I could enjoy the delights of your beautiful breasts and thighs crushed against me . . .'

She gasped. 'You did that? No, I do not believe it!' Then she saw that he was teasing her, and trying to hide his laughter.

'Elisavet told me, of course. She came in during the night and saw what you were doing. She told everyone that you were saving my life.'

'They prayed all night for you before the replica of the Miraculous Virgin. I rather think that had more to do with it,' she smiled.

'Maybe, and being a good Christian I would not deny it, but for me that night you were my miracle.' He reached out to pull her down to him. 'I was damnably rude to you, sweet Princess, and I shall burn in hell for it. Can you forgive me for being the most abominable male who ever drew breath? I mistrusted you for so long, and the fever confused my brain, making me forget how you had rescued me from certain death.'

'Of course.' Tingles of sparkling delight were dancing through her at his touch. He had done right not to trust her at first. Had she not been the same with him? When their lips met it was like the joining of two souls who had been enduring an eternity in search of one another. Heaven sprang between them, caught them in its arms and held them close. Safe. At peace. There would be no more misunderstandings.

'I cannot recall much about my illness. How long has it lasted?' The departure of his mouth from hers left her feeling cold and insecure.

'Nearly three weeks in all. You had a rash. I thought you might have typhus, but the spots soon went.'

'And you were still willing to nurse me even when you thought I had that foul disease? It is the most contagious and dangerous of fevers.'

'I know.'

'Ah, Princess, how I have wronged you.' His eyes were softer than she had ever seen them, like limpid green jewels.

'Did you – did you think of me when you were in that terrible gaol?' she whispered.

'Of course. You were my sun to light my days and nights. I looked at the streaming walls and saw your gold and scarlet hair, and I looked at the window bars and thought of your beautiful, soft curving breasts and hips. I thought of when we made love and how I wanted you again – and again. I cursed myself for the unkindness I had shown you, and I thought I would never be able to make it up to you.'

She was blushing even more now and could not meet his eyes. Laughing, he tugged her closer still, and seeded tiny, tender kisses on her nose and cheeks and forehead, and then a long, lingering kiss to blossom on her lips.

'Everything grows at a terrific rate when the rains come,' he whispered in her ear, and if she had any doubt about what he meant, they vanished as she felt his steely hardness pressed against her.

'Zardos! You must not do that!' she cried. 'You are not strong enough! It will make you ill again.'

'Then tell me how I stop doing it?' he teased. 'You should not be so gloriously desirable.'

Whispering in his ear now, she said, 'Do you really think it is right that I should be here with you? Away from the kitchens I mean . . . There are pots of vegetables to be prepared and the soup is burning for want of stirring . . .'

'Vegetables? Soup? What are they, *agapiménos*?'

He had called her beloved, and it thrilled her with a trillion delicious sensations. More than anything else in the universe, she wanted him to love, adore and treasure her as she did him, but she knew that she must tread carefully. He had spoken so soulfully of his lost love, the beautiful dancer who had died so tragically. He had warned her that he could never give his heart again. His body, yes, but not his heart. She knew that she loved him desperately, that she would never stop loving him. She wanted to live and die in his arms.

'*Agapiménos?* Do you not hear me? The vegetables can moulder and the soup burn to dust, I do not care. When I am with you, I think only of you.'

'And when you are away from me, what then?'

'I told you. In my prison I warmed myself with my memories of you. When I hungered, I thought of you, of your soft, sweet laughter, your tender heart, of how proud and fiery you can be and yet beneath it all you are so vulnerable, so easily hurt.'

She was silent, startled by his astuteness, for of course he was right. How many others had guessed that?

'It would be simpler if I had no heart.'

'Simpler for whom? Not for me, for then you would not be my sunrise.'

Tears slipped down her cheeks as he pulled her into his embrace. 'I never thought you would think of me like that. When you told me you could never love again, I thought – I thought . . .' Her voice was muffled.

'That I meant it? Perhaps I did, or it might have been

313

foolish bravado. My months in prison changed that. If I could have taken back those words, then I would have done, believe me. I wanted to tear out my tongue . . .'

'Stop!' She placed her fingers on his lips.' All that is past now, let it be forgotten. We are together, and we must make the most of the time we have left.'

'I know.' He pulled her into the bed, dewing her with ardent kisses and she loved every second of it, but she had no intention of letting him exhaust himself when he was still so weak. After enjoying his closeness, she told him what she was thinking. He objected, of course, but she would not submit. She loved him too much to risk his health.

'Later, when you are strong,' she whispered, and then she slipped from his arms not looking back, for, if she had, then she would have pleaded with him to make love to her.

The Catamite

'Where is time? The lightest breeze has taken time out
    of my mind.
These pines are forever, the breath
wafted by the young thyme eternal . . .

And the rhythm of our horses now
seems the same rhythm that still lives
under obscure hoofprints of ancient horses
left in this same holy ground

No, it's not an illusion
for us to ride a dream on this godlike day
when everything, visible and invisible, we and the
    heroes and the gods too
move forward inside the same eternal sphere.'

Sikelianos

CHAPTER TWENTY-TWO

Hassani was breathing raspingly. He had contracted a chill while travelling in the rain to watch the Pagan being executed. He might have thrown off the illness quickly had he been able to relish seeing that execution, but the rebel leader had eluded him yet again. He had cursed so violently and behaved so strangely that his body servants had been afraid. They thought he had lost his mind. The fever had followed, and with the care of an Arab physician he had recovered, save for a wheezing chest after any exertion.

The sound of tabor and drum announcing the arrival of the dancers, Hassani leaned back, his mouth crammed with *Rahat Lokum* in his favourite flavours, rose and mulberry, a white dust of powdered sugar sparkling on his chin and drifting down onto his flabby chest. Sticking his finger into his mouth to loosen a wedge of the Turkish Delight which had jammed behind a rotting tooth, he probed and pushed until it was free, then pulped it with one greedy bite.

Six dancers entered in shimmering robes of silvered lamé, their *shalwar* cloth-of-gold beaded with ruby spangles or rose samite edged with silver fringing. One was taller than the others and slightly more ungainly. This one would need extra tuition he thought, clumsy creature, and not only dancing tuition, either. He smacked his lips in anticipation, feeling a twinge in his loins. Yes, things were getting back into working order, he was delighted to say.

The tall dancer wore a rose and silver skirt trimmed with tinkling bells, a rose-velvet bodice embroidered with indigo silks and a heavy rose-silk veil secured by a tiny pillbox hat over streaming silver tresses. The long whirling and twisting limbs sent a shiver down his spine. What soft, smooth legs and soft pale skin . . . Bright-blue eyes, so rare, enticed him from above the *yashmak*, and the skirt swayed and whipped sideways to reveal that the dancer was naked beneath it. Hassani's heart jumped painfully and he leaned forward, losing interest in the giant box of *Rahat Lokum* which was at his elbow. Tonight he would bed this silver-haired dancer with the sky-blue eyes, and he would be able to perform as he had done half a year ago, before the murderous bitch, Alliya, had set upon him. How he had enjoyed watching the hounds devouring the remains of her carcase.

The dancer knelt at his feet, kissing his insteps ardently and running a beringed and painted hand up his inner thigh, lightly touching what was hardening there, before withdrawing as if burned. He roared with laughter at this maidenly modesty, and saliva dripped from the corners of his stale, sticky mouth.

'What is your name?' he leered.

'Arita.' The word was whispered coyly.

'What is your religion?' He cared nothing for a dancer's creed as a rule, but this time he had a special reason for asking.

'I am a Muslim, great lord.'

'You are not Jewish?'

'Indeed no, great lord!'

'Get on with your dancing. Show me more of your thighs.'

'Yes, great lord.'

The other dancers, seeing that little notice was being taken of them increased their efforts to catch the royal eye but failed. Arita held Hassani's attentions for the next hour, until he was burning, aching, throbbing, with lust.

Later, in his scented silken bed, he ran his fingers through the glorious moonlight-coloured hair and kissed the bright blue eyes which were the colour of the sky after a great storm.

'Arita, where did you get all this hair?' he asked in wonderment.

'I grew it, great lord,' Arita giggled.

'It must have taken you many years.'

'Yes, great lord, many.'

'How did my slave master find you?'

'I was sold by my lord, Benazzi, to Mullahdi Pasha, who tired of me, and sold me to a slave master, who then sold me to your slave master, great prince.'

'Why did Mullahdi Pasha tire of you? Was he mad?'

Arita giggled again, and whispered something in Hassani's jewelled and scented ear at which Hassani roared with laughter. So Mullahdi Pasha was impotent, the boastful old dog. Hassani slid his hot, cushiony hand along Arita's thigh, marvelling at its softness. Giggling, Arita leaned forward to unfasten the glittering, embroidered bolero into which were tucked the false breasts. Naked from the waist up, Arita's body was smooth and golden, the muscles sheeny with oil and delicate, but nothing obtrusive or vulgarly masculine. Again the dancer whispered in Hassani's ear, telling him of the specialities to which he would introduce him. It appeared that Arita's prowess and stamina were extraordinary, with a man or a girl.

'Let me show you, great prince, then watch me with others, anyone you care to bring and it will be done.' Arita sighed rapturously as Hassani's hand cultivated the desired place.

It was almost too much for the Turkish prince. The streaming silver hair, the girlish face and figure, the soft velvet flesh, and in the midst of it all, the one thing which no woman could ever give him. With surging passions driving themselves through his body he threw himself onto Arita, his chest heaving with a passionate emotion which he had rarely experienced before.

Seeing the Prince's violent response, power raced through Arita's veins, flowering in his brain as it always did at moments like these; and there had been many, ever since he had been seduced as a small boy. Sex reduced everyone to the same level, princes, lords, even kings

319

became as low and obsequious as peasants. Arita was aware that he was possessed of amazing powers, and that he would very soon have this bloated, drooling man eating out of his palm, but for the moment he was relishing his hold over Hassani, while the Turk groaned in a delirium of excess.

Afterwards, Hassani laughed to himself. When the Princess Musbah was found, as she would be soon, he would force her to endure a thousand terrors. He would humiliate and crush her, the proud, rebellious bitch. Tortured, raped by Arita until she screamed for mercy, lacerated – perhaps even the bastinado for her tiny white feet – then, when she was sobbing her heart out, he would have her flung over the balcony of this very room, to her death on the marble tiles below. He would say that she had chosen to take her own life rather than be his bride. By then, the Sultan would have his jewel, as Zebukar's treasures would have been released, and all would be as before, save that Hassani's troubles would be over, and he would be even richer.

The door swung open to reveal Arita who had returned with two young boys, both of them slender and beautiful. They were going to entertain Hassani as only they could. Really this Arita was incredible. Five hours had passed and still the silver-haired dancer was untired. Hassani leaned back to enjoy the exhibition, unable to take his eyes from the rippling silvered skeins of Arita's magnificent hair.

The Sultan's reinforcements had arrived. They were well-nourished, well-rested and eager for the battle to come. There was also the matter of revenge, for many of them had lost friends and family in the recent battles with the Greek insurgents. Bloodlust was a quintessential element of their characters, and lust they did, with the same vigour which they displayed in their love lives. There had been frequent clashes as they marched inland from the sea. The

Kleftsmen were everywhere, behind rocks and bushes, concealed in the clefts of hills and boulders, once, even lying on a river bed, breathing through reeds, and leaping out as the Turkish cavalrymen were crossing the river.

Their Sultan had told them not to return if they failed. He had told them, too, that the *Kleftes* were virtually wiped out, but it was plain that this had been an over-optimistic statement. After the great battle when the infidel Pagan had been captured, it was believed that Greece was won, finally and forever for the Turks. Greek morale had evaporated, the remaining *Kleftes* were broken, wounded, petrified; they had no leader, and without their Pagan who had united them they would be impotent as children. Or so it was thought.

Muhammad Baswar was taut with a passion for vengeance which was like a poison brewing deep inside him. Honours had been heaped upon him after his brilliant conquest of the *Kleftes* and their leader, this success a palliative which had partially compensated for the sudden death of his favourite concubine, Medisha. She had died in childbirth, and his son had been stillborn. He knew that men were sneering behind their hands because he had lost two sons and had none to replace them. His rusty-brown hands gripping the reins of his horse tightened into savage knots. Glory had been his, but he had lost his son, and he knew that Medisha would have survived childbed if he had not brought her with him to this bleak and hostile country. The thought of the rebel Pagan, tortured and broken, had been his compensation, and he had planned to watch his execution and report in full detail to the Sultan.

The Pagan's escape had made fools of them all. The Turks cannot keep their prisoners, people were saying. They can hold their *khoshab* and their tongues, but not their prisoners. Of course the reference to *khoshab* was intended for him, and he had fumed over it. What good was it that he was the greatest general Turkey had ever seen if the prison guards allowed the Pagan to evade them?

He had been told of the various tortures to which the Pagan had been submitted, the bastinado, the savage beatings on the soles of the feet; being hung by the thumbs, for two hours daily; being dropped into water until near drowning, after which he had been revived only to be submerged again – and again. Lashings and near-starvation, too, of course. He knew of the plan to wreak vengeance on the *Kleftes* leader, after which would come a period when Alexandros would be fed properly and kept in comfort so that when he went to his execution he would appear as strong and vigorous as he had been before his capture. It had seemed an excellent idea, and he had applauded it. There was no sense in taking a shambling, broken wreck to the scaffold, for who would see him as a man to be feared? If he were not fiercesome, then the Turks were not great to have brought him down.

His son. Often in his mind's eye, he imagined the boy as he would have been had he lived. Tall already, even though he would be too young to walk as yet. Dark, of course, and perhaps with the blaze of ivory hair inherited from his father, and which his grandfather before him had possessed. He had chosen a posthumous name for the boy, Muhammad Mulli, and he prayed to Allah for him just as if he were alive. He had seen the dead baby, the body blackened as if bruised, for Medisha had been in labour four days. His little black son who had suffocated to death . . .

Part of his revenge had been to take four Greek girls captive and rape them, before allowing them to be submitted to other suitable indignities. Naked, they had been led out by a chain round their necks and presented to his soldiers for their sport. All four were dead now.

The most disappointing moment of his sojourn in Greece had been his audiences with Prince Hassani. Knowing the man's kin, and the bold way in which he had uncovered the assassination plot in Constantinople, he had expected a fiery warlord with a sharp and cunning mind. Instead, he had found an obese and lecherous blockhead who was incapable of taking his thoughts from the boy who was sitting in his lap and who was fondling him openly. How long had Hassani been governor here? He was never good at dates, but surely it was not long enough to have reduced the man to a debauched, dull-witted old woman? The Sultan had received his reports on Hassani and Baswar had been given his orders. If Hassani continued to prevaricate, and Zebukar's treasure could not be released, Baswar had been given the power to remove Hassani in any way he saw fit. He would be replaced by a new governor, one selected most carefully by the Sultan, and the new governor would be given the hand of the Princess Musbah in marriage. Providing they had taken her prisoner by then . . . Baswar's mouth curved in a lascivious grin. Never had a woman become such a legend in her own time. English, yet she had the fire of Allah the Avenger in her veins; female, yet she behaved with the stamina and alacrity of a trained soldier. Hassani had been an imbecile to let her go into the convent, of course. From there, she had vanished from the face of the earth. Baswar had burned the convent to the ground a few weeks before, and tortured its Mother Superior. Having revealed nothing, she had died under torture. He himself had raped the youngest and prettiest of the nuns and then they had all been cast out without money or clothes. Watching them stagger out onto the plains, naked and sobbing, had been one of the sweetest moments of his life.

So soon afterwards that he suspected Allah's intervention, had come the spy who had told him of the Pagan's fortress hideout and the presence of the English girl there. He had rewarded the man generously, giving him a ruby ring, a gold chain for his neck and two new concubines for his household. (Baswar had taken their virginity first, of course, and given them a taste for perversions which the humble little spy would be hard-pressed to satisfy.)

Hindered by skirmishes and attacks from the Greek rebels, Baswar was at this very moment heading for the Pagan's fortress. He had orders to execute the Pagan himself before he escaped again, and he was to take the man's head back to Constantinople and present it to the Sultan personally. A box had been specially provided. He could not wait to see this extraordinary Englishwoman around whom such a strange and unbelievable legend had grown. If she were as beautiful as they said, he knew that he would want to bed her, but he had been given orders that she be kept in perfect health until after her marriage when Zebukar's fortune could be released to her husband. Secretly, Baswar was hoping that he would so please his royal master that he would be given the hand of the Princess in marriage, and not some moronic book-keeper who would be installed in Hassani's place. Already he felt proprietorial towards the girl. He knew that if she were given the choice between him and the bloated, decaying hulk of Hassani, she would choose him, Turkey's most renowned general. His master was a generous man with those who obeyed him to the letter. When Mahmud told Baswar that he could choose whatever he pleased as his reward for beheading the Pagan and recapturing the Princess, he would say, quite simply, that he wanted only her.

CHAPTER TWENTY-THREE

Flavia trembled violently as she slipped into bed with her lover. This would be the first time since his recovery that they had made love. Prior to this, she had refused to let him weaken himself, and although he had baulked, he had agreed in the end. But not tonight. When he tried to kiss her, and she pulled away, he had leapt from the bed and lashed his arms round her waist so that she could not move. Within seconds, he had stripped her of her clothes, the baggy white blouse, the embroidered peasant skirt, the petticoats, stockings and boots. Now the clothes were lying in a tangled heap across the room, and he was pulling her close to his naked body, so that she was lying pressed against his steely muscles, revelling in his beauty, in his male scent, in the way his arms made her his prisoner. She wanted to be his prisoner for ever. She wanted the world to stay away from their love-nest and never, ever intrude. If only they could forget war and the Turkish soldiers, Hassani and the Sultan, and what might lie ahead for them if the Turks won . . .

But no, they would not win. They must not. Now, when she practised her skills with bow and arrow, with dagger, sword and spear, she was no longer a girl dabbling with weapons which were meant for men, but deadly serious. So far, the *Kleftes* and their allies had slowed down the advance of Muhammad Baswar and his troops who had joined with the reinforcements freshly arrived by sea from Turkey. Nonetheless, their progress was sure even if it was, at times, slow. One day they would reach the fortress and then . . . .

'My beloved,' Zardos was whispering in her ear, his voice sweet honey. 'I know what you are thinking of. I know what you fear. I fear it too, but we must put it aside and give ourselves time for love. You are thinking that this might be our last time together, like this?'

She nodded, dumbly, tears like sequins in her eyes.

'If it is the very last time, then let us make it memorable. Do not spoil it with tears.' He hugged her tightly, kissing away the glittering sequins and licking them from his lips.

'I wish – I wish that I could have been your wife when I died,' Flavia said huskily.

'They will not kill you, my darling, you are too precious. They want you safe and alive to release Zebukar's fortune.'

'They will never capture me alive, Zardos! I shall kill myself before they get their hands on me. Could you imagine what life would be like married to Hassani? He is the most loathsome monster I have ever known!'

'You will become resigned, my darling. Women always have become so, whatever man they have to marry. It might not be so terrible. He is rich and he will be pleased when he has some of Zebukar's jewels in his keeping. Your life will be luxurious.'

'And what of you?' she cried. 'You speak as if it is a foregone conclusion that they will kill you and take me prisoner! Do you think that I could be happy in the most luxurious palace in the universe if you were not with me? How could you think that? I love you, oh I love you, and I want to be with you, not with some filthy old Turk! I shall die before they take me, I vow it!'

He felt her trembling in his arms, like some tender, fragile winged creature which was too delicate, too sensitive to survive in cold, harsh air. He knew what he would do if they tried to steal her from him for Hassani. Before he let them take her, knowing what sufferings she would be subjected to, he would kill her himself, and then take his own life, dying with her safe in his arms. No foul and degenerate Turk was going to get his greasy paws on Flavia, certainly not the rapist and assassin Muhammad Baswar, nor the odious Hassani. He did not tell her this, of course, nor would he. He would make sure that she died without any pain, in the way that he knew, and she would not even realize what was happening. He would pray for her, too, using her own favourite prayers, offering her soul into the keeping of the Miraculous Virgin whom she so adored.

Now he was fighting back his own tears. To think of her dead, breathless, lifeless, unable to speak or communicate with him. Unable to hear her saying that she loved him, unable to let her know how much he worshipped and adored her. It might be blasphemy, but *she* was his Miraculous Lady, and he treasured and revered every silken scrap of her sweet, smooth and adorable body. Such courage and fortitude throbbed in her heart; her eyes were bright with determination and fearlessness. Even for a men, she would have been a hero, for she had a hero's heart, and yet she was frail femininity, so soft and malleable, so generous and loving. Emotions rang through him, one after the other, and he knew that he must make this last time together as unforgettable for her as it would be for him. He cringed when he thought back to the first time he had made love to her, when he had been so arrogant and self-seeking, when he had thought of her as nothing more than a highly desirable women who could satisfy his lusts on a temporary basis. Well, they said the greatest fools were men who declared that they would never love again. His mermaid dancer was far from his thoughts and his heart these days; there was no room there for two women.

His kisses, made from passion and yearning and sorrow, were of the eternal kind, while she responded with her own desperate longing to capture eternity in his arms. For a time, they succeeded. Ravenous for his love-making, she curved herself into his body, wishing that she was part of him, wanting to be his flesh, his bone, his breath, his spirit. She could feel his heart pounding and she knew why; he wanted her. It seemed like years since they had last made love, long, long barren years of darkness and separation, living like troglodytes in airless caves without light, without heat. Now there was light, she was bathed in it, for she was back in his embrace; he was her blazing sun and she was inflamed with passion for him.

Her heart was thudding now, and she was tiny and delicate as crystal in his powerful arms, so delicate that she might well break and if she did she would not care. Only he had the power to break her, no one else, and she gave him that power willingly.

Seconds later, they were together, two bright forces linking, uniting, fusing into one being, one body, one love, never to be parted again, not even by death. It was even headier than she had thought it could be, and so stirring, so momentous that she thought it quite possible she might not survive it. And what if she should die now, die of love? Would it not be infinitely more marvellous than waiting to die when the Turkish armies came? She could not bear to endure another moment knowing what their fates were to be. When this was over, she would beg him to die with her, beg him to kill her now, before the enemy arrived. Thousand upon thousands were approaching, men fresh and eager for battle, armed to the teeth, with murder in their hearts. There would be a siege, but for how long could they survive such conditions? They were stocked up with all that they could find, but that had been limited for the countryside was barren after years of war and dispute.

Those who brought in food had been forced to do so at the dead of night for there were Turkish spies everywhere. The inhabitants of the fortress were more than tripled now that survivors of the village massacres and holocausts had swelled their ranks, and more than a dozen of the women were with child. Then there was Ezta who was expecting her baby any day . . . How long could they all survive a siege high up here without contact with the outside world? How long indeed. And afterwards, when they had to submit, as they inevitably would, the Turks would behave in their customary fashion, raping, hacking to death, destroying. Destroying all she held most dear in the universe . . . Oh, she would have given anything to know that Atalanta, brave and invincible, was on her way with her troops, her sword unsheathed to quell the Sultan's cohorts!

'Put it all from your mind,' Zardos whispered, drawing her thoughts back to love and passion. 'I can feel your unease, your sadness, but we shall overcome them.'

She did not know whether he referred to her emotions or to the Turks, but she wanted it to be both. Overcome them all, quash, vanquish, put down, whatever phrase he cared to use, that was what she wanted to do, and the fire filled her veins exactly as it had once filled Atalanta's, the warrior-queen who had never lost a battle.

'Bruise me, hurt me, I want to feel myself aching for days after this,' she told him. 'I want to remember, to relish it all. I want you, I long for you. Take me, hold me, devour me . . .'

'My lusty little queen, my warrior of love,' he chuckled, as if he were thinking of Atalanta too. 'Fight your battles in my arms, for there you will always win, always. You can conquer me with a glance, vanquish me with a hint of a smile, crush me with your silvery laugh. Can you not see that I am your prisoner?'

'So you will stir *my* soup and scrub *my* vegetables from now on, is that a promise?' she teased, and he roared with laughter, so she did too, but then she lay against him, her head on his dark-bronze shoulder, before he began to move inside her again, hard and persistent, brooking no interference, no hindrance. She thrust her hips hard against him, curving them up to meet his pressure, drawing him ever closer, absorbing him deep, deep within her so that they were forged into one indivisible being. How futile were words at such times and yet they must be said, for feelings can overwhelm if they are not set free.

'When we are out of this, when it is all over and Greece is free, we shall marry,' Zardos whispered. 'You will be my bride, my lady, and I will take you to meet my family, not that I have many relatives left. We shall have sons and daughters, and tell them of the days when Greece was enslaved and its rivers ran with the blood of patriots . . .

And of how we met and how I had some insane notion of holding you to ransom . . .'

'You did what!'

He had the grace to blush. 'Yes, I visualized you as a fat and pampered royal princess, and I knew how valuable you were to the Sultan and Hassani, so I was going to hold you to ransom.'

'What for?' she whispered.

'Either for gold to buy arms, or in exchange for the freedom of those of my men who were in Turkish gaols.'

'I see.' She pretended to be cool with him, which he could not bear.

'My darling, you know I could not do it! As soon as I saw you, so tiny and yet so brave, I loved you, despite what you may have thought at the time. How could I have handed you back to those monsters?'

'I thought then that they were the saints and you the monster,' she reminded him, ashamed as she recalled her behaviour in the early days she had spent in the fortress. 'It is still so hard to believe the horror stories that I keep hearing about Zebukar.'

Zardos made a sound which was something like a growl, a jealous growl.

'I want you to forget that you were ever married to another man. I burn when I think of you in his arms, in his bed!'

'But there is no need. For a time, when I was an innocent, my heart was his, but those days are gone forever. "When I was a child, I loved as a child, but now I am a woman, I love as a woman," ' she paraphrased the Bible. '*Your* woman, Zardos. You will be my first husband for the other one came to mean nothing to me. How could he? I meant nothing to him except as a symbol of political alliance, so that he could go on persecuting Greece. He never saw *me*, the real me. There is only one thing that grieves me about those days. I wanted so much to make friends with Zebukar's mother, but she was so cold towards me. She would never speak to me, or answer my messages.

330

I felt that I could have helped her if only she would let me, but she would have nothing to do with me. She seemed such a sad and lonely figure. Do you think she was jealous, imagining that I would steal her son's affections from her?'

Zardos looked deep into her eyes. 'So you do not know?'

Something in his tone filled her with alarm. 'Know what? Did something terrible happen to her? After Zebukar died, I never saw her again. Oh, tell me what you know!'

'Prepare yourself for grim news, my darling. The Princess Fira had an excellent reason for not speaking to you. Zebukar had ordered her tongue to be cut out so that she could not warn the British ambassadors what his plans were. She threatened to tell them, she tried to escape the palace, but her son caught her, and that was her punishment. He told her that if she tried to warn you, her hands would be the next to go.'

Flavia went white, her lover hugging her close. She knew that he was not lying, that every word he had spoken was true. All along, she had felt that there was something deeply tragic about her mother-in-law, but she had not conceived of anything so cruel, so unthinkable as that.

Later, when she was over the worst of the shock, they talked of Zardos's past, and to take her mind off the poor Princess Fira, he told her about his own ancestry.

'I have heard so much about you,' she said, 'and not only that you were the son of a goatherd! I heard you were the illegitimate son of a notorious bandit, all sorts of things yet no one seemed to know your true identity. But I want you to know this, my darling. I do not care what you were, or what your origins were. I see only you, the man I love.'

'Tales were spread deliberately so that my family name would be kept secret, for obvious reasons. The plan failed, alas. I can tell you the truth now. When the Venetians occupied Crete, which was then called Candia, it was governed by the so-called Duke of Crete and his council. The Duke, a Venetian, of course, was a passionate man, possessive, restless and something of a despot. A great despot, if the truth be known, but a man of great charm

331

and determination. They say that he behaved as if he had Borgia blood, but without the proclivity for murder.' Zardos grinned. 'He fell wildly in love with a Cretan girl, of excellent family. Her name was Leah, and she was very proud and very beautiful. She would have nothing to do with this interloper, this foreigner, so one day he abducted her as she walked in the gardens of her family's home. He carried her off into the mountains of Crete, the famous amethyst mountains where they say that Zeus himself was born, and there in the labyrinthine cave where the king of the gods took his first breath, high up on Mount Ida, the Duke made love to Leah. A son was born nine months later, by which time Leah was married to the Duke, but her heart was broken, and she died soon afterwards. The boy was raised as a Venetian, and when he grew to manhood, they gave him a Cretan bride to further establish the bond between the Cretans and their conquerors . . .'

By now Flavia was sure she knew what he was going to say. He was descended from that mating on Mount Ida. He had Venetian blood in his veins mingling with proud, fierce Cretan blood.

'Generations later, when the Turks conquered the Ventians and took Crete for themselves, Zardia, the Duke's direct descendant, escaped to Italy and married an Italian count. He was my great-great-grandfather. They returned to live in Greece later.'

'No wonder you are so dark, like a god carved from black basalt . . .' she touched the skeins of his ebony hair. 'But those emerald eyes, where do they come from?'

'My grandmother. She was Scottish.'

'Scottish!'

'Yes. Her name was Miranda MacGregor and she was the daughter of a clansman who fled Scotland during the troubles.'

'So my beautiful Greek hero has Italian and Celtic blood? Well, who would have believed it?' She kissed him soundly. 'Somewhere amongst my ancestors I have a Scottish chieftain too, a Stewart, if I recall.'

332

'Then we are blood brothers!' he teased, nibbling her ear, then her cheek. 'Perhaps we should celebrate this moment with a haggis-eating ceremony!'

She giggled. 'Is there such a thing?'

'But of course. All honest Scots have heard of it. A great haggis is cooked and then it is served to the people who wish to participate in the ceremony. Each one must eat all that he is given otherwise he is denounced as a traitor.'

'That is bad luck for him if he has a small appetite.'

'And he must drink all the whisky that is put before him, too. Then when the meal is finished, he has to dance a Celtic reel in a sprightly fashion, tireless as a young man, and if he becomes short of breath, then again he is denounced as a traitor and his sporran is cut off before the assembled company. A terrible humiliation, that is, with his name blackened for all time.'

By now Flavia could hardly stop laughing. 'Zardos, you have made this up!'

'No, I swear I have not. They say that men who have lost their sporrans in this way can never beget sons. Who would wish to endure such a punishment?' His eyes twinkled.

She pretended to look coy. 'You have never had to endure this humiliation have you, Zardos?' she asked.

'Never!' he laughed.

'Then give me a son, my darling, give me a son now, *now!*' she begged, and her tone was deadly serious.

Later, when they had made love a second time, she whispered, 'What shall we call him? A Scots name or a Greek one? Acteon was my father's name.'

'Then Acteon shall be part of it, but we want him to be renowned for famous deeds. What of Alexander?'

'Why not?' A strong name, but do not forget that he conquered Greece just as the Venetians and the Turks did. What of Zardos Acteon?'

He laughed. 'You want to immortalize me, because you love me so.'

'You have immortalized yourself with your own deeds,

my darling. Who will ever forget Lord Zardos, the leader of the *Kleftes*, the man who freed Greece of the Turkish yoke, the man who united all Greeks beneath his banner?' Tears sequinned her eyes again. One day, if she lived, she would tell their sons and daughters all there was to know about their heroic and fearless father. If she lived . . .

She thought of the message she had despatched the moment that their plight had been brought home to her. Leon, who was devoted to her, had vowed that he would die before he parted with her letter save to anyone but the man for whom it was intended. Smiling to herself, she thought of that man, her godfather, Sir Edward Codrington, one of England's greatest heroes who had been the captain of Nelson's ship *Orion* at Trafalgar. His son was now a midshipman in the family tradition of the Codringtons, sailing on his father's flagship, the *Asia*. Had she not been betrothed so young to Zebukar, it might well have been her godfather's son who had become her husband. She was glad, hugely glad, that he had not, but she liked Sir Edward. He was a staunch and trustworthy man and he was fond of her. He had never failed to send her gifts on her birthday and at Yuletide. She had not forgotten that he had been the only man to raise doubts about her marriage to Zebukar, and the only man who had written begging her to return to England when Zebukar died. She could recall his letter word for word.

'*My sweet goddaughter, Although you might feel that your Duty lies in Greece with the people of Your husband's Race, I beseech you to Return to Your Homeland and take up Your old Life here. You are dearly Loved, and not Forgotten. There is ever a Home for you in my Household and My Family will welcome you with Open Arms whenever you choose to Return. Let it be Soon, my dearest goddaughter.*'

He had been right, in one respect, but only one. If she had rushed back to England with her tail between her knees, she would never have met her darling Zardos and come to this eerie and unearthly fortress where spirits who should have died thousands of years ago still fired the hearts of those who were able to hear them.

And she had heard them. Oh yes, loudly, brightly, they spoke to her. Live. Love. Conquer. Fear nothing. Their commands sang in her head, Atalanta's commands, whispering the words which Flavia knew had been waiting for her ears for centuries. All those months she had spent wishing that she had a great army just like Atalanta's, along with the warrior-queen's power and authority, and then it had come to her, like a dagger of lightning. Her godfather and the British navy, they were her army! The political side of it did not occur to her at all, which was as well. She thought only of the people she loved, of her beloved Zardos's people, and how they needed help so desperately, and how it was, after all, within her power to save them.

CHAPTER TWENTY-FOUR

It was dark when they buried Ezta and her baby, swallowing their tears, creeping about like cautious creatures of the night. Over her body they placed a mound of stones to keep away the scavengers if the fortress should be captured by the Turks.

Away beneath them, far, far below, was Muhammad Baswar's camp, with eagle-eyed guards constantly watching them. Should anyone be so foolish as to show his head and shoulders, he would be shot by a Turkish sniper's flintlock pistol, wielded by the specially trained crackshot marksmen. Seven weeks of siege, and the Turks were as persistent as ever. Down there, they had plentiful supplies, and more were on their way. Their men were fresh and keen for there were plenty to take turns on watch.

In the fortress, nights were broken and restless, but they had given thanks for the well until one day the water drawn up was murky and stinking, and they knew that the Turks had found the source and poisoned it. Now they were dependent on their handful of goats for milk. Stores which had seemed generous when they brought them up the mountain were now depleted. The youngsters were always hungry, and four babies had been born other than poor Ezta's. Flavia knew now that the message to her godfather had failed to reach him. Perhaps he was in the Caribbean, or the Baltic seas on an expedition. If so, it could be months yet before he even read her letter.

She herself had made the wooden cross which she placed on Ezta's grave. Tears rolled down her face as she forced it in between the rocks and Zardos ensured that it was jammed tightly, so the wind would not buffet it. Ezta had bled to death. They had tried everything they could to save her. Flavia well knew that such a tragedy could as easily have happened in London with the most skilled physician on hand, but she blamed it on herself, on her own medical ineptitude, on the Turks, and on the siege. All that blood, thick and crimson, dying blood, like Zebukar's which had splashed on her when he was murdered . . . It had brought it all back, like a feverish disease only half-cured which had flared up again savagely. She had bathed the tiny dead infant which had been strangled by the cord which only seconds before had been keeping it alive. In the midst of life we are in death, she thought.

They had used all their arrows, firing down at the snipers, and they had no wood to make more. The seven weeks of siege seemed more like seven years, and the fortress which had been a joyous love-nest had swiftly become a gaol. Zardos was restless and fierily impatient. Where were the men who should have come to their aid by now? Where was Jacques-Pierre and his mercenaries who had ridden off on a sortie to delay the Turks' progress and who had not returned? Were they all slaughtered, or in hiding somewhere, having seen that the enemy numbers far outweighed their own? Unanswered questions buzzed in the air like hornets, preventing sleep, preventing relaxation.

The heat of early summer had increased, as if some malicious trickster were piling logs on an already blazing fire. It was intolerable, savaging their skins and turning their herbs and plants to tinder. When the well was poisoned, the plants died within a day, so there was no vegetation to feed the goats. Fortunately, there were bales of hay and dried grasses in store, but the way that these were vanishing was frightening.

When Flavia went into the kitchens to see what food was left, she found that she could not stay for long. Ezta's little ghost was everywhere, at the table, by the hearth, on the stool, in the larder. It was the ones who died who were the fortunate ones, for those who were left behind had to suffer their loss. Weeping in the privacy of her room,

337

Flavia found her fingers clenching into claws. She imagined them curving round the neck of Muhammad Baswar, tightening, crushing, squeezing his breath away until he crumpled to the earth, sagging, spiritless flesh. Then she saw Jacques-Pierre's flashing Gallic grin, his bright teasing eyes, and she thought of him and his die-hards doing just that, dying hard, fighting the ferocious men who were now encamped below them. Were those brave and loyal mercenaries lying dead somewhere, the carrion picking at their bones? She shuddered, hugging herself. She was so filled with despair, so low in spirit, that she had not thought of the Miraculous Virgin for days, nor prayed to her. She knew now that they had been abandoned by God.

When Zardos joined her, he was frowning.

'Mikos, one of the boys from Nauplinos, has a fever. He is burning up. If it spreads . . .'

She flung herself into his arms. During a siege, lack of water and food was the first worry; next was fever and disease.

'He did not drink any of the well water?'

'I don't think so. He was well yesterday. He was helping to feed the goats. He had supper last night, as usual, and seemed fit. He has been isolated anyway.'

'I must nurse him.'

'*No!*' His tone made her eyes open wide. 'You will not go near him. His friends can care for him. Dear God, was it not enough that you risked your life nursing me when I might have had typhus? You will not do it again, not for anyone. *Ever.*'

He crushed her in his embrace, his passion for her safety bringing fresh tears to her eyes. This was love, real, true love in all its nourishing, heartening beauty. She had known nothing like it before. Nor would she ever again, she knew. If anything happened to Zardos, if she survived him, she would go straight into a convent, anywhere, it did not matter. She would take her vows, and never leave the cloisters again. Love like this showed up the past for what it was, a tinsel fantasy. Oh she might have thought

338

that she was happy then, dreaming of her perfect Prince Zebukar. But that was emptiness, ice compared to the fire which devoured her now, the fire of the love she shared with this fearless, adorable Greek.

CHAPTER TWENTY-FIVE

The message was clear. It was signed by Muhammad Baswar and it said:

'*Send down Her Highness the Princess Musbah on pain of death.*'

Zardos's reply was in the singular:

'*Never!*'

Somehow, despite the craggy terrain, the Turks had heaved cannon into position with the aid of mules and tackle. At first, their aim fell far short, so they climbed higher during the night when the watchers on the ramparts of the fortress could not pick them off. At dawn, there were the cannons, so near that their noses could be seen down below. There had followed a clamorous and nerve-shredding day of ruthless firing. Firing upwards had never been easy, and sometimes proved impossible against gravity's downward thrust, but the explosions and the proximity of the guns was terrifying all the same and inevitably some of the balls were to hit their target. The explosions went on, and on, day after day, until some of the women were near hysteria. In every part of the fortress they could hear the deafening boom as the guns fired, then the eerie whistling as the balls whipped through the air towards them, followed by thunderous crashes as they landed. Part of the horror was in not knowing where they would land next.

More messages came from Baswar, one every morning and one every afternoon, all of them demanding the immediate surrender of the Princess Musbah.

'He will leave you alone if I go down,' Flavia said to Zardos, her eyes bright. 'The women cannot bear this much longer.'

'He is a Turk. You can't trust a word they say. He wants me dead, that I do know. Even if you went to him – God forbid! – he would not end his assault.'

'I could order him to do so! I could order him to take me to Hassani, *order* him to withdraw from here.'

'How simple it would be if that were so.' Zardos pulled her to him. 'You are a mere pawn to them. Hassani wants you back to salve his wounded pride. Hassani represents the Sultan here, it is true, and as such has a modicum of power, but Baswar has come directly from the Sultan, and the Grand Turk's orders overrule all others. Believe me, they want my death as much as they want you alive. Without you, they will never get their claws on Zebukar's fortune.'

Flavia did not reply. She was a princess, after all, and supposedly a princess of the Muslim faith. Her dead husband was first cousin to the Sultan, and Hassani was not. Muslims set great store by blood relations and bonds; they meant everything to them. She was Zebukar's widow and male relatives were commanded by the laws of Allah to protect and preserve widows. If only she could get to the Sultan and plead for Zardos's life and the release of the Greek prisoners who were in Turkish hands. The thought rang in her head like a celebratory bell. Never mind that afterwards she would be sacrificed to the bloated and debauched Hassani. If her beloved Zardos and his people were freed, what did her fate matter? Their stores were shockingly low; they had very little goats' milk now, for there was no water to give the goats. If only some rain would come but at this time of year it was unlikely. There had been a burst of violently hot days which scorched the skin and parched the earth. More of the children were ill, and the boy from Nauplinos had died of his fever. Unable to bury him in the now rock-hard garden area, they had strapped his body into a sheet and cast him down into the sea to the rear of the fortress, after saying prayers over the corpse. They did not know what had killed him, but Flavia was convinced that they were all going to die of the contagion, whatever it was. If they stayed here, they would die of starvation and disease, or be slaughtered by the Turks. What a choice! However, for her alone there was another choice, and, steeling herself over the next twenty-four hours, during which another of the children died, and three more sickened, she came to her decision.

She said nothing to Zardos, not one word, for she knew exactly what his reaction would be. When he was otherwise occupied one night, when the moon was nothing more than a narrow sliver of pearl, Flavia, heart thumping wildly, slipped on her dark hooded cloak and strong but silent shoes and slipped out along the chilly corridors of the fortress. On tiptoe, she went out into the night air via one of the small rear exits to the building. The men who were on watch were at the front of the fortress, their eyes fixed on the camp below and the cannon which were even closer now. They did not see the small, shadowy figure creeping along by the walls, making her way to a bolted and barred gate which allowed castle dwellers to make their way down the mountain by the nine hundred and ninety-nine steps. More than half of these steps had been blasted to fragments to ensure that the Turks could not use them.

Over cobbles of shattered stone and lumps of loose earth, along a terrifyingly tortuous and uneven track, sometimes slipping and sliding, her hands clinging to sods which came out by the roots quite alarmingly and feeling herself slither down foot after foot until her soles touched solid rock, she descended. It was a descent into hell, and much of the time she was on hands and knees, her skin scratched and bloody, her palms skinned, nails broken, eyes blinded by tears of heartbreak.

All the time, she clamped her mouth tightly shut so that no cry would alert the look-outs above her. Once, as a ragged stone knifed her breast, she thought that she had lost her footing completely. Intolerable pain leapt through her and the tears burst from her eyes. Scrabbling wildly, sure that she was to fall to her death, she managed to clutch at tough mountain grass and then a rough piece of rock which saved her from tragedy. She paused then, weeping hysterically, weeping for Zardos whom she would never see again, weeping for Greece and its agony, and for

342

her own anguish. Like a blow, it hit her. She would die without him, anyway, so she might as well die now . . . Yet she must not, for her life could save the Pagan and his people, she was sure of it. The Sultan was half-French, he was said to be a cultured man. He would hear her pleas; he would listen, she was sure of it. Baswar was his general, but his minion, too. In the Ottoman Empire, all men's fates were woven by the Sultan, so Baswar would not dare offend his master. He would have to take her to Constantinople, by boat across the Aegean. She had no idea how long the journey would take, but it was infinitely better than starving to death here, along with those whose lives she could save by carrying out her plan.

Zardos, oh, Zardos! His name was a benediction and a blessing, yet the very thought of him clove her heart like a thousand splinters. She had left him. She had left their mountain eyrie of love and dreams. When he found out, what would he do? How would he feel? She knew that if he had deserted her, she would want to die. But she had not deserted him . . . She had done this to save his life, to save the Greece that he loved. For a moment, her tears were like rain lashing her eyes, bright and sharp and hot, the torrent fed by the storm raging in her heart. How long would she survive without him? Weeks, days, hours? Minutes, probably. She felt sick and desperate and feeble-minded, as if she had been feverish for a very long time.

When the savage, clawed hands gripped her by the arms and shook her brutally, she burst out crying and her legs gave way.

Baswar was nothing like she had imagined. He had a cold face with malicious, lascivious eyes. She knew that he was visually stripping her of her cloak as she stood before him, yet he had treated her with the courtesy befitting her rank as the widow of a Muslim prince. He had listened to what she wanted to say, nodding his head now and then, as if giving her every consideration. Nonetheless, she felt as if she were losing ground fast. She could feel her courage and confidence ebbing away. She was floundering impotently. When she stammered to a halt, having said it all, he looked at her with the eyes of a rapacious, thieving jackal and gave a smile which chilled her soul.

'Renowned Princess, bride of Islam, if only it were in my power to take you to the Sultan, but I have my orders and they came from Allah's Representative on Earth himself, Mahmud II. I cannot intervene. It is not in my power.'

She knew then that even if he were the Sultan, he would not give her what she asked. He was bent on his own elevation; he was ruthless, cunning and probably heartless. Shivers of unease spangled her spine.

'What – what orders are they, General?' she whispered, her face pale as pearl.

'You are betrothed to His Highness, Prince Hassani, who awaits your presence for the purposes of the marriage ceremony. I do not need to tell you this, Your Highness. The Sultan, my master, wishes to see you married to Prince Hassani, and thus it will be, for no one disobeys Allah's Representative on Earth. No one.'

The blood felt as if it were spinning downwards, away from her head.

'I wish to be taken to the Sultan! I have something to tell him. You must take me to him! I command you to take me to him!'

Her nails speared her palms, for she was chillingly conscious of the two heavily-armed guards standing behind her, fingers curving round their daggers. She was trapped, but she could not blame anyone, for she had set the trap herself. She had been a fool to think these ruthless men would possess the honour and gallantry of her own countrymen. What did this callous giant of a man care if she were in distress, the tears flowing down her cheeks as she fell to her knees to plead with him? The expression in his eyes did not change one iota, not even when she tore at the hem of his robe and repeated her words through sobbing gasps. Even before they moved, she knew that the

344

guards were going to take a firm hold of her and this they did. Moments later, bound like a mummy, she was being flung clumsily into a litter which was hung with rich cerise silk. A litter fit for a princess, but she was a prisoner, a *prisoner*. The world went black.

Hassani could not believe what he saw. True, she was bedraggled and white as a corpse, her famous red-gold hair dusty and tangled, but nonetheless it was she, the Princess Musbah herself, regal, enraged and spitting like a hellcat. Luckily for him she was bound with ropes so she could not scratch out his eyes, for she looked as if she would delight in doing just that. He walked round her slowly, wonderingly, as if he had found some rare and incredible *objet d'art* and was struck speechless by it. Now and again he stabbed at her breast or her stomach with a jewelled finger and made a crowing sound which might have been spiteful laughter, or venomous triumph.

He had it all now. Zebukar's widow and Zebukar's treasure, the Sultan's esteem and Allah's Teardrop. They were all in his grasp. He had won. Not one second longer would be put off the marriage ceremony. It would go ahead this very day, in exactly the same form as the ceremony which the Princess had undergone with Zebukar, so that everyone involved would accept it as legal, the Muslim world and the people of her own land. Then he would bed her before witnesses so that the consummation could not be questioned and afterwards she could rot in his harem, for all he cared, the evil, cunning and rebellious bitch.

He winced as a pain stabbed him in a very intimate part, a curse festering on his breath. So much for that debauched he-bitch Arita, who had given him the foulest disease of the organ he prized most in all the world, and just when it had been recovering from Alliya's vicious attack. He had endured the so-called cures which were as vicious as the cause itself, and yet the pain had not abated. If anything, it was worsening and so was the noxious

discharge. Two of his *Kadines* were infected now and four
of his concubines (not that they mattered), but he had
been told by the physicians that he might not be able to
beget children after this. That had hit him like a hammer
blow. A man might have a harem of five hundred concubines but if he did not have a son then he might as well be
a woman himself, the lowest of the low, forsaken by Allah.
He shuddered as a fresh pain speared him.

He saw the eyes of the English girl watching him as if he
were a filthy cockroach. Her contemptuous gaze shook him
so deeply that he shoved her violently between the breasts.
She fell over and lay still.

Flavia woke to the sound of shouts and footsteps. In the
palace of the Silver Cicadas, for her, time had swept
backwards. Preparations were under way for her wedding,
but this time to Hassani and not to Zebukar. Inch by inch,
she was fading away, weakening, her spirits ebbing. She
hoped that she would not live to see the wedding; with
luck, she would not. Zardos was her life and they had
taken her life from her, hacked at the shining, silvery cord
which bound her to her beloved Pagan. Now they were
separated, adrift for eternity. Or would they meet again in
some distant, strange and unforeseeable future? The
ancient Greeks had believed in reincarnation, and while
she had lived in Atalanta's fortress, she had come to believe
in it herself. How could she have failed to do so in that
eerie and timeless place? Time, what was time? A measured
quantity of seconds, minutes, and hours, by which human-
ity organized and disciplined itself, sometimes with sweetness but just as often with harshness. 'I will see you
tonight, my darling.' Or, 'This woman has just a few hours
to live.' If only she could say the former, but she feared
that her fate was to be the latter. If the Miraculous Virgin
was kind, she would allow her to die before the wedding
night and Hassani would be cheated of his victory.

'Oh, Zardos, my beloved, why did I leave you? I was a

346

fool; will you ever forgive me? Look for me, look for me wherever we go after this, in the next life,' she whispered, and she ached with a sick, bruised feeling because he was not there to put his arms tightly round her and kiss away her grief, as only he could.

History was repeating itself, just as people said it did. The *halaiks* and *khalfas* were grim and silent. They had been forbidden to speak to her and the wedding robes which they had brought looked chillingly like the very ones she had worn to marry Zebukar. Then she saw that the material was different, not so fragile, but all the same she felt faint when they lowered the glittering confection over her head. It felt heavy as stone, stiff and rasping against her flesh, and the jewelled collar and headdress weighted her down intolerably. Glittering, diaphanous, shimmering silk the colour of pearls, beaded and jewelled with diamonds, amethyst and rubies. Where had it come from? Looted from some poor enemy queen or princess, probably. Their enemy, not hers. This time they did not give her a *muska*, a charm to avert evil, which was just as well, thought Flavia wryly, considering that she was marrying evil.

She did not know it, but this gown had been sent by the Sultan, care of Baswar, for this very moment, so that the Princess Musbah would go joyously to her wedding. He thought that she could be bought by riches and finery. If only he knew that she was not for sale.

She had been bathed, and massaged with creams and scented unguents, and her gown was drenched in some sickly perfume which she could not identify. Then they handed her a golden goblet studded with rubies and ordered her to drink the liquid which gleamed within. She had flung it across the room. They brought her another and held her down while the liquid was forced between her lips. It was bitter and acrid, a drug, or some sort of

347

aphrodisiac. If it had been poison, she would have drunk gladly.

She spat out as much as she could, but they kept on bringing more, and eventually some of it found its way into her stomach, even though she fought with all her strength. The scene blurred, and instead of a dozen faces above her, she saw two dozen, three dozen. Then, as if from an immense distance, she heard weird, malicious laughter. Someone was crowing gleefully over her subjugation.

Then, wonderingly, she heard the voice of Mother Marie-Thérèse, lilting, sweet with comfort, and she strained her ears to hear what the nun was saying.

'My mother made a vow to the Blessed Virgin. She said that if I, her only child, recovered from the fatal illness, then she would give up what was most dear to her. I did recover and she did give up what was most dear to her – and that was me.'

A sacrifice. Did it mean that a sacrifice was needed?

'Virgin of Miracles, I offer myself to you. Take me, do whatever you will with me. I am yours, yours . . .'

The soul-curdling laughter faded, as did the brightness in the scented chamber. A darkness began to spread across her vision, little by little, like a hand slipping slowly across her eyes. When it covered her sight completely, she lost consciousness.

It is said that hell hath no fury like a woman scorned, but what of man? What of Menelaus when he found that Helen had deserted him for Paris? He had begun the Trojan wars for vengeance. What of Samson's blind vengeance when Delilah deserted him? He had destroyed the temple of the Philistines with his bare hands. When Zardos searched his fortress with gathering horror and disbelief, finding not even a note from the vanished Flavia, he was devoured by so many emotions that for long moments he could not clarify his thoughts. He knew instantly what she had done. She had gone, his brave little warrior had gone. Their last

348

conversation told him everything. She truly believed that she could persuade the Sultan and his minions to withdraw from the siege and allow him and his fellow patriots to go free. A wave of utter helplessness swept through him, and he shuddered. Then it was gone, for which he thanked God. What he needed now was strength such as no man had ever possessed before, along with the ability to perform miracles . . . His sensual mouth twisted in a tortured smile. Where would she be now? Down below, in Baswar's camp? What would they do to her? Yes, she was the widow of a prince of Islam, but she was also the key to Zebukar's fortune and the entire universe knew how much the Sultan wanted Allah's Teardrop for his favourite, Medisha, who had recently borne him a son.

There were a number of options open to Zardos. He could muster the young men in the fortress and make a night raid upon the camp below, knowing that they were outnumbered by hundreds to one. He could leave one of the young men in charge here while he slipped away at dead of night, found some lone guard and made him reveal what Baswar had done with the Princess Musbah. He was almost positive that she would be on her way to Hassani, for only when the marriage ceremony was celebrated could Zebukar's fortune be released. The Turks were an anachronism. They considered other peoples' laws were there to be broken but they adhered too rigidly to their own.

Zardos clenched his fists, anger surging silently through him. *He* was going to be her second husband, not some debauched and depraved fat Muslim who would add his adored Flavia to a harem which was already overflowing with females, and males, too, in Hassani's case. Somehow he had to get to her before Hassani married her, or, failing that, rescue her before the marriage was consummated. If he arrived too late . . . An iciness coiled deep within him like a frozen dagger's blade. God knows what that devil would do to her; submit her to a selection of his infamous perversions no doubt, and then . . . He could not bear to think about it! Leaping to his feet, Zardos paced up and down the room.

For ten years he and his *Kleftsmen* had run rings around the Turks and now too many of his countrymen were in prisons, or dead, while Jacques-Pierre and his mercenaries had, so it seemed, vanished from the face of the earth. What ever he did, it looked as if he would have to do it alone, entirely alone. The enormity of it weighted him down, hung on him like a gigantic leech.

He strode into the mermaid chamber, which had been Flavia's when she first came to the fortress. Once, that room had been occupied by the beautiful dancer, Cassandra, who had worn shimmering mermaid gowns and combed her long silky hair like a magical siren sitting on the tumbling rocks below. Gritting himself, he went to the window to stare down at the rocks where the dancer had killed herself. The Turks had been responsible for that, too, but an equal guilt lay upon him, for he had failed to realize how frantic she was, how deeply her sensitive mind had been wounded. He had continued to love her passionately for two years after her tragic death, and not until Flavia's advent had he been able to put her from his mind and heart. How long would he grieve for Flavia if he lost her? Into eternity, came the answer, bright, harsh and true.

Turning, he gazed around the room, stricken with heady memories which were like a starburst inside him. What he needed now was a miracle: divine intervention. Alone against the might of Islam he was like a sparrow in a storm, but a wingless sparrow. The analogy brought another twisted smile to his lips. When he fell, as fall he must, would God see him die, and care?

CHAPTER TWENTY-SIX

In the mountains of Haksios, two days' march from Atalanta's fortress, Jacques-Pierre and his army were recovering from a savage skirmish with a band of Baswar's
reinforcements. Meeting by accident, for the French captain
had received no warning of their presence on his route, they
had clashed at dawn, fighting desperately for their lives.
More than a quarter of his men had been slaughtered.
Although it had stuck in his gullet, and would for ever more,
he had ordered a retreat, he and those of his men who could
run taking to their heels. He knew the Haksios mountains
intimately, so there they had made their camp while the
wounded recovered and cautious scouts scoured the
countryside trying to gather news of Baswar himself. Jacques-Pierre had a broken arm and a heart to match. His
plans which had been so brave and brilliant, had come to
nothing. He knew what Zardos Alexandros and his people
were suffering, and he was suffering likewise. News had
filtered through of the siege, for the Turks wished the Greeks
to know of their Pagan's fate. The water supply to the fortress
had been poisoned and the occupants of the fortress were
dying of a fever as contagious as the Black Death. In a few
more days, Baswar would take the fortress and carry the
Princess Musbah back to her betrothed, Hassani Pasha.
The Frenchman had trembled violently when he heard this.
It would mean the end of Greece. Zardos would be
beheaded, if he had not succumbed to the fever, and the
brave Princess would be rushed to Hassani's palace and
forced into marriage with him. By all accounts, Hassani was
a degenerate and vicious man, and the courageous little
Princess would have a desperately unhappy life with him.

It was unthinkable that he acknowledge it, nor would he
ever voice it, but he loved the Princess. Where some would

say that a woman's place was in the kitchen, he had always said that it was in his bed. So it had taken him long months before he realized that he loved the English girl with a pure but powerful emotion. He did not want to take her to his bed for she belonged to Zardos, but he loved her strongly and he cared, oh yes, he cared deeply about her fate. That was why he had altered the habit of a lifetime of battle and ordered his men to run like cowards. Too many Greeks had died and he knew that he and his men were one of the last contingents who could save Zardos and his woman.

Time was scarce and his arm was taking a damnable time healing. He wished desperately that he could contact their allies, but the Greek freedom fighters were scattered about like petals falling from a dying rose. He had done his best, sending out scouts to try to make contact where possible. God was the only one who knew what had become of those men. Gripping his bandaged arm to stop it aching, Jacques-Pierre strode up and down fretfully, unable to remove from his thoughts the image of the Princess being submitted to appalling sexual infamies in the bed of Hassani, the demon Pasha.

More than two dozen dead had now been cast down onto the rocks below, dashed into the foaming sea, falling into the bottle-green depths while prayers were said for their souls. The situation in Atalanta's fortress was hopeless. The youth who had brought in the disease had been the first to die and he had done so without being able to give any clue as to its cause. Now some were saying that it was a visitation from an angry god because Zardos had stolen the bride-to-be of another man. This was the first time that any of his followers had ever criticized Zardos, and it caused him intense anguish. Save her he had done, and from a hideous fate. Cherish her, yes, he had done that too, but not stolen her. No, never that.

The replica of the Miraculous Virgin had been brought

down from her tower room and placed in a central position, with candles alight at her feet and prayers recited day and night. Seeing her thus, remembering what Flavia had said about the replica: that it was only wood and fake glitter, tears drowned Zardos's thoughts. His Flavia, so indomitable, so perceptive, and he had spoken only half in jest when he had told her that women were made for stirring soup and scrubbing vegetables. God in Heaven, if only he could take back those words, and all those which had done her such injustice! His brave Princess, who had sacrificed herself for him and his countrymen. One day, there would be a statue of her in the capital of Greece. He would see to it, if he survived this; if Greece survived it.

The night was black and thick as shrouding when the rebels arrived, armed to the teeth and determined to wreak a savage vengeance on Muhammad Baswar and his men.

Zardos, who rarely slept long these days, was first to hear the echoing ring of steel on steel. Leaping to his feet, he headed for the nearest slitted window. It was futile. Too dark to see anything below. The clash and tintinnabulation of steel continued, sounding now like a fast-growing forest of bells ringing out release, deliverance, freedom.

Within minutes, Zardos and his most loyal aides were robed in black and slipping down the mountainside silently as nocturnal animals, all heavily armed and glowing for action.

Tents had been ignited by the rebels, and, by their gilded-scarlet light, Zardos assessed the battle. Untouched lay the silken tent of Muhammad Baswar, for it was surrounded by his bodyguard, each man well over six foot tall and brandishing an enormous scimitar. These were eunuchs who were prepared to die for their master. The rebels had startled the Turks, who had believed themselves secure in this land of crushed mutineers, and valuable time was lost while the enemy had ravelled their wits together. They had been half expecting a minor attack from Zardos and a handful of his men, but nothing like this; horde upon horde of healthy, vigorous and skilled mercenaries.

Zardos was grinning as he launched himself into the centre of the battle, aiming for Baswar's tent where the Turkish skunk was hiding out. The black eunuch guards who prided themselves on being able to slaughter any number of men single-handed, seeing the Greek rebel attacking the first of their number, did not entertain a second's panic.

Blood roared in Zardos's ears as he fought with the strength and courage of a man who refused to consider that he might fail. As he saw it, there was nothing more that he could lose. The first guard fell, an expression of shock freezing his features, a sword blade through his liver. The second guard stumbled on a rough stone jutting up from the earth and in that moment, Zardos plunged his sword into the black's side. With a bellow of fury, the remaining four guards lined up before him, their faces glinting like pearly basalt in the flames from the fiercely-burning tents. Oblivious of the rest of the battle, Zardos took on the guards like an avenging angel, wielding a sword arm which seemed incapable of tiring, and which appeared to possess supernatural strength.

From a split in the tent drapes, Baswar watched, his eyes bulging like those of a dead fish. He was determined to preserve his own life at all costs. He was hungry for honour and riches and the acclaim which would be his for his brilliant tactics in battle, and he could enjoy neither if he were dead. The Princess Musbah would by now be married to Hassani and it had been Baswar who had made this possible. He would not die before he had been honoured. Indeed, he would not die at all! Allah was on his side, of that he was sure. Allah would see that his favourite general won this day.

Afterwards, Zardos would not be able to remember where his energy came from, but come it had, in fierce, bright bolts like the electrical force of a great storm. In the years to come, men would talk in wonderment of the Pagan

354

and how, like a living Colossus of Rhodes, the great bronze statue of the sun god, Helios, he had fought with a superhuman and unearthly skill and vigour. To die a hero, what more could he do when there was nothing else left? And die a hero he would! One after the other, the huge, muscular eunuchs fell, littering the ground like fallen ebony idols, and then, when Zardos thought that, incredibly, he had won, the hand fell on his shoulder and he was a prisoner.

The scenario before her glittered as if gemmed with a trillion dazzling diamonds, yet overall there was a misty look about it as if a fragile veil was suspended from floor to ceiling. Trying to move her head, she found that it ached intolerably and her neck was stiff as if held in a clamp. Moving her hands carefully over her body, she found that she was dressed in a flimsy robe of soft silken gauze which was slit at the sides to reveal her thighs. Again she tried to focus on the shimmering, blurred scene before her. What was happening there? Where was she? Lying on something soft, like a bed. A bed? Memory began to filter back slowly, like sunshine through water, but it was fragmented and slow to form because of the powerful drugs. Zebukar. Yes, that was the name. She was married to Zebukar now, Zebukar her beloved husband. All her childhood she had yearned for this day, when she became his Princess. Violets. Suddenly she could smell the strong, almost nauseating smell of violets. How the Turks loved flower scents, but violets . . .? There was something horrible, deeply disturbing about that particular scent, since . . . Since what? She could not remember.

The faint tingling began in her toes. Life was returning as the drugs filtered away. Oh Zebukar, my husband, where are you? She tried to call his name, but she could not speak. Then she became frightened. Why had her voice gone like this? No one could hear her. She was paralysed.

355

The nasal droning of Turkish musical instruments began then, and the beat, beat of their dancing-drums. The shimmering mist seemed to lift a little so that she could see, behind it, moving figures gyrating gently to the undulating, eerie sound. Now she knew why there were pins and needles in her feet, for, having tried to move them, she had found that they were tightly bound. There were thongs round her ankles to tie them together so that she could not run away. Why should she want to run away from her darling Zebukar?

'Drink.' The hand came out of nowhere, pressing a goblet to her lips. Hoping that it would relieve the sand-dry throat, enabling her to speak again, she drank it all. It was sweet, sickly sherbet, orange-flavoured, and with an acrid aftertaste. Soon after, a strange, deep and vibrant longing rose in the pit of her stomach, an aching, yearning longing for her beloved. She wanted him to come and make love to her, oh, how she wanted it! She could barely wait. Then the beautiful dream began.

His hands began to caress her, surging possessively over her breasts and thighs, so that she melted with delight. He was here, her beloved was here! Soon she would be his. Soon. In her eagerness, she pushed against his palms, sighing his name, and this time she was able to make a sound, but it was faint and he did not hear the name she was saying.

'My darling, my beautiful, precious Rose of the West,' he said, his voice savouring what was to come. 'Oh, *hayatim*, my adored one, *sevgilim*, my beloved, my bride . . .'

Her eyes flew open, the light striking against them like midday sun. It was not Zebukar, her beloved! Terror replaced the blood in her veins. Now she knew who it was, and it was too late, too late . . . His mouth clamped down on hers, suffocating her, and the hands were brutal now, grasping her wrists, restraining her by force. Then someone began to laugh, a gurgling, triumphant laugh. It was the most horrifying sound she had ever heard.

The Miracle

'Until the day dawns and the shadows fade, turn again to me, my beloved . . . How beautiful you are, my love, how beautiful. Your eyes are like a dove's, your lips like scarlet ribbons, your voice is melodious, your cheeks the colour of a ripe pomegranate, your breasts are like twin gazelles browsing among lilies. Let me now approach the mountain of myrrh and the hill of frankincense, and there remain until the day breaks and shadows depart. You are all beautiful, my love. I find no fault in you.'

Song of Songs

CHAPTER TWENTY-SEVEN

Rumours spread like rain throughout Greece. The Pagan had died of a mysterious fever in his secret fortress hideout. The Pagan had launched a futile but incredibly heroic attack upon the Turkish army and had perished along with the last of the *Kleftsmen*. The bride of Prince Hassani had tricked the Pagan into falling in love with her, after which she had delivered him up to the Turks who had executed him. A beleaguered country, a desperate people, they were frantic with anxiety yet already assuming a taciturn acceptance of their harrowing fate. What would come next? The devouring of Greece by the incumbent enemy, Islamic fangs clamping, crushing, swallowing? Annihilation. Humiliation. The proudest of races, descended from the most valiant heroes the world has ever known, totally submerged by an alien creed, an alien dogma?

In the mountain villages and in the foothills, in the highest hamlets, in the highest mountains, the people prayed and wept, and prayed again. The churches were crammed with sighing, black-clad bodies, and the sight of the wayside shrines was obliterated by the faithful kneeling before them. Without their national hero, Zardos Alexandros, they were nothing, a lost and vanquished race, the conquered ones. Only he had been able to unite the *Kleftes*, the bandits and rebels, the mercenaries, the dashing and fearless young men willing to die to free Greece. The blood of Odysseus and Hector was in his veins, perhaps that of Alexander too; and of Perseus who had marched fearlessly into Minos's labyrinth to slay the Minotaur, so that no more Athenian youths and maids would be horribly sacrificed to it. And now Turkey, the Minotaur, had murdered Zardos, the modern-day Perseus.

In the village of Skathios, an old woman died. Ten years

before, she had vowed that she would not die until Greece was free. Everyone had believed her for she had been a formidable character, strong, vigorous, never having endured a moment's illness or pain in her life. She had reared five sons, and seen them all die fighting for Greece, fighting to free their homeland so that their mother might rejoice with them. Hearing of the death of the first son, she had wept. Hearing of the death of the second and third and fourth, she had nearly broken. When the fifth son died, slaughtered in the battle at which the Pagan was taken prisoner, she did not weep. Raising her eyes to Heaven, she said, 'The Lord giveth and the Lord taketh away. Blessed be the name of the Lord.' Soon after she fell sick of a wasting illness, a strange disease which was painless and caused her no discomfort, yet which robbed her body of flesh.

Now she was dead, her grave surrounded by sobbing villagers, men as well as women, and children too. She had not lived to see their country free, as she had vowed, and, strangely, their hopes had died with her. They were buried deep in the earth with her corpse.

In the bay of Nauplinos, a young village girl walking with her small brother saw a woman standing staring out to sea. The woman wore a plain, darkish robe which blew around her ankles although the day was still. Thinking that she was a stranger who was lost, the girl went up to her and spoke with great politeness, asking if she might be of assistance. The woman did not reply nor did she turn round. Repeating what she had said, the girl waited. She was sure, suddenly very sure, that she must wait and hear what the woman said. Urgency flowed through the child, along with a marvellous, glistening peace. She had never known such acute happiness.

The woman turned, in a spinning movement which was simultaneously deliberate, almost lingering, as if she wanted to show herself and yet did not.

The girl laughed out loud with delight when she saw the woman's face, and so did her brother, their faces becoming radiant with joy. The girl had seen that face before, during the Festival when the statue of the Miraculous Virgin was brought out into the streets and paraded for the faithful to adore. That festive face was painted and jewelled, cold, yet stunningly beautiful, while this face was warm and soft, glowing with life. Suddenly, the dark robe was not dark any more. It was shimmering like cloth of silver, brilliant with all the light in the firmament, every thread stitched with starlight, every seam coruscating with the moon's unearthly glow.

Now the children fell to their knees knowing that they were in a great presence, and for five long, unforgettable minutes they were allowed to revel in the beauty blazing before them. Nothing had ever been like this for them before, or ever would be again, not in this life. They knew this, despite their youth, their innocence, their sheltered, unworldly lives. Later, there would be a convent for the girl, a monastery for the boy, and years spent waiting, just to see the lady again.

When she had gone, drifting away like silvered mist, they heard her voice.

'Carry this message. Prayers must be said. Many, many prayers. Hours, days, weeks of prayers. Ask God, and it shall be given. I am the source of life.'

In their rough stone cottage, the children's story was greeted with scathing fury by their parents. Was it not bad enough that the Turks had won, that Zardos Alexandros was dead, without their children bringing shame on their family by telling such stupid lies? The children, curiously bold, refused to go to bed, refused to go to sleep, and kept repeating their message until their father begged the priest to come and talk to them. When he did, he went white, then grey. A boy of barely four and a girl of eight, talking of prayers, of God giving whatever was wanted, of a strange woman who called herself the source of life. If only life and its source were so simple! Everyone knew that the source of life was God, not some weak and mindless female.

'But she shone, *papás*! She shone, like – like the sun, like the stars!' the little girl cried, tears in her eyes. 'She was like the statue of the Miraculous Virgin – *just* like her! The same, the same exactly!'

The little boy nodded frantically, saying, 'Yes, yes, *papás*.'

'How could he know? The last time we saw the Blessed Virgin's statue, he was in swaddling clothes,' the priest sneered.

'That is so, *papás*, but I held him up to see the Virgin. I held him close to her as she was carried past our home,' cried the children's mother, her cheeks pink.

'So you think they are telling the truth, eh? You think that they have seen the Mother of God taking a stroll by the sea?' The priest smacked his forehead with his palm. 'Next they will be seeing hosts of angels and Christ himself! Yes, how about that, children? Jesu himself, walking by the sea, admiring the scenery. They say the view is the most splendid in the Morea, so why should he not come here? Why not God himself, indeed?'

'Father, you are not yourself!' The children's father said in a shocked voice.

The priest trembled, his grizzled beard shivering, beads of moisture glistening on it like rain. The loss of the Miraculous Virgin's statue had affected them all, as had the desecration of the convent and the rape and murder of the nuns who had lived there. He was a broken man, his faith gone. He knew that they were all doomed, that they must accept, finally and forever, the cruel mastery of their Islamic overlords, but he could not bring himself to speak of this to his flock. It smacked of feeble cowardice, and although he was a coward, he could not admit it verbally.

'*Papás*, do you think that my children are liars?' The mother's voice quavered.

'What else? Do *you* think they speak the truth? You are

their mother, *you* should know!' The priest's voice rattled out like spittle.

'I – I am not fitted to judge such holy things . . .' The mother crushed her rosary in her hands, feeling its imprint glowing warmly against her skin.

'There, you do believe them! You say it is holy!' The priest leaped to his feet. 'Who is better suited to judge, you or I?'

'But *papás* we have never tried to judge. We asked you. We still ask you. Do we dismiss this as childish nonsense, or do we accept it as a visitation from God's Holy Mother?'

The priest began to laugh, a choking, hiccoughing laugh.

'I cannot say, I cannot say! We must ask the Patriarch in Constantinople. Yes, ask him, ask him!'

The children's father gaped. 'But *papás*, the Turks hanged him, in retribution, do you not remember? They hanged him. He is dead.'

In the shocked silence which followed, the little boy suddenly yelped out loud.

'We not lie! No, *no*! We saw the lady, saw her glow like a star!'

Weeping, the mother gathered him up into her arms, she and her husband averting their eyes as the priest shambled out of the house, muttering to himself.

News of the visitation spread throughout the area swiftly, carried with the speed of astonishment and delight. The Mother of God had not forsaken them after all! A little while later, the children were released from enforced confinement in their parents' home, and on the first day they were allowed out, they were again visited by the Star Lady, which was what the little boy had christened her. This time, she told them where the statue of the Miraculous Virgin could be found, and she commanded her faithful to retrieve it.

'Where is it, then?' The priest glared at the little girl, his black eyes bulging like swollen olives.

She stepped back a pace, frightened of him.

'In the place of the silvcicas,' she whispered. 'Hidden there by a wicked man who stole it for himself. He thinks no one knows.'

'You lie! No such place exists!' the priest bellowed, enraged.

'Where – where did you say?' put in the children's mother, her face pale.

'The place of the silvcicas,' repeated the child, eyes wide.

'I know where that is!' cried the mother, triumphant. 'You remember who lived with the nuns? Surely you do, *papás*, you must have met her at some time? She often spoke to me when she came to buy our vegetables. The *princess*. You remember her, *papás*?'

Mute, the priest nodded, his palms shining with sweat.

'She came from that palace. The Palace of the Silver Cicadas. That is its proper name. The palace of Prince Zebukar, and Prince Bastan before him. Now Hassani lives there.' The woman shuddered.

'Yes, yes, that is the place!' cried the girl. 'And the Star Lady says we have to get the statue from there, and bring it back to its rightful home here, for she is unhappy that it is lost.'

'But the convent was burned to the ground. The lady did not know that, eh?' the priest growled, triumphant. 'Some Holy Mother she is if she does not know *that*! Have these children whipped soundly, for they are liars and in league with the devil!'

CHAPTER TWENTY-EIGHT

Muhammad Baswar's bodyguard, and some two hundred of his soldiers marched like Roman legions towards the Palace of the Silver Cicadas. On a magnificent white horse, bold and beautiful as a medieval knight's charger, sat Zardos Alexandros, called the Pagan. His feet were bound with cord and lashed beneath the horse's belly so that he could not leap off and run away, and his wrists were similarly bound. Turks came to watch the progress, shouting with delight at the sight of the captive, bellowing their congratulations to Baswar, who rode just ahead of the Pagan prisoner, wearing his famous black and white armour, and the enclosed black helmet with its hideous skull and crossbones motif. Turkish villagers and townsfolk ran forward to kiss the hem of his black cloak and cry, 'Allah preserve you, oh great general!' But Baswar behaved in his usual fashion, neither moving his head, acknowledging them, nor raising his visor with its chilling, death's-head symbol.

They had been marching at immense speed for a day and a half when the first gaggle of wild and desperate Greeks launched itself upon them. Alas, soon after, these men, having been deprived of their weapons, crude spears and pitchforks, farming and butchering implements, were in wrist chains, tramping behind the proud and conquering Turkish force. Again this happened, for there had been much talk of the appearance of the Virgin who had let it be known where the Turks had taken the statue of the Miraculous Virgin.

Her command that this statue be rescued and replaced in its rightful setting had fired every Greek who heard it.

Each fresh onslaught of avenging Greeks was treated as successfully as the last; their numbers were swiftly overcome and chains soon shackled their wrists. By that second night, more than six hundred Greek rebels were marching behind the Turkish force led by the proud and triumphant Baswar who, now and again, glanced behind him to grin delightedly at his infamous prisoner.

When the Palace of the Silver Cicadas came in sight, the soldiers felt as if they were returning home. With luck there would soon be somewhere to rest, good food and drink, time to talk and congratulate themselves on their massive victory. Their god had been with them, and he was still with them, of that they were sure. He had let his feelings be known. He had allowed his chosen ones to be the victors.

Silvery music could be heard in the violet-scented bed-chamber of Prince Hassani, sumptuous with its delicate silk hangings fringed with silver and gold, its radiant ivory and gold tiling with the beautiful motif of the silver cicada after which the palace was named and which had been the emblem of good Prince Bastan. It was the lilting, sensuous music of love, and behind a silvery veil, dancers swayed and pivoted to the haunting notes. Perhaps the tiny ghost of the dancer, Alliya, was whirling amongst them, for her spirit had been seen here and there throughout the palace, causing great unrest, and talk of dark omens, bringing Hassani out in an icy and painful sweat. Even though his physicians had assured him that no one had ever been physically harmed by one of the dead, he shook at the mere thought of further encounter with the shade of the vengeful Alliya.

On the vast and quilted silken bed lay the beautiful and legendary Princess Musbah, daughter of an English duke. She had just been heard to scream, to protest and scream again, but that was the concern of no one but her new husband, Hassani. He was laughing delightedly as he caressed her breasts, tearing the delicate gauze of her nightrobe and exposing her sculpted ivory bosom. Her

366

perfection was so breathtaking that he paused there to admire, as he would a marble statue of great beauty, or a jewel of immense value. Then, breathing raspingly, he caressed those breasts and pinched them, making his new bride writhe with pain and disgust. When his hands moved lower, she screamed again, as loud as she could, and cursed him, but he ignored it all. After all, was he not an expert at defiling and abusing the unwilling?

'Rose of the West, from now on you shall be known as the Rose of Islam. What an imbecile I was not to have you sooner! If I had known how superb you were, I would not have hesitated.'

'Get off me, you vile cur! When Zardos knows what you have done . . .'

'Zardos? That sick dog? He is General Baswar's prisoner now. Did you not know? His fortress has been blasted into the sky and everyone in it is dead. He was a coward when it came down to it and was easily captured. He is on his way here now, to be executed. You shall of course watch him being beheaded, that I promise you.'

'You're lying!' Flavia screamed, trying to pull her hands free, but only succeeding in tearing the skin where the ropes pulled tighter. 'Zardos will never be taken prisoner! *Never!* He will free Greece. He has sworn that he will!'

'Allah is on the side of the Faithful, not the skunks who masquerade as heroes in this land. We have won, Musbah, not them. They were not fit to overcome *us*.'

Tears rolled out of Flavia's eyes and down the sides of her face. 'I do not believe you! You're lying! You have always lied!'

'Believe what you like, but open your legs while you are doing it,' Hassani said crudely, taking a tiny jewelled knife from his belt and cutting the thongs round her ankles. Then, his hard, brutal hands digging into her thighs, he prised them open and in the next few moments submitted her to the greatest indignities she had yet known in this palace. When he had finished, she was scarlet-faced and nauseous with shock.

367

'You will get to like my fingers there, bride of mine,' Hassani giggled. 'And you will get to like what is coming next even more.'

Standing up, he began to tear off his clothes, the brilliant coloured silks with their flashing gems and sequins. When he stood before her, naked, she felt faint. He was grotesquely fat, his belly hanging down to his groin like a half deflated balloon, his legs spindly and crooked. And he smelt horrible, like a dead animal. Round his penis there was a crimson scar, livid, but thoroughly healed all the same. She did not have time to ponder on its cause, for he was climbing on top of her and stabbing his sharp bony knees into her thighs to force them wide, so that he could well and truly consummate the marriage, and let the Sultan be informed.

Behind the shimmering veil, the dancers had gone and in their place were palace officials and the ambassador from the Sultan, who were watching, witnesses to the consummation. After that the terms of Prince Zebukar's will could be put into effect and his treasures shared out as he had desired – with Allah's Teardrop, the world's largest diamond, on its way to Turkey and the Sultan.

Breaths taut, mouths wet, the officials watched as the gross and panting Hassani lowered himself onto the beautiful Princess Musbah, whose Titian hair was spread out around her like a cloak of sunshine. Lower and lower Hassani sank, his body almost touching that of his bride. There was an answering reaction in the groins of the officials, for who could watch such a voluptuous, white-skinned female being raped without wishing to do likewise? Was it not every man's right?

The hammering on the door of the bedchamber took them all by surprise. When it swung open and Muhammad Baswar strode in, fully armed in his hideous black and white armour with the brazen death's-head helmet, shock and stunned amazement took the place of lechery as the Sultan's most famous general strode up to the royal nuptial bed and picked Prince Hassani off his bride as if he were lifting a child. In one lithe movement, he flung him across the room so that he landed on the far side with a sickening crash, where he proceeded to whimper like a thrashed hound.

'*Treason!*' screamed the officials, leaping backwards, and scrambling for the door behind their screen of veiling, for none of them wished to tangle with Islam's most feared and dreaded general, who was reputed to have super-human strength.

No man went to Hassani's aid, so he continued to lie in a bruised and crushed heap, sobbing and wailing to Allah, and nursing his broken arm, while the Princess Musbah, her heart pounding in terror, looked up into the death's head mask of her new conqueror. So shocked that she could hardly breathe, so paralysed with fear that she thought her heart had stopped beating, she waited for Muhammad Baswar to continue what Hassani had begun, for surely that was why he was here, with his army, to make her his bride in place of Hassani and thereby lay claim to Zebukar's fortune?

CHAPTER TWENTY-NINE

Baswar's forces swarmed throughout the Palace of the Silver Cicadas, taking control of it in record time. Soon, men wearing Baswar's crest, the death's head, were everywhere, in the corridors, on guard, eating in the kitchens, guarding doors and gateways, talking through the grilles to the concubines in the royal harem, much to their astonishment and dismay, and the men's immense enjoyment.

Word soon reached the men's ears that Hassani had tried to stab their leader. The hated Prince had crept up behind him as he leaned over the Princess's bed, and, with a tiny dagger, in his unharmed hand, had plunged the weapon with all his force into their leader's back. Fortunately, the weapon had been deflected by the famous black and white armour, which was specially forged to protect its owner from such attacks. Turning, their leader had fought Hassani with his fists, not wishing to harm him, for he would be wanted as a witness, but Hassani had repeatedly plunged the dagger at his enemy, searching for a vulnerable spot, and eventually, to save his own life, their leader had been forced to kill the Prince.

No one grieved over Hassani's death, for rarely had any man been so despised and feared, even amongst his own people. As for a strong and just leader like the one who wore the death's-head armour, well, who would say no to his commanding them now? They would have nothing more to fear from their enemies with him in control, so there was excellent reason to rejoice, which is exactly what they were doing.

*

The Princess Musbah had not been raped by Baswar as she had feared. It would appear that he was willing to wait for a lawful marriage ceremony before he consummated their union. She was now sitting on a scarlet silk couch, sipping a soothing herbal tisane to restore her nerves, while her new conqueror massaged her ankles to make the blood flow in them again. Now and again the Princess exchanged a delighted glance with him and they would smile like long-lost lovers who had found each other after a long separation.

Baswar's black and white armour lay on the floor in a heap, the skull and crossbones averted from the Princess's gaze. Now its wearer was robed in white silk in the Turkish style, a robe which gave him ample room to move when he wished to fling his arms round the Princess and hug her passionately, or kiss her ardently and whisper that he adored and cherished her, and that they would never be parted again.

'Tell me again how you did it, Zardos,' Flavia whispered, her eyes alight with wonderment.

He responded as she wished, repeating the story, how he along with the survivors of the siege and Jacques-Pierre and his army, plus rebel bands of *Kleftes* who had got word via Leon that the Pagan was not dead but being attacked by Baswar, had launched themselves at the Turks. For all his bravado, Baswar had proved a coward, when, after some four or five hours of fierce and bloody hand-to-hand combat it became obvious that the Greeks were gaining the upper hand. Whether Baswar had tried to flee to save his own skin or to warn Hassani would never be clear, but as he had leapt astride his horse and headed away from the camp, a bullet from Jacques-Pierre's gun had felled him. Seeing that their leader was dead, the heart had gone out of the Turks, who had either tried to take to their heels, or put up a last desperate fight. None could be allowed to escape alive, for they would spread the word to Hassani and his forces, so, when battle was ended, every straggler, every wounded man, was put to the sword, or shot.

Flavia shivered when she heard this, although she knew that the Turks would have done the same, or worse, to the Greeks had they been given the chance.

'We felt that we were with God, that he was on our side when we fought. It was an uncanny feeling. I cannot explain it. We have always known that right was on our side, all these years, but somehow, fighting Baswar's troops, we felt that we were bound to win. It was almost as if we were given supernatural strength for the battle. I have never known anything like it before,' Zardos mused.

'So many people were praying for you, for us all. God was watching over you, my darling.' Flavia gazed at her lover adoringly.

'As I found out later. We then dressed ourselves in the Turks' armour, and Jacques-Pierre put on Baswar's famous armour, leading everyone to believe that he was the Islamic general. Like that, we marched here to this palace, and along the way we were joined by Greeks who were ravenous for our blood, until they saw that we were Greeks and we told them what was really happening. After that, they pretended to be our prisoners, and so our army was swelled into hundreds by the time we reached here. It was believed that we were Baswar and his men, of course, with hundreds of Greek prisoners, so the gates were opened wide for us, and in we came. We were able to take control with hardly any violence, and once established here, I donned Baswar's death's-head armour, assuming his identity, and marched into Hassani's room.'

'Where you saved me from the most hideous experience imaginable. I doubt I would have survived it!' Flavia clung to her lover, basking in the warm safety of his arms.

'Why were the Greeks coming here?' she then wanted to know.

'In Nauplinos, two children had a vision of the Blessed Virgin. At first it was treated with derision and they were scorned, then she appeared again and told them that the statue of the Miraculous Virgin was here in this palace and that she wanted her faithful to return it to its rightful home.'

'So it is *here*!' Flavia's face shone.

'It would appear so. My men are looking for it now.'

'Then we have won, we have won!' Tears formed in Flavia's peridot eyes as she leaned against her lover, rejoicing at the feel of his strong arms holding her close again.

'Not quite. We have conquered Hassani and this palace, but that is all. Next on the agenda is the Turkish Empire itself, my darling. Admiral Codrington's ships are gathering at Navarino now to sort out that little problem, but it is only a minor one, I do assure you.' His emerald eyes glittered with humour.

'Oh, Zardos, I do not have your optimism! What if we lose the battle? My godfather is a brilliant man, but what if he is outnumbered?'

'Codrington, you mean? He is your godfather?'

'Yes, indeed. Before the siege I sent him a message, you know, but I was sure it had not reached him. I asked him to come to our aid if it was at all possible. It was probably very unpolitical of me, but I could not see any other way out at the time.' She clung to him, remembering how she had longed to be Atalanta with an army at her command to free Greece. Had it been a premonition of this day when the British naval fleet arrived under the command of her godfather?

'When will we know?' she whispered.

'The moment the battle is over messengers will be on their way to us. Fast riders.'

'And what if the Turks win?' She shivered, unable to contemplate such tragedy, for them and for Greece.

'If they win, my beloved, well, we go into hiding, of course, and then we start again, in the very same way as we did before. We gather our forces, we gather our strength and we do not give up until the Turks are beaten, and our land is free of them. Are you with me if that happens? It will be a tough and dangerous life, no soft beds, no silken clothes and all the other luxuries that you women love so much.'

'I am with you, Zardos, always, and you are wrong! There will be everything a woman loves – you – and I am that woman.'

They found the statue of the Miraculous Virgin after a long search. She was in Hassani's treasure vault, where they had looked at the start, but she was not in the midst of his chests and caskets of jewels and gold. Behind a false wall, which had sounded hollow when Zardos struck it, they discovered the beautiful statue. It was totally unharmed, as heart-stopping as ever, and, so men said afterwards, for a fleeting moment there was a smile on the painted mouth as they drew out the figure to free it of its stone prison. Hassani had been so fearful of the statue that he had been unable to look at it once it was in his possession.

Flavia wept when she saw it, and because she was so very moved, so was Zardos. They knelt together before the symbol of love and peace and freedom, and they were praying for all three when the result of the battle of Navarino was brought to them.

Before the messenger entered, Flavia flung herself into her lover's arms.

'If we have lost, then I shall come with you wherever you go, my darling Pagan. Into the hills, the mountains, anywhere, and I shall fight beside you until we are free again. We shall never be parted, not after this. Never, come what may.'

The door swung open and the messenger was ushered in. He was covered in dust, had tears streaming down his face and was desperate for water. His voice was a croak as he began to speak.

On the west coast of the Peloponnese, which was then

374

known as the Morea, was a place known to the Greeks as Avarion, but which was to go down in history as Navarino.

It was October, 1827, and the harbour of Navarino was packed with Turkish and Egyptian ships, for the Egyptians too were members of the Ottoman Empire. Admiral Tahir Pasha was at the head of the Turkish fleet, the name of whose ships rang like battle cries, the *Warrior*, the *Lion*, the *Ihsania* under Hassen Bey, the *Souria*, a fifty-six-gun frigate accompanied by two frigates carrying forty-four guns each. The *Warrior* had sixty guns, the *Ihsania*, sixty-four. Battleships displaying seventy-four guns waited further north to be engaged should the necessity arise. The scent of coming battle was a reek in the air, acrid, barbaric and bloody, as noon approached, bifurcating the day. First, was morning, at peace, then afternoon, at war, but it had not started out like that.

Leon had been haggard and racked with a malarial-type fever when he finally reached London and Admiral Codrington. He had escaped from the mountain fortress just in time, before the surrounding area was swamped by Turkish troops. Hair wild and unkempt, clothes tattered and rough like those of a poor sheepherder, he had made his way to the coast, never losing sight, in his mind's eye, of the face of the Princess whom he idolized. It was only the thought of pleasing her and of carrying out her request which kept him going when his food ran out and he was faint from lack of sleep. He bought a berth on a clipper bound for Genoa where, having purchased a fast horse, he made his way at breakneck speed along the coast of Italy until past the Alps, where he sold his horse, buying another and setting off across France as if the devil were behind him. By then, he was feverish, but he kept going, once nearly losing his seat when he fell asleep in the saddle. When he had to stop to sleep, he raged at his feeble-mindedness, hating himself for such physical frailty. The money Flavia had given him was running short by the time he reached Calais, and he was forced to work his passage across the

Channel, which he did with gusto, despite his recent recovery from fever.

The last leg of the journey from Dover to London had seemed an eternity, and the horse he had purchased from a farmer in Dover proved to be wild of spirit and proud of it. He passed many people during his journey, pilgrims, merchants, farmers and their wives in ugly, creaking carts, troops of newly-enlisted soldiers being route-marched at a sweating speed. He noticed nothing, only the road ahead in all its rutted, pitted and dry dustiness. Not even the comparative chill of an English spring distracted him. He had vowed that he would not stop until he placed the Princess's message into the hands of Admiral Codrington, and that was what he intended to do.

The Admiral had been astonished and somewhat non-plussed at the sight of the dark, skeletal, gypsy-like youth who was ushered into his library by his shocked secretary, who then hovered in the background, fearful of the foreigner drawing a weapon. When Leon placed the Princess's message into Codrington's outstretched hand, the Greek almost collapsed, and had to be helped to a chair. The relief, the joy of accomplishment, had taken the strength from his legs. As soon as he was well again, he would return to Greece and join the mercenaries. There was no way he was going to linger in England while his country had need of him.

Codrington read his god-daughter's message with incre-dulity. He had believed Flavia to be in a convent making up her mind as to when she would marry the fat libertine, Hassani Pasha. All along, he had hoped that she would decide in the negative and return to England, but now there was this extraordinary letter. The girl was in some mountain fortress, in the company of the man they knew as the Pagan, and they were about to be besieged by Muhammad Baswar and his army. Flavia wrote that they expected the Turks to arrive any day and she prayed to God that Leon could get out of the Morea alive. Well, he had, though by the look of him, it was only half-alive.

God's wounds, how had the girl got herself into such a predicament? And how strangely the arrival of her plea for help had coincided with his latest orders, he reflected.

The Turks had brought in their Egyptian allies, under Ibrahim Pasha, while the Pagan, the one man who could rally and unite the remaining *Kleftes*, was believed to have died in a notorious Turkish gaol. Disjointed and desperate uprisings which were little more than tattered skirmishes had been put down by the Turks and Ibrahim Pasha's men, with a brutality excessive even for them. Heads were displayed on pikes, to rot in the blazing sunshine as deterrents. The heart of Greece had ceased to beat.

In London, the Greek problem had been one of the major issues in British politics for many months. There was an intense conflict of opinion. Because the Sultan was considered an ancient ally of Britain, some were reluctant to wage war on him, even now when the true state of affairs in Greece had been known for some time. Others were equally adamant that Britain could not stand by and see a beleaguered people wiped out by their oppressors. In the end, the latter opinion triumphed and the British fleet was despatched to Navarino under the command of Admiral Codrington. However, he had his orders. There must be no hasty moves. He must not fire the first shot. All must be done in a cautious and lawful manner, if one could call the proposed warfare lawful.

Thoughts had centred on the late Duke of Acteon's daughter. It was erroneously believed that, had her husband, Prince Zebukar, survived, then the bond with Britain would have been stronger, pressure could have been brought to bear on Zebukar, and, through him, on Mahmud II. As it was, that had not been possible, but fresh hopes had rested in the proposed marriage between the Princess and Hassani Pasha, until it became obvious that the Princess rejected this alliance out of hand. An ambassador had been sent to try and make her change her mind, but, on his arrival at the convent where she was supposed to be living, he had found it burned to the ground, and only the local people left to tell him what had become of the nuns. He had hurried home to England with this shocking news, and for a time it was not known whether the Princess was dead, or had been carried off by force. Either was unthinkable in the circumstances. A British woman treated so outrageously: it could not be allowed! When Codrington's god-daughter's letter was read out in the House, there was uproar.

Within a very short time, Great Britain, France and Russia had formed a triple alliance to go to the Princess's rescue. It was still hoped that the Turks and the Egyptians would be coerced by this show of power into reforming their savagery towards the stricken and starving Greeks, if they could not be pressured by peaceful means, to withdraw from that country entirely. If all else failed, it was to be war at sea.

That was how Flavia's godfather came to be entering the harbour of Navarino at noon on October 20th, 1827, in his flagship, the *Asia*, with a fleet of a dozen or so ships carrying between them some four hundred and sixty guns. Heading the Russian fleet was Admiral Heiden, who, Dutch by birth, had served in the Royal Navy and become a naturalized Russian in 1810. With Heiden was a diplomatic advisor, a Greek called Zatakazy. The name of his flagship was the *Azov*. The Comte de Rigny led the French in his flagship, the *Sirène*.

Codrington knew what he planned to do. His orders were to make a show of strength, to bring the Turks and Egyptians to heel, not to their knees, and he also had official but secret orders to rescue the Duke of Acteon's daughter and bring her back to London. So, when the first shots thundered out, no one was more surprised than he. Erupting like miniature volcanoes, they came from one of the Turkish vessels, killing several of the crew of the *Dartmouth*, one of the English ships nearby.

The *Dartmouth* had no choice but to retaliate, the *Sirène* following suit after being engaged by the Egyptian frigate, the *Ihsania*.

Because of the close proximity of the vessels it could not be a full-scale sea battle as at Trafalgar, which Codrington had relished so hugely. Here, it was a struggle for survival as well as one-upmanship – literally. One by one, the vessels fired at each other, to defend themselves or to protect a neighbour. Afterwards, no one could give an accurate, chronological account, detailing which ship had fired upon whom and when.

The enemy guns on shore fired at the French *Trident* as it entered the harbour, and because the *Scipion* had reduced sail too soon, she was temporarily slowed, thus not only delaying herself but the *Trident* and the *Breslau* too. These, no longer able to protect the *Sirène*, it now took the full horrifying brunt of the Turkish guns. Later, de Rigny would write to his sister,

'When I was able to get down at midnight between decks to see the victims, I found everywhere limbs and shoulders shattered without benefit of amputation. Poor unhappy creatures! I saw one of my brave men, the gunner who manned the gun in my cabin, with his thigh smashed, not yet bandaged because my surgeon had so much to do. "Well, my poor Daniel," I said, "you did your job today as I expected of you. Are you in great pain? We'll get you bandaged up." "There are others in greater need than mine, sir," he replied, "only tell me that you are satisfied with Daniel?"' De Rigny went on to say that his ships had behaved like angels in the face of the enemy, *'but then think of an English squadron and a French squadron side by side on the same target – poor target! I imagine the Turks have lost not less than three thousand men.'*

And it was so.

A superbly heroic battle in the grand tradition, with the enemy decimated and put to flight, it was to change the history of Greece, and hasten all that the Pagan and the Greek people had been fighting for through long decades.

As soon as the battle was over and he had carried out his naval obligations, Codrington headed for the Palace of the Silver Cicadas with a small company of his men to protect him should there be any savage Turks encountered on their journey.

'Dear godfather!' Flavia cried, running to kiss the victorious Admiral whose face was pink with pleasure at seeing her safe and well.

'Egad, Flavia, ye've had us all pacing the deck chawing at our fingers wondering for your safety! 'Tis good to see you looking so well. And this is the man they're all talking about, eh?' Codrington transferred his gaze to Zardos.

'Yes, godfather, this is the man I love, the man they call the Pagan, but as you'll soon find out, he's nothing of the sort!' Flavia grinned happily.

'I don't know what your dear papa would have made of all this, m'dear. Indeed I don't!' Codrington guffawed, while pumping Zardos's hand energetically. 'First a Muslim, and now a Pagan!'

'Oh, you know what papa was like, godfather. He'd have loved every minute of it and he'd have done exactly the same in my place.'

'Yes, I suppose he would.' The Admiral tweaked his brows. 'Now I've a little matter to ask of ye, Lord Alexandros. I have in my possession a document from His Majesty the King of England. If we lost the battle, then it would have been of no importance, but as we won, it is vital. A governor will be needed while Greece puts itself to rights during the Turkish withdrawal. A man is needed who can unite the Greek people and restore the country to peace and prosperity again. It was the unanimous decision of His Majesty's government that you be that governor. If ye'll agree, of course? There will be an English title in honour of your courage and bravery in recent years and for the work ye'll be doing on England's behalf. Between you and me, ye'll be getting 'em out of a very sticky corner, m'lord, but that's for your ears only, d'you hear? How do ye fancy being a duke, eh?'

'The title has little interest for me,' Zardos said firmly, 'but the governorship does. Believe me, I have dreamed of such a moment!'

Flavia was gazing at her lover open-mouthed. Zardos, the Governor of Greece, and herself beside him able to help as she had always longed to do. Then a thought occurred to her.

'But, godfather, there are no available dukedoms in England, are there?'

'With respect, m'dear, ye've been absent quite a while. Your distant relation, that skulking curmudgeon, if ye'll forgive the foul language, has died. Set upon by ruffians in a London backstreet while he was about his disgusting habits. He's now been well buried and without leaving an heir. So the duchy of Audlington is available again. It seemed only right that Acteon's daughter should inherit it. That is, if she decided to marry her Greek hero.'

'The thought of refusing his proposal never crossed my mind.' Flavia grinned. 'Not even when he told me that he was going to hold me to ransom to the Turks, nor when he said that my place was in the kitchen scrubbing vegetables and making soup.'

'What's that?' the good Admiral blustered, ready to take great umbrage on his god-daughter's behalf. 'Ransom? Kitchens, eh, *eh*?' He blinked at Zardos.

Flavia took her godfather's arm. 'I am only teasing, godfather. Preparations are under way for our wedding, and I want you to give me away, if you would. Please tell me that you will stay for that?'

'Stay for your wedding? Why, of course, m'dear! Your father would never have forgiven me if I did otherwise.'

Linking her other arm into her lover's, and smiling up at him adoringly, Flavia led the two men into dinner.

'After dinner is over, godfather, we will show you Muhammad Baswar's black and white armour. It is hideous!' She shuddered, thinking of the death's-head emblem and its ruthless owner. 'And you will want to see the beautiful statue of the Miraculous Virgin, will you not? It is all intact, even down to the Lion Rubies. Tomorrow, it returns to Nauplinos where it belongs and it is to stay in a church there until the convent has been rebuilt to house it. We could not have won the war without the Virgin's intercession, we are quite sure of that.' Flavia's eyes shone as she smiled at her godfather. Then she turned her gaze to her beloved Pagan, remembering how they had met, how they had sparred with one another so fiercely until love had conquered them both.

How magnificent he was, her lover, turning this humble table into an Olympian feast with his brilliant good looks and god-like build, and how she adored him. As if reading her thoughts, his hand reached out for hers, grasping it tightly, while a sweet and joyous emotion sprang between them. Never had those remarkable emerald eyes held such tender devotion as they gazed into Flavia's peridot ones. They were in possession of one of life's greatest blessings, the love between a man and a woman. Not lust, which is temporary and fickle, but true, deep and abiding love.

Here in this very room she had once sat beside Prince Zebukar at the beginning of her life in Greece, when her beliefs had been so totally different, when she was little more than a child filled with dreams. But she had learned that some dreams can come true, despite what sceptics say, and that miracles still do happen, especially if you pray for them.

Holding her future husband's hand tightly, and revelling in his tender, adoring gaze, she knew that she was in the possession of the greatest gift that heaven can bestow, and that in itself was a miracle.

ROYAL SLAVE

Julia Fitzgerald

Author of VENUS RISING, SLAVE LADY and
SALAMANDER

HEART OF FIRE

They captured her one night on the dark and rocky
coast of Cornwall as she was eloping with the man
she had vowed to marry.

FLAME OF LOVE

Cassia Morbilly – a woman of fire and flame – she
had given her heart and body once in love and
thought that it would be forever. Until they
auctioned her in the slave markets of
Constantinople to be a Sultan's plaything . . .

Futura Publications
Historical Romance
0 7088 1405 0

All Futura Books are available at your bookshop or
newsagent, or can be ordered from the following address:
Futura Books, Cash Sales Department,
P.O. Box 11, Falmouth, Cornwall.

Please send cheque or postal order (no currency), and
allow 55p for postage and packing for the first book
plus 22p for the second book and 14p for each additional
book ordered up to a maximum charge of £1.75 in U.K.

Customers in Eire and B.F.P.O. please allow 55p for
the first book, 22p for the second book plus 14p per
copy for the next 7 books, thereafter 8p per book.

Overseas customers please allow £1 for postage and
packing for the first book and 25p per copy for each
additional book.